SEAL
OF THE
SAND DWELLER

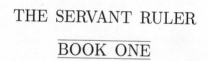

THE SERVANT RULER

BOOK ONE

R. RUSHING

DOMINIA PRESS

Published by Dominia Press
Copyright © 2018 by R. Rushing

ISBN-10: 0-9989299-1-3
ISBN-13: 978-0-9989299-1-0

Cover Illustration by Joel Durham
Cover Design by Derek Taylor
Book Layout by StewartDesign.studio

A praise to Elohim, the God of my life

For Ben, my husband and the love of my life

He called down famine on the land
and destroyed all their supplies of food;
and he sent a man before them—
Joseph, sold as a slave.
They bruised his feet with shackles,
his neck was put in irons,
till what he foretold came to pass,
till the word of the Lord proved him true.
The king sent and released him,
the ruler of peoples set him free.
He made him master of his household,
ruler over all he possessed,
to instruct his princes as he pleased
and teach his elders wisdom.

Psalm 105:16-22

CHAPTER ONE

YOSEPH

SQUINTING AT THE TORCHLIGHT, YOSEPH raised his head from the slab of wood. The taste of blood in his mouth, the beast's clopping hooves, the raucous laughter of the men. All of it a reminder of the caravan that forced him into Egypt and the traders that sold him as a slave. But he was no longer a mere slave. No, things were far worse than that.

The guards drew him from the Great Prison a few days ago. They'd traveled through the night with only a sliver of moon to guide them through a mild sandstorm. A gust of wind flickered out a torch, and one of the men stumbled in the dark, growling a low curse. The beast came to a halt, and a gate groaned. Winter would not relent, and the east desert winds were at their worst. Hot in the daytime, numbing at night.

Yoseph lay on his side, gripping the slab of wood that dragged him and gritting his teeth. His bones took in the shock of every dip and bump in the rutted road. Even if they hadn't strapped him down like a carcass, they'd trussed him like a dressed ox. His bound limbs were swollen, bloodied, and numb. The party came to a halt, and one of the guards addressed the palace gate attendant. When the beast moved forward again, the ground beneath Yoseph gave way to a smooth limestone surface.

Elohim be praised.

He unclenched a little, licking his cracked lips. His flesh burned from the cold gusts of wind, and his limbs throbbed in the bonds. If he could see the king's cupbearer, Lord Hetnu would allay his fears. The remnant of an old prayer ran through his mind though he could not grasp the words. Something prayed traveling through Edom, where Uncle Esau might have slaughtered them all had he not remembered mercy and love for a brother. Yoseph prayed such mercy would find him today.

Qareg led the party, using his spear as a walking stick. He was a mid-ranking soldier titled Greatest of Fifty and fresh in from the borders. He came to second at the garrison in the warden's absence, but it was the Going Forth of Min, and he handed off his duties to set out with the escorting guards, catching the tail end of the winter festival.

The men sang for most of the journey, using military ration chips to barter for warm jugs of beer. The lot of them merry, except for Yoseph, whom Qareg deemed unfit for the luxuries of food and warmth. He'd been summoned to the palace by royal edict, and Qareg assured him he was a man going to his death.

Celery leaves from the festival littered the ground and blew across Yoseph's chest. He shivered against the chill, inhaling their lush scent as the guards crushed them underfoot. He gambled Qareg lied about the edict, but even Qareg would tell the truth if he thought it would hurt a man more.

They'd reached the palace compound in the dead of night. Only the wind howling through the trees and the slab of wood dragging over stone broke the silence. They passed through a lit archway where dim torchlight flickered on the king's royal name cartouched in the ceiling.

Sekhamaat Khakheperre Senuseret

Yoseph stared at the symbols fading from sight as the beast dragged him on. Darkness obscured the great structures of the king's house, all but the walls of the king's treasury lit with torches and shining like gold in the firelight. Another sharp wind stung his limbs, pelting him with sand and pebbles. The punishing blasts guttered out the great torches around the treasury walls, but the scene was lost to him when they pulled into a courtyard. The harsh winds ceased.

Qareg cut him loose from the slab and yanked him to his feet. He fell over like a beam, and Qareg dragged him to a wall by the bonds at his wrists. He sucked in a breath for dignity sake and glanced up at the crowd he'd drawn. He yelped. The sharp poke in his neck drew blood. Not for the first time, Qareg had used his spear to amuse himself. He drew laughter from the gold-clad youths on the balcony. They flocked around an ornately dressed prince holding a wine jug and followed him out of Yoseph's line of sight.

Qareg nudged the spear tip deeper. Yoseph hissed, pressing his head against the wall. Blood trickled down his neck. The journey to the king's house was grueling, but Qareg's attentions had worn him thin enough to think death might bring relief.

Remember the cupbearer. He promised.

His heart raced. Qareg would see him executed before dawn, and Lord Hetnu would never know he'd arrived.

A tall Cushite trotting toward them stopped short at a gatehouse to bark at the men within. "You there! Get yourselves alert, or I'll hang you by your heels from the palace walls!" Three guards knocked into each other with sluggish salutes, and he hastened by. His muscled gut was tight like scales on a croc's back, his thick arms tattooed with the symbol of the king's elite guard. He approached with the measured grace of a warrior, one who could kill with a single blow.

Qareg gave the spear shaft a little twist. Yoseph let out a sharp breath. A warmth splattered across the top of his head, and laughter echoed from above. He caught the scent of urine as it ran down his face and sputtered it from his lips. Such a comfort to know the young lords on the balcony had dined on such a fine, sweet wine.

The Cushite guard shooed the youths away, waving a staff as long and as black as he, etched in gold hieroglyphs. It was a staff of precedence whose bearer was not to be challenged or hindered in his actions. Yoseph seized with hope. Such deference was not extended to one about to be executed.

"Qareg." The Cushite spread his feet. "What do you do here?"

Qareg broke into a flat grin, palpable with rancor. "Sabni, my old comrade from the borders. I come to drop off a troublesome prisoner with my crew."

"You lie like the coward you are, Qareg." Yoseph bucked at the sharp kick to his ribs and doubled over, wheezing. So much for exemplary behavior, but with the last of his slipping dignity, he told the truth.

"The king's prisoners are not to be spoilt in such a manner." Sabni motioned to the guards behind Qareg. "Release him."

The guards came forward.

"Hold off." Qareg raised a hand. "He's just a dirty sand dweller 'bout to be executed." He'd hissed the reminder in Yoseph's ear all the way to the king's house. Now he stood, blocking anyone who might prove otherwise.

Yoseph held his ribs where Qareg kicked him and addressed the king's guard. "A clean kilt and a razor, Master, I beg you." It was a bold request, but useless if this man had come to execute him.

Qareg squatted and grabbed a hunk of Yoseph's matted hair. He winced.

"This sand dweller's the warden's pet. He's clean enough. The royal princes just gave him the best washing he's ever had." He yanked Yoseph's head back, hocking spit in his face. "That's the second best."

"Cut him loose!" the guard Sabni snapped at the men.

Qareg shot up, facing him. "I reckon you think yourself peerless since you guard the monarch. But I remember when you was a stick of a boy wettin' your reed mat."

The sun was rising, and workers filled the yard, tending their duties and eyeing the rising confrontation between the two men. Yoseph squinted at a wide-eyed scribe staring down at him from a rooftop before stepping back out of view. Sabni's grip tightened on the staff while Qareg yapped on, puffing his chest.

"You've no right to command me. I'm a man of the land. You're a Cushite dog, a prisoner of war. For a fact, I hear they lopped off your father's head."

Sabni cracked Qareg in the jaw. His head snapped back,

and Yoseph's lips twitched. If this Sabni refused his request of a kilt and razor, at least he'd given a dying man his last wish.

Elohim be praised.

Qareg staggered back and whipped out a jagged flint dagger.

"What goes on here?" The sharp tone brought them both up short. It was Lord Hetnu. The king's cupbearer was wrapped in a thick pelt. He was still rail thin and irritable as the first day he entered the Great Prison where Yoseph personally tended him. "Pummel each other on your own time." He shot a look at Sabni.

Hetnu reprimanded the men, and Yoseph pushed himself upright. He willed Lord Hetnu to acknowledge him, wordlessly begging for recognition or some assurance— anything to prove Qareg wrong.

"Indeed, my Lord." Qareg sheathed his dagger. "My comrades and I was deliverin' this prisoner as instructed when we was harassed by this so-called king's guard." He worked his jaw. "I would like to lodge my official complaint."

"Is that so?" Hetnu's gaze swept over him. "I see you assist the warden at the garrison of the Great Prison." He indicated the insignia on Qareg's armband. "What is your name?"

"Qareg, my lord." He gave a perfunctory bow, grinning.

"Qareg," Hetnu echoed. "I shall remember that name. You are especially mouthy for one of your rank. Are you not?"

Qareg blinked. His flat grin faltered.

"I observed you were instructed to cut this man's bonds and refused to do so. Why is that, Qareg?" Hetnu tapped a fly whisk against his thigh and threw a withering glance at the prison guards. They rushed forward to cut Yoseph's bonds, and he gasped like a man coming up for air.

"Yoseph's a wild savage," Qareg hedged. "We had to tie him up."

"Now you are lying," Hetnu countered in a voice sing-song with irritation. "One more word from you, and I'll see you returned to the king's prison as a guest."

"But I'm to assist in this criminal's execution."

"That won't be necessary." Hetnu waved him off. He glanced down and gasped. "By Horus, look at the man's feet!"

Sabni stepped up beside him. "I'll get Imehy to bring his salves."

"Do so immediately, but mention this to no one. I need him standing in the king's presence this morning."

"No need to trouble His Majesty." Qareg insisted. "He's a criminal. I can snap his neck and have done."

"I suppose that would be the final flourish since you've half-killed him already. But he's the king's prisoner not a feasting goose for a meal." Hetnu scowled, adjusting the pelt around his shoulders. "There is a proper way of doing things."

The words raised a cold knot in Yoseph's gut. And still Hetnu would not so much as look at him but struck at the air with his fly whisk. "Get these garrison brutes out of my sight, Sabni! Get them out before I have them all whipped!" He shot Qareg a scathing look and stomped off toward the inner dwellings of the palace, giving Yoseph no assurance at all that Qareg's words were a lie.

THE SUN WARMED THE MORNING AIR AND glinted off the Cushite's gold armband as he made long strides ahead of the litter. Yoseph caught sight of Sabni's puckered mouth. His face still radiated anger from his encounter with Qareg.

It was the usual effect of an encounter with Qareg.

The healer-slave Imehy kept pace beside the tall Cushite, his head bobbing in cadence with legs that moved with childlike vigor. He was odd-shaped for a dwarf with long arms and a stretched torso that gave the impression of a tall-short man.

Yoseph rubbed his thumbs across numb fingertips. The prison warden meant well in overpraising him as a prisoner and slave who could manage a garrison with his hands tied. And as soon as he left the garrison on business, Qareg took up the challenge. He kept Yoseph bound in rough hemp, untying his hands only to let him tally prison supplies. But his feet Qareg tied so tight, that at sundry times he could not walk or stand.

Imehy let out a string of curses at the bloody rope wounds at his ankles, then fetched unguents and bandages. Sabni allowed him a razor and kilt after all and even called for a chair. It was a kindness Yoseph had not expected. He clung to the arms of the litter as the palace guards jostled him past a myriad of avenues, archways, and courtyards at a bone-rattling pace. They went up a ramp and entered the wide corridor inside a great building.

Huge colored columns capped with designs of flowering rushes and lotuses centered the passageway where they lowered the chair. Sabni motioned where to sit, and Yoseph's chains clattered against the polished basalt floor as he hobbled to the base of a column. He sat, clenching at the cold stone and the pain that shot up his legs. Imehy had soaked his foot bandages in a rank concoction that rivaled the floral scents of the corridor. The polished faces of passing courtiers pinched in distaste.

Yoseph peeked between the wall of guards surrounding him. Across from where he sat, servants hurried to and fro from a set of blue lacquered doors, muffling and releasing sounds from within a room. An ennead of gods scowled down from the ceiling. Horus, the falcon headed god, stood between his parents, Osiris of the dead and Isis, his consort. Among them were Montu of war, Thoth of writing, and Hathor, goddess of love and music. All of them, adorned in gold raiment and rendered as cold as the floor on which Yoseph sat.

The pent-up anger he'd clung to for years while in the king's prison seeped out of him. At the garrison, he'd railed against the injustice done to him, then watched the gate for two more years after Hetnu left. But today, he might be given the chance to defend himself to the king.

He scoffed at his hope. Would the truth be enough? Would a king regard the plea of a slave who dared to speak against the wife of his former master? Lady Kemsiyet was a noblewoman. He was nothing. He stared at the large blue doors, his gut roiling. The king of the whole land was in that room and might order him struck down for a morning's amusement.

The tap on Yoseph's shoulder was Imehy. "Open your mouth." The dwarf stood over him, pinching something between his fingers.

Yoseph stuck out his tongue, accepting the powder.

"For your discomfort." Imehy patted Yoseph's back with all the confidence of a sought-after physician though he stunk of the ox stalls. But at the sound of quick approaching footsteps, the dwarf stood as erect as the guards.

Lord Hetnu was freshly appareled in a short Punt-styled wig. Beneath his glittering cloisonné-jeweled belt, he wore a sheer kilt, starched sharp enough to cut. He came to stand near Yoseph and sniffed. "What's that stench?"

"Special bandages. It's my own work." Imehy stuck out his chest like a proud youth.

Lord Hetnu plucked a flower from a nearby vase and stuffed it beneath his nose. Gold bangles clashed at his wrists. He glared at Yoseph, at the nicks and cuts he'd laid to himself with trembling hands and a sharp razor. "You shaved, I see." His eyes picked over him like vultures. "And nearly ruined yourself in the process." His gaze snagged on the clean kilt before he shot a look at Sabni. He sniffed the flower again.

"I also gave him herbs for fever." Imehy bowed. "If it please my lord."

"It pleases your lord very much. Give him more."

"Too much will make him sick to his stomach."

"Anyone can see he's already sick. As long as he can stand and interpret the king's dream. That is all I need."

Yoseph drew in a sharp breath. "Am I not here to plead my case before the king?"

Hetnu held him in a hard glare and sucked in his cheeks. "You will approach the good god and stand at a respectable distance. You will prostrate yourself on your belly and rise to speak only when you are given leave to do so. You shall not lift your gaze to his royal person nor offer opinion, nor beg for freedom, which I trust as a good slave, you should know."

Yoseph gave a short nod.

"You shall keep to your dream interpretation. It shall be abbreviated and succinct. Do I make myself clear?"

"Yes, Master."

Hetnu relaxed his stiff shoulders. "I am harsh, Yoseph." He flicked a gaze to Sabni. "But I am fair. If you obey me in these things, then I shall personally speak to the king about your release. But if you shame me before His Majesty, then you will be sorry you were ever born to see this day." He let his threat settle, then sniffed and struck Imehy on the head. "And that smell. I should whip you for it!" He jammed his knuckles into his nostrils and turned to Sabni. "Bring him in the formal manner into the king's presence. I will not have Potipherah picking me apart for any breach of protocol. No matter how badly he reeks."

Shortly after Hetnu left, the large blue doors opened, and the guards hauled Yoseph to his feet. He pressed the back of his hand to his mouth. But his empty stomach had nothing to repel. There would be no chance for a merciful death if he failed. Yet there was a great chance he would fail.

He hadn't interpreted a dream in years.

THE GUARDS BROUGHT YOSEPH INTO THE HALL. He glimpsed the crowded room and lowered his head. Servants darted around officials who stood or sat on stools near braziers, and the hum of conversation buzzed in his ears. The stink of his bandages drew more attention than his rattling chains. The courtiers cleared a path, hurling curt remarks. He must thank Imehy for that later.

Qareg's abuse left his legs with only the memory of walking. The guards gripping his arms kept him upright. They stopped some distance from a stone platform that stretched the width of the room, crowded from end to end with priests and officials. Clerestory windows slanting curtains of sunlight divided the approaching suppliant from the throne.

Squinting through the dust-littered haze, Yoseph made out the shape of a Tesem. The dog wore a jasper-studded collar and lay on the platform's edge. He yawned, flexing a paw over a spell etched in stone.

"You may look upon my person, dog."

The words were for Yoseph. He tried to bow but stumbled like a drunkard when the guards released him. Sabni took his arm again.

"If the wild one's feet trouble him, he can always gnaw them off." The jibe caused a low rumble of laughter. Yoseph stole a sideways glance at the prince slumped in the chair on the crowded platform. He'd directed the party of young lords on the balcony. His eyes were as red as the fat tassels dancing on the edge of his Babylonian-styled kilt. He tapped the rim of his wine jug for a slave to top off. "Gods, I can smell him from here."

"If he's wild, Ameny, then he has much in common with you, my dear brother."

The small, rasping voice above Yoseph's head stirred more laughter. Derogative terms like wild one and sand dweller marked nearly all the border-crossers coming down from the north.

"Mentuser, give him your stool before he topples over."

Yoseph turned from the blinding light as a dark, lanky man stepped down from the platform with a camp stool, his lips moving in the silent spells of protection and health cast by physicians. Upon his chest lay the bright gold and jasper medallion indicating him to be a pure priest of Sakhmet, a physician of the most specialized healing skill.

Mincing forward with a sharp grunt, Yoseph reached the stool and lowered himself with the help of the guards. Shafts of sunlight warmed his back as he swiped watery eyes, adjusting to the change of light. He looked up and trained the shock from his countenance.

The king was young like the guard Sabni, but gaunt, with arms like sticks and legs like poles. He toyed with a cylinder seal hanging from his emaciated chest, then dropped it to tighten a shawl over his sharp shoulders. His slitted gaze was full of contempt.

"Enough, Hau." He waved a loose gesture to the monstrously tall slave behind him with a gold bull ring in his nose and skin white, like sand. The slave drew in a massive shield fan and stepped back against a column.

"I've had a dream that no one can interpret." The king thumbed a lapis signet ring on his left hand. "But I've heard it said that when you hear a dream, you can."

"I cannot do it, Majesty. But God will give the king the answer he desires."

He must.

The king's face lit with brusque amusement. He huffed a weak chuckle. "Oh, will he now?" He beckoned to servants who pushed forward with trays of food to mount the platform. The sovereign picked over the fare, tearing off a chunk of bread to dip into one of the steaming pots. He waved the rest away, all but one pot from which he supped. The room hung in near silence as he made a great show of cleaning his teeth with a silver pick before dropping it onto the tray and dismissing it. His gaze darted furtively about the chamber.

While they all waited, Yoseph met the calculating regard of a priest assessing him. He wore a leopard-skin pelt slung across his chest, the slightest movement of his long skirt releasing the scent of myrrh. He raised blue-dyed fingers to his lips, whispering to the men standing near him. He conferred as if he told them, as if he knew the Asiatic dog had lost the ear of his god, and his gift of dream-telling had long since dried up.

The king's face went rigid at their whispers, and Yoseph's lips burned to tell that he no longer understood dreams. That he no longer had them. But his heart raced, and his tongue sat thick in his mouth. Either God had turned from him, altogether, or had shut his mouth to preserve him from haste.

Lord Hetnu also overheard the men and dropped to his knees beside the king. He pleaded in vehement whispers and gestures until the sovereign snatched his arm away. Hetnu stood and withdrew a step back from the throne. Clasping his hands, he shut his eyes as his lips moved in a silent plea to Horus.

"You are very sure of this god that has done so little for you."

Yoseph held his breath at the king's carping tone. Such was enough to warn a free man of trouble, and a slave of impending death. Silence stung the air. But instead of calling for executioners, the sovereign leaned back on his throne and gave a sharp exhale.

"In my dream I stood on the river bank when out of it came seven cows. They were fat and sleek and grazed among reeds. After them, seven other cows came up, as scrawny and ugly as creatures of Set." He coughed into his fist, and Hetnu was beside him in an instant with a silver cup. But the king refused it, and his cough grew spasmodic.

The physician, Mentuser, rushed to the throne with

three others garbed in the long green-trimmed robes of royal healers. They surrounded the king, uttering spells and prayers as his phlegmy lungs expectorated. His brown skin reddened as coughs racked his feeble frame.

Among the wordless concern spreading about the hall were a few quick glances passed back and forth. Coughing sickness was a common malady, brought on by exposure to sandstorms or swamp-fever. A few recovered. Many did not. The king's coughing fit had been expected, and judging by the subtle smirks on some faces, hoped for.

The blue-fingered priest drew near the physicians laboring over the king. He dared to touch the back of the throne, raising a brow in cool curiosity.

Mentuser tucked a black dolomite bowl beneath the king's chin and urged him to spit. One of the physicians shifted, revealing a kilt speckled with red drops. Sabni stood beside Yoseph, clenching his fists. His stricken countenance conveyed that the king was not only sick but dying.

When his coughing subsided, Mentuser waved the other physicians away and tugged at the king's arm to lift him from the chair. But he resisted with the last of his strength.

The blue-fingered priest addressed the king in a voice loud enough for the whole room to hear. "Majesty, do not consort with dogs who weary you."

"He does not weary me, Potipherah. Not as you wish he did." The king's voice cracked with phlegm. He swallowed and fought to control another bout of coughing as he clutched his seal pendant. His mask of composure slipped, revealing a torment in his strained face. "But this dream..."

Lord Hetnu knelt to lift a cup to the king's mouth before he could finish. The cupbearer spoke in low tones of admonishment until the king pushed the cup down.

"I had another dream also. Seven heads of grain, full and good, growing on a single stalk. After them, seven other heads sprouted, withered and thin. They were scorched by the east wind. The thin heads of grain swallowed up the seven good heads." He took a breath. "I told the magicians and my priests, I told the astrologers also, but none could explain it to me."

"Nor can a barbarian explain if the gods do not." Potipherah folded his arms and paced a few steps away.

The cupbearer cut a sharp look at him, then pinned Yoseph with an anxious glare. "Well?!"

Yoseph stood, clinging to the shoulders of the guards. His blocked understanding now gushed like a stream and his thoughts ran clear. God had delivered him, for his skin pricked with the meaning of the king's dream.

Elohim be praised

"The dreams of the king are one and the same. God has revealed what he is about to do."

The king slid to the edge of his seat and grasped the ivory arms of his throne, his whole body still and listening.

"The seven good cows are seven years and the seven good ears of grain are seven years. It is one and the same. The seven lean ugly cows that came afterward are seven years and so are the seven worthless heads of grain scorched by the east wind. They are seven years of famine."

"A blasphemous lie, Khakheperre. I warn you," the priest griped.

"I am no liar," Yoseph countered. "God has shown the king what he is about to do. Seven years of great abundance are coming throughout the land of Egypt."

The hall swelled with dissonant shouts of both rejoicing and censure. Sabni steadied Yoseph as he rocked on his feet. Cupping hands to his mouth, he strained to be heard above the clamor. "But seven years of famine will follow, then all the abundance will be forgotten and severe famine will ravage the land." He stumbled back to the stool, hissing at the pain in his feet.

The hall was in uproar, but the king sat paralyzed, his eyes wide.

Potipherah stepped forward, pumping a blue fist in the air and shouting. "Who is this dog come before us? Who is this sand dweller attempting such deception? He should be quartered and hung from the walls! He should be weighted with stones and flung into the river!"

While he barked at the crowd, the sovereign dragged his gaze from Yoseph to look around the hall. He raised a hand for silence, and Yoseph rushed to fill the lull.

"The reason the dream was given to the king in two forms is that the matter has been firmly decided by God, and God will do it soon."

"Which god?" Potipherah snapped.

Yoseph swallowed. "Mine."

There was some laughter behind him, but the king's face grew hard. His gaze narrowed.

"I'll hold you to it then, sand dweller. You're just like all the rest, trying to flatter your way into my coffers and favor, toying with me because I'm ill." He leaned back on his throne, a scowl pulling at his gaunt cheeks. "I'll wait to see if your words prove true. And if they do not, my executioners will flay you with a skill that will leave you screaming long after you're dead." The king gave a sharp gesture, and the guards plucked Yoseph up like a stick doll and hauled him back toward the great blue doors.

CHAPTER TWO

ASENAT

TRIUMPH SHONE IN MEPI'S EYES AS HIS comrades shuffled off to board games and mid-morning naps with the taste of hearty debate still on their tongues. The old father smacked the back of Asenat's hand with a pert kiss before placing it in the crook of his arm.

"There, you see? I've proved to those old goats that you rank with queens in learning." He snapped his shoulders back and for a moment seemed a younger man.

She gave a tenuous smile. Mepi sprang the debate on her as soon as she entered the quiet palace garden, parading her before the retired priests of the residence, all of whom knew of her father. But the king's house was full of courtiers and administrators and servants. She stroked her bald head, certain that her appearance was as nondescript as any scribe or priest. Even when, by chance, someone realized she was a girl, no one paid her any mind. Yet this was the first time Mepi had singled her out. And that was dangerous.

Mepi struck out with his walking stick, pulling her down the path beside him. He boasted of her talents, then came to an abrupt stop, jolting her from the rhythm of their pace.

"What's wrong, my Ibis?" Asenat drew in her brows.

"I've left something out that should have been put away." He squeezed her fingers. "We must return to my office."

"Tell me what it is, and I'll do it for you."

"No, my dove. It's private information from the king that not even your eyes may see." His brow creased with alarming distress.

"Do you mean those sealed documents I checked for you yesterday? I saw you nodding off in your chair, and I put them away. You must have opened your secret compartment at least five times in my presence without realizing it." She pecked his smooth cheek and whispered in his ear. "All your secrets remain with Thoth." She grinned, trying to draw a smile from him, but his dumbfounded expression dimmed to one of concern.

"Oh, my dear, but you must tell no one of this. No one." He clutched her hand, looking away. "What a fool I've been."

"It's nothing, Mepi. I'm only here for a short time each year. Let us not spoil it with fretting."

He gave a wan smile at her plea, and they resumed their stroll, but his joy had dulled, and he festered in guilt.

Asenat festered in her own, playing at being the daughter of this venerable old priest. Lady Benu was the only name she gave when she wrote from Iunu, requesting information on the gods. But a friendship grew out of her correspondence with Mepi. He invited her to visit, and she remembered the day he met her on the palace water steps, embracing her like a long-lost daughter. She wept in his arms, knowing then how the gods had cheated her.

Her real father was first prophet of the god Amun and chief counselor to the sovereign. He was titled illustriously, Potipherah. Even Asenat called him this, preferring it above his given name, preferring it above calling him Father.

Mepi should have been her father. He would have loved her, not hidden her away in the great temple of Iunu to grieve her mother's death among scholars and servants. Mepi was the father of her heart and she, the daughter of his. This was the third year she returned to the king's house to drink of his paternal companionship. She squeezed his hand. Potipherah must never find out.

"So, what do you think of the criminal we saw in the king's morning hall?" she asked, chasing away dark thoughts. If anything happened to Mepi, she would never forgive herself. "You wouldn't believe how ratty his appearance was, earlier in the courtyard. The guards from the king's garrison had just brought him in through the east gate." She had risen at sunrise to watch the morning activity from a rooftop in one of the palace courtyards. There would be no such freedom allotted to her when she returned to Iunu.

She'd peered over the edge of the roof as the young lords on the adjacent balcony moved on. That sort was nothing but trouble after a night of carousing down by the river pubs. The guards in the courtyard below were in some heated confrontation, making it easy for her to examine the wrongdoer propped against the wall. She glared shamelessly. Perhaps there would be an execution. That would give her something to recall during her long structured days at the Iunu temple. She studied the Asiatic with fascination, then pulled back from the wall, realizing he watched her as much as she watched him.

The savage.

Mepi smiled. "He looked nothing like the way you described him to me. They say he had a good interpretation of the king's dream, the poor fellow."

"And what wrongdoer would not devise a good interpretation to save himself?" The king's morning hall was in uproar by the time she and Mepi had entered. And there on the platform's edge was her father, Potipherah, stirring his usual dissension. "I suppose the barbarian must be credited for taking care to groom himself before meeting the king."

Mepi gave a throaty chuckle. "No prisoner is given such privilege as to groom himself, my dove, not even the prominent men in the place of confinement within the king's garrison, and this one an Asiatic slave. Did you notice his feet wrapped in bandages? He had some great help in his corner, I think."

Asenat had locked eyes with the Asiatic when they took him from the hall. She was unnerved by an awareness that passed between them.

A sparrow darted by her head as she and Mepi stopped near the likeness of the war goddess Pakhet, shaded by a blooming persea. She turned to study their surroundings. "Mepi, this is not the usual path we take."

"I know, my dear." He covered her fingers clenching his linen shawl. "But I wanted to bring you by the Horus columns today, and pass you beneath the goddess for luck."

"For luck? But why?" She fidgeted. This was a main thoroughfare, well-manicured with trees, paved roads, and stone benches. Courtiers often gathered here to vaunt their wealth and connections. It was the very place she and Mepi avoided in order to obscure her from the eyes of those in the king's house. But a few nodded in Mepi's direction and passed her curious glances. She looked the part of a lanky scribe with her shaved head and loose robes, but this grew harder to pull off each year as her body rounded with feminine curves. She took on a practiced masculine gait, holding Mepi's elbow so as to appear to help him walk. "Let me call a chair."

"And ruin my joy of being with you? No, indeed."

She should remind him of their agreement, and they should remove from this place, but he was so proud of her today and she could not disturb his joy.

"I was moved that the Asiatic risked death to speak what he believes," Mepi said as they passed beneath a shading row of acacia trees. "I have seen vile men in priestly garments who milk the poor like cattle. Perhaps my guilt is as great as theirs, in that I did nothing to stop it when I could have spoken up." He cast her a half-smile, his eyes full of regret. "Give me another chance, I ask the gods. I would be like the fearless Asiatic we saw today."

"But too many agree that the king's dreams point to his death."

"Yes, yes. Priests and sages, all carrion birds claiming to know the sovereign's Horus dream. But such a dream is from the gods, and the king alone must confirm the interpretation. And the priests haven't given Khakheperre so much as that. Let them come out and say he's dying instead of spreading rumors. All this fasting and elaborate portending, yet not one of them has produced a sign from the gods."

It would be a shame to see King Khakheperre cut down in the flower of life. His passion for the written word inspired him to build a new scroll room and ignore the work on his burial tomb. This lavish feat rivaled the houses of learning found at the great temples. The wisdom of the ages was being gathered from Crete, Anatolia, Babylon, and all the places of the known world.

And it was dear Mepi who guided the project as overseer of the king's scroll room and collector of ancient works. This was the true work of his heart, to salvage the forgotten dictums of old kings, the words of sages and maverick scribes who refused to paint flowery histories and wrote the truth as they saw it.

"Potipherah was irritated at the mention of the Asiatic's god." Mepi gave a covert smile. "This god has been mentioned before though you will not find him in the more popular texts. It was an embarrassment you see. He came down from the North to protect a woman, and she an Asiatic. The king who, at first, tried to take her into his harem was forced to honor the woman by sending her and her husband away from the land with many gifts."

"I've never heard this."

"As you may well not have heard it but for me. It appears this unseen Elohim will not be silenced." The corners of his mouth tugged up with a look of veiled satisfaction. He'd been a lector priest from his youth, yet now, in the twilight of his life, Mepi spoke of another god. Asenat did not inquire further. This was too much for her ears.

"Well, I suppose the Asiatic's dream interpretation will give the jaded courtiers some excitement. I thank you for sneaking me in to see him."

Mepi snorted. "Sneak you in? Come now. Two baldies walk into the king's crowded morning hall. What's to sneak? It's common enough for one my age, but you resemble a freshly plucked goose. The king might have ordered you skewered and cooked, and no one would have been the wiser." He harrumphed. "Shaving off your pretty hair."

"You've never seen my hair."

"Doesn't matter. You hide everything pretty about yourself."

"I'll shave as bald as an acolyte if it brings me back to you each year." She raised her chin. Her time with Mepi was too precious. With her father's spies lurking in every corner of the king's house, it was best she dull her feminine features. "No argument, please. We have agreed I would don this disguise when I come to see you at court."

"I've not agreed. You've insisted."

"I've never denied being a woman."

"You've never had to. No one's asked." He glanced down the front of her loose robes. "Yet."

She always came in the winter when it was easier to hide her budding shape under shawls and cloaks and the thicker linen of scribes. "What does it matter? I'm more than a mere female."

"A mere female? My dear, females have given birth to the world. They are not inferior." Mepi slowed his steps and propped his walking stick on the cast of one of the ram-head sphinxes lining the avenue. He dug into the pouch at his waist. "But you cannot blame my attempt to dissuade you."

He handed her a sealed scroll. "Let me persuade you to remain at the level of a beginning acolyte for some time before plunging into something that cannot be reversed. The life of a priestess of Pakhet is stringent, and I fear I may lose you forever."

Asenat's mouth hung agape. She recognized the clay seal on the document. Pakhet was a temple and cult exclusive to female priestesses serving the goddess of war. Only women of superior breeding who read were accepted if they passed a rigorous writing exam. She broke the seal and unrolled the scroll. "The high priestess of Pakhet has offered me a position in the temple on an entry level of service." She shook her head. "But I haven't even applied. I have no sponsor."

"You most certainly do have a sponsor. One who is well received by the king himself and who is an ardent admirer of your talent. I've personally extolled your abilities to the high priestess."

Asenat pulled Mepi into an embrace that took him off balance. She sniffed back tears. That Mepi should think so well of her. That he should give her such hope of a life away from Iunu. It was more than she had dared to dream.

Mepi chuckled and pushed her back. He grinned like a sated cat and called to a passing courtier. "See here, Nebsumenu!"

The man that passed them kept walking, but Mepi called after him again. "Nebsumenu," he beckoned, loud enough for all the Nebsumenus in the palace to hear. "Nebsumenu, come, come!"

The man looked back and fought down his glower. He ordered his guards to wait and started back toward them. The sheerness of his linen bespoke his rank. His movement drew the attention of two pinch-faced mothers with gold charms and beads swinging from their throats. They scooted forward on a shaded bench to peer, and Asenat fought the urge to run.

"Greetings, my lord." Mepi stood ramrod straight with his chin out, squeezing Asenat's fingers in the crook of his arm.

"Greetings." Asenat bowed at his approach. His intense regard fixed on her, and the amusement in his rich bronze-colored eyes heated the top of her bald head and cheeks. Mepi raised his chin offering a faint smile as though Lord Nebsumenu should guess who she was. Asenat lowered her gaze to the cloisonné hieroglyph pendant on his fragrant chest and swallowed. He was too observant and her throaty greeting had not fooled him. He knew she was a girl.

Her nose was too full, her lips were too full and her eyes large, like the painted girls in pleasure houses. How she hated her face.

"It says Keeper of the King's Treasury." He touched his pendant with a hennaed fingertip.

"I can read perfectly well, thank you."

"Can you, now?" He arched his brows. "Most women don't bother with the tedious task of learning to read."

"Neither do most rich men who think the work dull and save it for scribes."

He gave a hearty laugh, and she tried not to smile. Those rich-colored eyes made him handsome, along with a natural elegance born to his station. He glanced at Mepi. "This is the girl you mentioned, Lady Benu? She's enchanting."

"You've heard of me?"

"Mepi speaks of nothing else. How long will you be staying?"

She smiled. An answer stuck in her throat.

"She always returns to me in due time." Mepi gripped her trembling hand, but it did not calm her.

"Good." Nebsumenu looked over her face. "Good. See that she does. I shall mention her to the king." He bowed and walked off.

Asenat pressed a hand to her fluttering stomach, and Nebsumenu looked back a second time to chuckle at her appearance. She was an amusement to him. One he would not soon forget.

OVER EIGHT HUNDRED COURTIERS RESIDED IN the palace compound. The host of administrative buildings, parks, lakes, and industry courtyards made it a city unto itself, and there was the king's dwelling set deep within its own private walls. Past the southern palace walls lay an expanse of rich land intricately cut up by canals, groves, and homes of the affluent. To the north was the true city named after the province, Itjtawy, *of the knife.*

Mepi was among the most venerable dwellers in the king's house and given a handsome suite of rooms. Asenat tried to convince him to take a chair home, but he refused. By the time they reached his door, he was grinning in defiance though struggling to catch his breath.

The door opened. "There you are!" Henhenit cast a tight-lipped look over Mepi's shoulder. Asenat avoided the matron's scowl, concentrating on the tiny flesh moles dotting her cheeks. She was a slave, but well in command of her domain, and the master had missed his midday nap. "We returned from the day's washing to find a guest in the receiving hall," she said with strained emphasis.

Mepi's nap would be further delayed, driving the dagger of guilt deeper into Asenat. The old father remained in high spirits though he shuffled forward with obvious fatigue. His young man, Wenen, helped him to the hall.

Asenat fell into step behind Mepi's stooped gait, pulling Henhenit close to whisper in her ear. Henhenit reared back in clear objection of her request, but Asenat sent her a pleading look. She released her breath only when Henhenit stalked off in silent protest.

Wenen helped Mepi to his chair and raised the master's swollen feet to a stool.

Asenat started for her room but caught a glimpse of the visitor, squared her shoulders, and went to stand behind Mepi's chair. She offered a grudging nod. The message she sent was the same as always. *You are not wanted here.*

"Prince Dagi, how pleasant of you to come and see me," Mepi exulted through his fatigue while Asenat shifted her jaw at the little troubler. He left the balcony this morning in the company of other young lords and Prince Ameny, the king's full blood brother. Dagi was known for grazing a few softhearted courtiers when his gambling funds ran low. Asenat glared at him in warning. He would do no such thing to Mepi.

"Henhenit promised me some of her date bread and a woven strap for my bow." Dagi's tone was as apologetic as any liar's. At just fifteen, his form was athletic. He always wore a small silver bracelet and a choker of carnelian and rock crystal dung beetles to show off his muscular neck. His face held the promise of handsomeness, but there was a meanness in his small eyes and in his upper lip that jutted out in some unknown defiance. "I thought it best to stay and greet you, Mepi." He gripped the hemp sack tight enough to crush any bread inside.

"You are welcome here as always, my lord," Mepi's voice was full of warmth. "Have a cup of cinnamon milk with me."

"Yes, I will."

Asenat looked away, holding her patience. The privileges of royalty were wasted on the pack of cubs roaming the palace. Their distant blood ties to the throne brought undeserved merit. Dagi ignored her existence, though occasionally he distinguished her from other inanimate objects referring to her as "the girl" or "the bald one."

He sipped the cup of milk Wenen handed him, keeping a firm grip on the sack stuck in his armpit. He'd been waiting here alone, and Asenat's gaze flitted about the room as she wondered what the little gambler had taken.

Mepi's words dragged out in intermittent conversation. She and Dagi glared at each other until Mepi broke up their staring contest with a loud snore.

Dagi stood. "I will keep you no longer, old father. You look tired."

Mepi's head bounced upward in response. "But you've just arrived. Finish your milk."

Dagi gulped down the rest of the milk and wiped his mouth on his arm. "I will come again later when we can speak alone." He kissed Mepi on the head before sending Asenat a last spiteful glare from which she did not shrink away.

He left, and she'd won though it was foolish to be at odds with anyone here. Dagi could drag her name like a fire cloth through a field, and he would if he got wind of her identity. But for now he was too wild and caught up in the revelry of his own youth to give her a second look.

Mepi snored softly, and Asenat knelt before his chair. "My Ibis." She shook his arm and his grey lashes fluttered open.

He smiled. "There you are, my dove. You just missed Prince Dagi, come to visit." He patted her cheek, and her eyes welled with tears. He was so childlike today, but he was happy. Of course, she would forgive his speaking of her too much. She prayed she would be with him again before he took his journey into the West.

Wenen helped Mepi up and Asenat embraced him again. "I love you, my Ibis." She sniffed back tears of guilt for what she planned to do.

"And I love you, my dove." He patted her arm as Wenen led him off to rest.

She walked into the guest room and passed Henhenit who stripped the linen from her couch. She continued to the far side of the chamber where a little terrace overlooked a small courtyard.

"He loves you, my lady. We all do. Do not leave him in such a manner, I beg you."

Henhenit's plea tore at Asenat's heart, but she would not turn to answer it. She struggled with leaving Mepi while the likes of Dagi paraded around the palace. Mepi meant no harm in praising her. He was proud, unlike Potipherah who hid her away like a shameful secret. But Lord Nebsumenu said he would speak of her to the king, and no one speaking of Potipherah's secrets could stay safe. She would not risk Mepi's safety, not when it was said that even the sovereign bewared the great high priest of Iunu.

Henhenit's kiss on the back of her head drove tears from her eyes, but Asenat did not move until she heard the matron leave the room.

She knelt by her travel sack to retrieve a little box of rings with which she would barter her way downriver and back to Iunu. Alarmed by its soundless light weight, she shook the box, then opened it.

Empty.

Her breath came in short bursts. She sat back on her heels, stiff and silent. She remembered the sack pressed in Dagi's armpit, his time alone in Mepi's dwelling, and she struck her thigh. That little reprobate had filched something after all.

CHAPTER THREE

HETNU

AFTER THE INCIDENT IN THE KING'S MORNING hall, Hetnu passed his duties to an under-butler and took his barge upriver to a place he seldom frequented, his own sprawling estate. He ascended his water steps as his house steward met him under the shade of a doum palm tree and passed him a note.

Hetnu closed it in his fist and followed his steward down a shaded path, his senses lulled by the swinging counterweight of Nen's jeweled collar. He glanced once or twice at the formal gardens ruined by drought in the last few years. They held the promise of a colorful display if the seasonal winds would relent.

Nen led him to his private garden off the main sleeping chamber where Hetnu took a single step forward and stopped. "What's this?" He gestured toward the fertile delight before him, so lush and verdant despite the hard east winds.

"Does my lord not remember the challenge he accepted from the king's architect?"

Hetnu narrowed his eyes at the hint of mockery in Nen's tone. "You are dismissed." He waved off his steward and entered his garden to inspect the changes with a glower. All the world knew he'd accepted the challenge of the king's half-breed architect. Kitjau boasted his gardening skills, despite the low river levels.

Hetnu looked over the improvements to his garden and sucked in his cheeks. The wild limbs of his favorite persea had not been altered. And new walls were added to deter eavesdropping servants and keep out the eyes of the vulgar. He was forced to give that braggart his inward grudging approval. It vexed him that the winters grew colder each year, yet somehow that barbarian, Kitjau had done more for a garden than all the gods had done for the whole of Egypt. He did not approve of how Kitjau often steered the sovereign away from preparing his tomb and directed his attention to building gardens and a scroll room. Khakheperre was better off without him.

Hetnu made his way to a shaded corner near a brightly tiled fish pool and sank onto a bench. The cacophony of birdsong hid the catch in his throat as he checked his surroundings. Finding himself alone, he lay back on the stone bench and let out a howl of agony. He wept, swabbing kohl-streaked tears until his knuckles blackened and his belly heaved dry hiccups. He'd had enough dealings with foreigners to last a lifetime.

His well-meant efforts to save the king made matters worse. He was a fool to bargain with a condemned man who was bound to exaggerate. What else could one expect from a slave more likely to receive death than favor?

Proclaiming one year of blessed harvest would have been enough to give the king time to deal with the raptors of his court. Even two years would have been forgivable. But seven years?

Preposterous.

Hetnu couldn't remember seven consecutive years of good harvest that occurred either by prophecy or by chance. He shook with fresh grief and blubbered his misery anew. This was his reward for attempting to show kindness to a lowly slave. Yoseph had made a laughingstock of the king in his most desperate time of need.

Everyone knew Khakheperre suffered bouts of sickness, but, as a god, it was the king's duty to prove the favor of the great gods and maintain Ma'at or divine order over the land. The harvests had been poor for the last few years, and now men whispered that the gods did not favor Khakheperre, that he was not fit to rule.

The governors took the king's poor health as an opportunity to filch what rightfully belonged to him. They purloined Khakheperre's taxes, turning his land into their own little kingdoms instead of working to curtail the chaos that accompanied low food supplies. They'd grown fat and sought to break his authority when his health took a turn for the worse. Now they expected him to die.

Hetnu sat up, full of misery at the chaos overtaking the land. The message Nen passed him was still crumpled in his hand. He broke the seal and read its contents, then tossed it in the direction of a fishpond. Someone was out to make a bigger laughingstock of him than he had made of himself this morning. But he was through making bargains and reclined again on the bench, covering his face. Footsteps approached.

"Go away, Nen. And do not come out until you are called for."

"I didn't expect you to call and so came of my own volition."

Hetnu shot upright at the familiar voice, almost smacking his face against a taut brown paunch. He hadn't seen his friend's mischievous grin in years. "Djehuti!" He leapt into a crushing embrace, tolerating hearty back slaps with good cheer.

Djehuti's laughter rang out against the walls of the garden. "Don't they feed you in the king's house?" He nudged Hetnu back. "You're no more than a stick in a kilt."

"A heavily jeweled stick, I hope you'll take note." Hetnu sniffed, pulling a mask of arrogance to compensate for his watery smile. The presence of his childhood friend warmed his heart.

"I suppose they must weigh you down with something to keep the sand storms from taking you off." Djehuti turned Hetnu in a half embrace and bellowed toward the house. "Nen, get yourself out here, man!"

Nen stepped from the shadows of the doorway.

"Be a good man and fetch us a meal." Djehuti slapped his belly.

"I'm not hungry," Hetnu protested.

"Your underfed frame says otherwise." Djehuti gestured toward Nen. "And tell the cooks to make it a good one. Your master's cross with me."

"I am not cross!" Hetnu carped. "Fetch Imini also, and bring my head herbs."

Nen bowed at the instructions and left.

"Now don't blame poor Nen for letting me into your private garden." Djehuti steered Hetnu to a sitting area under a tamarisk tree. "I forced him."

"He shall lose his position immediately. Take him with you when you depart."

Djehuti plopped down into a cushioned chair. "Yes,

indeed, I'll take him. He's the discerning sort. And this garden, how beautiful." Djehuti clasped his hands. "A fit retreat for the gods themselves."

Hetnu harrumphed and stretched out on a couch. He gave no response to the compliment of Kitjau's improvements but flung off his wig. A red hennaed braid slapped his shoulder. Djehuti followed suit, revealing a shining egg of a pate, nestled in a ring of tight red curls. It was a fashion to henna one's grey hair though Hetnu hardly considered himself an aged man.

"This Imini you spoke of, is she your woman?" Djehuti leaned forward. "It's about time you found some distraction from your duties. But tell me of the mad Asiatic who charmed the king out of executing him this morning."

Hetnu gripped his forehead. "You've heard of my disgrace already, have you? It's why you find me here weeping like a newborn. May my foolishness soon be forgotten."

"On the contrary, it's spreading like fire through the city. Prosperity after so many lean years. I shall be the first to send up a harvest thank-offering to Min and Renenutet. May we all live to see it."

Hetnu groaned at Djehuti's misplaced enthusiasm. Potipherah was probably having a good laugh. He would be sure to turn the event in the king's morning hall to his advantage.

The sound of little footsteps scampered down the path. Hetnu sat up on an elbow and cracked a smile. Djehuti turned in his chair. "And who is this little beauty?"

"Isn't she a treasure?" Hetnu clapped a hand to his chest at the tot coming their way. Nen followed and set down the tray of warm water and herbs, but Hetnu had quite forgotten his headache at the sight of his little dear one.

Imini stepped forward like a princess. Her head perfumed

and shaved to a sidelock of thin, oiled braids, clicking with carnelian beads and fish charms for spells of protection. She beamed a smile, bright against the shock of her rich, dark skin, her limbs decked in red and yellow beads.

"I found her wailing on the docks one night, sitting in her own excrement with a face full of snot and tears," Hetnu said. "Poor little thing. I took pity and had one of my servants extract her from the dead woman wrapped around her. That was over a year ago and she's brought nothing but joy to my heart ever since."

At a soft word from Nen, she turned and gave Djehuti a little bow then started for Hetnu's arms. His heart swelled.

"She bows to me as though I were an afterthought." Djehuti blustered in mock protest.

"You are." Hetnu set her on his lap to spread her little beaded apron across her thighs. Her nurse had thoughtfully dressed her in the outfit he'd purchased while touring the Walls of the Ruler on the king's business. "I am her whole world."

"Nonsense. She ignores us both. Sell her to me at once." Djehuti waggled his brows until Imini giggled.

Servants brought out a feast and Djehuti fell on the food before they could lay out the trays. "Eat," he ordered, stuffing his mouth until his jowls expanded.

Hetnu smiled at his friend's unrefined manners. From their youth, Djehuti gorged on his food like a man at war and was just as greedy now as when they were boys. No man could hold back change, and at their age there was precious little that did not change. It was an encroaching beast, devouring a man's life and ritual, telling him he was getting old. Useless. Djehuti's crude manners gave Hetnu a sense of peace. They were something time had not changed.

Imini's nurse came to retrieve her, but Hetnu sent her away, satisfied to let the child nap on the couch beside him as he talked.

"I must thank you again for the appointment you've sent my way." Djehuti kissed his fingertips between bites of meat.

"Nonsense, your appointment as governor to the province of the Upper Laurels is well deserved and needed. I merely pointed out to the king your work as mayor, and that you have the right blood in your veins for the position. I only wish that we could have moved you farther south where the king meets his greatest resistance. The Sons of the South give Khakheperre nothing but trouble." Djehuti surpassed his well-born half brothers in talent, proving himself resourceful, despite his inferior circumstances of birth.

"I've been working hard to show my gratitude in a way I hope the king will not forget."

Hetnu inclined his ear toward his friend. "What news have you?"

"Well." Djehuti scooted his bulk forward. "You know Deduamen, of the Min province."

"An utter cud chewer!"

"Yes, yes, Hetnu, but he too is of royal bloo—"

"Of the most uncanny, prolific lot I know! Sister and daughter-wives that produce just the right number of pups to keep their line going in the fashion of kings. But they are not kings, mind you, and it should never have been allowed."

"Such is the practice of many a rich man, claiming himself part of a royal line. It's foolishness, I agree, but Deduamen's family has behaved well enough in their province—"

"Which should never have come into their hands!" Hetnu's nostrils flared. "If Khakheperre's forefathers had obliterated the line of their rivals, then he would not have to suffer this humiliation. Deduamen and his whole family are like dangerous pets the good god is now forced to tolerate!"

"Hetnu, would you let me finish?"

Hetnu crossed his arms. Deduamen's growing popularity among the southern governors had all the stink of Potipherah behind it. "Well?" He motioned. "Go on, then."

Djehuti's eyes glittered as he broke into a smile. "Deduamen's oldest daughter has just died in childbirth."

"The poor girl," Hetnu said without inflection. "But what does that matter when he has two daughters to spare? Twins, I hear." A king had every right to marry or approve the marriage of those nobly born, though Deduamen dared to keep his girls from court. Khakheperre's father should have taken better care with such threat facing his son.

"Twins to be exact." Djehuti winked. "Appipa and A'at are their names, and I hear Appipa is as lovely as a spring morning, as beautiful as Hathor herself."

"Who would know with the girls so secure in their father's lair? He's probably keeping them for himself and for his son."

"Not anymore. They've vanished."

Hetnu jerked upright, grasping the side of the couch. "You know this first hand?"

"Almost."

Hetnu slumped. "Almost? Don't entertain me with one of your childlike exaggerations, Djehuti." He expelled a gust of air and leaned back. "You were always excitable when we were boys, and you've worsened with age. The girls are probably closed up in mourning for their dead sister. How can you be so numb-skulled, man?"

"The anonymous note I—"

"An anonymous note?" Hetnu pointed to the fish pond. "There's mine. Add it to your collection."

Djehuti rose to pluck the note from a bush near the pond, and Hetnu was torn between amusement and annoyance when he did not laugh but studied the note, running his tongue over his lower lip.

"I'd put a watch at the palace gates if I were you."

Hetnu searched his face. "You can't be serious."

"Servants are selling out their masters for pittance. If Potipherah is hiding a child—"

"It's foolishness." Hetnu snatched the note from Djehuti and threw it on a tray.

"Then let a spy handle it. Better yet, let me."

Hetnu cackled, but for the first time, Djehuti's jolly face darkened with a scowl.

"Search out a far-fetched matter, Hetnu. Especially when the stakes are high." The words cut through Hetnu's laughter like a knife.

"You are overexcited."

"But no longer a boy. And you can be sure that if I say a thing is so, it is so."

"We shall see." Hetnu avoided his intense gaze. "How is your son, Rudi?" He could have struck himself as soon as the question left his mouth. It was a poor change of subject, one that had kept him at odds with Djehuti for years.

"You speak as if Rudi were my only son." Djehuti bristled. "I remind you I have two more."

"Then I'm sorry for you, but if you hadn't married your slave—"

"Must we go over this, again?"

"The king has asked for Rudi. I think there is an opportunity at court." Hetnu crossed his arms, unable to hold back the scorn brimming at his lips. "Any number of noblewomen would have married you after your first wife died and given Za'amun and Meru the proper blood. Instead they are seen as the sons of slaves."

"Do you see them this way?"

"Of course I do. They are nothing like Rudi, whom the king himself has called for, but coarse like their mother who keeps the strife going between them."

"My mother was a slave, you old coot!"

"Yes, and one who knew her place, unlike your wife. You cannot deny that Rudi has character while those other two miscreants do not."

"My wife has every right to insist on the best for her sons."

"But must she be so jealous? So imperial?" Hetnu sucked his teeth. "Don't expect me to speak in her behalf. If I have anything to do with it, she and her sons will never come to court."

"She has no desire to come."

"Then good for all of us."

Imini groaned, and Hetnu scooped her up in his arms. He pulled the thumb from her mouth. "No, my love, you will ruin your teeth with that." She moaned against his chest.

"All this talk of correct blood, Hetnu. Yet you love this Cushite tot who is not of your body. Hypocrite."

Hetnu rocked Imini in his arms. "I admit I am where she is concerned, but she has time yet to be trained. Your sons are as rotten as their preposterous mother."

The fighting look in Djehuti's eyes fell away. He dropped his shoulders and let out a breath. "Yes, she has failed me in this, I will admit. But if I could just get my younger boys to court like Rudi, they would be compelled to improve."

Hetnu held up his hand in protest. "I will not assist you in this. Let us drop the matter."

"I have a proposition for you."

"Please. No bargains."

"What if I delivered Deduamen's daughters to the palace water steps? Or even Potipherah's girl?" Djehuti picked up the crumpled note and made a show of reading it, then waved it about. "Potipherah with a daughter by his deceased wife. A daughter he's kept hidden. A daughter the sovereign knows nothing about." He sat back slowly. "It's treason my friend, treason by the king's chief priest and counselor."

Hetnu remained silent. Djehuti well understood the hope of his composed hatred.

"Come now, Hetnu, just think of the revenge you could have on that old fox if this were true. The powerful high priest of Iunu, who has caused both you and the king great distress, finally brought to heel."

"I've made my last bargain in the king's morning hall. I'll make no more."

"But a daughter makes a man guarded, protective." Djehuti's gaze shifted to Imini. "You've proven that yourself."

Hetnu's resolve weakened. How long had he prayed for some doom to overtake Potipherah who flourished while the king's health withered? What he would not give to have that note prove true. Potipherah's daughter, hiding in the palace.

Imini awakened, and he set the child down to pick flowers. He looked up to find Djehuti holding a faint smile. "You are a wretched old snake charmer. Of course, I'd give my right arm to crush Potipherah. And if I did not love you so, Djehuti, I would hate you for your cunning. But, if you could give me any real proof—"

"You'd break that silly oath you swore never to help my sons rise at court," Djehuti finished, bursting with a vigor that sapped Hetnu's strength to deny him. "Then consider it done, old friend." He leaned forward, his face split with a grin. "Consider it done."

HETNU HURRIED THROUGH THE CORRIDORS toward the king's meeting room, gripping two jugs of wine. He'd lost track of time, having accepted Djehuti's bargain just to shut him up.

Potipherah with a daughter. Indeed. What madness had overtaken him to indulge Djehuti in such a manner?

The king was meeting with his top counselors, three of whom supported him with unquestionable loyalty throughout these trying years in the land.

Mentuser came from a long line of meticulous royal healers. He was long-limbed and solemn and kept the sovereign's health with medical skill and the sacred spells he muttered to his patron goddess, Sakhmet.

The treasurer, Nebsumenu, was a dashing yet steady man of great talent who worked the king's funds to pull resources from what seemed to be thin air. This was crucial with the land suffering a mild famine and the swindling governors holding back more than their fair share of grain and goods.

Then there was Resnakt, who was both a royal sealer and attendant of the broad hall, in line to become the hall's leader when Lord Reniqer took his retirement. Resnakt had done very well for a young man who was of an age with the sovereign and recently promoted by Lord Nebsumenu to deputy treasurer.

These three counselors bore the coveted title "Intimate Friend of the King" behind their names, but were affectionately known as The King's Watchmen.

Despite these good men surrounding Khakheperre, Hetnu could not reach the good god's side quickly enough. The hypostyle hall in the king's corridor was a maze of columns, and he stopped to catch his breath and set down the wine jugs he carried. Leaning against one of the colorful monoliths, Hetnu heard low grating voices. He peeked around the column and there saw the reason his heart always gave warning to stay close beside the king.

Potipherah.

The priest cornered some poor soul obscured from Hetnu's view, hissing threats and jabbing thick blue fingers into his victim's chest. A scoundrel in his natural habitat.

Hetnu drew back against the column. There were probably a number of palace servants spying for the high priest, but to witness such intimidation in the king's house proved one thing true. The sicker Khakheperre became, the bolder Potipherah grew.

All high priests were the scourge of kings, yet, before he died, Khakheperre's father titled Potipherah Father of the God, giving him a permanent position of counsel that not even Khakheperre could revoke. Potipherah had become a beast to be wary of, holding little sway with the sovereign but great influence with his enemies.

By the time Hetnu pushed off the column and stepped out to shame the brute, Potipherah had already shoved his victim ahead. Hetnu picked up his jugs of wine and followed, glancing over the lower servants in the meeting room to see which of them seemed shaken. He was livid at Potipherah's state of calm, but the issue would have to be dealt with later.

The meeting was about to commence, and Hetnu moved to the polished ebon sideboard and broke the clay seal on one of the jugs. He decanted the wine into silver bowls, adding garlic and honey to the king's bowl for his cough and a little sea water to Prince Khakure's wine. Khakure watched him from over his father's shoulder. He was eight years old and his father's Staff of Old Age, Khakheperre's heir and co-regent.

Co-regency became a safe-fall for kings when the first of the line was treacherously murdered. Khakheperre instructed his son on the formal behavior of a king, but he was ever the loving father despite his waning strength, and today he sat Khakure on his lap.

"That's a pretty trinket dangling from your waist, Resnakt." The king lifted two bowls from the tray Hetnu presented.

Resnakt unhooked the little figure of Ma'at from his belt and Khakure hopped down to fetch it.

Hetnu returned with another tray of bowls for the counselors. Indeed, it was a fine piece. The skin of the goddess was sculpted in polished peridot. Wings of dark red jasper stretched from behind the solid gold sheath she wore. A rare piece, and a rare hand that mastered the hard gem.

"Remarkable." The king turned the jeweled trinket over in his hand.

Resnakt shrugged. "A gift from fawning relatives I wear for luck." He grinned, giving a perfunctory nod. "Keep it, Majesty."

"Nonsense." The king passed it to his physician. "Exquisite don't you think?"

"I could carve the good god one of these."

The king chortled. "You and that old surgical knife of yours are never parted, Mentuser. But until you can carve one from a gem, this shall belong only to Resnakt." The king passed the trinket back. Resnakt hooked it to his belt, stealing a glance at Nebsumenu.

Hetnu proffered the wine tray and fought down a grin at Resnakt's embarrassment. No man in his right mind wished to outdo his sovereign.

"What entertainment we had in the morning hall."

Hetnu ground his teeth at Potipherah's mockery, yet he held the proper bow.

"I wonder where the Asiatic overheard the '*Tradition of the Seven Lean Years.*' Someone must have practiced the story with him." Potipherah slid his gaze to Hetnu, then back to the king. "The tale was set down by King Djoser eons ago." He sat forward to hover over the tray of wine bowls. "You should have known better, Hetnu," Potipherah mumbled, "having once been a tutor, yourself."

"Take your wine, Potipherah," the king ordered, his words as tight as the grip on his son.

Potipherah plucked up one of the bowls and reclined with a satisfied smile.

Nebsumenu took the last bowl, and Hetnu gripped the tray, hard pressed not to bash the priest in the head before he took his place on the left side of the king's chair. He balled his fist. A mortifying swell of water rose in his eyes.

He hadn't realized how similar Yoseph's interpretation was to that of King Djoser's. The famed stele explaining the seven lean years could still be found in the south at Abu for the world to behold. Yoseph had not only lied. He lied badly.

"Return the Asiatic to prison," Potipherah said. "Better yet, I'll take him back to Iunu and teach that jackanapes to interpret dreams." He snorted and sipped his wine.

"He is my prisoner, Potipherah, not yours."

The sharp defiance in the king's voice tore at Hetnu's heart. He should have left Yoseph in the garrison. Better to have let him rot and tell lies to himself than to the king at such a dangerous time as this.

"Your garrison has spoilt the dog," Potipherah said. "I've heard he practically runs the place. What a golden tongue he must have. He could use some humbling. Don't you agree, Lord Nebsumenu?"

"I don't know." The king's treasurer lowered his wine bowl to his lap. "What if the Asiatic's words prove true after all?"

"'Grain was scant. Fruits were dried up and everything they eat was short. Men robbed their companions and infants wailed. Youths and courtiers in want and old men in sorrow with their legs crouched to the ground.'"

Potipherah recited the ancient text, leaving a chill in the room. It spoke of famine and chaos in days gone by. But if the gods didn't work a miracle, if the land was forced to endure another year of famine, chaos would soon return.

The priest tossed his empty bowl on the tray. "These words from the venerable Djoser, I believe, not some filthy sand dweller, smelling of sweat and dung."

"Resnakt, Khakure has a request of you." The king

nudged his son, and Potipherah's face twitched at the abrupt dismissal.

"By all means, speak, Majesty." Resnakt nodded as the king touched his son on the shoulder.

"I will be chadding downriver next year to inspect my likeness and name on the Walls of the Ruler, and I thought your sons would like to join me on the excursion."

"You do me great honor, Majesty. The boys will be delighted." Resnakt dipped his head, and Khakure's grin stretched almost to his long ears.

Hetnu bit back a grimace. Resnakt's sons were the children of concubines. It was not Ma'at for such base-borns to surround the royal heir. Djehuti's head would bloat to bursting if he ever got wind of this.

"Let us come to the point of this meeting," Potipherah cut in. "Ma'at is absent from the land and there is need of a vizier."

"The king is due a grace period!" Hetnu snapped, unable to stop himself.

Potipherah glanced at the ceiling. "Will someone inform the counseling cupbearer that there has been a grace period for a little more than two years."

"I had not known that I was under a time restriction." The king clutched the cylinder pendant at his chest. The vizier's seal was his power-in-action on the land. Placed in the wrong hands, Khakheperre would be no more than the jeweled trinket of the goddess Ma'at he'd handled.

"Since there is no vizier, it is my duty as father of the god to seek the governors' counsel on filling the position, unless the good god can sway the court by the Front of the Year ceremony. It is the law, Majesty, recorded in the last ordinance of your father."

"With your persuasion, I'm sure!" Hetnu clipped out.

The king raised a hand, and Hetnu mashed his lips while Resnakt and Nebsumenu argued heroically on his behalf. But it was no use. The ordinance had been carefully sewn in as a condition to Khakheperre's rule, along with Potipherah's authority.

"There are governors in the north His Majesty might consider."

Potipherah shook his head at Nebsumenu's suggestion. "None are eligible, being so late with their grain tax. Their yields are as low as the governors in the south."

"I'll have none of the arrogant southern governors as a vizier."

"None are worthy, Majesty." Potipherah's gaze followed the king as he reached for his wine bowl. "Except one."

"And who might that be?"

"Why, the king's most dedicated servant who sits peacefully on his lands and who is caught up on all back tribute due the king."

The priest shot Hetnu a sidelong glance that filled him with dread, then addressed the king.

"Your faithful governor of the Min province, Lord Deduamen."

Hetnu touched the back of the king's chair to steady himself at Potipherah's words. Surely, the world had come to an end.

CHAPTER FOUR

YOSEPH

YOSEPH LAY ON THE FLOOR OF THE STOREROOM.
The sun's heat baked the mud brick walls of the room full
of trunks, bolts of coarse fabric, and bundled papyri stalks.
Still, the place was a luxury compared to the hole Qareg
stuck him in at the garrison.

After being hauled out of the king's presence, he'd spent
a day in the palace lockdown. Sabni came for him that
night, this time without a litter, without guards, or a torch.
He unlatched the bolt and shot a warning look across the
cell as he stepped inside, pressing a finger to his lips.

Stay quiet.

Sabni pulled him from the floor and stretched Yoseph's
arm over his shoulders. The two of them moved in deep
shadows across the palace grounds. Once or twice they
stopped to wait against a wall for nearby voices to fade.
They sprinted from the light of torches a few times, panting
hard by the time they reached the storerooms by a temple
wall. Sabni shoved him into one of the rooms and latched
the bolt with no explanation.

Yoseph stared at the storeroom's thatched ceiling. How

long had he been here? Eight days? Ten? In his sleep, he ran for his father's camp just beyond Egypt's borders, then awakened from the lucid dreams with an old misery gripping his heart.

Elohim would protect him. Elohim would deliver him and make them set him free. He'd prayed himself dry, begging God to hear. He could no longer remember the faces of those he loved.

He understood that he was to remain quiet in this place and spent his days studying the sounds of passing servants and young men dicing against the walls.

Why had the king hidden him away?

At night, a slave brought food and dumped his pot. But for the last few nights, he'd heard whispers outside the storerooms, footfalls that were quiet and careful with enough deliberation to wake a man from his sleep.

Someone fumbled at the latch on the door and Yoseph sat up. Perhaps it was Hetnu come to announce him a free man. But it was the sour-faced slave with his meal. He was late tonight and had eaten half of the bread he tossed across the room onto the dirt floor. He set down a mug of beer, splashing its contents just inside the doorway, dumped the pot, then left, bolting the door behind him.

Yoseph scooped up his meal, limped to a stack of trunks against a wall and climbed them. He sat, chewing the half eaten loaf, chasing each bite down with a sip of beer as he peered into the darkness. The treasury torches were out again, but the king's coffers were protected by an army of guards and his dwelling by a great many walls.

Yoseph drained the contents of his cup and climbed down to lie among the bolts of fabric. He was drifting off when he heard whispers at the door. Someone strained at the latch, then struck the bolt. The door creaked open, and two men stepped into the room. One of them had a cudgel. Yoseph sat upright, catching the sour grin on one of their faces. His blood pulsed in his ears. There was nowhere to run.

CHAPTER FIVE

SABNI

THE THRILL OF A HARD RUN THUDDED IN THE boy's chest. He stopped to catch his breath, bracing sweaty palms on his knees. His was the victory, being so far ahead of the other boys he raced home.

The city glowed, a lantern against the night sky. Wai, with its spires and temples. Wai, where his father ruled as leader among a network of small provinces, though none compared to Kerma, the great capital city of Cush, farther south of Egypt. But the discovery of gold within Wai's borders had increased its renown.

There were no guards on the wall tonight, but the gates would soon close. The boy peered into the city, seeing his mother's concerned face as she turned from the doorway of their house, tugging his little sister's hand. He loped toward the city gate until a strange light glinted off the gold medallion bouncing on his chest.

A man blocked his path with a torch as bright and fiendish as the look in his eyes. The boy recognized the squat-faced grin creeping across his face.

Qareg.

He hurled the torch over the wall, setting the city ablaze.
The boy stepped back and screamed.

"Fire!"

Sabni shot upright on his sleeping mat, grabbing his dagger in one fluid motion. He leapt up, running.

Outside the barracks, bright tongues of fire licked the night sky in the distance. Sabni staggered to a halt as men rushed by him, sloshing leather buckets of water. Amidst shouts and confusion, his chest tightened. "Mother," he whispered.

Dropping his weapon, he took off past the organized lines of men with leather buckets and ran straight for the cluster of burning storerooms. "Mother!" he shouted, dancing around falling beams. He coughed as the smoke choked out his strength and his memories gushed like the life-blood of vanquished prey. This was no haze-filled dream.

The city of Wai had been razed to the ground.

He dropped to his knees. Flames shot up like pillars around him. Embers nipped his flesh, and the roar of fire drowned the wail that tore from his throat. How could he let them make him forget?

Men beyond the wall of flames called out to him. He could not speak or move. He was numb to all things but the buried memory Qareg had drawn from him with cruel words.

I heard they lopped off your father's head.

The words echoed in his mind, peeling back memories like rotting flesh.

He fell forward on the ground, squeezing his eyes shut. That night in Wai, the fire took whatever the marauders failed to plunder. Sabni wept into the dirt. Let it take him also.

A sharp thump cut through the roar of flames, and he raised his head. Another thump. He crawled to one of the storerooms whose roof had caught fire. Sucking in a breath, he staggered to his feet to kick at the door. It gave way and bumped an obstacle. A wall of smoke rushed at him. He squinted and waved his arms, almost missing the unconscious man inside. The Asiatic, Yoseph.

Sabni reached for the rope that bound the man's feet. Tugging the dead weight, he pulled the man from the building just before the roof caved in. The fire chased them, granting no retreat. He dragged the slave by sheer strength of will around obstacles of burning residue littering the ground.

The air thinned, and Sabni coughed with the heat at his back. He collapsed and smacked the ground, heaving air into his burning lungs. There were shouts. Footfalls pounded toward him. Cool hands gripped his arms and legs and dragged him farther from the flames. His world went black.

CHAPTER SIX

HETNU

HETNU SUCKED IN A BREATH AND COUGHED. The upper north garden was one of the places least affected by last night's fire. Still, the air smelled as scorched as a cooking pot left over flames too long. He tapped his jaw with the hound game piece. Mepi was sharp as flint for a man of his years, and Hetnu was tempted to unload the dread that sat like a sack of stones in his chest, but the old father was long past the age of bearing such ills.

After the meeting the king held with his counselors, Hetnu had seen the two marks on Khakheperre's chest beneath his jeweled collar, marks as blue as Potipherah's fingers. Would the priest dare to go so far? Hetnu's lips burned to speak his suspicions, but he took a sip of pekha to squelch the temptation.

"You must show me your new gardens." Mepi rolled the jackal game piece between his fingers before placing it in the next slot on the game board. "I hear Kitjau has worked a wonder upon them."

Hetnu tapped his game piece on the table, drawing on

his patience. "If one more person asks to see Kitjau's work in my garden, I'll rip the whole thing out."

"You should have known better than to accept his challenge." Mepi chuckled. "Kitjau is the king's finest gardener and architect."

"It's his Egyptian side, I assure you." Hetnu moved his game piece farther down the board. "That mongrel from Byblos won't get any compliment from me. He's supposed to be a prisoner of war."

"Politics." Mepi glanced up. "Claiming him a prisoner was the only way to keep him safe. He's behaved and done well for himself."

"Khakheperre's father, Osiris Amenemhat, did him well. He should have never been allowed to study with the royal architects."

"You cannot deny Kitjau's talent, and if the river ever rises enough to fill the palace canals again, he'll prove his genius in the new gardens."

"Bah!" Hetnu waved off Mepi's words. "We've yet to see it. He already has the run of the king's house. Hammers where he will and the king says nothing."

Nor had the king said a word about Yoseph's interpretation of his Horus dream. But the provincial governors made comments enough, some staying on to take bets on whether the Asiatic's words would prove true. In the meantime, they drained the sovereign's wine stores, and this with the Festival of the Ruler hard upon them in a few days.

And there was Deduamen who would arrive at the front of the year to be installed as vizier. Hetnu's blood boiled at the sheer possibility of the king's blood-enemy holding such power. Djehuti's ridiculous plan to find Deduamen's twin daughters was a last string of hope. The king's power tottered like a stone on the edge of a cliff. This was Potipherah's vengeful retribution for anyone trying to undo his plotting. Something must be done. And soon.

Mepi's servant woman, Henhenit, sat some distance away in the shade of a tree with Imini in her lap. She took it upon herself to teach the child finger songs and little dances to distract her from sucking her thumb. Hetnu was proud of his little darling who enraptured the whole court. She was but three years of age, yet understood the power of her own charm. Not even that cold fish, Weret, the god's wife, could resist and called for Imini once or twice to hear her sweet voice.

Mepi's head hung low on his shoulders as he looked over the game board, but Hetnu wasn't cowed. The old father was merciless at the game of Hounds and Jackals with that deceiving slow hand of his. Hetnu waited his turn, thumbing an ivory jackal game piece with amethyst eyes and ears outlined in fine gold, set against a mother of pearl collar at the jackal's neck. "Exquisite." He stroked the figure's carved teeth.

"It was Osiris Amenemhat who gave them to me, you know. I was his favorite."

"Yes, you old showy windbag. You were his favorite everything." Hetnu took another pull of pekha, nursing the chilled cup in his hands. The tarty fruit drink was a rare treat with such poor harvests in the past three years. Hetnu drained his cup, then divided the rest between himself and Mepi while he hummed along with Imini's little tune.

"I warn you, I'm well acquainted with each game piece and will know you have taken one," Mepi said without looking up.

"Don't blame me for seeking compensation. You never let me win."

"You once tutored the king, Hetnu. And I have tutored you. Stop whining and master the game."

Hetnu chuckled. "Well said, Master. You are still the brightest and the best of the residence."

Mepi harrumphed. "And I'm still watching my game pieces. You were a light-fingered child and took several of my best reed pens among other things."

Hetnu sat erect. "You knew? Then how did I avoid getting my back beaten raw by that awful stick of yours?"

"I had no children then. You were an amusement to me, like a curious little monkey."

Hetnu grimaced at such an account of his youth and observed a woman who knelt by Henhenit in light conversation. She stroked Imini's back as she drifted off to sleep. He frowned.

"Leave Yimenet be." Mepi pinned him with a firm look. "Tend your game."

"She's Ameny's woman."

"Is it that or because she's from Crete?"

Hetnu stole another look at the slender bright-skinned lady dressed in high court fashion. A reprimand perched on the tip of his tongue.

"She lacks friends, Hetnu. Let her make one."

The lady nodded a greeting at them.

Hetnu pursed his lips, glaring at her until she left. He glanced up at Mepi. "Don't stare at me like that."

"You have a classic case of Egyptian conceit, and every foreigner in your path must suffer for it. That poor girl can command the color of her skin no better than Imini."

"Please, leave Imini out of this."

"All right, Sabni, then. He, like Imini, is Cushite. You've always been unreasonably hard on him though he's truer to the king than most, foreigner or no."

"Khakheperre is distracted by such a friendship."

"Was that your excuse for sending Sabni to the northern borders? It was a cruel thing to do to a boy pampered in the bosom of a prince."

"I did it to protect Khakheperre. Who could tell what Sabni remembered from his childhood? He came here as a slave and in time might have put a dagger in Khakheperre's back." Hetnu plucked a hound from the board. "I sent him to the borders that the gods might test him. He returned a champion. Let that be the end of it."

Mepi snorted, and for a few moments they put their tension into the game before he spoke again. "Their friendship is unique."

"It is dangerous." Hetnu bit his tongue. The king warned him not to speak of Sabni's past, but he had his own opinion of the good god's cavalier favor extended to that barbarian.

"And that Asiatic dream teller you brought in. You had no part in that fire that almost devoured him last night, I take it. I had hoped the poor fellow was in some less danger of being disposed of after giving us all such a good foretelling of a profitable harvest. But someone appears to share your view of foreigners."

Hetnu turned his palms down on the table and pushed back. "Shall I fetch your stick, master? Perhaps you'd like to take a few strokes across my back for every foreigner I do not trust."

"A stick across your back did little good when you were young. I doubt it would soften your rough hide now. But mark my word, Sabni will do the king good in the end."

Hetnu held back his objection as Mepi crunched on his traditional morning treat of cucumbers and crackers.

"You said then."

"Mmmh?" Mepi drained his cup of pekha.

"You said I amused you in my youth and that you had no children *then*. Your age is a miracle in itself. Don't tell me the gods have performed another and that you've now fathered a child." He chuckled, but Mepi's mouth hung open a fraction.

"I have a child, a foster daughter." His tone was guarded. "She is an intelligent girl. Visits me at the palace from time to time."

Hetnu examined Mepi's closed face. "My, but you are tight-lipped about the girl. I've been told Potipherah has a daughter also." He slapped Mepi's hand and leaned back to snicker. "There. Can you believe it? And she, scholarly and no illegitimate, resides here in the palace." Hetnu's eyes watered with laughter. "That crocodile with a daughter. Come now, Mepi. She must be the ugliest hind part of a water horse or weigh as much as one."

"Who told you such nonsense?"

His sharp tone stifled Hetnu's laughter. "An anonymous note left at my estate. You don't believe me? I am the very mouth of Nekhen and lie not. Call me a fool, but I've even tightened the watch on the palace gates."

Mepi stood. "Forgive me, Hetnu. I must leave you now."

Hetnu stood with him. "Have I offended you in some way?"

"No, no. It's past time for my nap, that's all. My joints have been aching all morning."

"Why did you not say so?" Hetnu stepped around the table ready to assist Mepi, but he raced for his litter.

Henhenit rushed forward to set Imini down and scoop

up the game board and pieces. She bowed, then ran after Mepi's chair moving at an unusually fast pace.

Imini was sour, having her nap cut short. She howled, and Hetnu took her up in his arms. He rubbed her back, relieved that his house steward, Nen, hurried toward them. "Take her," Hetnu ordered, bouncing the child in his arms to break her wails. But Nen stopped short, and the triangular curls of his wig dipped forward as he bowed.

"Master. Lord Djehuti insists you make your way to the palace quay. He bids you retrieve the package immediately."

"What package?"

"He said you would certainly know it on sight."

Hetnu snatched the note from Nen. "What nonsense. How should I identify a package I know nothing about?" Imini screeched and climbed him like a tree. "Take her!" He tugged at her arms as she clung to his pectoral. Something jabbed him in the shoulder, and she let out a cry of protest as he pried one of Mepi's game pieces from her fingers, all the peace of the morning shattered.

"Hire a chair, man! Get the child home!" His voice as hysterical in his ears as Imini's screeching.

Nen took Imini from him and bowed, then hurried off as her sleepy wails echoed against the garden wall. Hetnu blew wind from his cheeks, adjusting his wig before he snapped open Djehuti's note.

Lord Cupbearer,

The package awaits at the palace quay. If you do not find it, it will find you. I've promised you something, and I've delivered. See that you deliver on your promise as well.

Ever your servant,
Djehuti

Hetnu frowned, in no mood for Djehuti's wild schemes, but went in the direction of the quay. If this was a waste of his time, Djehuti would hear about it.

GUARDS PATROLLED THE PARAPETED HIGH walls of the quay. The walls enclosed a river landing of fifteen stone piers large enough to house eight to ten vessels each. Bustling with activity, the palace quay was the busiest place in the king's house and the main entrance for both visitors and imported materials.

Here were the tell-tale signs of a king's wealth, based on how often imported treasures came in. Long ago, and once or twice in Hetnu's youth, every pier was full. But now, less than half were active, and three stored the barges of the governors and nobles visiting from the provinces.

Hetnu strode through the gate and passed the shading yew tree, then stepped back just in time to miss a heavy rope falling from a scaffold. He scanned the area, cursing Djehuti's note.

There were over a hundred wrapped objects strewn on the docks. Any one of them could be this "package" Djehuti spoke of. The porters were staring at him. A foreman winked, and Hetnu drew in his brows, checking the front of his kilt, then behind him. Two painted trunks sat in the shade of the yew he passed. He went to lift one of the lids when someone slapped his hand away.

"Put that down. It's not yours."

He was dumbstruck by the exquisite girl who drew herself up to a dainty height near his chin. Her hair was a bush of spiraled red-brown curls, cascading over her shoulders. His mouth fell open at her honey-colored eyes. Her perfect face was bright with animation, stealing his ability to speak.

"And are you Hetnu, the king's cupbearer?"

"Yes. I am." He tried a commanding tone despite the girl's uncommon allure. "I'm looking for a package delivered by a friend."

"Then look no further," the beauty said as a second girl came up behind her. "We are your package."

Hetnu blinked at the second girl who was a plainer likeness of the first, but with darker brown eyes and a round face, her hair wooly and thick against her collarbone. His gaze volleyed between the girls who were the same, but different. He gasped, slapping a hand to his chest.

By Horus, Djehuti had done it.

The first girl gave a pert smile and spoke the words he was too shocked to utter. "We are the twin daughters of Lord Deduamen. And we have come to marry the king."

CHAPTER SEVEN

POTIPHERAH

POTIPHERAH ENTERED HIS CHAMBER. HIS SLAVE, Khons, dabbed the sweat from his brow. The wind blew hot today, and the air was thick with sand. His spies gave reports, proving themselves as useless as his priests. And he was in no mood to interpret the frivolous dreams of courtiers. He dismissed those waiting to attend him and splayed his fingers for Khons' inspection, wincing at a touch. He sat in a cushioned chair and removed his rings while Khons gathered his herbs and jars.

A head above most priests, Potipherah was as hale as a stonecutter, keeping his body supple through wrestling whenever time would allow. Yet one trivial ailment plagued him.

On his best days, he cracked nuts with his bare hands, but his fingers gave him fickle allegiance in the winter and at sundry times like this. They grew cold, turning so pale in their coloring that not even his rings could hide their ghastly appearance. Khons' solution was the best to date, a concoction of a few herbs, blue lotus, and woad plant that worked like nothing else.

The world concluded his blue fingers were a result of his celestial contact with the gods, and the rumors had gotten him no small merit. Courtiers clamored for his attention. Some came from as far as Byblos to worship with gifts from their coffers and have their dreams interpreted. He was the first prophet of Amun, privy counselor of the heavens, and father of the god. It was fitting that he inspire such awe, so he kept his ailment private.

He winced as Khons pricked his spasming fingers with bone and copper pins. "You should rejoice the gods have not chosen you to be a man of power." He smiled at his slave, expecting no response. Oh, what he might have gleaned from this skilled man had he not arrived so late that day at the slaver's block where Khons staggered forward half dazed, his tongue severed and his mouth stuffed with bloody rags.

Potipherah had used such methods once or twice, attempting to bestow mercy on fools, but a deed on such a one as Khons was barbaric.

He bore himself like one born to privilege, and only among the king's harem were there one or two girls of such coloring with the same tight, slanted eyes. Yet, the message lingering in Khons' countenance was always the same.

I have given up but have not the courage to end my own life.

He deftly plucked out the pins and Potipherah released a breath he hadn't realized he'd been holding. Khons massaged his wrists, and the pain in his throbbing fingers subsided.

Khakheperre had brought this frustration on him. He should have left the running of his government to wiser men as his father had done. His cupbearer's poor attempt at summoning a makeshift dream teller lacked dignity. The desperation of drawing a wild sand dweller from the place of confinement at the garrison. Did Hetnu actually think such a thin scheme would work?

Potipherah still flushed from the insult. As if he would allow one crumb of his status to be negated by the word of a prisoner and slave. His attempt to have the Asiatic dog burned in the storerooms might have failed, but Khakheperre could take it as a warning. Even in his own house, he could hide nothing.

And where was that imbecile Deduamen he'd ordered to the palace? His was the only bloodline in the kingdom pure enough to challenge the king's. Potipherah had ordered the southern governors to hold back their grain tax, while he personally stuffed Deduamen's coffers and paid his provincial taxes. Khakheperre had little choice but to accept him as vizier.

It was Deduamen's forefather, Mentuhotep, who united the two kingdoms and Khakheperre's who murdered him. But when the first Amenemhat king took the crown for his own line, he in turn was murdered. Placing Deduamen as vizier would remind Khakheperre that the tables might turn again if he demanded too much of the provinces.

Potipherah allowed Khons to guide his fingers through the holes of two watertight boxes. He sat patiently as Khons put his supplies away and directed the slave to lay the towel in his lap. He would let his fingers soak a bit longer and turn the rich blue that mystified the courtiers.

"Dismiss your man."

Potipherah looked up and frowned. He drew his fingers from the boxes to wrap them in the linen towel. His uninvited guest wore a short tanned leather kilt, dotted with turquoise and gold beads. How irritating that a prince of the realm would deck himself in some tribal apron of an enemy desert clan. But for this one, it was common enough.

"What do you want, Ameny?"

"It seems the mystery of your magic fingers is revealed." He took a seat across from Potipherah as he patted his fingers dry.

"You are in a bold and playful mood, prince. But I am not your playmate." The dye treatment was ruined. He would have to apply it again later.

"I want you to make me king."

Potipherah's shoulders shook with the chuckle building in his chest. "My dear prince, there are some miracles that not even the gods can bring about."

"I mean it. Make me king, or I will expose your little secret."

Potipherah rose and took a few steps to his wine pitcher. He decanted wine into two bowls and sent a covert wink to Khons, who eyed him warily from the doorway. Potipherah brought a bowl over to Ameny, and the prince gulped down the wine before he could return to his seat.

He supposed one must tolerate the machinations of a jaded prince from time to time and sat facing Ameny as he tended to the ruined dye treatment on his fingers. "You may divulge this secret begging at your lips. But take care with threats, prince."

"You have a daughter."

Potipherah shrugged at the words and took a sip of wine. "A wealthy man may have a hundred daughters and sons which he may or may not choose to acknowledge."

"But this is the daughter of the wife you were rumored to have murdered."

"Tell me Ameny, do you believe every rumor someone can use to milk gold from you?"

"It's no rumor. I heard it from one of your priests come down from Iunu."

"Don't be ridiculous."

"Senib. That's his name. He described her to me as a lanky, dark-skinned girl about seventeen years of age. A tight watch is usually kept on her." He smiled. "Seems your daughter is misplaced."

"Senib you say?" Potipherah took another sip of wine. "I don't recall the name. There are over a thousand priests at Iunu. It would be easy to imitate one." He rose to refill their empty bowls. "No, prince, I fear you have been duped."

"The province lords are ready to rip my brother to shreds if death doesn't take Khakheperre first. Either way, his time is at an end. I must be the next king, and I require your assistance in this."

Potipherah lingered at the wine tray while Ameny rambled on, rising from his chair to pace. He boasted of his qualities, dangling himself like a cheap trinket at a peddler's booth.

Potipherah took up the prince's empty bowl and refilled it, half listening. But as for Senib, who apparently left his temple post to go fortune hunting with the business of the high priest... He was a dead man.

"She's well past the age of marrying, though still of great value, I'm sure." Ameny leaned against a pillar.

Potipherah brought the prince another bowl of wine. "I have no daughter, fool."

"Not where you can find her, I'm sure." He took the bowl, raising it to his lips. "But do lay hands on the girl before I do, for I'll make you a grandfather if I can."

Potipherah struck him across the face. Wine splattered on Ameny's chest. Then drops of blood. He dropped to the floor and writhed like a fish, cradling his nose, his eyes wide.

"Y-you have struck me! You have struck a god!" His voice shook. "It is not permitted!"

Potipherah snapped his fingers and Khons disappeared from the doorway. "But I see that your blood is as red as a commoner's. So I must conclude that you are not a god but the drunken sot the world knows you to be."

Ameny touched the bump on the bridge of his nose. "It's bwoken!"

Potipherah shook out his hand and poured wine on Ameny's face. "No doubt you slipped in my chamber." He crossed the room to toss Ameny the blue stained rag he'd dried his hands with, then fingered through a box of potsherd on his desk. He could order Ameny's death, but his own miserable existence seemed punishment enough.

Khons rushed in with a basket of tinctures, and Potipherah glanced at the acolyte that followed him. Khety stood frozen in the doorway and nearly leapt from his skin when Ameny yelped as Khons snapped his nose back into place. Potipherah scratched out a message on the potsherd and beckoned the young man near. He inched closer, his gaze fluttering upward, away from the scene on the floor. "You do understand, Khety, that a position such as yours is not for one faint of heart." Potipherah held out the message.

Khety nodded and took the scratched note. "And shall I f-fetch a c-covered litter for His Majesty, my lord?"

Potipherah sighed. "I suppose you should. But after you've seen to the prince, chad downriver on the fastest skiff you can find and deliver my message. Tell the lectors at the temple to find my daughter.

"Or else."

CHAPTER EIGHT

SABNI

SABNI STOOD AT THE THRESHOLD OF THE KING'S leisure room, gripping the copper-headed axe. A slave propping Khakheperre's chair cushions blocked the king's view of him. One of the dogs bellowed as the musicians sat in a small circle, delighting with their skill on the double flute and harp. The drummer matched his strokes to the rhythm of a pretty slave girl massaging oil into the king's calves and feet.

Hetnu stood in a far corner, his rigid back and jerking limbs suggesting his usual annoyance with something as he shuffled jars in the king's wine cabinet.

Lord Resnakt hovered over the king, handing off the sovereign's crown to a servant before deftly removing his wig. Khakheperre humored Resnakt's boast in his superior styling abilities by appointing him keeper of the royal diadem, some ancient title for the king's wig dresser. By the Festival of the Ruler, Resnakt had worked wonders on the royal noggin. Even now, his perpetually grinning face turned severe as he inspected curls and placed the king's wig on a cedar stand.

Sabni slipped the small axe he held into the thicket of a tall potted plant just inside the doorway. He intended to build up the king's strength, but Khakheperre was looking less hollow in the cheeks and Sabni had no stomach for training today.

His dreams of late were nightmares, driving him to the brink of madness. The king's house was home to him and watching over Khakheperre his life's work, yet he was at war with himself.

He should have been made a slave when he was hauled downriver with the rest of the booty from Cush, but Khakheperre took him in like a little brother.

He loved the king, and he loved the world he knew before coming to the palace. He stepped back from the doorway, unsure now if he could love them both. No one had seen him enter. It was best to leave, spend the day with Kijau and wear himself out working off this misery in the new central gardens. He would make his excuses later.

"Well, if you're going to be a genuine guard today..." Khakheperre called over his shoulder.

The king's acknowledgment propelled him forward into the room with an energetic gait though his stomach quivered. He wasn't ready to face the good god now. Hetnu turned with a half grunt in his direction while Resnakt looked with greedy eyes upon the exchange. His promotion to Nebsumenu's deputy treasurer had raised him to new heights and esteem in the king's eyes. It was clear he'd never seen Khakheperre speak so casually to a guard.

Sabni gave a formal bow, though he knew it peeved Khakheperre for him to do so in such a setting, but Resnakt's probing gaze warned him to take care. "I'm sorry, Majesty, but the borders taught me that you are first my king." Sabni stood in a military pose of respect, meeting the king's gaze with a silent plea for him to play along.

Khakheperre shot him a look of reproach but pulled his legs back, signaling to the girl at his feet to withdraw. She patted his limbs with a linen towel and gathered her oils.

The king clapped. "All out."

The musicians muffled their instruments, and three guards, half hidden in shadows took on animation, filing out behind the musicians and slaves.

"Hetnu, stay and serve wine."

Hetnu held his bow at the king's request until Resnakt caught on that the order to leave included him. His face flashed with insult between his capitulating smiles, but he bowed and padded lightly to the doors, closing them as he left.

Four remained in the room though the mute slave could be counted more beautiful beast than man. Hau was nearly half the height of the column he stood beside, with a nose that took up most of his face. He gave his usual bovine smile and kept the air circulating with his fan.

Sabni met Khakheperre's gaze. They waited for the sound of footsteps in the corridor to recede before he flopped on the couch across from the king's chair.

"You're looking better today, Heperre." Sabni used the king's shortened name when they talked in private, but his greeting felt awkward today, forced.

Brave One padded over for a pet. Sabni stroked the Tesem's short, speckled coat, uncurling his tightly coiled tail. He'd trained four war dogs as hunters on the borders and brought them back as gifts. They barked or growled if at any time they felt the king under threat.

Brave One had a particular nose for danger, but spent

more time on his belly than in training. Sabni stroked the dog's head, then pulled his hand away. "The dogs are getting lazy, Heperre. They need to be run."

"I'll find someone to do it." The king leaned back into his cushions and stared at the ceiling.

Sabni huffed. He'd find someone himself.

Hetnu brought over three pitchers of wine along with two cups for the delta grape and a bowl for his old favorite, the doum palm.

Sabni cringed. His emotions were too volatile for drink, but Khakheperre would insist on it.

"You are crazed." The king grinned, his eyes full of excitement as he filled his own cup from a pitcher. "Charging into a thick cloud of smoke like a bull giving chase."

Sabni forced a smile. Khakheperre had been sickly from their youth, but he was hale and so performed athletic feats that made Khakheperre vigorous of heart. The king's admiration of his strength was always humbling, but today it cut like a dull blade.

Qareg's insult that morning in the courtyard had shaken him. It was the first news he'd heard of his father since being brought down to the king's house. Not even on the northern borders had anyone ever spoken of the razed city of Cush. Now Sabni wondered how much Heperre really knew about Wai and if he commanded others not to speak of it.

What of his mother? His little sister? Sabni's throat constricted. What vengeful god had set him down in the house of his enemy to mock him? Or had he been sent here for revenge? But Khakheperre had been a boy when his people were annihilated. Perhaps, then, his father had done it.

Hetnu passed Sabni a cup of wine, a rare sign of his approval. Sabni accepted the cup, though Hetnu's favor never lasted long, especially toward him.

"So, you dragged him from the circle of flaming buildings?" The king's voice hinted at awe.

"A handful of dilapidated storerooms. It was nothing." Sabni took a sip of wine and nursed his cup. He could never reveal the madness that overcame him that night, nor the pall it left on his soul.

Khakheperre leaned back as though he'd just devoured a satisfying meal.

"You'll retell it to one of my scribes. It's worth a good reading, like Montu swooping down to save the five children from Set. The priests were pestering me to get rid of those miserable thatch-roofed buildings anyway." Khakheperre swirled the contents of his cup. The smile died on his lips. "Where did you hide him?"

"In the barracks, near me. But he won't be safe there for long. It was an oil fire. He was bound and gagged when I dragged him from the storeroom." Sabni sat up and poured himself more wine in the room's silence. "My guess is that someone tried to cook the Asiatic dream teller."

The king repeated the words, meting them out with care. "C-cook the dream teller." His face pinched, and he spasmed. Sabni opened his mouth to call for a physician, but Heperre burst into laughter.

Sabni's jaw slackened. The king's chuckle was contagious, and he found himself joining in. Together, their laughter grew vibrant. One look at Hetnu's sour face and they both doubled over, swiping tears until their chortles ebbed to frenzied gasps of air and then subsided like a short-lived reprieve.

Heperre narrowed his eyes in a far-off look. "Put him out in the open, near a heavily trafficked area."

Sabni nodded.

"A few of Ameny's followers pelted those storerooms with dung and rotten fruit a few days ago. Now I see who they were after." Hetnu poured himself a bowl of wine. "If you had let me in on the Asiatic's whereabouts, this might have all been prevented."

"I must speak to my brother about the reckless behavior he inspires." The king reached for his cup.

"Why bother, when we know this was Potipherah's doing?" Hetnu crossed his arms and scowled.

Sabni exchanged a forbearing glance with the king. Any mention of Potipherah from Hetnu meant dramatics were sure to follow. And he was drinking.

"Do you forget his injustice to me?" Hetnu struck himself in the chest. "He stole something very precious from me, Heperre."

"Everyone knows you never poisoned my father, Hetnu."

"Yet I was sent to prison, grouped with that miserable baker, my good name tarnished, Heperre, tarnished." His voice took on the familiar quaver that accompanied a promise of tears. "Potipherah tried to separate me from you. And I am angry for it!"

"I can well understand that." Sabni stretched out on the couch again, and one of the dogs came over to lick his hand. Hetnu had gotten a taste of his own medicine, but nothing could match a trip to the borders where Hetnu had sent him.

"Fight him, Heperre!" Hetnu punched at the air, twisting his wig askew and sloshing wine from his half empty bowl.

The king slouched in his chair, covering his face. It was

better to let Hetnu wear himself out rather than to interrupt his passionate lamenting. But the wine was unusually good tonight, and Hetnu eventually settled into the trance of clicking beetles and other sounds of the night coming from the garden.

The king closed his eyes and thumbed his seal ring. "I'm going to marry one of my harem girls. I shall make her a queen."

"You're drunk." Hetnu refilled his wine bowl.

"But determined."

"Then, by all means, be determined to love all the girls in your harem. Not even half of them are pregnant. Better still, tend to Deduamen's daughters who miraculously showed up on your water steps. They should be near fat with child, yet you haven't so much as seen them."

"They've just arrived four days ago, Hetnu."

"No matter. You've shown more interest in that Asiatic than anyone, almost sending your best watchdog to stand guard for a slave."

"What?" Sabni turned to the king, but Heperre looked away from him sheepishly. Of course, Brave One would sniff out any danger, but he'd never known Heperre to go so far.

"I've not a care in the world for the sand dweller and would sooner cut off his head, but I promised to wait for his words to fail. It would not be Ma'at to dispatch him sooner." The king talked into his cup as he always did when he was unsure of himself. Or when he utterly lied.

"What's this talk about the Asiatic molesting his master's wife?" Sabni changed the subject for Heperre's sake.

"Potiphar's wife," Hetnu clarified. "That is, he held the

title of Potiphar under the rule of His Majesty's father, then advanced to Commander in Chief of the Ptah division of soldiers, stationed near the Walls of the Ruler. Commander Nebitef."

"Nebitef?" The king hiked his brows.

"I toured the borders under him. One of your finest," Sabni said.

"His wife is...Lady Kemsiyet." Hetnu looked between them, and Khakheperre harrumphed.

"Then the slave's case for freedom gets stronger by the hour."

Sabni smothered a chuckle. Lady Kemsiyet was a popular courtier... but not the best example of a devoted wife. "No wonder the commander stays so near your borders. He chooses the lesser evil."

"It's too strange that Nebitef sent a slave to prison instead of to the mines. He'll explain himself."

Sabni closed his eyes as the king chattered on, expressing an uncanny interest in the Asiatic, Yoseph.

After a while the heady wine silenced them all, and there was only the occasional howl from one of the dogs and the steady swishing of Hau's fan. Hetnu stirred once or twice, humming some old hymn in wine-laden indifference. Then a thought struck Sabni like an arrow in the chest.

He sat up, half expecting either the king or Hetnu to discern the wicked plan sent straight to him from the dark god, Set. But only the dog at his feet shifted, and Hetnu and Heperre never opened their eyes. Sabni's chest heaved as he reached for the last of the wine in his pitcher. But Brave One could smell the dark intent clouding his heart. And for the first time, the dog snapped at him and growled.

CHAPTER NINE

HETNU

HETNU KEPT HIS PROMISE AND ASSIGNED Djehuti's two younger sons the low position of palace messenger. Nevertheless, Djehuti was delighted, but Hetnu hoped his promise to keep his younger boys in check was earnestly meant.

Hetnu sat facing the door of his office. He stroked Mepi's game piece in one hand. In the other, he held the reed pen aloft as he bent over a tally of the summer grape harvest. Last year's harvest fell short, and he would have to concentrate on varied date and palm wines again this year. He chafed, remembering Yoseph's declaration of seven years of abundant harvest. Seven years indeed.

It was embarrassing to see the king go down to the temple water steps to check for this promised miracle. The provincial governors laughed at Khakheperre who would not be counseled. And there was nothing to do but hope Yoseph's words would prove true.

Nen entered the office, and Hetnu took the note he extended. It was rare that his house steward left the estate other than to bring Imini to him. "Is all well?" Breaking the note's seal, he leveled a glare at Nen. "If it's another request from Appipa I shall cast it into the brazier. And you along with it."

He afforded Deduamen's twin daughters every luxury as the king's guests. A'at required nothing, but Appipa constantly needed her jewelry polished or her furnishings changed. She sent messages to his office and to his home ten times a day, informing him that she was ready to see the king. The girl was already queen in her own mind.

"The note is not from Lady Appipa, my lord, but from one of your spies."

Hetnu huffed, still miffed about the anonymous note that Nen accepted on his behalf about Potipherah having a daughter. He turned the message over to check the secret markings his spies knew to leave. "I wonder how they are toying with me now. Emptying my purse while fattening their own with the nonsense they send me." Hetnu glanced over the contents of the message and furrowed his brow. He dismissed Nen, read the note again, then paced.

The two most notorious gossips in the kingdom had stopped him in the corridors this morning. Ladies Ipwet and Sahathor cornered him with their canes, insisting they heard screams coming from Potipherah's suite a few nights previous. They claimed Prince Ameny was rushed from the priest's rooms to a covered litter, holding a bloodied cloth to his nose. But the two old biddies were known to excite scandal at every opportunity, and Hetnu believed not a word they told him. But this note confirmed the bloody cloth they spoke of and that Ameny had taken a vessel to chad downriver with his nose swollen and marked blue.

Marked blue.

Hetnu diverted his anger from the possibility of

Potipherah mishandling both Khakheperre and his brother, Ameny. If the high priest had any less power, such actions would have meant his death. But there was a deeper issue here. Could Potipherah have struck Ameny in anger? Had Ameny threatened him in any way? The prince was certainly brazen enough to try. Hetnu rubbed his knuckles across his chin. A few possibilities began to spark in the back of his mind.

Mepi's game piece rolled off the slanted writing tray. He caught it just in time and wrinkled his brow. Mepi should have inquired about it by now. Hetnu turned it over, remembering the old father's abrupt departure from their garden game of Hounds and Jackals. The sculptured little jackal grinned at him as he recalled the little quip he made about Potipherah's daughter. He stroked his fly whisk across his chest, and Djehuti's advice came to mind.

Search out a far-fetched matter. Especially when the stakes are high.

"No." He rejected the thought that flashed his mind. "Mepi would never do such a thing." Yet he stopped pacing to tuck the game piece under his belt. It was time to pay a visit to the old father in the king's scroll room.

THERE WAS SOME MERIT IN BUILDING A depository for storing records, and it was a king's right to do so. Khakheperre ordered copies made of all the written works from all the great temples in the land. And the temples responded like slugs in fulfilling his request. Yet, he sent the same request out to the neighboring kingdoms in search of culture and art, and the response was tremendous.

Hetnu stood at the threshold of the gallery, halting

the guards he brought with him. The white flecks in the polished quartz floor captured a ghost of color from some of the hanging faience tiles. Columns were spaced throughout, extending to the second story of the room that could be accessed from a set of stairs on both sides of the long gallery with walls full of cubbies, packed with scrolls between works of art. He directed some of the guards to different exits and pressed through the crowd with three guards in tow. He took the set of stairs to the upper level that were closest to Mepi's workroom.

The place had become a den of foreigners, contaminating the people of the land with stories of inferior cultures and gods, playing inferior music, and displaying inferior art to the courtiers of the king's house. It was one of the reasons Hetnu never came here.

"Wait for me and space yourselves out," he instructed the guards when they reached the upper level. "Keep an eye out for any suspicious looking female." It was a ridiculous order. May the gods prove him wrong on the festering premonition in the back of his mind.

He passed through a room full of scribes at writing palettes and came into a second room where he found Mepi immersed in some study with an assistant beside him. Hetnu waded toward them through a sea of scrolls in baskets on the floor. The robed scribe stood with his back to the room's entrance and lacked the manners to turn at his approach.

The way Mepi peered at him seemed strange.

"I've come to return your game piece." Hetnu moved closer, searching the old father's face. "And while I'm here, send this fellow beside you to fetch that daughter you've been hiding from me."

Hetnu tapped the young man's shoulder, and he spun around and shoved Hetnu with a force that sent him reeling back. Hetnu crashed into the baskets and lay amongst a heap of scattered scrolls. He blinked, open-mouthed at the ceiling. The sound of sandals slapped the floor as the young man raced from the room.

Mepi offered no assistance, called for no help, but crossed his arms, sending Hetnu a baleful glare. "There, fool! You've scared her away!"

CHAPTER TEN

ASENAT

THE GUARD'S GLARE BURNED THE BACK OF
Asenat's neck. She descended the stairs from the upper
level. Her heart flitted like a trapped bird in her chest.
Scanning the gallery, she expected to be stopped at any
moment.

A female musician locked eyes with her from across the
lower level and shook her menat necklace full of colored
stones and faience beads, drawing the crowd's attention.
She struck up a popular tune on the harp, and the other
troupe players joined in.

The guard at the top of the stairs clapped in rhythm as
Asenat descended. She ducked into one of the rooms on the
lower floor, pressed her back to a wall, then pushed off. Her
legs shook but she forced herself to the exit. If she didn't
hurry, they would find her.

The grounds of the central gardens were being remodeled,
but there was a path to an untouched cluster of trees that
she remembered. She fought the urge to run and made
herself walk past the groups of courtiers, resuming the
cumbersome stroll of a man.

She passed Prince Dagi who sat beneath a tree with his friends. Some beads were missing from his red and white choker, along with the silver bracelet he always wore. He'd been gambling again. How she would love to kick him, to bring him to account for the rings he'd stolen. She should have been back in Iunu by now.

She had asked Mepi for the funds to return home, but he begged her to stay on a little longer. How could she refuse him after he'd seen to her entry into Pakhet? But after that, some private apprehension seemed to plague him. He kept her hands busy and their walks short, avoiding the quay and the palace guards at nearly all cost. Did he know they were looking for her?

Her legs were aching by the time she reached the small chapel of Hathor nestled in a copse of sycamore trees. The outside of the stone structure was hot to the touch in the midday sun, but few knew of the cool shadows within. Asenat made a quick bow to the image of the cow-horned goddess inside the chapel and hurried to the darkest recess behind it.

She pressed herself against a cool wall and tried to catch her breath. What had gotten into her? Mepi spoke of her too often. First to the retired priests, then to Lord Nebsumenu. The air thickened with the scent of the king's myrrh when the man came into Mepi's workroom and took her by the shoulder. She shoved him and ran.

"You're in some sort of trouble, aren't you?"

Asenat startled. At first, she thought the echoing voice came from the goddess. Then a woman stepped around the statue. She squinted her gaze.

"You." She addressed the female who led the musical troupe in the gallery of the scroll room, a shapely, bright-skinned Minoan in a fat, sumptuous wig. Asenat squared her shoulders. "It just so happens that I'm in no trouble at all. And I don't like being followed."

"I know trouble when I see it." The woman sauntered over, and the bars of sunlight she passed revealed the deep green color of her eyes. "You weren't complaining when I drew that guard's attention away from you."

"You weren't following me then. I'm complaining now."

"I watched over you." She touched her fingertips to her hips, and her limbs glittered with tinkling charms like an advertisement for the gods. Asenat shot a look at the doorway, and the woman went to stand at the chapel entrance. She stretched her arms across the span of it as if to block an attempt to exit.

Asenat frowned. "Planning to turn me in, are you? You'll have to share the reward."

"You mean with the princes sitting beneath the tree?" She nestled her back against the doorway. "I gave them a few rings. They'll get drunk and forget the whole matter."

Asenat folded her arms across her stomach.

"You'd better come with me if you know what's best for you." The woman shaded her eyes, looking out over the grounds. "You won't get away without help."

There was something highhanded and mocking in her manner. Asenat considered her words but thought better of putting her trust in such a woman and moved toward the door. Either the Minoan would move out of her way, or she would be toppled over.

The woman cupped her hand to her mouth and called out to someone on the grounds. "Guards, come here! Yes, you. I order you here now."

Asenat was ready to call her bluff but heard male voices

and footsteps approaching. She scooted behind the statue, stinging with humiliation at the dirty trick.

"Why so many guards about today?" the woman asked, her tone flirting, as she stroked her menat necklace.

"We are looking for a bald female scribe dressed in plain white apparel."

Asenat held her breath. There was no other way out of the chapel. She would be caught. Then what?

"Well, you've disturbed my prayers," the woman said. "Now go and fetch my litter against the wall. There, the blue one. Call it for me, and be about your business."

Asenat fell limp against the likeness of Hathor. The sound of footsteps receded before she gave a sharp whisper. "You might have warned me first."

"You didn't seem to be in the mood for listening." The woman reached up to pluck a leaf from a nearby tree. She pushed off the doorway. "If it weren't for me, you would have run straight into their grasp. There was nothing more I could do."

"I'll find my own way out, thank you. Just draw them away."

"You'll do no such thing unless you want to get caught." The woman came toward her. "The king's cupbearer is a very thorough man. I saw him going up the stairs in the scroll room with guards. By now, he will have sent a message to check for you at all the palace exits."

A tight ball knotted in Asenat's stomach. She let out a breath. She had shoved, of all people, the king's cupbearer. "All right then, what do you suggest?"

The woman untied an elaborate turquoise girdle from her waist, then pulled silver bracelets from her arms. "Put these on. Hurry."

Asenat slid the bracelets on and wrapped the girdle around her waist. The woman pulled the heavy wig from her head and thick dark locks fell down her back. She took off her pectoral and drew a lock of hair over her shoulder to cover a bruise at her collarbone.

"Professional hazard." She smirked. "I'm a bull jumper."

"Why are you helping me?" Asenat shifted at the woman's tug at her waist, securing the turquoise studded girdle, then readjusting the heavy wig slipping off Asenat's bald head.

"Does your pride need so much soothing after all I've done?" She moved to the doorway. "Come."

The covered litter waited at the chapel steps. Asenat got in behind the Minoan.

"Lay on your side. Cover your face with the cushions. I will say that my lady has a headache." She spoke as if the whole thing were a game.

"Lower the curtains." Asenat reached to tug one down. The woman slapped her hand away.

"No. They will stop us if we draw the curtains. We'll conceal nothing. Snore a little." She smacked Asenat's bottom. "I said relax and snore."

They performed their way past three guard checks with Asenat's face buried in cushions. The shouts of river porters and docking scribes rose in her ears, flooding her with relief as they neared the palace quay. The sooner she got away from the king's house, the better. But the litter took a sharp turn at some point, and the sounds of the quay faded.

Asenat raised her head. "We're going in the wrong direction."

The woman shoved her down. "I wouldn't dare take you

to the quay when the palace guards are actually doing their work today."

"Then where are you taking me?" Asenat demanded.

"Back to the palace, of course, where it's safe."

CHAPTER ELEVEN

SABNI

SABNI WALKED IN THE SHADE OF THE CRUMBLING Horus columns casting long shadows all the way down the main thoroughfare. Built by one of Khakheperre's forefathers who established Itjtawy as his royal seat, the columns proclaimed the supreme rule of hereditary kings. Now crumbling monoliths, they marked a juncture of intricate avenues within the compound and littered the roads with debris.

Sabni took one of the smaller lanes until it ended, then turned down the dusty, dirt-packed roads of the worker's district. He passed several courtyards of industry and came upon a row of one-room dwellings assigned to privileged slaves. Bile rose in his throat at the shame he was about to bring on himself.

Imehy's new corner dwelling was quite a step up from sleeping in the ox stalls. There was probably little peace here with the bustle of wagons coming off the rutted road, but Imehy's serenity was not the main concern.

Sabni pulled back the rawhide flap and stepped inside, flaring his nostrils at the scent of pungent herbs and vinegar. Imehy labored over the slave, Yoseph, who muttered and groaned in Egyptian and in his native tongue as he thrashed in a troubled sleep. Sabni drew in his brows. "What happened?"

"No one checked his wounds after the fire. That's what happened. They're dirty, and now he's fevered!" Imehy scowled and pointed to a bruise on his thigh where he'd been kicked by the unconscious man on the reed mat. "And this for all my troubles." He limped to a table to retrieve a liquid mixture in a bowl. "You told me I was to watch him, to tend his feet. That's all. I've wasted all my best herbs on him, and this is the last of what I have. It'll either cure him or kill him."

Sabni dragged the Asiatic away from the wall and held down his hot limbs. Imehy fastened his short legs around the man's head, then pulled out his lip to pour a foul concoction down his throat.

"We'll see that your herbs are replaced. And I'll have someone check on you more often and bring what you need. We must keep a step ahead of Potipherah," Sabni whispered.

Imehy gave a curt nod. They both knew the king couldn't send a palace guard. That would suggest the Asiatic was important. The palace lockup wasn't a good enough place to hide him, either. Bribed guards might be waiting to bring the man to a neat accident.

Such shame that the good god should need cunning in his own house. Khakheperre's power crumbled like the Horus columns.

The Asiatic settled down, and Sabni brushed dirt from his hands. There were three woven rugs on the floor, a low table full of pots and jars, pegs on the wall, and two chests in a far corner. "Nice place, here. You were long overdue for some comforts, I think." A wave of guilt rolled over him. He'd secured this place for Imehy, but after tonight, Imehy might lose it again.

"I'm not stupid because I'm small, you know." Imehy pointed a stubby finger. "I took the king's agent for all I could get out of him. And just remember to mention how well the Asiatic fared in my care." Imehy threw himself against the wall and dragged his hands down his face. "He's going to die, I just know it. And I'll be the one blamed and lose my reputation."

"What reputation? You tend animals in the stalls."

"My talents far exceed my limitations. And what should you know about it when your art is one of hurting men? Mine is one of healing them."

The words smarted more than Sabni could let on. "You're in a rank mood, little man." He tossed Imehy a silver ring. "Go get yourself a tankard of rot-gut down at the river pubs. I'll stay, and if he fades, let them blame me." He held a weak smile while Imehy fingered the fine silver ring. It could keep a man drunk for a month if he bartered well with it.

"All right." Imehy stuck the ring in his pouch. "But you'll have to deal with me if anyone else touches him." He snatched a vegetable-fiber wig hanging from a crude peg on the mud brick wall. Placing it on his head, he strutted out like a man about town.

The flap slapped against the doorway, and Sabni dropped his grin, going straight for the chests in the far corner of the room. He rooted their contents, found what he needed, then sat back on his heels and shuddered.

Dwarves dominated the art of jewelry making, even

Imehy who preferred mixing herbs to handling metals indulged in the craft from time to time. The long thin pin Sabni pinched between his fingers was used to secure a heavy counterweight to a pectoral necklace. It would do the trick.

He stood up, his pulse throbbing as he considered the turn of events in his favor. The Asiatic breathed evenly in his sleep. The kill would be easy.

Sabni raised the pin to a beam of light. On the borders, a soldier had once threatened to reveal Qareg's corruption. He jerked and died in his sleep when Qareg pushed a pin like this through the man's ear canal. Sabni had seen it all from his mat but was smart enough to feign sleep when Qareg hovered over him.

And now this trite and petty effort at revenge that no one would care about. His was the effort of a coward gone mad. He might never know who had destroyed Wai, but on behalf of those assaulted and murdered, revenge of some kind, to someone, was due. Sabni watched the sleeping Asiatic, wishing someone had paid him this kindness when his world was razed to the ground. More than a week had passed since he'd saved Yoseph's life from the fire at the storerooms. Now he was going to take this man's life. Yet if killing would serve as some small blood-price for the lives lost in Wai, if it would cool his fevered mind and conscience, then murder was Ma'at. Khakheperre would feel but a little pain at loosing his favored Asiatic, and Yoseph would feel none.

Dusk had fallen, and Sabni swiped his sweat-soaked face. There was the promise of a half-moon rising. He could wait till then. Yes, he could wait. He moved across the room, away from the Asiatic, then slid down the wall and wept.

A bad dream awakened him, and he leapt up fumbling for the bronze pin he'd worked into his kilt. "Make it quick and get out," he whispered, rolling the pin between his fingers. This man had done him no wrong. But this was no time to be deterred by one's own guilt. He swallowed dryly. Retreat was vile.

He crossed the dirt-packed floor to the Asiatic who sat upright against the rough wall, unconscious. Not uncommon for sick men on the verge of death. The moonlight turned his skin pale. He breathed in uneven patterns and shallow gasps. Sabni squatted beside him, clutching the pin. He raised it, and the Asiatic lurched forward to retch, knocking it from his hand. Sabni leaned back and grabbed a pot just in time. He fetched a ladle of water.

Yoseph rinsed his mouth and spit, then drank and coughed between gasps of air. Sabni flooded with a strange relief, then guilt. The Asiatic's regard clung to him as he gulped down more water and lowered the ladle. "So, why don't you tell me your dream, Sabni?" His voice grated with inquiry. "I have all night to listen."

CHAPTER TWELVE

YOSEPH

YOSEPH CALLED TO THE GIRL PULLING AWAY from the edge of the rooftop. Her diaphanous garments waved like a pennant in the wind. The fragrance of cardamom and almond floated above his head.

A hard smack stung his cheek. He opened his eyes. Two body servants hovered over him, twin-dressed in short red kilts with polished collars of beaten silver.

"Such a luxury to dream, but the vile Asiatic is going on a trip today." The servant glaring at Yoseph bore his same coloring and facial features.

"You're an Asiatic, yourself, Ukem." His companion furrowed his brow.

"Yes, but I'm not a vile one."

They laughed in chorus, nudging Yoseph to join in as they rushed him to a bath stall. The two men chirped like magpies as they stripped, splashed, shaved, plucked and struck him if he tried to offer assistance. They near drowned him in fragrant oil. The Asiatic, Ukem, eyed him with particular disdain.

Imehy had taken him through a massage regimen to

restore circulation to his legs, and his foot canker was healing well. But the two body servants walked far ahead, ignoring his need to rest. He limped to a bench, and the men doubled back to curse and strike him. He blocked a few slaps until the pain in his feet subsided, but his legs were fatigued by the time they reached the brightly muraled wall.

Guards patrolled the perimeter and a few archers higher up gave them cursory glances as Yoseph followed the body servants around to a thicket of bushes where they blindfolded him. His two companions grew quiet, and he heard stone grating before they pulled him through an opening in the wall. Exotic birdsong and floral scents assaulted his senses. Dappled sunlight warmed his skin. He stumbled over a bush.

"Imbecile!" One of the servants yanked him upright. "Keep up!"

Heat radiated on his face and chest when they stopped. Grating stone, again. A rush of cool air and a sense of darkness struck him as he stepped inside a chamber. He heard the crackle of torches. The wall behind him closed.

"Remove your blindfold."

Yoseph obeyed the deep voice, working out the knot in the tight strip of cloth that covered his eyes.

The steward stroked him with a quick look. "Come."

Yoseph kept pace with the broad, polished back in front of him. They traveled down a narrow corridor lit with torches. The steward stopped to push against a wall, revealing a concealed opening. He led Yoseph into a small room full of precious furnishings, instructing him to wait beside a column. At the great number of voices in the distance, Yoseph's stomach coiled into knots. He inhaled, filling his lungs. He had been a steward over Nebitef's estate when he was Potiphar of the king's house. He knew how to speak to great men. He knew how to conduct himself.

Elohim guide me.

His gut fluttered. This interview with the king must go better than the last.

The steward reappeared, crooking a finger at him. They passed two rooms in a blur before reaching a large chamber. Servants busied themselves refilling the wine cups of men decked in fine kilts and formal wigs.

"Ah, there you are."

Yoseph lowered himself to the floor at the king's regard. "Majesty." He flinched at a dog's wet nose pressed against the back of his neck.

"Brave One, where are your manners?" The king whistled, and the dog trotted away. "Get up Yoseph. Sit."

Yoseph took the stool in the middle of the room full of officials. He sat erect, keeping his face clear of expression as was proper for a slave. All eyes were on him. Lord Hetnu was absent, as was the formidable blue-fingered priest who called for his execution.

"Brave One remembers you from the morning hall." The king pet the dog beside him. His eyes shifted down. "Your feet, no better I see."

"Much better, Majesty." Yoseph crossed his ankles in a vain effort to hide his rope wounds. Some of his toenails had gone black. Two were missing. But his feet were better.

The king nodded. "You look much improved."

The sovereign looked much better, himself, a little fatter in his robes. The string of his false beard lay against cheeks that were thin, but no longer gaunt. He called over his shoulder. "Mentuser, make sure you send someone to care for his feet."

The physician Yoseph remembered from the morning hall gave a respectful nod, and the king continued. "I've heard you were an excellent steward for your former master."

Yoseph followed the direction of the king's gaze. Not far from where he sat, his former master, Lord Nebitef, stood in a military kilt with a long dagger strapped to his waist. He crossed his arms over his neat muscular form and held Yoseph's gaze below his tight drawn brows.

"Assuming we have these good and bad years you spoke of," the king said. "Tell me how you think the coming harvests should be handled."

Yoseph blinked and cleared his throat. The room went still, and the servants pouring wine no longer pretended disinterest. Nebitef signaled with an indistinct nod toward him, and he exhaled a deep shaking breath.

"Let the king appoint commissioners over the land to take a fifth of the harvest during the seven years of abundance." He paused, trying not to rush his words. "They should collect all the food of these good years that are coming and store up the grain in the king's name. It should be kept in the cities for food and held in reserve for the country to use during the seven years of famine. This way, the country will not be ruined."

The room remained silent for a beat, then broke into mumbles and low laughter. He'd done well.

Elohim be praised.

An impressive looking man leaned to whisper to the king. He had a finely shaped, cropped beard that only a man of high rank would dare. He held the sovereign's rapt attention as he spoke, then gave a little smile. Yoseph sat straighter on his stool, gripping it. The king would speak now. The king would reward him or laugh at him. The king would call his guards and have him escorted back to the borders. For this, he'd prayed.

"You may go."

The order came not from the king but from the man beside the sovereign, waving him off with a gesture. Yoseph obediently bowed himself out of the room, determined not to limp on his tender foot.

"Well done," the steward called from the other side of the column.

Yoseph followed him back through the two rooms to the secret corridor, clutching his heart. Perhaps he'd been too forward, too hasty. Perhaps they were laughing at him now. The steward left him outside at the garden wall. He fought to slow his breath. The king might release him today or tomorrow. Or the king might forget him altogether. The sun warmed his head as he came down the path and found the body servants dicing against a wall.

"Oh, you again." Ukem looked over his shoulder. He finished the throw and didn't bother with the blindfold.

Yoseph followed the king's body servants through an alleyway. A few slaves lingered in the shade of the narrow-spaced buildings. Two females pulled at each other's hair in a vicious fight that no one attended. Farther down, four servants huddled in an alcove, sleeping off the effect of heavy drink. Yoseph's brows knitted to a frown. He never would have tolerated such slackness as steward of Lord Nebitef's estate.

The body servants stopped near the intersection at the Horus columns, refusing to go farther. "There's your place." Ukem shooed him in the direction of the slave dwellings. "Off with you."

Yoseph limped across the road. Someone called to him.

"Sand dweller!"

A missile of rotten fruit exploded on his shoulder. The young lords near the columns doubled over laughing as flies attacked the filth. Yoseph wiped the slime from his arm.

He'd come to know Prince Dagi well, having become the young lord's daily target practice whenever he stepped from Imehy's dwelling. He bowed to the chuckling prince whose red and white choker danced at his neck. His aim was getting better.

CHAPTER THIRTEEN

KEMSIYET

LORD RENIQER STRUCK THE FLOOR WITH HIS staff and announced Lady Kemsiyet. She minced forward with her name still ringing off the walls of the broad hall. Her slaves had stained her lips red like poppies, and powdered her face with a hint of gold dust to perfection. Her seamstress added a train of shells and silver disks to her beadnet dress. It dragged across the tiles, imitating the gentle timbre of a sistrum.

The small crowd in the front of the hall parted to let her through. Her status as wife of a high ranking official should have long secured her place in the queen's ornate, a select group of women attending the god's wife. There was only some old rumor about a presumptuous slave that hindered her progress, but like the crowd who parted for her approach to the front of the hall, it was all behind her now.

Kemsiyet lowered herself to the floor then rose with the help of hall attendants. She raised a demure gaze to the throne. This was a long awaited day. It would be the most memorable of her life.

"Lady Kemsiyet, I wish to know, did the slave Yoseph attempt to rape you, or not?"

The soft smile froze on her lips at the king's question. She looked left, then right, searching the room for the god's wife, Queen Weret. She was not present, nor were her ladies, nor was there a single female in the hall beside herself. The king wore his Ma'at crown, tapping his palm with his Ames scepter, often used to pronounce judgment.

She swooned in the arms of an attendant, peeking at the king who glared at her.

"Get her up!" His hard voice resounded in the hall.

Reniqer's staff struck the stone block, jolting her. His voice rang clear.

"Enters the privy counselor of the heavens. He who is great in regarding and who is chief of secrets of the heavens, the first prophet of Amun, Potipherah of Iunu."

Kemsiyet crooked her neck as the attendant raised her to her feet. The entrance of the high priest drew everyone's gaze but the king's. The hall attendants fanned her, and she stalled further, requesting a cup of water. She held out, sipping it slowly until the king directed his next question elsewhere.

"So, you mean to tell me that you promoted Yoseph to watch over your entire household? That he distinguished himself year after year?"

Kemsiyet went rigid at the name she'd washed from her memory. She glanced to where the king addressed his question and swayed on her feet. There stood the man she hadn't seen in years, her husband, Nebitef. She stumbled.

"You will not faint again, Lady Kemsiyet," the king clipped out, aiming his scepter like a weapon.

She pressed knuckles to her forehead and found her

footing, outraged that a lady's delicacies were not to be attended.

"Yes, Majesty," her husband answered. "Yoseph's god blessed him. Whatever he did succeeded, and I could find no fault in him."

Kemsiyet mashed her lips flat. That was the trouble between them. Her husband found no fault in Yoseph. Only in her.

The king leaned back in his chair, scoffing as he turned the scepter in his hand. "Then explain why you've taken a faithful servant and cast him into a garrison prison."

"It was my pride." Nebitef pressed his fists to his sides. Kemsiyet raised her chin at the stern look he shot her.

"It was not Ma'at to kill a man for my wife's lie."

Her jaw dropped, and she fluttered her lashes in disbelief. *How dare he.*

"And what kind of prisoner was he?" The king addressed the warden of the garrison, standing beside Nebitef.

"Yoseph came to the Great Prison as a convict, but Lord Nebitef recommended him highly as a manager. He was so efficient at his work that there was hardly anything left for me to do."

"Perhaps I should make him warden, then, instead of you," the king said, and the warden blustered amidst the laughter in the hall.

"The point is, Majesty, that he is exceptionally attentive."

"That is no more than the duty of all slaves. But if you value him so, then why did he arrive at my house in such a state? His feet were near ruined. I am against such abuse."

"I only heard of the incident when I returned to the garrison. That thick-headed oaf was in charge."

"I believe the warden speaks of his assistant, Qareg."

SEAL OF THE SAND DWELLER

Lord Hetnu set a cup of wine on a tray beside the king. "I met him when he brought Yoseph to His Majesty's house and almost ordered him strung up myself."

Kemsiyet chafed. She was on trial and her conduct brought into question for her dealings with an Asiatic dog, one the whole world seemed ready to defend.

"Qareg was jealous of Yoseph, Majesty," the warden added. "Always has been. I had no choice but to leave him in charge while I went to fetch a proper assistant. Yoseph was to tend the books."

"He can read?" the king asked.

"A little hieroglyphs, but he does numbers. One of Yoseph is worth ten Qaregs, and I shall make that rascal a resident of your most gracious prison if you will allow. Qareg has abused his authority and your prisoner."

"You may do so."

Kemsiyet raised her chin, ready to defend herself when the king glanced at her. He ignored her and addressed her husband.

"So, you believed the word of a slave above your wife?" The king's inquiry hinted in amazement.

"I have preferred the woman I love in all things but this."

A derisive burst of air escaped Kemsiyet's lips. "You speak of love but chose a slave over me." She prepared to release her full fury on Nebitef but glanced sideways at the blue fingers touching her shoulder.

"I would beg the good god to consider the words of your loyal servant, Lady Kemsiyet," Potipherah, spoke up for her. He was, at present, her sole ally in the room.

"Do not call such a woman loyal," the king said. "She cannot be loyal to me if she is not loyal to her husband."

"But she is a lady of the realm, Majesty. And for her word to be disregarded would not be Ma'at."

Nebitef, that scoundrel of a husband, came to stand beside her. She met his gaze, ready to receive his apology, but he offered none. Instead, he knelt, facing the king.

"I offer the good god my resignation. I thought I was a just man, but I have failed."

The king glowered at Nebitef's confession and rolled his tongue in his cheek as he tapped his palm with the Ames scepter. Kemsiyet shifted on her feet at his glare. A sovereign would not condemn a noblewoman on the word of a slave. He would not.

"Since only the gods saw the exchange between Lady Kemsiyet and the slave, Yoseph, I will let them judge the matter. Lady Kemsiyet may speak as she finds."

Kemsiyet exhaled.

"But as for you Nebitef." The king leaned forward, his mouth flat with disapproval. "My prisons are reserved for my prisoners, not for the prison of your guilt."

"Well said, Majesty," Nebitef answered. "And again, I offer my resignation."

"And I do not accept it, but you will walk out the embarrassment of this error." The king huffed, waving his scepter in a sharp gesture. "Is this not a sight to be seen, one of the commanders of my army wetting his kilt before me and before his peers."

Kemsiyet sent her husband a baleful glare, snatching the linen patch he offered. She sniffed, sopping the kohled tears running down her gold-powdered cheeks.

CHAPTER FOURTEEN

POTIPHERAH

THE BIRDS CHIRPED IN THE LAVISH GARDEN, and bees flitted between blooms. Potipherah gave an indulgent smile for the sake of his talkative hostess.

He'd received no news on the whereabouts of his daughter, but it was a busy time with the temple in preparation for the Front of the Year ceremonies, and she was probably traveling between his estates.

He meant to squash that slippery sand dweller like a bug under his thumb for giving the king's supporters false hope and distracting Khakheperre from the business of dying, something Potipherah wished the king to do very soon. By the time the priest sent his spies to slit the Asiatic's throat, he'd been moved from the slave quarters.

The reading at the water steps had affirmed that an exceptional harvest was forthcoming, but this was of no great concern since a profitable harvest was any fool's guess. However, the good reading emboldened Khakheperre, who courted his counselors in his personal chambers and summoned the Asiatic dream teller again. Potipherah received no invitation to the event.

Then there was the nonsense of walking into the broad hall to find Khakheperre painting the Asiatic something short of a god. Shortly thereafter, Khakheperre tucked the sand dweller away in his personal dwelling to tend the royal dogs.

Potipherah stirred the sweet minty beer in his ivory cup and took another sip. If the good god continued with these games, he'd snap Khakheperre like a dry reed.

Lady Satweret tapped his finger, drawing Potipherah from his musings. She'd been touching his hands in irreverent awe all afternoon, chatting and darting about like a plover, picking meat from the teeth of a croc. And he'd graciously left his jaws open.

For now.

Satweret was utterly thrilled to entertain a high priest in her home. He knew because she'd told him this for the hundredth time while plying him with ravenous inquiry for details on Lady Kemsiyet's humiliation in the broad hall. But the feral light in the lady's pretty, painted eyes grew dim when he enshrined Kemsiyet in glowing praise.

Of course, he lied. Kemsiyet was a pampered trollop like most great ladies of the realm who suffered neglect from their husbands. But his lie offered blissful intervals of silence from Satweret's gaping hole of a mouth. She offered delightful refreshment in the pleasant shade of her garden, then worked him like a cheap peddler, insisting that he interpret every dream she could pull from her beetle-sized brain.

After she wrung him dry, she plunked a heavy feldspar ring in his lap, raising her gaze like a worshipful pup. "I am so pleased with the interpretations you give to my dreams, Holy Father." She clasped her hands at her chest.

He glanced at her simpering smile and pressed the exquisite gold-mounted gem onto the first joint of his thumb. She was a fetching little dimwit with a heart shaped face bordered in triangular curls, but she also knew the worth of a good stone.

"Will you use the ring to feed the poor, Holy Father?"

"Most certainly not." He wiggled his fingers as the sunlight glinted off the rich green stone. "I shall have it resized and added to my meager collection." He splayed his blue fingers decked in flashing rings, and her dunce-laden face broke into a pained expression of hysterical tittering.

"Tell me, Lady Satweret, where did you find such an exquisite shade of vermillion?" he asked, attempting to rein in another onslaught of mindless banter. She stroked the straps of her brightly colored sheath-dress, and he relished the silence as she appeared to actually think.

"I remember now. My cloth dyers purchased the color from a caravan near the province of the Cow Thigh." She gave a pretty pout. "I should have beaten them for not buying the whole lot of it. No one has seen its like since."

"Then I'll devote myself to finding it for you. The color suits you very well."

She called for more refreshments. When her slaves didn't respond, she walked back to the shaded alcove of her porch. If he had to destroy her husband, the sweet little bird of a woman would be crushed underfoot. But this type of thing must be done from time to time, and he popped a wine-soaked date in his mouth to console himself.

She reached her porch and gave a little cry as a man leapt from the shadows and yanked her into a sound kiss.

Potipherah sat forward. Now here was something. He had no idea Nebsumenu was so in love with his little wife, and a smile broke on his lips. The treasurer's undoing would be easy.

The lovers held their embrace, and Satweret stroked the thin beard at her husband's jaw and whispered against his throat. He shoved her back, and his head snapped up.

Potipherah greeted the naked look of astonishment on Nebsumenu's countenance with a wave of blue fingers.

Nebsumenu banished his sweet little wife to the inside of the house, then swaggered down the garden path, unable to wash the chagrin from his face.

"Greetings my lord treasurer," Potipherah said over the rim of his cup.

"I am honored to receive the first prophet of Amun in my home."

"I wouldn't have to grace your home if you answered my messages."

Nebsumenu reached for one of the treats on a nearby tray. "I haven't received any."

"Lying poorly keeps one from greatness, Nebsumenu. I'm very thorough with my messengers. Two messages were sent. Both turned away."

"Then I will put it to you in simple terms, priest. You have run the king just as you ran his father. It is too much that you should hold all the reins and all the glory. You've had the world at your beck long enough. I will not follow you. I will go another way."

He paced, and it was clear he'd practiced this speech for some time. Potipherah folded his hands, letting the silence fall between them before he answered. "Well, stop standing there like I'm going to take a rod to you. Sit."

There was almost a flash of relief in Nebsumenu's face as he sat with stiff politeness.

"So, you think to put this old Iunu priest out to pasture, do you? I suppose it appears to be any man's dice with both the king and the land in such a poor state."

"Everyone knows Khakheperre's on his way out."

"And so, therefore, you think that I am too? My dear man, I still hold all the dice in my hand, and I assure you that I feel my full vigor."

"Then share a portion. If you don't, we will simply take them from you."

"Don't attempt riddles as if I don't know that 'we' includes yourself, that melancholy butcher, Mentuser, and that hyena-faced Resnakt. Anyone can see the three of you playing fetch and throw with your eyes whenever you're near the king. You're no better than common thieves, and that curly headed imbecile Resnakt wearing his stolen little trinket on his belt right in the king's face. You think I didn't notice?"

Khakheperre thought his governors were the chief cause of his poverty. But with no vizier the responsibilities of the office were divided and there was little accountability for Nebsumenu's watch over the king's two houses of gold. With no one to hold him in check, Nebsumenu dipped into the king's coffers.

Often.

"And where would Khakheperre be without us?" Nebsumenu defended. "We've protected him."

"To milk him dry till there's nothing left?

"That is our business. You'd be wise to move out of the way."

Potipherah laughed under his breath, though his chest heaved with disappointment. The king's polished treasurer was no more than a thief with his heart set on the loot. It was sad to see a talented man stoop to such base desires. He was merely greedy and could not see his position for its true worth. The king's son, Khakure, was the real prize. A boy king to mold to one's will was a chance that came once in a few lifetimes, and Nebsumenu was a fool not to see it. He was impressive in a crisp white kilt with all his trappings of gold, but he was no challenge, no threat at all.

Potipherah raised his hands in surrender. "I'll do better than move out of your way. I'll give you the reins as you insist though you'll strangle yourself with them soon enough."

"You can afford the generosity. You have Deduamen on your side. Make him vizier and run the provinces. We will run the king."

"Deduamen." Potipherah huffed. "You may dispatch him with my blessing. Your wife has more sense in her little finger. Or perhaps you might join *him* to your little ragtag group. He's about your caliber."

Doubt played across Nebsumenu's face. He opened his mouth to speak, then paused to find words. "Swear to me that you are sincere in moving out of our way, that you won't interfere."

"I have no need of swearing. I keep my word well enough. There'll be no bloodshed unless you initiate it."

"Then you'll let the sand dweller be?"

Potipherah hiked his brows. "So you plan to use this Yoseph in some way." He glanced over the treasurer with a sharp smile. "All right then. I'll let him live, and I'll let you steal to bursting. But you have crossed me Nebsumenu, and in the end, you will be sorry for it."

CHAPTER FIFTEEN

ASENAT

ASENAT WATCHED THE SMALL MINOAN WOMAN strutting the length of the balcony in a suite of rooms more lavish than Mepi's. She struck the poor slave boy who chased her with a shading pole, scolding him for either being in her way or for not shading her enough as she paced.

It was the pile of hair she clutched atop her head that made her so short-tempered. Several times a day, the lady tersely ordered her maids to pin it up, comb it out, or restyle it. All efforts were made, except the most sensible in a season of such heat. To cut it off.

"My lady, come back to your lessons," Asenat called, only to be flagged to silence. She was rightly named Yimenet and was as elusive as her namesake, the goddess, consort to Amun.

Asenat returned to her writing as Yimenet tinkled and paced in her trinkets and elaborate girdle of turquoise and silver, colors always worn by musicians. She was rarely parted from her menat necklace, a privilege granted to musicians dedicated to the goddess Hathor. Exquisite on the harp, she kept it propped against a wall most days. Again, she claimed to be a bull jumper, explaining away the bruise marks on her limbs.

She was generous in her provision of three dresses, a wig and painted jewelry that relegated Asenat to the look of a skilled laborer belonging to the middle class. Yimenet had claimed a desire for writing lessons and agreed to pay for them. But she never sat more than a few minutes before she was up pacing again. The fine sheets of papyri were going to waste. Asenat snatched up a piece, burnished it, and began stroking out symbols to keep her sanity.

Yimenet warned her the guards would be watching if she tried to return to Mepi. She said women were being stopped and questioned in the corridors. It had been seven days since the event in the scroll room and they still searched for her. Asenat scoffed under her breath and wondered if her father had even noticed her absence from the Iunu temple.

"I ordered an embroidered sheath-dress for the Front of the Year ceremonies," Yimenet said, impatient. "If the seamstress doesn't get here in time, I'll have nothing to wear."

Asenat sent sharp, stiff strokes across the page at Yimenet's complaint. At least she could venture around the palace and find another seamstress to attend her. Asenat had only seen a few places in the palace compound and one or two of Mepi's favorite gardens. Now she was sorry for it. She was stuck here in Yimenet's dwelling, unsure if she was a guest or a captive.

"And what have we here?"

Asenat flinched at the warm breath tickling the back of her neck. A lean pock-faced man came to stand in front of her. His legs were sinewy beneath a short leather kilt, his scent like that of a stale washrag under the ointment he wore. His searching eyes chilled her to the core.

Yimenet hurled an ivory cup that bounced off his shoulder. "Get out, you castrated goat!" His face rippled with embarrassment from his wide low forehead to his narrow, soft jaw. She'd labeled him what he was despite his manly swagger. A eunuch. "How dare you enter my chamber unannounced. I might have been indecent."

"And who in the palace has not seen you indecent before?" He turned, inspecting the room.

Asenat tucked her chin. She could feel him watching her.

"I see you've finally done something worthy of your lord's money. Something besides preening yourself with trinkets and lying on your back. Good."

Asenat filled her reed pen with ink-soot, resisting the urge to look up. He stood at her writing palette.

"Female scribes are quite uncommon, Yimenet. Where did you find this one?" He squatted and cupped Asenat's chin. "It puts me in mind of the king's cupbearer who had half of the guards chasing after some female scribe."

Asenat exchanged an anxious look with Yimenet when Urshe glanced around.

"Turned out to be some effeminate priest in the end." He laughed but his words unnerved them.

"Remove yourself from my dwelling, Urshe," Yimenet demanded. "My master would beat you for being here."

"I shall remove myself and inform the master of your new scribe when he returns." He moved toward the door, and Yimenet moved so quick to block him that Asenat thought her claims of bull jumping might hold true.

"I'm learning to write. It's a surprise Urshe, and you will spoil it."

His potent regard moved over her. She moved in closer and walked fingers up his chest. No eunuch ever stood so near a woman with such hunger in his eyes.

There was a brief silence before Yimenet pulled his head down to hers. Her kiss held him prisoner while she kept her free arm rigid as if holding all her contempt for him there.

He trembled, trying to pull her deeper into an embrace, but she laughed against his mouth and shoved him back.

His eyes flashed a soul-torment that made Asenat wish she were elsewhere.

"Tell my master about the girl in my room Urshe, and I'll tell him about our kiss." Her cold smile expressed a triumph while his face grew redder than the Syrian cushions scattered on the floor. Asenat held her breath when he started for the door then stopped to level a venomous glare, first at Yimenet.

Then, at her.

CHAPTER SIXTEEN

HETNU

THE WINE FOR THE FRONT OF THE YEAR ceremony must be exemplary, and Hetnu had spent the better part of the day checking the stock brought up from the royal vineyards. He pressed his throbbing temples, unable to concentrate on his duties, and handed over his seal to a docking steward to sign off on supplies. How could he concentrate when the king was being forced to give way to a vizier that was not of his choosing? Deduamen was expected to arrive any day now.

Hetnu made his way to the threshold of the king's leisure room and stopped dead in his tracks. The scene unfolding before him was the stuff of nightmares he replayed a thousand times in his sleep.

Khakheperre swung the pole, knocking the dagger from Sabni's hand. Sabni grabbed an axe, Khakheperre, the adze. The king swung upward, sparking the blades.

Hetnu's world expanded and retracted again. He rushed forward with a vase as Sabni gave a war cry.

Hetnu brought the pot down on Sabni's head. He crashed to the floor, and Khakheperre doubled over, gripping his middle. Hetnu snatched a cloth from a table, ready to staunch a flow of blood. "Mentuser!" He yelled at the top of his lungs, rushing toward the king.

Khakheperre straightened, sputtering laughter. Prince Khakure laughed from the far side of the room and knocked over a fort model. And Kitjau, that blasted foreigner, hid his chortle behind his hand. Hau stood by a column smiling blandly, without so much as disturbing the rhythm of his fan.

Only Sabni sat on the floor, spewing curses and rubbing the swelling lump on his head. "You old fool! Would guards be right outside the door if this were a real fight? Dull blades, only dull blades are used when—"

"When what? When assaulting your king? When pulling on his waning strength?" Hetnu pivoted. "Are you hurt, Majesty?"

Khakheperre waved him off, unable to suppress his chuckles. Sabni kicked at shards and rose from the floor.

Hetnu went to the wine cabinet, humiliated by the unending cycles of laughter behind him.

"Don't be such a grandmother, Hetnu," the king said from across the room. "It's only Sabni."

Only Sabni.

Hetnu shook a wine jar with more temper than skill and peered over his shoulder at the good god brushing pottery shards from that Cushite's kilt.

"I ordered the exercise. Who else could I trust but Sabni to be hard on me?"

Hetnu poured himself a cup of wine and gulped it. His hands trembled. When he entered, he hadn't noticed the furniture stacked against the wall, the rugs and floor-pelts rolled back. He saw nothing but a weapon raised to split the king in two.

Kitjau helped Khakure gather the wooden blocks from the floor, while Khakheperre passed Sabni his personal jug of wine. That oaf had the gall to take a swig and pass it back.

Hetnu batted his stinging eyes. How long had this dangerous play with weapons gone on without his knowing? "The good god makes me feel like a cast-off sandal. You might have informed your faithful cupbearer." His attempt at a show of outrage was overlooked when servants bustled into the chamber to restore the room under Kitjau's direction. Hetnu's chest expanded in a hot flush as that mutt from Byblos strode past him. "Shouldn't you be mucking dirt somewhere?"

Kitjau answered with a smirk and a chuckle. He left the room with Prince Khakure and closed the door.

"Perhaps the cupbearer should stop his sulking, and take note of the king's improved health." Sabni brushed pottery shards from his shoulders.

Hetnu cut him a sharp look then glanced sideways. His eyes grew wide. "By Horus and Worsret." He slapped his forehead. When had Khakheperre's bones taken on such meat? "Mentuser's prayers to Sakhmet are working."

"Not Sakhmet, Hetnu," Sabni shook his head. "The lion goddess has had her chance to heal the king. This is the work of Yoseph's god, Elohim."

The king gave a broad grin. "The land is healing, Hetnu, and so am I. Let the governors see now that I am Horus in the flesh and the shape of Re himself."

Hetnu took a step forward, awed by the king's appearance. Sabni shoved a chair beneath him. He sat.

"And there's more, you old coot." Sabni slapped his shoulder. "Add this to the flourishing crops, and

Deduamen's elusive daughters floating into the palace quay like two gifts from the heavens."

Khakheperre swung his leg over the arm of the chair like a carefree youth. "And to think, I only kept the Asiatic around to buy myself time. But even Nebsumenu agrees that his plan for the crops is impressive. I'm inclined to agree with Sabni. It's the work of Yoseph's god."

Yoseph's god. The words alarmed Hetnu. The king had been spending too much time with Yoseph since he took the Asiatic in to tend his dogs. This Elohim was said to need no temples due to his greatness and Hetnu wondered if Khakheperre had gone out to seek him when he took one of his harem girls and a slew of guard into the desert one night without explanation. Hetnu would mention his concerns to Lord Nebsumenu. The treasurer was the king's closest counselor. He would encourage the sovereign to keep some balance.

"Just wait till the governors see the change in me, Hetnu. They will handle me more carefully."

"Most of them are here for the ceremonies, Majesty, except for Governor Nakht who keeps to himself. Your southern governors don't like him."

"May old Nakht live forever then." The king wiped his brow with a cloth. "Anyone who is enemy to the Sons of the South is friend to me."

Sabni shook his head. "There's something in the air, Heperre, and no one can deny it started when Yoseph interpreted your dream."

"Well, then remember my part in it." Hetnu raised his chin. "I was the one who brought him to you."

The king nodded. "Your part is duly noted, my beloved and selfless cupbearer."

"However, somewhere in the city, there's a bald effeminate priest living in fear of being identified as Potipherah's daughter." Sabni nudged the king into a chuckle and left the room.

Hetnu puckered his lips. The joke was running rampant among the guards. "I tell you it was a girl in Mepi's office."

"I appreciate your love and diligence nonetheless, Hetnu. You have brought Deduamen's daughters to me and Yoseph, whom I find trustworthy, being neither a thief nor a back-turner."

"If I have pleased the good god, then I wish him to hear my words."

"Go on, dear one."

Hetnu lowered his gaze to gather strength, then looked Khakheperre in the eye. "You put yourself in danger training with Sabni. He is not a man of the land but a Cushite. Get another guard to train you."

"I'll hear no adverse words against Sabni."

"He is the son of your father's enemy."

"Be quiet!" The king pressed his lips to a thin line. "It was never proven that his father was enemy to mine. Sabni and I are both dark sons of this land. Do not stir my displeasure on the matter, Hetnu, but sit in your chair. You may instruct me in all else but Sabni, for I love him as I love you."

"Oh, you love me, do you? Then what of this outrageous news I hear of you making a harem girl one of your queens?"

"I told you I would do as much."

"That's no excuse, Khakheperre. I didn't believe you could do something so foolish as this. The match gives you no political advantage whatsoever."

"I love her."

"Love, bah! You could have loved her just as well by keeping her in her sphere. You have Deduamen's daughters. Marry them."

"I plan to."

"Which one?"

"Both if it pleases you!"

"Pleases me? Well, that's a first in light of your recent activity. Please me then by punishing that detestable thief, Potipherah, for his rough handling of your person. I saw him accost you in the hall before the meeting with your counselors. I saw his blue mark on your skin. That such a thing should happen in your own house!" Hetnu shook, unable to hold his outrage any longer. "Potipherah should be stuffed into a sack and flung in the river!"

The king's face flinched with embarrassment, then anger. Then shame.

"It has always been thus with kings, Hetnu. I would that my forefather had not murdered Mentuhotep and left the throne and its cares to him. The crown is a gilded cage from which I cannot break free. And my son will be caged, after me. How can I bring such a one as Potipherah to account for his offenses?" He fingered the vizier's seal at his chest. "I've doubted there would be enough guards to follow me if I opposed him." The king gave a far-off look. "I had but one weapon left in the corridor that day. My anger. Though it was foolish to provoke Potipherah.

"Yoseph interpreted my dream and gave me boldness, and more hope than I could dream of. But if this is not the work of Yoseph's god on my body, if I should relapse and die, Potipherah will have Khakure. I must make the way safe for my son, even if he cannot be a true king." The sovereign's mouth pressed to a grim line. "But oh, what I would not give to have your words hold true about Potipherah's having a daughter. For I would love to hold his child like chaff, the way he holds mine."

CHAPTER SEVENTEEN

ASENAT

THE FRONT OF THE YEAR CEREMONIES DREW
courtiers and noble families from every province, as well
as emissaries from Crete, Mesopotamia, Punt, and a few
favored tribes from the northern borders. The palace
corridors were a crush of white and glittering gold. Shrills
of occasional laughter rose from the babble of the crowd.
The sovereign was to announce a new vizier today.

There was hardly room enough to wave a fan, and the
cloying perfume of courtiers churned Asenat's stomach. The
crowd moved as one man, and the long, trapping sheath-
dress she wore trimmed the length of her strides to petite
steps. Tight straps tugged at her shoulders, adding to the
neck strain of her ostrich-plumed headdress.

Many of the noblemen donned short, fat plumes of black
or white atop their wigs for the formal event while the
ladies preferred the long, slender plumes of brown or grey.
Asenat's was dyed one of the more daring shades of red,
and she longed to rip it off. But it held the wig to her
shaved head. An itching torment, but a necessity due to a
recent and troubling encounter.

She had to leave the king's house, and soon.

Yimenet was to blame. She'd been gone on a shopping spree for several days and appeared this morning to drop off her purchases and pick up her slaves. She made quick apologies, ushering her girls into the corridor before Asenat could get in a word.

She sat at the writing palette on the floor, letting her fingers express her irritation at being relegated to the level of a house pet. If Dagi hadn't stolen her rings, she'd be back at Iunu, packing her belongings for the temple of Pakhet.

"I've been thinking about you."

The low grating voice was Urshe's. Once again, she hadn't heard him enter the room.

He grinned, revealing a row of gapped teeth.

"What do you want?" She kept her voice even and her hands busy.

"I want to talk to you." He crouched down, and it took all of her efforts not to scoot back. He was slim and virile with a deliberate intrusive manner. There was nothing eunuch about him.

"Lady Yimenet keeps me busy."

"Apparently, you fail to hold her interest."

He was too close. She used a sheet of papyrus as a shield against his breath on her face.

"And where is the beautiful trollop anyway?"

"If you mean Lady Yimenet, I don't know."

"I suppose you think a man labeled a eunuch is completely useless."

There was something vulnerable in the timbre of his voice. She glanced up. "No more than a woman who writes with no one to read what she says."

He yanked her into a slimy kiss before she could stop him. His grip on her was vile, like that of a desperate vagrant.

She broke loose, swinging.

He weaved away from her intended slap with her wig in his hand.

"My father would kill you with his bare hands!" She knocked the back of her hand against her burning lips.

"And who is your father?" He stood up, inspecting the shadow of growth on her head. "I think that you are not a good tutor. I think that you are not a tutor at all with that high-class, lower kingdom dialect you've been hiding."

She threw a cushion at him. "I'll call the guards if you don't get out."

He held up his hands. "I assure you I know better than to molest a woman of noble birth. But as for the guards, I'll get them myself." He winked and left the room.

Asenat still shuddered at the memory of his assault though she was cocooned in the crowded corridor. She stroked the fine silver pendant hanging from beneath a heavy jasper pectoral, sorry to have taken Yimenet's new purchases, but she needed them to barter her way back to Iunu and would have to repay Yimenet later.

Asenat half-listened to the talk of the crowd on the hopeful harvest and the king's failing health that kept him closed off from court. A few girls chattered how romantic it was that he had elevated a common girl from his harem, and the throng's pace slowed even more. They'd reached a narrow archway that led to yet another corridor near a gate. Asenat took a second look.

A gate. One that led out to the palace quay.

A guard was settling some dispute, and courtiers passed

through without being questioned. Asenat moistened her lips, working her way to the edge of the press. This was her chance.

She met Urshe's gaze with her first step toward the gate. But the woman he argued with waved an angry finger in his face, drawing his attention.

Yimenet.

He grabbed her finger, and she shrieked. The crowd laughed and the guard was forced to intervene. Asenat pushed back into the drove, her heart pounding in her chest.

"Watch where you're going, girl!"

She arched at the poke in her back. The old woman clamped down on her shoulder, hopping like a dancer. "You stepped on my crooked toe."

"I'm sorry, Mother." Asenat glanced at the altercation near the gate. "Let me move you to a bench to rest." She pushed deeper into the crowd, ducking her head, but the old mother's grip held her fast.

"And lose our place in line? No, indeed."

A second old woman poked her way through the crush with a gold-capped cane. She was dressed much like the first, swathed in white linen and a heavy wig, her limbs ringed in gold.

These two Asenat remembered glaring at her from the bench the day she met Lord Nebsumenu. She peeked over her shoulder.

Urshe leered in her direction.

"Have you ever seen such a get-up, Ipwet?" One of the old mothers tugged Asenat by the arm, turning her to get a better view. "Why, she looks the part of a sheathed ostrich."

"It's too tight around the stomach. Too loose around her small breasts."

The second mother tsk'd. "You are right. We should beat her seamstress."

"Her legs are too long for such a style as this. And look here, Sahathor." The scowling old mother touched her cane to the unfinished hem of Asenat's sheath-dress.

"Atrocious." Sahathor flashed a look of disbelief. "Let's show the others."

They gripped Asenat's arms. "Come, hoyden. Don't just stand there, lead us on." Ipwet banged her cane and motioned forward.

Asenat glanced back. Urshe was pushing toward her through the crowd. She nudged toward the doors of the broad hall, dragging the matrons with her.

Lady Ipwet hiked her painted brows after a few minutes of overbearing questions in the crowded hall, her face a mixture of insult and utter fascination. "Do I understand that despite the attention you draw to yourself in such a get-up that you refuse to tell us your name?"

Asenat's gaze shifted toward the hall's entrance where Urshe's lips moved rapidly as he spoke to a guard. Asenat twisted her wrist in Ipwet's grip. "Dear Mother, I cannot say who I am. Not now." Her refusal provoked an astonished whoop from Lady Sahathor while Ipwet drew herself up and narrowed her eyes.

"Perhaps you do not know who we are, girl. We are among the king's intimates, those closest to the sovereign's ear."

Sahathor motioned a few courtiers over, inviting them to make a game of guessing Asenat's identity.

"She's a lost princess," one of the courtiers decided.

"No," said another. "A goddess in disguise."

"No, not a goddess." Ipwet struck the nobleman in the

chest with her fan. "A goddess would be more classically dressed."

Urshe found Asenat in the army of plumed headdresses and pointed her out to a guard. Her heart almost leaped from her chest.

"Well, if you won't tell us who you are, girl, then we will simply ask the king," Sahathor warned.

Urshe and the guard no longer stood at the back of the hall. Asenat pulled her wrist free of Sahathor's grip and pressed toward an exit near where she stood, but a flood of courtiers erupted through the doorway, pushing her back. She squeezed her eyes shut, clenching.

"Are you all right, my dear?" A man stood facing her with a heavy long wig of silver-beaded tips resting on his chest. He dabbed sweat from his brow and from the fat rolls at his neck. "I am Mayor Ubenresh." He bowed slightly. "Or soon will be if the sovereign favors me." He opened his mouth to say more, but his eyes widened. A girl came up beside them for whom the term "pretty" would have been a poor choice of words. Her bright brown eyes shone with interest. Her own natural red-brown curls fell to her shoulders beneath ribbon-bound braids caught up in tiny bells. Beside her was a girl dressed in identical fashion but with far less beauty and self-possession than the first. Her hair was not so red or curly but stretched with heat and fragrant oil.

"She is A'at. I am Appipa." The prettier one introduced herself. "You've heard of me? I am to be the king's next wife." She squared her shoulders. "And my father will be vizier."

"Sister," A'at chided in a loud whisper. "We are not to speak of that."

Appipa shrugged. "I don't care if the world knows it." Her gaze flitted around to see who was listening. She heaved a dramatic sigh and raised Asenat's arm to examine a variety of bracelets, then dropped it.

Her pretty eyes were full of avarice. Jewelry was ever the sign of one's status among the noble class, and neither Appipa nor her sister, A'at, wore anything like the pieces Asenat had borrowed from Yimenet.

"Would you like to wear my headdress?"

Excitement flickered in Appipa's gaze. "I'll try it on." It was a quick exchange that Asenat was happy to make, hardly noticeable in the crowded hall.

"You may stay beside me." A touch of delight filtered through Appipa's hauteur. "And if you are a good sort of person, you may join my ornate when I am queen."

A'at looked heavenward at her sister's declaration, but the long sound of a trumpet shifted their attention with the crowd's.

The leader of the broad hall struck the stone block. The sound of drums and pipes filled the hall, and the crowd crushed them back as it parted to make an aisle.

Drummers marched in double rows of ten. Lord Ubenresh worked his way beside Appipa, but she wiggled away to see the Cushite dancers flowing into the hall waving colorful flags on rods. The herald's voice rang out above the musicians, leading the king's administrators through the wide doors at the back of the great chamber.

"Seshemtawy who is Horus and who is Ma'at caused to appear by the Two Ladies, Mighty Bull of his mother, Son of Re, Lord of the Two Lands."

Asenat fought for space to see the king's entry. He was resplendent in his double crown of red and white, his crook and flail crushed to his chest. Ten officials in stiff white kilts bore him in on a gold and ivory litter. They lowered the chair at the front of the hall and the sovereign dismounted.

"Hetepnetjeru who is the Golden Falcon, appeasing the gods. Senuseret, Man of Worsret. Khakheperre, the soul of Re come into being." The dancers bowed, and the herald prostrated himself. The music ceased as the king ascended the platform where sat his great wife Queen Khenemetneferhedjet and his co-regent, Prince Khakure, his son.

"Glorious," Appipa whispered in the reverent silence.

There was something strange about the sovereign's appearance that Asenat could not account for. Swathed in embroidered robes, he almost disappeared from her sight among the forty counselors mounting the platform to cluster around his throne.

Asenat's father came forward. He glittered in bracelets and a pectoral of chalcedony and jasper that stretched across his shoulders and chest. His voice rang with clarity and confidence as he began a prayer to Horus for the king.

Asenat squinted at the man who stepped through the doorway at the back of the platform. Her eyes widened.

The Asiatic.

But a messenger squeezed by him and pushed forward to kneel beside the king. The sovereign leaned toward him as he whispered. Potipherah continued his litany to the gods, and Asenat lost sight of the Asiatic on the crowded platform. Now would be a good time to leave. She glanced again at the sovereign. He gave a little smile in her direction. She lowered her head. Of course, her eyes were playing tricks. Appipa gripped her arm.

"Do you see how he keeps glancing in this direction? He cannot take his gaze from me. Today I will be queen."

The words gave Asenat some relief.

"Not queen, Appipa. He already has a queen," A'at told her.

"Nonsense. Our blood is better than his. I shall be queen."

"Appipa, be silent." A'at's scolding was lost on Appipa's heap of self-assurance.

Potipherah concluded his supplication to the gods, and the king passed off his scepter to an attendant and lurched from his throne.

"My council tells me that I must accept the worthiest of my governors to become vizier." He came to the edge of the platform, addressing the crowd. "But today I say that you shall choose him yourselves."

Potipherah's locked jaws and down-turned mouth told Asenat he'd not expected such words. Even the king's cupbearer raised his brows.

"The dreams that I thought meant my death could not be interpreted by my priests, and I thought the blame was mine. But an unknown god came to test my worthiness."

The throng of courtiers stirred and mumbled as the king motioned, and the Asiatic emerged from the group of officials and priests on the platform. He'd altered greatly in his appearance since she'd last seen him in the king's morning hall. Dressed like a prince, he wore a pleated kilt with silver cuffs at his wrists and feet. The king brought him forward and grasped his shoulder.

"The gods sent a prophet from my prisons who gave meaning to my Horus dreams. I waited for his words to fail as the words of false speakers do." The king released the Asiatic to toy with the girdle at his waist. When he opened his robes, the courtiers gasped, and Asenat with them.

She had seen the king at the door of death, blighted and

coughing blood. But now his body was healed and filled in where his ribs once stuck out. He was lean, but there was no sign of sickness upon him.

What miracle was this?

The murmurs in the crowd swelled to shouts of praise.

"Excel in thy greatness, Majesty!" the courtiers cried.

"Live apart, oh excellent one!"

The hall rang with deafening cheers for several minutes until the sovereign shouted. "Look to your lands! For the river will rise to exemplary levels this year, and your fields shall burst with abundance!" He pulled the Asiatic up beside him. "The gods find me worthy, and if you do also then know that this Yoseph is the man who interpreted my dream. He is a true priest, giving all the credit to his god. So I ask, can we find this man's equal? A man in whom is the spirit of God? Tell me, shall I make this man vizier?"

The hall swelled with the deafening cheers and wild shouts of the courtiers. Khakheperre shook the Asiatic's shoulders, laughing.

His cupbearer fainted dead away.

Several courtiers around Asenat declared there was nothing like this to be seen in all the ceremonies that ever took place in the broad hall. A king with a miracle of the gods performed on his body. Khakheperre's sovereignty would not be soon questioned again.

While the crowd cheered, Potipherah stepped forward with his fists balled in the folds of his long, pleated skirt. He spoke to the king through clenched teeth, but Khakheperre laughed and gave him a hearty slap on the chest, then stepped down from the platform. He pushed his way through the crowd. Asenat's eyes widened. He was coming in her direction.

Appipa snatched one of the bracelets she'd been eyeing, scratching Asenat's arm. She clamped it on her own wrist. "He comes, you see?" Her voice shook. "He comes for me now."

Asenat closed her eyes at the king's approach. The scent of lotus essence and frankincense filled the air as she fought for space to lower herself at the king's approach. Only Appipa dared to remain standing in the red-plumed headdress.

"Majesty, I am delighted." Appipa addressed the sovereign.

Asenat held her bow, trying to make herself as small as possible. She would not dare look up, not even when the king's robe brushed her cheek. A tug at her wrist filled her with dread and brought her to her feet. Her gaze clung to the seal necklace at the king's chest. She glanced up and held her breath as the sovereign inspected her face. A slow tight smile broke on his lips.

"Come, daughter."

She tried to get the words out. She tried to tell the king that she was the wrong girl. He wanted Appipa, the pretty girl with the red-plumed headdress, not her.

He dragged Asenat to the front of the hall, his rings pinching her flesh as she stumbled behind him. As they approached, her father became very still, his expression unreadable.

"Tell me, Potipherah, when did you plan on presenting your daughter to me?"

Asenat kept her eyes down. Her pulse boomed in her ears. This was not happening. It was a bad dream.

"My daughter has come to court a number of times, Majesty." Potipherah spoke in the matter-of-fact tone of a smooth liar. "She often travels with me." He could call on any priest or servant to confirm this. "If the records do not show her presence, then the blame is mine. As you see, she is dressed to present herself, and besides, who could keep their child from your all-seeing eye?"

"Or who would dare to keep their child from me?" The king glanced down at her frayed hem. He stroked her wrist with his thumb in the pregnant silence and looked between the two of them. "I will take your daughter as my ward and make myself better acquainted with her."

"You honor my house, Majesty."

Potipherah bowed, and the king drew her past him. Asenat exhaled a shaking breath and glanced back. The look of heated anger on her father's face she would never forget.

CHAPTER EIGHTEEN

HETNU

FOOTSTEPS APPROACHED, AND HETNU BALLED
himself tighter into the woven blanket. "Whoever you are,
get out," he said with a catch in his voice. "Leave me alone."

Someone kicked an empty wine jug across the floor. "A
man could kill himself in this confounded tomb of yours."

Something ripped, and Hetnu shot straight up, slapping
a hand to his face. Beams of blinding sunlight streamed
into his room from his porch. He ground his teeth. "My
curtains from Crete! What is the meaning of this? Nen!"
He roared for his steward, clutching his head that someone
had obviously impaled before sticking it back on his neck.
He squinted through his fingers splayed across his face and
moaned.

A man in the brown leather kilt of an army commander
stood facing him with arms akimbo.

"Oh. It's you." Hetnu arched the covers over his head and
threw himself back on his couch. "Get out of my chamber,
Nebitef. You are not welcome here."

"What's this game you're playing? The king is asking
where you are."

Hetnu flipped back his covers, pinch-faced and furious, then sat up, gripping the edge of his mattress, waiting for the nausea to pass. "Tell Khakheperre, if my resignation hasn't reached him, that I've retired. The ways of the good god are too high for me." His voice quavered, and a long, groaning burp erupted from his gut. He rocked himself up from the couch holding his head and shuffling forward, kicking at empty wine jugs in his path. He scratched at the sheet-marked side of his face, pulling away a few strands of hair stuck to his cheek. He'd refused his body servant's offer to work out the tangle hanging down his back from a drunken slumber of more than two days.

He wanted to die.

"And as for you, Nebitef, you've brought humiliation on us both by overpraising that Asiatic." He plucked two wine bowls from the floor and tossed them on a low table, then reached for a half-full pitcher.

Nebitef harrumphed and sat across from him. "You're a fine snake of a friend. Yoseph cared for you while you wept like a babe in the garrison."

"I have no wish to recall such days, thank you." Hetnu raised his chin.

"He told you the meaning of your dream and gave you hope."

"I gave him hope also, bringing him to the king."

"Two years later."

"And two years too soon," Hetnu grumbled, raising his bowl of wine to his mouth.

"The words I spoke to the king were truth." Nebitef poured himself a drink. "I've freed my foolish wife from her lie. And myself from a well-deserved prison of guilt."

Hetnu grimaced. "Still. The world is a dung heap when

from among a host of nobles, a foreign slave is chosen to become vizier."

"By the term nobles, I take it you mean those greedy, self-anointed overlords, divvying up the land. I remember when we were a country united."

"United or no, I won't have that scarred and leather-skinned sand dweller commanding me. I will not have it."

They argued back and forth until Hetnu grew quiet, drawing vigor from Nebitef's mounting anger. He let the commander rage on and raised his bowl to take another sip. Nebitef slapped it from his hand.

"Why, you broken down cow! The king no longer hangs on your breast and all you can do is swill wine like nourishing soup!"

Hetnu dabbed the splattered wine from his chest and face. He poured himself another bowl.

"And then you faint like a woman before the whole court. I should deal with you myself for such a display."

Hetnu slammed his fist on the table. "By all means throw me back into prison, then. I'm well acquainted with the territory!"

"Don't change the subject." Nebitef aimed a thick finger at his face. "You've coddled Khakheperre all his life."

"He was a sick child."

"That's no excuse. He's a man. A king. Even a soldier worth his weight knows he must take risks. You've never given Khakheperre room to prove himself. No wonder he took such a leap."

"It was foolish of him."

"It was brilliant."

Hetnu clenched every muscle in his body. He knew nothing of Yoseph speaking to the king's counselors, nothing of Khakheperre's talks with that barbarian in his private garden. He'd been left out again. And again the deception cut him to his heart. "I've already put in my resignation. Your time is wasted here. Let Khakheperre play with his new toy of a vizier if he wishes. I'll not attend it."

"Yoseph is no ordinary man. He is above reproach in all things, and his god is as great as he claims. You cannot blame the king for taking hold of this."

"And a dangerous hold that Asiatic must have on *you*, defending him above your own wife. Such a thing is shameful for a man once Potiphar of a king's house."

"It was high time I bore a little shame. Kemsiyet is spoilt and good for nothing but jewels and parties, but Yoseph will serve the king well. He will not serve himself with the king's attention as you have, sheltering him like some tot on your knee."

The stinging remark caught Hetnu off guard. He blinked back tears. "I love Khakheperre like my own—"

"Like your own what?" Nebitef yanked Hetnu's wrist, pulling him across the table. "The king is the son of a god, not the son of a cupbearer." He shoved Hetnu's hand back. "Know your place!"

Hetnu bristled, then slumped at Nebitef's reproach. "Khakheperre is my life."

Nebitef exhaled, softening his voice. "You must allow him to leave his own mark upon the land, not yours. It is time to let him go."

"Then I was correct to turn in my resignation." Hetnu sniffed at the cutting truth. Khakheperre no longer needed him. Things were turning in the good god's favor. The watchmen and a few well-meaning administrators would be enough to get him through.

"You will most certainly not resign." Nebitef raked him with a scathing look. "You will train this Asiatic to be the best vizier the land has ever seen, and you will do it for your selfless love of Khakheperre."

"I will consider your words, Nebitef, but do not push me, for the decision is mine alone to make. Besides, Khakheperre has probably received my resignation by now."

Nebitef pushed back from the table. He pulled a scroll from his belt, and Hetnu recognized the clay seal.

"What's that you're holding? Why, you scoundrel. I believe it's my resignation!"

Before Hetnu's shock could turn to full ire, Nebitef tossed the document into a low burning brazier, gave a flourishing bow, then headed for the door. "Enough of your whining, old hound. Get back to work."

Chapter Nineteen

Yoseph

YOSEPH TOOK MEASURED STEPS UP THE walkway leading into the king's garden and blew a trembling breath from his nostrils. Who could have known that by the season of Akhet, within four months of his summons to the king's house, that the sovereign would not send him back to the borders, but instead name him vizier?

Lord Hetnu had overseen his preparation for this casual garden party, ordering the body servants to scrub, oil, and scrape him raw. The permanent scars on his arms were fairly easy to cover with bracelets and armbands, but there was nothing to be done for the marks on his back. Every slave received a portion of those though his were thankfully few in number. The rope scars at his ankles were covered with jeweled cuffs of electrum, lined with soft wool.

Hetnu assigned him an elegant pair of leather sandals that folded over his slow-growing toenails, and only a strong wind could stir the starched kilt he wore. His formal wig was tapered at his earlobes, stinging from the quick piercings Hetnu ordered. He insisted gold rosette studs were the minimum requirement for a fashionable lord. And then there was the heavy cylinder seal of vizier, dancing on his chest.

The king moved him from the slave quarters and succored him with the dog keepers in his personal dwelling. On the day he was named vizier, he was moved again to the most luxurious set of rooms he'd ever seen, walls trimmed in gold and covered with colorful murals.

Imehy tended his feet, and Sabni came often to see him. Their companionship steadied him among the courtiers who revered him with curiosity and a dreamlike awe. He'd long forgotten the dreams he told in his angry youth, dreams of bowing sheaves and stars. But he never dared imagine himself in a place so exalted as this.

Reaching the garden entrance, Yoseph went numb at the sight of white and gold decked courtiers in almost every corner of the manicured grounds. He forced cheer onto his countenance. Today he would meet the members of the elite, those closest to the king's favor where he would now be intimately placed. His gut churned and clenched when the herald bowed and struck a staff against a block of white quartz.

"It is the vizier. Leader of All Kilts and Setem priest, Overseer of the Six Great Houses, Overseer of the Six Law Courts, Mouth of Nekhen, Priest of Ma'at and Master of the Secret of Hearing Alone, Lord Yoseph."

The string of stately appellations followed by his foreign name brought a few chuckles from the scattered crowd. He held a smile. The world had come out to gape at him, and his bowels quaked.

It grew quiet as a small, naked child with gold bracelets toddled up to him with outstretched arms. Yoseph reached down to pick her up, glad for the grounding weight. She reared back to look at him and worried her brows in a myriad of expressions. He braced for a wail, but she clutched his nose to pull herself forward and give him a sloppy kiss. Laughter erupted, and the hum of the crowd returned.

"As you see, you are welcome here, Lord Yoseph." The god's wife beckoned him from a couch beneath a wide, tasseled canopy. He pressed through the drove, nodding at his name on the lips of courtiers.

A nurse took the tot from his arms, and there was no way to hide the vizier's seal at his chest to which all eyes were drawn. He genuflected to the god's wife, who was united with the white crown and Mistress of the Two Lands. "Queen Khenemetneferhedjet." He had practiced the name a thousand times, forcing out any slip of his native accent. The queen, who was the king's sister and six years her brother-husband's senior, followed his every gesture with a cool smile. He drew to mind Hetnu's warning to take care with the god's great wife, who was as spiteful as a snake.

"I am Queen Weret to those I allow." She extended her brown hand and he bowed, touching it to his forehead.

"You see, Weret, he is handsome just as I told you." The king's younger sister-wife, Queen Khnemet had spoken. Her compliment filled him with an old dread. His looks never ceased to bring him attention and sometimes trouble, like a curse one could not shake off.

"Majesty." He bowed to the king's second wife, who wore her hair pulled back in a braided hairpiece. Queen Khnemet donned a pretty diadem of lotus flowers made of marbled lapis and deep red carnelian stones across her high forehead. A thin line of kohl rimmed her small, assessing eyes. She turned, indicating the nurse holding the child who approached him. "If you keep flirting with my daughter,

Lord Yoseph, I shall betroth her to you." She puckered her lips, giggling from her throat.

"Has he any brothers?" The question arose from the cluster of females standing beneath the shade of Queen Weret's canopy.

"No," he answered, provoking a chorus of disapproval from the queen's ladies. A derisive snort made him glance over his shoulder. Prince Ameny swayed on his feet, holding a jeweled wine jug. He stood among the white-clad courtiers in his Byblos styled garment of blue and yellow stripes. The bridge of his nose was no longer straight. Yoseph bowed to the king's brother and to Prince Dagi, standing behind him. The young coward was easy to spot in the red and white choker he always wore.

These two Yoseph understood even without Hetnu's explanation. Dagi was a brash boy, barely into his manhood, and the king's poor distant relative. Prince Ameny, the king's brother, was declared by Hetnu to be a harmless drunk, living in the lap of luxury. But rich and jaded men were never harmless. They spoilt the lives of others and were dangerous to any beneath their rank.

"I can certainly see your struggle in resisting him, Kemsiyet."

Queen Weret's address brought Yoseph to sharp attention. She cut a look sideways, though her ladies stood behind her. Hetnu had assured him the former Potiphar's wife was not one of the queen's ornate, nor among the king's intimates, but the malicious smile on Queen Weret's face told Yoseph all he needed to know. The queen invited the wife of Lord Nebitef, his former master, to make sport of him. But he would have spared even Kemsiyet from this embarrassment.

"It's his word against mine." Kemsiyet gripped the canopy pole, her voice trembling.

"Don't be foolish. It's the king's word against yours, and his word wins." Weret waved her forward. "Come, bow before your vizier."

Kemsiyet obeyed, pouting like a child. She was a lying woman, given the liberty to continue lying because no one had caught her the first time. She bowed, avoiding his gaze.

Laughter spurted from Weret's pressed lips. Her gaze shot between the two of them. In one blow, she had both amused herself and deepened Kemsiyet's undiminished hate.

Yoseph made his recovery by turning to greet the king's newest wife. Neferet was a harem girl made queen. He'd met her while discussing Elohim with the king while he tended the sovereign's dogs. Some distance away from Weret's waspish sting, she cradled her budding, pregnant belly. He bowed, and the girl's smile brimmed with silent solidarity. They were both new arrivals to the king's inner circle.

Queen Weret was not finished toying with him and patted the seat beside her. But Prince Ameny pushed by him and took the seat with triumph gleaming in his reddened eyes.

"It is not you that I have invited to sit, Ameny." Amusement colored her voice.

"He's not vizier yet," Ameny slurred, giving Yoseph a cold, half-lidded stare above the crooked bridge of his nose. "You'd better not let this dirty sand dweller too near you, Weret." He stroked his thin mustache, narrowing his eyes.

Weret slapped his arm. "You go too far."

"Well, then I take it back. He's not dirty," the prince mumbled, pulling his wine jug to his mouth. "Today."

A servant approached to inform Yoseph that the king required his presence. He bowed in respect to Queen Weret, who had already turned to converse with someone else.

Yoseph started down the path, spotting Hetnu in the distance with a little Cushite child on his lap. She enraptured the crowd around her, performing a little finger song, and for once, Hetnu smiled as he chatted with the king's other guests.

"May I walk with you, Lord Yoseph?"

Yoseph clasped his wrist behind his back, nodding at the lovely courtier who came up beside him.

"You handled that well." She smiled, flashing pretty eyes covered in complimenting shades of malachite from her brows to the ridge of her nose.

"You are kind," he said, keeping his own counsel at the ruffling experience. "As a slave, I've heard far worse."

"I was glad for Kemsiyet's setting down." She crossed her arms, exposing a set of matching amethyst bracelets. "I am no gossip, I assure you, my lord. It's just that lying is like milk to her. There will be those who'll feast on her words for the mere talk of scandal. I hope you can stomach it."

"I've stomached worse."

"Of course, you have. And you've avoided our dear queen's sharp teeth fairly well. Weret likes to leave marks for the fun of it."

"No doubt I'll find several upon my person before retiring tonight. Lady...?"

"Qatsenut."

"Qatsenut." He repeated her name, catching her blush as she turned into a profile of strong and graceful features. "I thank you for your warning."

She stopped respectfully a few feet from the king's pavilion. "Perhaps I might be of some assistance to you here at court."

"I would be delighted, Lady Qatsenut, if you should find the time to do so."

She left him as another herald announced his approach.

"Come, sit." The king beckoned Yoseph closer, cracking nuts for his son Khakure who wiggled in his lap. The sovereign wore a bright nemes headdress and less jewelry than the servants surrounding him. Gold rimmed the hem of his plain, sheer kilt.

"Majesties." Yoseph bowed.

The king tapped his son's leg. "Jump down, Khakure, and greet your new counselor who will also be a father to you."

Khakure obeyed, and the king whisked almond shells from his lap.

"But don't I have enough fathers already?" Khakure flattened his brows.

"This one will be of great service to you. Trust me." The king instructed Yoseph to sit, and Khakure stood in front of him.

"Watch this." The prince set his small hands on Yoseph's knees and leaned forward to balance his weight with his feet off the ground. "Sabni taught me." He strained, then lowered his feet again.

"Well done, Majesty." Yoseph instantly liked the child who bore the mark of his father's large ears and dour expression.

"Do you think I will be a good king?" Khakure wriggled into Yoseph's lap to examine his seal necklace closer.

"You will be a very good king."

"Run along now to your nurse, Khakure," the king ordered. "Tell the watchmen to come sit with me."

The boy jumped down from Yoseph's lap and started running down the path when his father called to him. "Khakure, do not forget yourself."

The prince slid to a stop, turned, and gave two quick nods that Yoseph suspected were hasty bows, then ran back toward the crowd. There was a father's pride in the king's face. Then he scowled.

Yoseph turned in the direction of his gaze.

Prince Ameny staggered toward them.

"What was this mess done at court, Khakheperre?" He slurred, raising his jug. "Making a sand dweller vizier? Were I here—"

"Were you here, you'd be drunk on my wine as you are now. Sit, Ameny, and do not say another word. No, not in one of the chairs, on the cushions behind me where you can sleep it off." The king directed his brother with a sharp gesture to a distant shaded corner of the pavilion, laden with cushions. He half turned in his seat to ensure that Ameny obeyed. "Brotherly love," he mumbled, eyeing Yoseph and blowing wind from his cheeks.

Footsteps came up the paved walkway. A blend of spikenard and myrrh tickled Yoseph's nose. He rose to bow and greet the three men, then cringed inwardly at his mistake. Hetnu had drilled him on the gestures of a high lord. He was no longer a slave, but a slave's habits were engrained in him and hard to break.

"Yoseph, here are my dearest friends and counselors, Nebsumenu my treasurer, Resnakt, one of my royal sealers and Mentuser, my physician who keeps my health.

"Oh praise me for keeping your health now, Majesty, but

you've given all of my credit to Yoseph's god." Mentuser's long face broke into a late grin. "And for the miracle he has wrought on the good god's person, I surrender it." Mentuser sent Yoseph a sharp smile. "I'll send someone to tend your feet."

"No, Mentuser. Go yourself since you are the best that I have."

Mentuser nodded at the king's order. "As the good god wishes."

Servants set down a stand in the middle of their group and brought a wide metal bowl filled with grilled meat and vegetables. The men scooted closer with platters and long prongs with which to spear the food and serve themselves. Yoseph's gaze strayed again and again to Lord Nebsumenu. The treasurer's eloquent manner was as impressive as Yoseph remembered when he was called to speak before the king's counselors. He owed this man much for speaking so well of him.

"I still grieve the loss his Majesty suffered on the nursery balcony." Nebsumenu filled his platter and glanced at the king.

Yoseph had heard about the tragic balcony accident. One of the king's lower wives and three of his children had fallen to their deaths.

"Yes. It burns my soul, knowing that I try to keep safe all those within my care. No less, my lower wives and children."

"Such would be enough to shake any man, Majesty. Let me close off the place in honor of your loss. No one will ever fall from it again."

The king sat thoughtfully and nodded. "It seems a just

memorial." He gave a half-smile. "What would I do without you, Nebsumenu?"

"I cannot answer since I will always be at your side, Majesty." The treasurer gave a brief smile, and the men moved on to small talk of their families and cattle and vineyards. Soft snores arose from the corner where Prince Ameny slept, and Yoseph sat tongue-tied, a gnat among such great men.

"My new vizier must begin work, and I mean to have him perform it well. Nebsumenu has volunteered himself as instructor."

Yoseph exchanged a friendly nod with the king's treasurer who smiled, stroking his beard as the king cleared his throat.

"But I have decided that Yoseph will perform the work alone." The sovereign mumbled into a cup. Nebsumenu's smile faltered.

"However, you will all give him a tour of your offices. He shall meet with your staff so that he may understand when he begins his own work how the waters flow."

"The good god cannot be serious." Nebsumenu held a pleasant but strained expression. "The man is untrained. You cannot put such important work in his hands."

The king spit out a piece of bone over his shoulder and jabbed at a chunk of meat with his prong. "I'd have Khakure or the lowest girl from my harem as vizier before that pretender, Deduamen that Potipherah tried to thrust on me. Yoseph has managed a great estate and one of my garrisons very well. The help of the men in his cabinet should be enough."

Resnakt leaned forward. "Yes, but managing a kingdom?"

"I am sure that I can perform what the good god bids

me," Yoseph cut in and sat up straighter. He would show these great men what he could do. He would show them the king had chosen well.

The king nodded his approval.

"Then we shall help direct his office and watch over our new vizier." Nebsumenu brightened. "It will be much easier on him."

"And he'll far better enjoy the pleasures of his status without being so overwhelmed," Resnakt chimed in.

"I've already secured the pleasures of his status." The king allowed a servant to wipe his mouth and hands with a damp cloth. "I'm giving him all five estates that belonged to the vizier before him, and he shall have grounds near Gesy on the west bank and taxes collected from the towns there." He leaned to touch Yoseph's knee. "And there is a mansion on the bend of the river, near the province of The Scepter that I seldom visit. It shall be yours along with eight coffers from my treasury after the first harvest."

Yoseph nodded, trying to swallow the beef in his mouth. He felt sick.

"It seems the good god has made his vizier richer than all of us." Mentuser's lighthearted comment bore hints of outrage, while Resnakt's gleaming smile grew feral. Yoseph chewed, forcing himself to concentrate on the grilled leeks and onions on his platter. His mother had pleaded with Naphtali and Dan from her sickbed to care for him after her death. The strained look of compliance on their faces was the same look passing between the watchmen, now.

"As you see," the king assured them, "I take my administrators seriously, and you will do the same. I have said this man shall be my vizier. If he is poor at his work, then I shall know you have not supported him. If he is excellent, I shall know that you have helped him. He is your master, and you will see that he has whatever he desires." The king drank his wine, as if to escape any complaint. Nebsumenu nodded his capitulation, then flashed a look at the other men.

Yoseph chewed a piece of meat and lowered his gaze at the glances passing between the watchmen. The king had called him their master and it was clear that the word did not sit well.

CHAPTER TWENTY

POTIPHERAH

Something in the air unsettled Potipherah. The way the early crops lay thick and heavy with grain, the way the dates and olives weighted down the trees, the grapes hanging like jewels on the vine. It was as though the world had taken on a verdant sheen in the hot, dry season of Akhet.

Though he was father of the god, Potipherah had not been invited to the king's garden party given for his sand-dwelling dog, Yoseph. It was an insult Khakheperre had been careful to pay him. But neither was he discouraged, playing the amiable host at his own clandestine banquet.

He invited the Sons of the South, a select group of governors who embodied the traditions of the land. These were the keepers of Ta-shema, the corn lands where the grain was grown. The gold of Cush traveled to the king's house through their provinces, and Khakheperre was forced to handle these southern governors with the greatest of care. Besides this, the years of poor harvest had increased their provincial power and left the king at their mercy.

Ta-mehu, the northern lands were less important with

networks of marshlands, pastures for cattle, and vineyards. There were quarries and trade routes in the eastern desert, but the true wealth of the land was in the south.

Potipherah did the provincial governors a great service in corralling them. Instead of their constant squabbling and skirmishes with each other, he directed their petty jealousies where they could make the most impact.

At the king.

But his hard work had almost been blown to the wind by the uproarious approval of the Asiatic in the broad hall. Thus he checked on his little flock to ensure the governors still answered to him and not to the king's restored health which some called a miracle.

"What do you say to this Asiatic's prophecy that has already proven itself in the land?" Lord Wegaf asked from his place farther down the table.

Potipherah delayed answering and served himself from the tray of braised ox tails. "The people are excited by the possibility of wealth an abundant harvest can bring, as am I, Lord Wegaf, and as you should be. We are long past due." He let his words settle in the room, regarding some of the more doubtful governors.

The men dined a few more minutes, engaging in light conversation. "You've insulted us, Potipherah, as much as the king has. None of us knew you had a daughter."

Potipherah took a sip of wine. Lord Sonebau had been chafing at the bit all evening. "You did not know about my daughter because I did not wish you to know." He glanced around the table, looking for more signs of challenge. "I'm sure every one of us here has secrets. But now you have the advantage of knowing one more of mine."

"How do we know you haven't positioned your daughter

Asenat to become queen?" Sonebau inquired, his tone cool and accusing.

"Because I didn't know she was coming." Potipherah shrugged, and his innocent answer roused laughter.

"Then perhaps you cannot control the girl."

"My daughter is intelligent and headstrong as are the sons and daughters of all wealthy men, but understand that she will work in our interest. As you see, it is not I who positioned her here, but the gods themselves. The girl has studied all her life at the great temple and is trained to serve."

"Is it true that you struck the king's brother Ameny?"

Potipherah touched his blue knuckles to his lips. "It is not Ma'at to strike a royal prince, Lord Wegaf," he answered, letting the expectancy in the room dim a little. "But I think we can all agree that Prince Ameny was a little too pretty for his own good." The room erupted in laughter, and he allowed himself the indulgence of a small smile.

"And what about Deduamen?" Sonebau cut through the room's lightened mood. "He was supposed to be here days ago."

"What harm can it do to let the king ride his Asiatic donkey? Deduamen will eventually be vizier."

"But it cannot be good that Khakheperre has a vizier of his own choosing." Sonebau looked around the room to garner support. "And the sand dweller's god is powerful."

"And are our gods not powerful?" Potipherah asked. "What can an Asiatic's one god hold to our ennead of gods and the hundreds of lesser deities who support the work of the great gods?"

"Not even you can deny the blessing of the Asiatic's god on the king's body." Sonebau pressed his challenge.

"The king has been healthy before, Lord Sonebau. How long do you think this will last?" Potipherah raised his cup. "May the Asiatic's word make us wealthier than ever."

His toast caught them off guard, but they raised their silver cups, joining him.

"But as for the sand dweller's success, not even Horus himself could keep him from bumbling." There was laughter. Potipherah was satisfied he'd won them over, despite the scowl on Sonebau's face. "Khakheperre will slit his own throat in the end for having made such a choice, and our own hands will remain clean. All we must do is wait."

CHAPTER TWENTY ONE

HETNU

HETNU'S MOUTH DROPPED OPEN AT THE KING'S words. "You mean you walked right into the crowd and plucked her up?" He hiked his brows. "She is here?!"

Khakheperre fingered one of the braided wigs Resnakt styled for him, grinning from ear to ear. "She is here. Yet another miracle since Yoseph came to my house, and this to your credit, my dear cupbearer, for we all made light of your words." The king raised a cup in toast. "Oh, had you but seen the hidden terror on Potipherah's face when I brought his daughter forward before the whole court. Only a god could have aligned such a moment in my favor. The girl is important to him."

Hetnu gave a sharp exhale, pressing his hand to his chest. They'd teased him so long about the scribe in Mepi's chamber that he'd begun to believe he only imagined it to be a woman. But it was a woman after all, a girl. And not just any girl, but the daughter of that scoundrel, Potipherah. Hetnu swallowed, waiting for his tongue to catch up with his shock. "W-what will the good god do with the girl?"

"Why give her to you, of course."

"To me?"

Khakheperre reached forward, touching Hetnu's arm. "Yes. You have begged for revenge since my father died and Potipherah had you thrown into prison with that wicked baker. I love you, my good father, never forget it."

Tears welled in his eyes at the king's gentle rebuke. He'd been away from Heperre's side too long. He was still needed. Such praise from the good god was like a cool drink of water.

"The presence of Potipherah's daughter in my house has secured my safety and authority."

"But what shall I do with her?"

The king chuckled. "I would not burden your life with marriage to such a girl, but she is yours to direct. Marry her off to some Cushite or Anatolian emissary. Send her to Crete. I don't care. As long as Potipherah suffers. I leave her in your hands."

HETNU WAS OUT OF THE KING'S CHAMBER IN NO time, strutting through the corridors and swinging his arms like hinged battle axes. He stopped for no one, not even the gossiping mothers Ipwet and Sahathor, who tried to wave him down with their canes. Potipherah had stolen something from him, and now he would see the priest groan in pain as he had. He would show no consideration for the offspring of such a man.

No respect. No mercy.

He reached the suite of rooms where the girl was kept and entered, promising himself this luxury would be the first thing to go. He warned the servant not to announce him as he passed through a sleeping chamber to a little garden courtyard. The girl sat with her back facing the house. Garbed in a scribe's robe, she wore nary a wig or a piece of jewelry. Her shaved, oiled head sparkled in the sunlight as she leaned over a writing tray.

So this was the one who'd knocked him flat in Mepi's workroom.

He would let her get a good look at his face, for she would never forget it after today. He cleared his throat to speak, and she put up a hand for silence, searching the documents strewn on the stone pavement around her.

That was quite enough. He struck his shoulder with his fly whisk to keep his temper. "First, you need a lesson in manners. And then one in feminine deportment. Hanging over your work in such a vulgar fashion. Were I an assassin, you'd be dead."

"Nonsense. I heard you come in." She met his gaze, and shock ripped through him. He fell back a step.

"Is anything wrong, my lord?"

He could not answer, only stare. When she pushed him in Mepi's office, he had no time to notice her face. But now he would never forget it. Time had kindly erased the memory of his beloved, yet here was her perfect face before him. The very thing that Potipherah had stolen from him in his youth.

His heart's desire.

Rudet.

"Are you all right my lord?" The girl rose from the floor, and his vision of Rudet's petite frame was deposed by this taller thinner form. But her face. Her face was one he had loved for all time.

She wiped ink from her fingers with a rag and brought him water.

He could not take his gaze from her while pretending to drink from the cup she gave him. Potipherah had made a fool of him, but now he saw how the gods had made him yet a bigger fool. He went to a chair and sat, placing the cup on the floor beside him.

"Your mother would turn in her coffin to see you wigless and your fingers and garments stained with ink." He forced out choppy words to keep the quaver from his voice. "Here on, you shall comport yourself like a well-bred lady."

"My mother is stiff in her coffin." She huffed. "And will not so much as turn unless a grave-robber turns her."

He could have struck her for such disrespect, but it was as though Rudet's ka, her soul's potency, had traveled back to the world of the living.

The girl returned to her work and took up her pen. She must have sensed his offense for she glanced over her shoulder looking down. "My mother's sweetness did not pass to me, my lord."

He took a moment to recover and went to stand near her as she labored over a text. "You wrote these? All?"

"From memory, yes."

"You have the hand of the goddess Sefchet, herself. You were an instructor at the temple."

She gave a stiff nod, and he looked over her, thinking how easy it must have been for her father to hide her at the Iunu temple. A reclusive, sour-faced girl. "Prepare to use your talents here in the king's house."

"I will do what you ask on one condition."

"You shall do what I command with no conditions attached."

"Then I would like to make a request."

"Yet I find myself in no mood to take your requests at present—"

"I request that you not let my father near me."

He should have insisted on as much, himself.

"He's had nothing to do with me." Bitterness riddled her words while she made herself busy, wiping ink from her fingertips with a damp cloth.

"But you are nobly born and have a duty to your king, a duty you will pay." He waited for her to argue, but she was wise enough not to challenge him. "And as for your request for distance from your father..." He paused, noting the first trace of anxiety in her eyes. "Very well."

Her shoulders slumped, and he nearly fled to the doorway to keep from losing his heart completely.

"Thank you, my lord." The words rushed from her lips on a sharp exhale. "And I wish you to know I came to the palace without my father's knowledge."

He sensed the peace offering she laid before him and searched her haunting face. "That may or may not be the case," he said as harshly as his heart would allow. "But your father is no friend to the king."

"Neither is he a friend to me," she said, taking up her reed pen again.

"WELL?!" KHAKHEPERRE LURCHED FORWARD gripping the arms of his chair.

Hetnu started in shock. He'd strolled aimlessly through the corridors, intending to mull the matter over, but his traitorous feet brought him right back to the king's leisure room. He swallowed hard at the hunger for retribution in Khakheperre's eyes. A hunger he could no longer serve.

"I believe..." He cleared his throat. "I believe this god of Yoseph has sent this girl to you for a purpose."

The king narrowed his gaze.

"I think she was brought here to give you strength over your enemy."

The king looked away and was very still. This was not going well.

"Then why not take strength over my enemy through her?"

Hetnu moved to the wine cabinet. "And anger this unknown god who's placed her in your lap? Or do you mean to put this god's wrath on my shoulders instead of yours?"

"I am king, and I gave you an order."

"You are king, and you gave her to me as a gift. If you have trusted me, Heperre, then trust me still. But do not ask me to perform your injustice for you." His voice nearly cracked in terror. "That is the truth of it."

"You walk a thin line, speaking to me in such a manner. Have I not done this for you? Have I not placed the heart of an enemy who is both yours and mine in the palm of your hand?"

Hetnu's heart hammered. He could not lose Rudet again. He must fight for her daughter. He swallowed and sent up a quick prayer to the gods, even to Yoseph's god if he would hear. "I walk as your justice here, Majesty. I shall protect you even from yourself if I must." He braced for Khakheperre's retort, but the king's face went blank, and by some miracle he raised his hand in surrender and chortled.

Hetnu could have watered his kilt.

"All right, Hetnu. What shall I do with the girl then?"

Hetnu poured two cups of wine. "You have placed her in my care. Allow me to decide. I shall see that she serves you circumspectly." He was still shaking. "She is an intelligent girl who reads and writes with peculiar exactness."

"And how do you know she will not spy for her father?" The king glared.

"She hates him, did I not tell you, and wishes no communication with him. We'll place her in a highly visible position where her every move will be scrutinized."

"Well, don't think about placing her in my bed. I'm humiliated enough with Deduamen's girl batting her eyes at me."

"You have my heart's thanks, Majesty." Hetnu bowed deeply.

"Then move quickly, dear one, for I'd rather have her head."

CHAPTER TWENTY TWO

YIMENET

YIMENET WEAVED THROUGH THE CROWD AT the palace quay, taking in the colorful woven rugs slung over the side of vessels and the pleasant scents of canopied perfume stalls. The once empty jetties overflowed with vessels bearing casks of Syrian wines, colored cloth from Byblos, and almost anything else the courtiers desired. Wealthy merchants from Egypt and from neighboring kingdoms fought against the swelling tides to chont upriver to the king's house. Word had gotten out that the river would overflow its banks to the perfect heights. Abundance was coming again to Egypt, and the world wanted its share.

In the midst of the crowd, Yimenet spotted the strong back and handsome form that set her heart aflutter. She slowed her pace to catch her breath. Ameny would not like it that she'd run like a thief, even toward him.

She brought a lock of hair over her shoulder and kissed her menat necklace, then sent up a quick prayer to the goddess and sauntered up behind him to slip her hand around to his hard, oiled chest. One was not permitted to touch a royal prince in such a way, but Ameny was so much more to her than that. He covered her hand with his own as he conversed with the other men, and she pressed her ear to his back to catch the resonance of his voice. Warmth flooded her belly. Even if she'd been a proper courtier, she would have traded her status ten times over to be his lover.

Ameny dismissed the men, and she bit her lip, smiling with thoughts of taking him to her couch to prove just how much she missed him. He pulled her around his fragrant form to face him, and her mouth fell open.

"My lord!" She reached for his crooked nose. He caught her hand and kissed it. "Who has done this? You will tell me who has dared to strike a god." She flung her perfumed hair back over her shoulder, stomping her foot in a pretty display of indignation.

"Never mind it. A mere tavern brawl, my love." He leaned to rest a kiss on her forehead. "I've missed you." He held her hand against his chest, and she tried to pull it free as he searched her face.

"My lord, do not stare at me so. It is not becoming for a god. What will others think?"

"That you are my woman." His low and sensual voice titillated her senses as he stroked her dark tresses.

She leaned into him, deeming the torture of keeping her hair ready for his touch a worthy cause. She almost forgot his crooked nose, until his gaze left hers to glance some distance behind her. She turned to see what captured his attention, but he pulled her through the crowd toward the pylon gates.

"Who's that fat man on the verge of tipping your vessel?" she asked. "I've never seen him before."

"That's Senib, a renegade priest I've had brought up from Iunu. He eats like a herd of oxen but swears that he's full of talent." Ameny gave a light scowl. "All these questions. You're a nosy little thing today. Afraid I'm taking a male lover?" He pushed forward, and some instinct made her steal another glance behind them.

She caught sight of Urshe, whose eyes glinted with a look of revenge. He broke into a slow smile. Her stomach dropped. "Urshe is a liar, my lord."

"And what is he lying about, my little dove?" Ameny's easy tone chilled her blood.

"Ameny, listen to me."

A group of court ladies passed them in an archway. He stopped to flirt and chat, locking her wrist in his grip. She fought down a whimper, tugging and plucking at his hold. He struck her until her ears rang, never losing the stride of his banter with the ladies.

She held still and lowered her gaze until he bowed and dismissed them, then yanked her forward.

It was in the less crowded corridors where she blocked a few blows on the way to his chamber. But not all of them. No, that would not be safe to do. Ameny was the king's brother and did whatever he pleased.

The guards at the door of his dwelling stepped to the side as he dragged her into his chamber. He flung her to the floor, and she held her breath until he passed the box where he kept his oiled whip.

He went to pick a fresh switch from a bush on his terrace and sniffed, swiping a drop of blood from his nose. He picked the switch clean without looking up and she knew what kind of beating this was going to be.

It was time to jump the bull.

"Take off your clothes, Yimenet."

"Ameny please." She shrieked, grabbing for the switch he swung at her face. "Listen to me!"

"Do you know how much you've cost me? Who was the girl in your rooms?" He laid three strikes to her thigh before she leapt out of reach.

"Let me explain." She'd lost none of her acrobatic strength and dodged a few swings whistling through the air. He motioned for her to continue while he caught his breath. "I did not know who she was. I swear it. I took her in because I wanted to learn to write you poems."

"You were hiding her."

"Yes, my lord. She was on the run from someone but I had no way of knowing from whom. You returned to the palace, then you left again. I tried to keep her for you." At the deflated croak in her voice, his eyes flickered with doubt. She summoned tears. "I didn't know how long you would be gone."

"She was the daughter of the most powerful man in the kingdom, and now she's slipped right through my fingers. With her beside me, I might be king." He staggered to a stool and sat, staring blankly.

Yimenet knelt before him. He sniffed, and she swiped another trickle of blood from his nose.

"Potipherah did this to me." He pointed to his face.

"And I will kill him for it." She met his gaze evenly, despite the welts stinging her thighs.

He cracked a smile and cupped her chin. "I believe you would. I could not bear it if you were false with me, Yimenet. I need you."

"I know." She leaned forward, letting him take her mouth in a kiss like fire. She held his face to hers, recognizing the familiar pattern of footsteps coming toward them.

"Be careful of comely little vipers my lord," Urshe said from the doorway. "They carry the strongest poison."

"I should beat you for making me think her a spy." Ameny rose, moving toward Urshe who shot him a bold look and took a chair in the room.

"I'm sure she is." Urshe challenged her narrowed gaze on him. "But this time I have proof that she performed opposite to my lord's best interests."

Ameny did not correct Urshe's forward behavior or command him to leave but went to the door and closed it. That pocked-faced scoundrel winked at her, and she felt her first fluttering of fear.

Ameny stood between them, nodding for Urshe to continue.

"I followed Yimenet on the day she found Potipherah's daughter."

"How dare you." Yimenet clenched her jaws, unable to draw Ameny's attention. She feared moments like this when Urshe's influence on him was sometimes stronger than her own.

"I came to her chamber to find she'd acquired a tutor. She supplied the girl with wigs, writing supplies, jewelry, everything she needed. If Yimenet's intentions were as pure as she states, she should have informed me."

"Informed you?" Yimenet huffed. "I am Ameny's woman, not yours." She turned to the prince, finding her chance. "And why should that gelded beast follow me around when you've instructed him to keep his distance from me? Ask him how many times he's approached me in an unsavory manor, as if that dirty rag could coax me away from you."

Ameny looked between them. He was as jealous as he was beautiful, despite the new crook in his nose. "And why did you say nothing of this before?"

Yimenet tossed her hair over her shoulder. "If I told you of every fool who made advances, you would have no one in your employ. I cannot help it that I am beautiful."

Urshe fumbled under Ameny's glare. That was his mistake. "Ask her about her missing jewels." Urshe blinked rapidly, rushing his words. "She helped the girl escape, I tell you."

"I was so ashamed." Yimenet shook her head. "You gave me so many precious things, and now most are gone."

"Oh but that sounds suspicious, my dear girl. I know you guard your treasures, afraid that I might tire of you." Ameny's eyes searched her. She'd overdone it, but she held her face contrite. He moved to the polished box where he kept the whip and she fought the urge to run.

Urshe cocked a smile in her direction. Ameny shook out his whip. Sharp gold pebbles studded its many tentacles, reminding Yimenet of the times he used it on a few unfortunate men. He raised the whip above her head. Every muscle in her body tensed.

Urshe stepped up beside Ameny. "I'd teach that little trollop of yours a lesson if I were you, my lord."

The whip flashed and snapped. She yelped. But it was Urshe's arm that bloomed red. The second blow struck his chest, and his tardy attempt at escape was almost comical. He tripped on a rug. Ameny flayed him until he whimpered and curled into a ball.

Yimenet pressed her hands to her mouth to cover her laughter.

That is until Ameny picked up the switch again.

And turned to her.

CHAPTER TWENTY THREE

DEDUAMEN

"I DEMAND WE MOVE FASTER DOWNRIVER."
Deduamen pushed himself up from the shaded pavilion on
deck. "Get these vessels out of my way."

"I did warn my lord..." The barge captain put up a
hand. "...His Majesty, that the river traffic is heavy with
early date and olive harvests coming in. If His Majesty
had taken my suggestion to travel on the smaller of his
barge—"

"How dare you!" Deduamen squared his shoulders. "The
line of my fathers was that of kings, and I shall arrive at the
palace in splendor equal to that pretender, Khakheperre."

He'd invested a great sum in his new vessel. An
abundance of green and red pennants flagged at the mast,
the deck of imported cedar planks, gold veneer, and ivory
inlays, juniper, and ebony for the ship's rails. All of it a
worthy expense though his vessel was unequal to any of
Khakheperre's pleasure barges.

It was larger.

Deduamen glanced over the congested river traffic and
scowled at his army of smartly dressed rowers sitting at

their leisure on deck. "Set a few men on a skiff with one of my coffers and pay the crowd to get out of my way."

"But there is no place for even the crowd to move."

"Do as I have ordered." Deduamen glared at the captain who bowed and turned on his heels.

A few months had passed since Potipherah's missive ordered him downriver. But the hard, east winds had delayed him in reaching the king's house for the Front of the Year ceremony along with other life events that left him sour.

His sister-wife at least, gave him the girls and Hotepi before she died, but his eldest daughter, whom he next took to wife, died before delivering his unborn heir. He was sure the gods of the afterlife would judge her harshly for such a selfish act, yet it was important he grieve the appropriate amount of days. Then there was the promise of a burgeoning harvest this year, and he dare not set sail before instructing his field supervisors on the proper handling of his profits.

On top of these delays, his twin daughters, Appipa and A'at, had vanished. He'd thought himself kind in giving them time to grieve their older sister's death before taking one of them to wife. But when they'd gone missing from the elaborate burial ceremony, he returned home to discover one of his smaller vessels missing, along with a handful of guards, two trunks of the girls' clothing and their jewelry. His nerves were on edge.

His girls were a gold mine of royal blood, and there was a terrible rumor going round that they'd gone down to the king's house. He would not believe his daughters could do such a cruel thing to him. Yet Potipherah assured him the office of vizier awaited him, and he could afford no more delays.

His son, Hotepi, came to stand beside him at the ship's rail, and he touched the stubble where the boy's youth-lock had been shorn. Deduamen's eyes misted over, remembering how well Hotepi bore up through the circumcision ceremony. At thirteen, he was now considered a man.

"What are you thinking, Father?"

"Oh, nothing." Deduamen crooked a smile and regarded his son, so like him in manner and appearance. "This time next year, you will be taller than I am."

This time next year, you will be king.

Deduamen had first thought to take the crown for himself once Khakheperre fell from power. But Hotepi would be the greatest king ever known to Egypt if he stood beside his son as advisor and vizier. To see greatness restored to his royal bloodline and that pretender Khakheperre dashed against a cliff would be enough to satisfy his revenge. Chadding downriver to Itjtawy had brought them closer to reclaiming the throne than his family had been in generations. He sniffed, striking a happy tear. This was no time to ruin his kohl when his barge sat like flotsam in the water.

"Look Father. A nobleman is calling to you."

Deduamen looked to where Hotepi indicated. The old man waving at him wore gold bracelets and fine apparel but had a grotesquely humped back. Deduamen grimaced at the misshapen beast.

"May I be of assistance, my lord? I see your men are handing out barter bread trying to clear a path, but I think I can do better."

"See here. I need to get downriver. Out of my way, old rag, or I'll tear you asunder." Deduamen waved him off.

"Oh, Father." Hotepi tugged at his arm. "Look at his vessel."

Deduamen took note. The sleek little marvel near his barge danced on the water like an energetic bull. Hewn from the acacia wood of Cush, it was inlaid with ebony. Deduamen had never seen the like.

"Yes, my lord, let the young god come down for a closer look." The hump-backed interloper motioned, and Deduamen reigned in his impatience for Hotepi's sake.

"No," he called down. "But I thank you for your offer."

The old man nodded, then signaled with a sharp whistle. His men swung their oars at the crafts near them, knocking people from rafts, tipping skiffs, and smaller vessels.

Hotepi cheered, and Deduamen was pleased at his son's delight.

"You see, my lord? Save your bartering bread. We'll get you downriver in no time."

Deduamen raised his voice above the complaints of those near overturned crafts. "I admit you are a thinking man for one so decrepit."

"Then come aboard, my lord. Come aboard, and we're sure to get you to the king's house."

Deduamen furrowed his brow. "How did you know I was going there?"

"But where else would such a worthy vessel be going?" The old man shrugged.

Hotepi tugged Deduamen's arm, his eyes bright with anticipation. "Can we ride with him, Father?"

Deduamen embraced the boy's shoulder. "All right."

"Grand and pleasant." The old man clapped his thick hands and drew his craft closer.

Deduamen spoke to his barge captain before boarding with two guards and a servant. "Send my things downriver to the palace. But make sure your arrival is soon following."

He'd paid in gold debens for this pleasure barge, and by Horus, the world was going to see it.

They boarded the handsome little craft, and their host ambled across the deck on uneven bowed legs with a gait as vulgar as the hump in his back.

"I am Lord Nakht, of the Shrine Province." He bowed and then forced a bow on the lively boy beside him. "This is my son, Nodjme."

Deduamen huffed. "Why the Shrine is no province at all, but a dust blown patch of broken buildings and ancient relics."

"It is that, my lord." Nakht bobbed his head in agreement. "But I have high hopes for it as governor there.

"And are you going to the king's house yourself, Nakht?"

"I wouldn't dare grace the king's house, being so hideous to look upon. To appear there with all the godlike lords and the gleaming Sons of the South is not fitting for one such as I. But I'm looking for a long lost friend who may be there."

Deduamen nodded approval but was distracted by the boy Nodjme, staring at Hotepi. Deduamen drew his son tighter to his side. Hotepi was not to be tainted with such low association.

Nakht led them to a shaded pavilion on deck.

"Look, Father. He's a limping old goat," Hotepi exclaimed, doubling over with laughter.

Nodjme turned and raised a fist to Hotepi. Deduamen shrieked, but Nakht caught his son's arm, rattling the boy with surprising strength.

"I was not aware you kept wild animals on your craft." Deduamen mashed Hotepi to his chest. "Might I have known, we would never have boarded."

Nakht struck the boy Nodjme who rocked back from the blow.

"But Father, he insulted you."

"And if the young god says I am a limping old goat, then I am a limping old goat." He struck the boy again, and Deduamen relaxed, a bit more satisfied at Nakht's instant correction of his ill-mannered son.

"He is too sensitive, my lord, and knows not how to treat his betters." Nakht shook the little miscreant by the shoulder. "I will bring him to discipline for it."

"Then let us see it now," Hotepi said. "It's been a boring trip thus far."

Nakht's dark expression lifted. "An excellent suggestion, my lord. A whipping's lesson is never better than when accompanied by open humiliation." Nakht called for a rod and looked toward Hotepi, who governed his strokes.

Nodjme yowled until Deduamen was satisfied and urged Hotepi to mercy. The young rascal staggered off, gasping with tears.

Deduamen leaned down to his son's ear. "You see here a man of impeccable judgment. Make note of it, Hotepi, for this is the type of man a good king seeks to have in his corner."

Nakht kept his word, charging his oarsmen to use whatever means possible to get them downriver. While they supped on chilled beer and crackers baked with cheese, Nakht called for his singer, who raised his strong tenor voice above the splashing and boisterous complaints of the vulgar beyond their view. He poked fun at himself so that Hotepi might have a moment of laughter, despite the droning whimpers of that wild terror, Nodjme, from the far side of the craft. Such devout servitude drew Deduamen to decision.

"Mark this day, Nakht, for great fortune has come to your house."

"To me, my lord? But your servant is not worthy of your regard as the young god Hotepi has so studiously noted."

"Yet you have entertained the most royal blood in the land, and I charge you to prepare yourself for great reward." Deduamen plucked a handful of grapes from a bowl. "I am on my way to the king's house to be made vizier and have a mind to place you in my cabinet." He glanced at Nakht, expecting some delight in his countenance. "Well, what's wrong, man?"

"I'm afraid, my lord, that my promotion into your service must suffer some delay."

"And why is that?"

"Because chadding downriver I had chance to hear that the position of vizier has already been filled."

CHAPTER TWENTY FOUR

YOSEPH

KITJAU, THE KING'S ARCHITECT, CUT A SIDELONG glance at Yoseph. "Is that what Nebsumenu told you, that the torches lighting the king's two houses of gold are never extinguished?" He peered at the lake, stroking his lip as if to measure his next words. "The treasury torches have gone out several times since Khakheperre became king."

Yoseph scrubbed his brow and gripped the stone bench on which they sat. "Why have you not mentioned this to the king?"

"I am no one here, so I shut my mouth and do what I love. But one can see anything from a scaffold."

Yoseph looked for some indication of a lie in Kitjau's expression. "If you think someone is stealing from the royal coffers, tell the king."

Kitjau huffed dry laughter. "A man takes a great risk in telling the plain truth. Or did you not learn as much with Lady Kemsiyet when you were her slave? Favor is a precarious perch here. I'm a poor exile torn from Byblos, but I wish to repay the kindness Khakheperre has shown me. Yet, I must stay in his favor as much as the men stealing from him for my own survival and for the good of Byblos." Kitjau turned to him with unnerving regard. "But you have the favor of your god, Yoseph. And as the king's vizier you hold great power."

Yoseph looked out on the placid lake. Lord Nebsumenu had assured him of the strictures applied to any entry or exit of the king's treasury. The guards at the gate checked everything down to a worker's meal and the contents of ink pots. This too was recorded at the gate by scribes. Nebsumenu claimed the same rules applied to him. He was passionate and persuading enough to make Yoseph think he'd only imagined what he'd seen at night from the storeroom's high window. Now Kitjau confirmed the thieving was real.

"And if you think this only goes on at night, then come to the Horus columns when you can. You will see their conduct is blatant."

Yoseph flexed a muscle in his jaw when Kitjau patted his shoulder and left. What did Kitjau think he could do? The king's watchmen had given him the required tours of their offices, skimming over their work and standing him before their cabinet members to be smirked at. But what could one expect from men who usually ordered slaves and were now being ordered to serve one? This power Kitjau claimed he had did not exist.

Nonetheless, Nebsumenu was the easiest to forgive. Yoseph had met several times with the king's treasurer and strolled beside the adept courtier this morning. He insisted his wife, Satweret, be first to entertain the new vizier. He spoke of the king's limited funds and how important it would be for Yoseph to keep to the treasury records he would provide. He cajoled and flattered, offering once again his own men to fill vacancies in the slow-growing cabinet of the new vizier. It was hard to deny such an obliging, pleasant man, but the king was Yoseph's master now, and he would run his cabinet as the sovereign instructed. After their stroll, Nebsumenu left him by the lake, magnanimous and deferential to the last though the stiff manner of his departure suggested he was not used to being refused.

Not once had he offered a tour of the king's treasury.

Kitjau joined Yoseph on the stone bench when Nebsumenu left, spilling righteous indignation. His accusation weighed Yoseph down like boulders. He'd wanted to impress the well-spoken treasurer who'd set guards at his door to keep him safe. But perhaps he was not being kept safe. Perhaps he was being watched. He'd survived the attacks of his tormentors, Kemsiyet's lies, Qareg's abuse and the fire in the palace storerooms. Yet even here in the place of the good god's favor his life might be in no less danger.

Yoseph glanced over his shoulder. Imehy approached with irritation flashing in his face.

"You've forgotten your treatment today."

"Then let's tend to it now." Yoseph shot up from the shaded bench, and the dwarf almost double-timed his steps to keep up. Mentuser, the king's physician, never came to tend his feet, and now Imehy took particular ownership of them. Since given the title of minor healer and herald of the vizier, Imehy strutted about in a pristine kilt and silver chain at his neck. Sabni remarked he'd become arrogant beyond measure, but Yoseph insisted Imehy have the position despite Hetnu's protest. The dwarf tended his care when no palace physician deigned to lay a finger on him.

"But I would never think of taking a position with the royal jewelers, my lord. I would never accept their offer when you have been so good to me."

"What offer was that again?" Yoseph blinked, drawing in his far-off thoughts.

"Nothing of importance, my lord." Imehy stopped short at his doorway and folded his hands at his waist. "I see your mind is elsewhere. I'll return later to tend to your feet."

Yoseph forced a nod. Imehy bowed and left. He, along with Hetnu and Sabni, had taken it upon himself to school Yoseph on the manners of a high lord. He was not to please but to be pleased. He was not to oblige, but he was to be obliged.

He entered his chamber, and his steward informed him of a waiting visitor. Treasury guards at his door were one thing, uninvited guests were another. He would take his steward to task for this later and entered the main hall prepared to dismiss the insistent intruder. But the sight before him nearly stole his breath.

Lady Qatsenut whom he'd met at the king's garden party, was a vision of loveliness, moving from his entrance hall to his leisure room. The blue lotus flower behind her ear was out of season but matched the faience beads of her overdress. Yoseph wondered what poor gardener she'd coaxed to conjure it for her. No wonder the guards and his steward had let her in. How could they resist? She flitted about with a basket of pink mignonettes and white heliotropes, adding them to vases scattered around the room.

"My Lord Vizier." She looked up, smiling. "How long have you been standing there?" She was even more beautiful than he first remembered. He pushed off the doorway.

She put down her basket and brushed her hands, glancing over the scar on his forearm.

The ladies loved his scars.

"You cannot know the popularity you've gained with the new harvest upon us." She fluttered her lashes. "Peasants rejoice in the streets."

"I am warmed by your enthusiasm." He let the silence hang between them, inhaling her sweet scent as she sauntered past him toward the balcony.

"I see the estate of the vizier is being repaired." She indicated the walled, ramped, and pillared mansion across from their view, swarming with workers on scaffolds.

"Kitjau insists on it despite his work on the king's new gardens and the Horus columns. I'm overwhelmed."

"But never show that you are overwhelmed, my lord." Her laughing eyes were very pretty with a design of brown flowers on the outer edges, subtle against her amber-colored skin. Attraction resonated between them in the silence before she drew her gaze away. "And what is this pile of loot in the corner?" She stepped in front of him to investigate the stacked gifts from courtiers. Her back radiated an inviting warmth in the snug sheath and beadnet dress revealing her curves. She stepped back, and his arms itched to embrace her. An image of Kemsiyet splashed him like cold water, and he widened the small space between them.

Elohim be praised.

"I see the courtiers are eager to be remembered of you." She encircled her own waist, turning to him. A tease flickered in her eyes, or perhaps it was insult.

"I have half a mind to send it all back. Having been a slave for so long. I have no need of such things."

"You have no need to be so humble, my lord. You are vizier. Let the world grovel at your feet for a change."

He chuckled and gave a nod, sure now that everyone he met was determined to mold him to the haughtiness of his elevated rank.

"I'll let you know which are the best gifts." She half turned, lifting a finger of instruction. "That will give clue as to how great a favor will be requested. And if you have any invitations, I will choose the best parties for you. And also, you shall need a tutor."

"The king would thank you himself for your diligence, Lady Qatsenut."

They both turned at the voice coming from the doorway. Hetnu entered the room, his gaze measuring the distance between them. "But Duaf has been appointed the vizier's food taster, and there is already a tutor assigned. So you see, Lord Yoseph will have plenty of servants to care for his social and private needs."

Qatsenut picked through a stack of gifts. "And who might this tutor be?"

"These are the crown's concerns, Lady Qatsenut, not yours."

"And are these the words of the king, Lord Hetnu? Or yours?"

Yoseph raised his brows at her boldness with the scathing cupbearer. Such a woman could make a man drunk with love.

"Yes. Well..." Hetnu pivoted, changing directions. "You look very well, Lord Yoseph." His eyes flashed outrage from Qatsenut's challenge, but he held his composure. Duaf entered the room.

"Lunch is ready, my lord. Honey-roasted guinea fowl with barley and leeks, sugared papyrus with fruited yogurt."

The welcome interruption broke the tension in the room.

"Would the two of you care to join me for a midday meal?" Yoseph offered.

"I would love to." Qatsenut clapped her hands together.

"I'm afraid the vizier has work to do." Hetnu came up beside her, offering his arm. She refused to take it, and he placed his hand in the center of her back and pushed her to the door. "Perhaps some other time, Lady Qatsenut, when the vizier is less busy." He escorted her out of the room, and the sound of their heated squabble erupted in the corridor.

YOSEPH SPIT THE GRIT FROM HIS MOUTH. THE pit was clouded with dust. He'd donned a workman's kilt and should have been hard to distinguish among the men shoveling and hauling dirt up the ramp.

His disguise hadn't worked.

Prince Dagi was the first to spot him, having perched himself high on a granite likeness of the god Horus. He was more vocal at drawing the interest of passing courtiers than a market-crier. Even Lady Kemsiyet and her followers ventured out on a balcony. Her dramatic gestures shook the beads on her wig. The thrust of her arms toward the pit told Yoseph she was cutting him to shreds with her tongue. And why not, when the king had given Lord Nebitef's wife the liberty to speak in her own defense? Her lies seemed to win her a new level of popularity.

Yoseph shoveled at the base of the columns with the rest of the men. Now that he'd been discovered, he would never hear the end of this. Kitjau had begged him not to lower himself to such a task, but Kitjau's indictment against the king's treasurer was no small matter. Yoseph had a clear and close view of the treasury gates from where he stood. If Nebsumenu was stealing from the royal coffers in broad daylight, he must see it for himself. In his dirty workmen's kilt he appeared no more than the unlearned barbarian the world thought him to be. Things could get no worse.

"Look, Sabni, the king's new vizier is finally put to his proper work!"

Yoseph cringed and glanced over his shoulder as Sabni advanced with a strained smile. Dagi's insult stirred laughter from the gawking courtiers standing around.

"Come down from the statue, Prince Dagi. It's too high."

Dagi chortled and flagged off Sabni's plea. Sabni pushed through the crowd gathering like gnats to a bruised piece of fruit. Chagrin shone through his hard smile. He came to the edge of the pit and cleared his throat. "My Lord Yoseph," he bellowed, his lofty tone a clear attempt to lend dignity to the disastrous scene. "You are late for your training with the staff and dagger."

"He trains better with shovels and rocks!"

Yoseph gripped the shovel. The crowd roared at Dagi's jest. If only the young prince would fall from the statue and graciously break his neck.

"Come down, Sabni." Yoseph beckoned. "The king has sent me to inspect the state of the Horus columns." Both of them knew this was not the inspection the king had in mind.

Sabni started down the ramp, cutting a sharp look at Kitjau through his tight smile. As he pushed past the other workers in the pit, Nebsumenu emerged from the treasury courtyard, flanked by the cheerful Resnakt and the dour Mentuser on either side.

"My lord, why are you here in such a state?" Sabni

leaned into Yoseph with a harsh whisper. "As vizier, you should excite respect on the king's behalf. An execution of dignity is paramount."

Yoseph traded places with Sabni, moving him closer to the base of the column. "Take a look at this."

Sabni sniffed. "It's rotting. Must have struck a vein of water."

"Rotting from the inside out," Yoseph said, his gaze fixed on the treasury gate as Nebsumenu emerged with the king's other watchmen trailing him. He carried two sacks in his arms. Yoseph glanced at Kitjau on the scaffold then back at the treasury gates. No clerk raised his pen. No guard stopped the king's watchmen nor checked Nebsumenu's sacks as they moved off.

They were getting away.

"Lord Nebsumenu!" Yoseph shouted, cupping his dirty hands to his mouth. Nebsumenu looked around and approached the rail on the upper level walkway, straining to see who called him. He looked down into the worker's pit. Sabni shifted behind Yoseph, muffling a curse.

"You see me here, Yoseph, doing the king's business." Yoseph grinned, waving like a happy farmer. Had he ever uttered something so stupid?

Nebsumenu narrowed his gaze, leaning forward against the rail. Lord Resnakt whispered in his ear, and recognition dawned on the treasurer's face. He gave some low remark that made even Lord Mentuser break into laughter.

Sabni groaned.

Nebsumenu cupped a hand to his mouth. "Greetings, Lord Yoseph. Your dedication to detail surpasses my own. You are a most worthy vizier." There was a catch of laughter in his voice. He flourished a bow and left with the other watchmen.

Yoseph exhaled a shuddered breath as Sabni tugged his shoulder. "My lord, if you wish to impress the king's watchmen of your worthiness as vizier, I fear you have gone about it in the wrong way."

CHAPTER TWENTY FIVE

NEBSUMENU

NEBSUMENU GROOMED HIS THIN BEARD WITH A small ivory comb. His hard glower forced a response from Resnakt.

"All right, all right, I'll stop wearing it altogether then." Resnakt pulled the Ma'at charm from his belt and slammed it on the tray beside him. His irritation clashed with the peaceful setting of his garden terrace. "Stop hounding me about it!"

Beneath the shade of a tree, Mentuser whittled a piece of wood with his favorite old scalpel. He waved off the glazed pheasant legs a servant presented, lost in carving his little figurine. Today was one of his ritual fasting days to the goddess, and he sang hymns to Sakhmet.

Nebsumenu pursed his lips at Resnakt's spoilt behavior. He'd lately begun styling the king's wigs and was proving himself a valuable influence on the sovereign as were his boys who companioned Prince Khakure. As a reward, Nebsumenu let Resnakt handpick a little something from one of the treasure rooms, but Resnakt's fingers were more slippery than he realized. "You should have told me about the trinket you took."

"It was just a little thing laying about." Resnakt sucked his teeth. "No one would even miss it."

Nebsumenu exhaled through his nostrils. "Don't let it happen again." No use arguing with Resnakt. Despite that bright smile and easy manner, the fresh-faced fool was as stubborn as a donkey. He tried a gentler approach.

"You're a broad hall attendant. Wear it at home where no one can see it." He wore the charm all the time, either on his belt or as an earring. Even the king had noticed it at their meeting, but Potipherah had guessed its origin. Nebsumenu blew wind from his cheeks, and Mentuser shot him a cool smile. He'd flattered Resnakt with the position of deputy treasurer because of his status in the broad hall. His cheerful smile made him well-liked, and they needed him to control the traffic through the corridors at night. But moments like these made Nebsumenu doubt Resnakt was worth the trouble.

Mentuser brushed away wood shavings from his kilt. "There'll be no more hard east winds to blame for the treasury torches being out at night. Take care boy, or you'll get us all chopped to pieces over something as small as a trinket."

Resnakt sat up gesturing broadly. "Why not strike Khakheperre and get it over with?"

"And tamper with our good fortune? I've talked the king into closing off the nursery balcony. That should be enough. We'll leave Khakheperre where he is." Nebsumenu pinched his lips together at Resnakt's foolish suggestion. Mentuser chuckled and shook his head.

He was the only one capable of speeding the king's journey into the West. But as the king's trusted physician,

SEAL OF THE SAND DWELLER

Mentuser had made vows to Sakhmet to bring no harm to any royal blood, yet Resnakt's enthusiasm to murder the king amused him as did all things depraved. For the right compensation, Mentuser had sped the journey of a few courtiers on their way to the afterlife. But only if the bloodline was far enough away from that of the good god.

"Poor Deduamen." Mentuser clucked. "Arriving to take on the role of vizier to find it already occupied. Khakheperre has the upper hand now. The sand dweller's his man."

"The sand dweller's *our* man. He just doesn't know it yet." Nebsumenu gave a silent chuckle. "Made a fool of himself at the Horus columns. I've never had a pet vizier, but he's just what we need."

"Perhaps so, but it would be wise to cut off visits to the king's coffers in broad daylight. My prayers to Sakhmet can only do so much. I'll not mock the goddess further." Mentuser shook his scalpel at Nebsumenu. "And if you can't get the sand dweller to accept help, he can't be watched."

"Don't worry about it, Mentuser. He wants to impress me. I'll bring him round," Nebsumenu assured. "I've already placed a couple of guards at his door, and I'll be sure to set a few spies in his cabinet to keep an eye on him. And if things ever go wrong, we can dump the blame on him. It's perfect."

Mentuser shot both of them a warning look. "He's got the king's seal around his neck, regardless of how dumb you think he is, Nebsumenu. That alone is a danger."

"It's not a king's seal, but the seal of a sand dweller. The novelty will wear." Nebsumenu sent a covert smile to Resnakt. "He probably won't last a year."

"And if he gets too sharp, we'll cut him to pieces with that rusty old scalpel of yours. Aye Mentuser?"

Mentuser grinned at Resnakt and raised his favorite knife. "Keeps my hands strong. It pleases the goddess."

"Well, I've seen your work. You're a bloody butcher if ever I saw one." Resnakt huffed, lifting his cup of wine. "Our new vizier doesn't know how lucky he is you haven't come to check on his feet."

Mentuser snorted. "As if I'd stoop to tend a dirty sand dweller."

"He'll be far easier to dispose of. No royal blood there, Mentuser."

Nebsumenu reached for a pheasant leg from the tray. "Leave him be, Resnakt. Yoseph's no threat. Killing doesn't suit our work, and stealing requires cool nerves. I've told Potipherah there would be no bloodshed, so there will be none."

"Potipherah's one who should be treated and watched with care." Mentuser blew on his little figurine. "He's far too silent. Probably toying with us."

Resnakt's six sons came tearing up the steps to the terrace, all of them soaking wet.

"Father! There is a skiff pulling into your secret water steps." Bebi, the oldest, wrung water from his sidelock. "We were playing bowl under water, and it nearly bumped into us."

"Bebi!" Resnakt sat up in his chair. "You're not to play that game. And stay away from the floating dock. The fishnets are stored there." Resnakt tugged his son's sidelock. "Go and kiss your uncles, all of you."

Nebsumenu greeted the boys in the playful manner they'd come to expect of him, and Mentuser gave a quick grin, accepting their hugs, and wiping away traces of mud smeared on the back of his neck.

Resnakt had gotten all six of his sons on three concubines in less than two years. He had some romantic notion of legitimizing the boys and bringing them to court without the benefit of a high-born mother's blood. Mentuser and Nebsumenu took bets on whether his charm could pull it off.

A dense branch of sycamore blocked the terrace stairway. Nebsumenu expected the mounting footsteps were those of a servant, then saw who it was and swore a vulgar curse. Mentuser gripped his scalpel.

"A luxurious den of thieves if ever I've seen one."

Resnakt scooted forward in his chair to kneel.

"Don't bother." Ameny put up a hand to stop him, inspecting the pleasant shade of the terrace and the garden below. "Fine grounds." The prince took a stool and helped himself to the pile of pheasant legs, uninhibited by the tense silence his presence caused. He took a ravenous bite of the meat and waved it about as he talked. "As for the concealed water steps, Resnakt, you really must do better."

Resnakt fumbled for a response, and Nebsumenu spoke up to put him out of his tongue-tied misery. "You find us holding a meeting, my lord, on how best to serve the king." He shot a look at the others.

"Or on how best to serve yourselves to that which belongs to him," Ameny challenged with a lump of meat in his jaw. He grabbed another pheasant leg and got up to circle the group, stopping to swipe a streak of mud from one of the boys' chins. "And these, I take, are the mongrels your breeders pump out, aye, Resnakt? I give you credit. Your mark is on all of them."

"Bebi, take your brothers and leave," Resnakt snapped. The boys ran off, and for a minute, there was only the sound of chirping birds until Ameny flung his pheasant bone into the bushes.

"If this silence is the best you can all do, then you certainly need my assistance."

"I don't know, Ameny." Nebsumenu glanced at the prince's crooked nose. "Perhaps you could do far better with Potipherah's support. Or did you try with him, already?"

"Never mind that, Nebsumenu. I want in."

"*In* to what, my lord?"

"*In* to my brother's coffers with the rest of you. I can get you the thing that will win even Potipherah's capitulation."

"And what's that?" Resnakt asked.

"Potipherah's daughter, of course."

"There's our prince," Nebsumenu said. "Always looking to get under a woman's skirt."

"And succeeding, Nebsumenu. Succeeding."

"You're a lecher, Ameny."

"It's a lecher's touch you need. Potipherah's daughter is a sheltered innocent. Doesn't know her front from her back with that reed pen in her hand."

"A learned girl. Rare thing." Mentuser nodded, glancing at Nebsumenu. "Not a nitwit like your little Satweret."

"She's pretty, and she pleases me. Leave her alone." Nebsumenu defended his little wife, but he was on the lookout for a second one. One who could converse about something more than the latest court fashion. He'd passed Asenat in the corridors with Hetnu once or twice. Who would have guessed such a graceful form lay beneath those loose temple robes? Those large eyes held promise. There would be intelligent conversations with that one. And a great inheritance from her father. Yes. He liked the girl.

"She's rare, alright, but nothing's as rare as her father's

support," Ameny said. "If I can get Potipherah's daughter, you'll hold him by the nostrils."

"We could well use that in our corner." Mentuser cast a glance at Nebsumenu. "But the king has not so much as let the girl see the light of day without Hetnu guarding her every move."

"I'll get my chance," Ameny said. "Just get me a small share from my brother's coffers, and you won't be sorry."

Nebsumenu stroked his thin beard. So Ameny had found out about their occasional dips into the king's treasures. Khakheperre was pliable and far too free-thinking. He seldom found fault with his no-account brother. That could be a problem. But Ameny had unlimited access to the king. And that could be useful.

"We'll let you in." Nebsumenu raised his cup of wine. It was best to keep Ameny close and quiet for the time being. If a few trinkets from his brother's coffers soothed his pride, then so be it. One eye on Prince Ameny, the other on the sand dweller, if they needed to watch him at all.

CHAPTER TWENTY SIX

YOSEPH

YOSEPH PUSHED HIMSELF UPRIGHT ON HIS sleeping couch and wiped the side of his face.

Dry.

The dream felt as real as the day the guards brought him to the courtyard in the king's house. Except this time, it wasn't the young princes urinating on his head from a balcony, but the king's watchmen.

"Watered wine," he said, over his shoulder.

The body servant shuffled forward from his sleeping mat in the doorway to obey the order.

"Thank you." Yoseph took the cup, sensing the slave's disapproval. Anyone in servitude long enough repelled excessive gratitude. Yoseph scoffed under his breath. He was no different. The duty to serve and please became life itself. He emptied the cup and handed it back. "Leave me."

The door closed, swathing Yoseph in the darkness of his sleeping chamber. Beyond the sheer curtain tenting his couch, moonlight lit a cheerful Delta scene on the wall and floor pelts, plants, and low tables spread around the room. He stroked the old scar on his forearm. His fears

cornered him here in the darkness of such naked solitude.
Temptation whispered.

Keep quiet and manage the king's house.

He'd kept quiet in the storerooms, and still someone
tried to burn him alive.

Yet there was some merit to staying quiet as Kitjau had
done. Yoseph let out a slow breath. He could do the same.
He would be left to enjoy his pleasure barge, estates and
untold wealth.

*And how long would that last before you are, once again,
made a scapegoat for another man's lie?*

The king's watchmen mocked him with their flattery in
spite of the king's favor. Or because of it. Despite the great
favor he'd held with his former master Nebitef, one lie from
Kemsiyet, his wife, had changed things overnight. Yoseph
had run Nebitef's estate with a prosperous hand. He knew
he could run the king's house with the same order.

*But the king has not made you house steward. The king
has made you vizier.*

Panic tightened his chest. Kitjau thought that only a few
low-ranking officials knew of the watchmen's thieving, but
he was wrong. The palace slaves knew. And they watched
him, the king's new vizier, to see what kind of man he
was. Whether he would reveal the truth or join the lie by
keeping his mouth shut.

His father, Jacob, a devout follower of Elohim, warned
him to cling to truth and take no part in lies though he
claimed to have once been a liar himself. A good one. A
slick one. He said that lies had torn his family to shreds,
that lies did not hold.

A derisive sound escaped Yoseph's lips. How could this
be so when Kemsiyet's lie had sent him to prison for so

long, and Qareg's lies had placed him in bonds? Lies had forced him to Egypt. No, in this one thing, his father was wrong. Lies had their own power.

How clever he'd once thought himself, bringing his father the news of warring wives and sons with an arrogance that only added to the rift in their camp. He gripped the side of his couch and licked at bitter tears. If he'd kept his mouth shut, they might have all been spared a few nights of contention in the camp, a few episodes of revenge. They might have loved him better if he had simply said nothing.

CHAPTER TWENTY SEVEN

POTIPHERAH

POTIPHERAH STUDIED THE DOCUMENTS BEFORE him and sniffed at the air, rank with wine. He glanced up. "Back again?"

Ameny stood before him, disheveled in a wrinkled kilt. His eyes were full to the brim of drink. He chewed natron, permitted only to priests. It did nothing to hide his rancid breath.

"I came as soon as I received your message."

"The request was for your presence tomorrow, not tonight." Potipherah scratched down a few more orders for the temple, then applied his seal to the clay tablets. "It's a wonder that your brother keeps you so close and in his own house. But then again, if Khakheperre let your leash out any farther, you'd break your own neck." Potipherah pushed the work aside and laced his fingers together to study the prince. "You seem quite hale despite your appearance. It teaches me something."

"And what is that?" Ameny grabbed a stool to sit across from him.

"That when next I break something of yours, I should keep on breaking."

Ameny forced a laugh. "You won't be rid of me, Potipherah, until I am ready."

"Your repeated intrusions into my chamber gives me every sign that you *are* ready."

"I came to persuade you to reconsider my offer. I have inside knowledge of the watchmen. You need me."

Potipherah snorted. "I need you not now, nor ever. That desert rat of a vizier is far more worth my time than you are."

"The throne is rightfully mine. Amun is foremost, that is the meaning of my name. I was meant to be king."

Potipherah nodded slowly. "That is true, but Ma'at is best served with your brother as king."

"I am the eldest."

"And the least sensible. Even your father saw as much and knew himself better off in the hands of a weak-bodied son than in yours. But besides your dysfunctions, I bear you grudge for devising a scheme against my daughter. Everyone knows you have your little savage from Crete. It's a shame you tried to switch her to death. Such pretty, bright skin. On occasion, I've seen her bruised as blue as my fingers."

Potipherah examined his rings. "Perhaps you should pander your charms on Deduamen's catty little trollop, Appipa. Now, there's one who could stand a switching or two. But I'll have no more dealings in that corner."

After pumping resources into Deduamen's province to ensure he was eligible for the position of vizier, after praising him to the Sons of the South, after pushing his worthiness on the king, Deduamen arrived at the palace too late. Potipherah was through with the feckless wonder.

"Khakheperre has plans for Deduamen's girl."

"Come now, Ameny. Your brother's plans have never stopped you before. And he's moving far too slow for that hot-blooded little sweetmeat. Appipa will snap at any royal blood advancing in her direction."

The veiled look of interest on Ameny's face proved the suggestion was already worming its way into his licentious mind. It was just the humiliation Deduamen deserved for his incompetence.

"I'll consider introducing myself." Ameny shifted on the stool. "But why have you called for me?"

"I received a note from governor Nakht of the Shrine province. He is looking for a priest he thinks to be in your care. A one called Senib."

Ameny broke into a slow smile. "So, you remember Senib after all. Tell Nakht I wouldn't part with him for anything. Senib is a man full of talents."

"Full of talents and full of lies. Calling himself a priest, now, is he? Let me assure you that fat charlatan has claimed every skill from priest, to cook, to scribe."

"He's gifted."

"He's an idiot praising you to the skies while eating you out of your food stores. Though if it's any consolation, he is a good singer."

"You require his presence?"

"No dear prince, I require his head. Bring it to me in a hemp sack, and I'll see what I can do for you."

"I've given Senib my word that he's safe in my dwelling. I am not a man who gives his word and does not carry it out."

Potipherah chortled dryly. "Let me guess. Senib read my note aloud to you, filled your cup with wine several times, and encouraged you to come to me, tonight. He'll probably be gone by the time you return to your chamber. Nevertheless, his head is what I require in payment for any services on your behalf."

Doubt played across Ameny's face. He stood up. "I think I'm safer with Senib in my pouch than you, Potipherah."

"I'll never be in your pouch, Ameny. This is my final offer to you."

Ameny burped through pursed lips, teetered and bowed. But he staggered toward the door with such determination that if by chance Senib hadn't fled for his life, Potipherah might have that fat rascal's head within the hour.

Chapter Twenty Eight

——⊷⊶►◄⊷(▣)⊶►◄⊷⊶——

Ameny

AMENY REMOVED HIS LEATHER SANDALS AND drew a mounted battle-axe from the wall of his entrance hall. He'd left Senib feasting and singing with Yimenet. But it was dark, and the fat priest would be asleep with a belly full of food by now. An easy kill.

Entering Senib's room, Ameny squinted in the dark to focus on the obscure lump on the couch. He dragged the axe forward, smiling. Potipherah said nothing about the head being unmarked. One solid blow above the shoulders should be enough.

Ameny heaved the axe and brought it down, bracing for the crunch of bone. When a cloud of feathers flew up, he released a string of curses and smashed the furnishings in the room.

Senib was gone.

Ameny plucked the note from the floor. His lips moved over the written symbols as he carried the message to an oil lamp in his entrance hall.

To my lord, Prince Ameny, Lion of Itjtawy, Beloved of Set and rightful heir to the throne,

I am, first of all, grateful for the sumptuous dwelling and meals that you have so graciously provided and admit I encouraged your immediate interview with the priest. After reading his note, I thought it best to remove myself and thus any temptation you might have to betray me to Potipherah.

But do not take this as a harmful assessment of your character any more than what it truly is, for I might betray you also were I wearing your jeweled sandals and had a chance at the throne.

I shall ever remember your hospitality and the hearty victuals and wine we supped together. Should you become wholly disconnected from Potipherah, and I say this knowing that he may very well kill you as well as myself for exposing the truth about his daughter, you shall find me once again by your side with an advantageous proposition that would suit both of us.

Let me warn you too, good prince that I am not a willfully killing man though the art of poison is truly my gift. I warn you that any servant you send after me will be outwitted and may well meet his early demise. On this wise, do not send your best men. Take care, my lord, and value me a little more when next we meet.

Ever your humble servant,
Senib

A drop of blood splattered on the note. Ameny swiped his nose, leaving a red streak on his arm. Senib was his best connection to Potipherah's daughter, and now he was gone. Uneven footsteps approached. "Who's there?" Ameny barked, raising the oil lamp to find Urshe limping toward him.

"Master, I heard an angry noise. I came to see what has happened."

Urshe had grown more submissive after a taste of the whip and learned the importance of directing his gaze away from Yimenet, keeping her name off his lips. Ameny didn't like his blustering accusations against her. For a fact, he didn't like Urshe at all. Turning the note in his hand, he wondered if Senib might care to practice his boast in the art of poison.

Ameny plucked a few pieces of jewelry from a dish and tossed them to Urshe. "Senib is gone. I want you to track him down and bring him back to me. If you don't find him, don't bother returning at all."

CHAPTER TWENTY NINE

YOSEPH

DUAF HAD PERSONALLY OVERSEEN THE preparation of a mouthwatering breakfast, but Yoseph's nerves were too on edge to indulge in such a feast. The king received his first report and called for him. The summons gave Yoseph hope on what they might discuss in private. It also gave him a chance to escape Lord Hetnu.

At the start of each morning, the king's cupbearer appeared at the foot of his sleeping couch to instruct him on the running of the king's government. Yoseph tolerated Hetnu's cutting little jibes. But, in truth, Hetnu only voiced what others would think of an Asiatic vizier who did not know the work of his office. Hetnu held a wealth of knowledge despite his discourteous manner, and Yoseph headed for the king's meeting room with one particular lesson hammering his mind.

The term 'two houses' expressed the king's sovereign rule over the northern and southern provinces because there had been civil war in the land. The two houses of silver governed the royal granaries and natural resources. But all tributary offerings, from the gold of Cush to the lapis of Sinai, were governed by the two houses of gold. Its chief location, the king's coffers behind the treasury walls in the palace. Its chief overseer, not the treasurer, Lord Nebsumenu, but the vizier. And Hetnu had been the first to tell Yoseph this.

"My lord."

Yoseph slowed his steps to let Imehy catch up to him in the corridor.

"I'm on my way to meet with the royal jewelers."

Yoseph smiled at Imehy's contained excitement. He'd seen the dwarf's remarkable cunning with simple stones and beads and urged him to reconsider the offer the royal jewelers made to him. "They're courting you for a position in their ranks. Be sure to show them what a stall-worker can do."

Imehy nodded his thanks and walked off with a strut that suggested he would do just that. He would be at home among the royal jewelers, most of whom were also dwarves.

Yoseph neared the king's hall as a nuance of bitter memories wafted by him like the scent of old wounds. He could still see Asher's smirk. He could feel Gad's stinging smack on his chest, a hard shake of his thin shoulders. Little tattler, they would call him when he reported their escapades to Father. Yes, he was certainly that.

He was the little tattler in the camp, the weakling, a poor desperate boy, fearing the loss of his father's love and attention after his mother's death. He had no one else. They told him he had no one else and kept him from Leah to prove it.

He blew out the wounding memory with a ragged exhale. There was greater sense in staying quiet on the matter of the king's coffers, but he knew he would not do it. This private meeting with the king must bear fruit. He would go slowly. He would be careful. The king would be made to see the errors with his own eyes.

Reaching the king's corridor, Yoseph navigated the wide columns. In the distance, Hetnu's voice resounded as he rounded on some poor under-butler, and Yoseph shook his head, almost missing the steps rushing toward him. Lord Nebitef pulled him to the side. He hadn't spoken to his former master in years and braced for confrontation.

"Take care when you enter the king's chamber," Nebitef whispered, his gaze stern. "Nebsumenu has it out for you." He gave Yoseph's arm a firm shake and moved off without another word.

Yoseph entered the meeting room and the king gave a limp smile. "It seems you've offended my treasurer. There were ample mistakes found in your report." He shot an awkward glance at Nebsumenu who sat beside him, thrusting the document forward like a threat.

"Who assisted you with this refuse? It mentions a tributary gift of two hundred and fifty bars of lapis and five hundred debens of silver from Anatolian kingdoms. I have no such amount recorded on the treasury books. Someone is either a thief or a liar." He threw the report down. "I had no idea my treasury scribes were so faulty in their calculations."

After a pleasant lunch together, Nebsumenu had passed him a report, assuring him it was the most accurate to date. The treasurer told him to present it to the king, but Yoseph had not taken the treasurer's suggestion. "The report was not collected by the scribes of the treasury." Yoseph's gaze shifted, and it was hard not to shrink back at Nebsumenu's hostile glare.

"And is the word of my scribes not good enough for you then, my Lord Asiatic?!"

An anger swelled in Yoseph's chest. He kept his voice steady. "I called on the talents of Lord Gebi for assistance."

"You had no right to check with a mere field leader!"

Yoseph addressed the king, whose gaze darted between them over the rim of a cup. "Gebi is your overseer of the lower fields and of your tributary offering. He holds a dual office under both the house of silver and the house of gold."

The king blinked with a slow nod that suggested he never knew this.

"I used the same method to give an accurate report at the estate of my former master, Lord Nebitef. Incoming goods were checked and counted several times downriver and again in the palace quay by myself and Lord Gebi."

A look of astonishment flashed on Nebsumenu's face. "My scribes tend the tally of the king's incoming tribute," the treasurer snapped. "Gebi is not needed!"

"I had trouble getting the attention of your scribes, Lord Nebsumenu." He had trouble getting their respect.

"Fetch this Gebi here!" Nebsumenu snapped at a guard, without so much as a look in the king's direction. The three of them waited in awkward silence, the treasurer's behavior foul, the sovereign slumping like a scolded prince.

Yoseph knew what it was like to be manipulated by those more powerful, to be surrounded by liars, to be sheltered, yet alone. Still, it was dangerous for a king to fear his administrators, and more dangerous when his administrators held him in such low regard.

Lord Gebi entered the meeting room and threw himself on his belly, his eyes wide with terror.

"Rise," the king instructed with forced joviality. "What mischief have you caused between my treasurer and vizier?"

Gebi tripped over an apology before hearing the charges, raising his hands in defense. "The fault is mine, Majesty. Solely mine."

"Of course it is!" Nebsumenu snapped. "You've confused the number of figs in the trees with the number of silver bars on a ship. His work is too much for him, Majesty."

Yoseph clasped his wrist behind his back. Gebi was excellent in his work which was exactly why he held a dual office in both houses. Everyone knew this. Everyone, that is, but the king.

"Then you must apologize to my treasurer, Gebi." Khakheperre's placating tone did nothing to soothe Nebsumenu.

"You'd think a house steward would know how to tend his lord's business without causing a stir."

Yoseph squared his shoulders at Nebsumenu's pointed insult. "I remind the lord treasurer that I am now vizier, yet even a house steward uses all resources possible to gather information on what rightfully belongs to his master." Yoseph addressed the king. "I assure you, Majesty, that my findings can be verified."

"And why should my vizier have to find other means?" Khakheperre forced a boldness into his tone. He dismissed Gebi and turned to Nebsumenu. "Have I not ordered that he is to know everything about the palace?"

"The king's funds are a private matter for his most trusted officials." Nebsumenu twisted his chair, using his shoulders to block the king's attention from all but his influence. "We do not know this Asiatic. Look at his carelessness already. Forget this wild scheme of making him vizier. It is not too late to cancel the ceremony, Majesty."

"You go too far, Nebsumenu." The king rose and moved away from his treasurer. "I have given you an order to obey this man. You will not give him reports from your scribes, but you will allow him entrance into my coffers." The command was forced, his glance between them skittish. He was trying to be brave, trying to command as a king should. "Let us test your skill, Yoseph. I have not tallied my coffers since my father's death. You will tour them and give report of what you find."

Nebsumenu leapt up like a desert hare. "If I have offended His Majesty in any way. Or if the king doubts my ability to handle his funds after all this time—"

"That is not the point!" The king struck his thigh. "Both of you will work together to serve me and that is the end of it."

Yoseph made his way back through the forest of columns in the king's corridor. Despite Nebsumenu's charm and elegance, despite his high standing with the king, Kitjau had not lied about him. But the king deserved a true account of his holdings. And how could Yoseph do less, having been the steward of a great estate, one in far better shape than the king's house.

Someone dogged his steps. And as soon as they were out of earshot of the king's chamber and sight of the guards, Nebsumenu yanked him around by the shoulder.

"My Lord Sand Dweller, let me explain how things work here and how they have worked for hundreds of years."

"You are stealing, my lord. I urge you to stop."

The treasurer moved in close, his voice a heated whisper. "The king's best men guard his life and, for doing so, are allowed a compensation of sorts. What I do in the treasury and what I say is delivered to the treasury is all you need to know. The rest is my business."

"And mine is the king's." Yoseph pulled back from Nebsumenu's grasp. The treasurer grabbed him again.

"Do you know who keeps this mass of crumbling glory afloat, who secures Khakheperre to the throne? Me. It wasn't the king or your god that made you vizier. It was me. Thus, your business is whatever I tell you it is." He shoved Yoseph against a column.

Yoseph balled his fists to keep the cool, subservient control he had learned as a slave. But oh, to cast it off for a moment.

A trace of red and white in the corner of his vision drew his gaze sideways. His shame deepened the more as Prince Dagi stood silent and transfixed by his humiliation.

"You see, sand dweller?" Nebsumenu gave him a pat on the cheek. "No one will stand up for you here." He stepped back with a deep mocking bow, then strode past Dagi, patting the prince on the back. His laughter echoed in the corridor.

CHAPTER THIRTY

A'AT

A'AT LOOKED UP AT THE SOUND OF A SHARP slap. A slave girl caressed her jaw as tears slid down her cheeks. "You are dismissed." A'at motioned for the girl to leave, then cut her sister a look of reproof. That was the third time today the girl found herself on the receiving end of Appipa's impatience.

Appipa threw a comb at the girl's back as she trotted from the room. "And take that with you. Come back when you can style a wig properly." She gave a frustrated grunt and threw herself back on the cushions.

"Appipa, take care. She is one of Queen Weret's slaves."

"Good, I hope the mark on her face shows the queen I'm tired of being ignored." She shot up from the cushions, scowling. "And that leather-faced Weret knows the king will take one look at me and forget about her."

A'at said nothing. That might well be the case. Hetnu informed Appipa she'd been added to Queen Weret's ornate of ladies. Yet Weret had not summoned her. It was no wonder when Appipa was so beautiful, wielding her looks like a warrior swings a mace on a battlefield.

Hetnu had tucked them away in a spacious dwelling full of beautiful furnishings, pelts and floors painted in lotus and fish patterns. Appipa received a continuous flow of love letters from Lord Ubenresh whom they'd met in the broad hall. But the admiration of merely one man was not enough for her. She stared in the bronze shield all day, practicing pretty expressions and conversations she might have with the king. Always restless when not the center of attention.

"Your time will come soon, dear." A'at crossed the room and touched her sister's shoulder. "Be patient."

Appipa yanked away. "I've been patient long enough. I am meant to be queen."

"The time is not yet." A'at tugged one of her sister's pretty curls. "And your harsh treatment of others promises that you will be a hated queen."

"Hated by servants?" Appipa harrumphed. "What does it matter?"

"It matters much when they lay out your clothes and prepare your meals." Her words were lost on Appipa who stared into space and bit her lower lip.

"I can taste it in my mouth, A'at."

A'at could not be angry at her sister's craving for attention. It was only natural that such exquisite beauty should show some weakness of character. Appipa would always shine wherever she was, and A'at found her purpose in being her advisor and comforter. But lately, she failed to balance Appipa's excitable temperament.

"Why is the king taking so long? Am I not the daughter of his enemy?" She turned to A'at with eyes sparkling like a beautiful moonlit river. "Am I not the daughter of Deduamen, his blood-rival? I've come all this way. I've thrown myself at his feet."

"You are not the sole daughter of a king's enemy."

Appipa narrowed her eyes. "Don't compare yourself with me, A'at. It will only make you miserable in the end. It is not your lot to be pretty."

The words stung, but A'at allowed Appipa to peck her on the cheek. "I was not speaking of myself, but Lady Asenat whom the king took from the broad hall on the day he announced his vizier."

"Yes. That deceitful cow usurped my place in front of the whole court." Appipa moaned. "How embarrassing. But at least we are out from under father's thumb and breathing the fresh air." She flashed A'at a look of obstinacy in her locked jaws. "He'll not get a son on me. And don't you dare think of going back to him. Not now, when I need you beside me."

She took a sudden step back, her gaze focused on the doorway. A'at turned to see who entered their room. "Fathe—"

He struck her across the face before she could turn to embrace him.

"Unfaithful girl!" Deduamen gripped her shoulder. "Do you know how much I had to bribe the guards at your door just to enter here?" He raised his hand to strike again. "How dare you drag your sister away from the protection of her home!"

"It was me who dragged A'at, Father." Appipa came up beside her. It was the boldest she'd ever been, and their father's face rippled in a look of disbelief.

"Can we go now?" Hotepi, their younger brother whined as he entered the room. "I want to talk to the other princes."

Deduamen pivoted. "And give Khakheperre reason to rejoice when a fatal mishap is planned for the son of his rival? You are my sole heir, Hotepi. We must be cautious."

Hotepi closed the door and flopped in a nearby chair to pick at a bowl of fruit while Father droned on about being the last of an ancient and royal line on the verge of being snuffed out. That was the closest their brother ever came to a scolding.

Neither did Appipa ever received slaps or harsh words so as not to disturb the "spirit of her beauty," as their father called it. For Appipa he saved his adoration, for Hotepi his pride. A'at held her stinging cheek. He reserved his vexation for none but her.

He sidled over to Appipa like a jilted lover. "How could you do such a thing? The king has tried to keep me away from you, refusing me access to my own sweet girl." Appipa crossed her arms.

"I'll not end up like my older sister, who labored to give you a child only to be taken in death herself." She stepped back when Father reached for her.

"It is the way of our family, Appipa, to keep alive our ancient bloodline."

"Then it is time for this way to end, for I will not see my children born with a cleft lip or twisted as mother had."

"Keep your voice low girl," Father whispered. "Do you want the world to hear?" He flicked a sharp look over her, then back at the door. "It cannot be helped if the mixture of our royal blood is sometimes too rich, but we have always neatly disposed of the imperfect."

"If they weren't born dead already."

"Then I will take A'at for Hotepi. And you may let your shame end here in the house of the usurper."

A'at's heart throbbed in her chest at the threat. Appipa held out a hand to her. She ran to take it.

"You shall not have her." Appipa raised her chin. "I will need her beside me when I am queen."

A'at quaked, squeezing her eyes shut, waiting for her father to unleash his fury. She opened them at his mournful cry. He'd sunk to the floor.

"So what am I to do now?" He rocked himself on his knees. "You have ruined us, Appipa, you and your evil sister. Our line is no more." He covered his face and sobbed.

Appipa knelt beside him. "And how long do you think the usurper kings will sit back and allow our line to continue, knowing that we are a threat to them? For years our family has planned to take back the throne, yet our presence here today is the closest we've come."

With breathtaking command A'at would never dare, Appipa took Father's face in her hands and stroked his wet cheeks. All silent, except for Hotepi who shuffled across the room, tossing grapes to catch them in his mouth, his standard response to almost every family crisis.

"My beauty cannot be for nothing, Father." Appipa thumbed a tear from his face. "The king was a fool to choose an Asiatic for his vizier, but what is that to us? You will have to wait a little longer, and I will mix our blood with the usurper's." She kissed him on the head. "Then we will plan for Hotepi."

Deduamen sniffed. "You are right my girl. Something is better than nothing. But oh, what I have lost because of your older sister's untimely death." He shook an angry fist. "May Ammut eat out her heart for delaying me." He stood, swiping his eyes when someone knocked at the door.

A'at went to open it wide enough to take the note from the servant.

Appipa put up her hand. "If it's another message from Lord Ubenresh, I'll not read it."

"It is not," A'at assured. Appipa snatched the scroll

from her and unrolled it. She read, her lips moving in silence. Mother had insisted they learn a little reading. She said it was fitting if they were ever to become queens.

"Well, what is it girl?" their father demanded.

"Yes, Appipa, tell us." A'at clasped her hands.

Appipa did not answer at first, but held the note to her chest and laughed. "I have received an invitation to dine with the king's brother, Ameny. There, Father, you see? Prince Ameny is quite unique among the king's brothers. He has the king's ear, and I shall use it to our advantage."

Deduamen nodded. "Yes, he is a leader of sorts, and I've taken a liking to quite a few of his wigs."

"Then I must go and speak to him on your behalf." Appipa embraced him, and they rejoiced.

A'at pressed her lips together. "I do not think you should dine with Prince Ameny. Lord Hetnu warned us to stay clear of him. It will do you no good to draw the king's attention while being courted by his brother."

"I will draw the king's attention in any way that I can." Appipa snorted. "And what do you know about it? No one ever looks at you." Appipa narrowed her eyes, tucking the invitation in her beaded girdle as if A'at was no longer worthy to see it. "I will take the prince up on his offer."

She threw on a few pieces of jewelry, pausing at the bracelet she took from Lady Asenat in the broad hall. She put it on. "And perhaps I'd better go and have another look at Lady Asenat, just in case."

"We are not permitted to leave the chamber." A'at panicked at her sister's wild defiance.

"Perhaps *you* are not permitted to leave the chamber, A'at." She swept by their father and Hotepi. "But let them try and stop me."

CHAPTER THIRTY ONE

ASENAT

ASENAT WAS STUNNED BY HER REFLECTION IN the bronze. The gold chain looped around her hips. The carnelian pendant hanging at her breasts. Instead of minimizing her large eyes, the dressing servants widened them with kohl and malachite. She reached to adjust the netted covering of gold rosettes on her shoulder-length wig when Hetnu slapped her hand.

"Don't touch my work." His imperious glare met hers in the bronze. "You know nothing of fashion with your bald head and temple robes."

"Why don't you wear all of this? Then you can teach the Asiatic how to read as well." She'd heard about the Asiatic shoveling dirt at the Horus columns with the workers. She had no desire to waste the king's good sheets of papyri on such an ignorant, exalted slave.

"Tut-tut, girl. If you don't appreciate this position the king chooses to bestow on you, then I can recall at least three Libyan princes to whom the sovereign has promised Egyptian wives. You may take your pick of them."

Asenat searched the cupbearer's eyes to see if he jested. He did not.

"The writing materials have been set up in the vizier's chamber." He pushed her from the suite. "And mind that tongue of yours." The door closed behind her, and she was challenged to mind her tongue that very moment.

A few ill-mannered princes stopped dicing to call out crude remarks and whistle at her. A guard bowed, and she followed him through the corridor. A lump of grinning cheek stuck out from his face. Impertinent. Yet she was glad for an escort with the memory of Urshe's slimy kiss still fresh in her mind. She had no doubt that it was Urshe who told the king about her, that day in the broad hall. She envisioned that urchin's gap-toothed smile and seethed. How he must be rejoicing now. She bumped into a passing courtier.

"Lord Nebsumenu." She stumbled back, and he caught her arm.

"Lady Asenat?"

Her gaze intercepted his look of disbelief.

"You are quite beautiful."

She flushed at the compliment, unaccustomed to the fashion of court that Hetnu forced on her.

"I will see the lady to her destination," Lord Nebsumenu informed the guard, then turned to her. "Where to?"

"The vizier's chamber."

His pleasant smile grew stiff. He held her in a gentle grip as they walked, remaining silent. Stopping some distance away from two guards flanking a black-columned doorway, he leaned close. "There's something you should know. This Asiatic cannot be trusted. You must be careful."

"I understand your concern, my lord." She couldn't think beyond the intoxicating blend of myrrh he wore.

"You've heard the stories then, how he tried to rape his master's wife?"

"Lord Hetnu assures me the rumors are unfounded. But I'd sooner trust a hungry jackal than let that sand dweller near me." Her gaze flicked to the thin sculpted beard lifting with Nebsumenu's smile.

"Good. We all have a king to protect."

"Agreed, my lord."

His beautiful bronze-colored eyes searched hers, and his kiss surprised her. It would have lingered had she not pulled back. Unlike Urshe's, it was soft. His hold, gentle. She flooded with warmth and looked away from the fire banked in his eyes, embarrassed at what he'd awakened in her.

"For strength, Lady Benu," he teased in light reprimand for the name she'd given him when they first met. He walked her to the vizier's door, but her legs would hardly hold her up. How she wished men would stop kissing her.

"I AM HERE TO SEE THE VIZIER." ASENAT followed the servant past the entrance hall, pressing her stomach to quiet her nerves. He announced her, and she entered the bright yellow chamber lined with columns, colorful tiled walls, and a balcony. Lion pelts were scattered on the floor, and flowers flowed from vases on veneered chests, tables, and stands. The Asiatic looked up from where he sat at a low, polished table, and she almost missed a step.

Even without his skin buffed and oiled, without his wig of thin braids rimmed in jasper, or the amethyst collar laying at his well-formed chest, he would have been strikingly handsome.

She disliked him immediately.

"Lady Asenat." He beckoned her forward without a hint of foreign dialect in his address. "The king's cupbearer has praised you greatly."

She answered with a straight-faced look and a nod, preferring to keep her distance, but he indicated a cushion beside him. She took it, wondering how deep his rope wounds were under the shining electrum cuffs covering his wrists. His gaze warmed her cheek while she selected a few reed pens near the ridiculous stack of pressed papyri at her side. She burnished a sheet of it with a piece of ivory, mumbling the customary prayer to Sefchet. That so much should be wasted on a savage when potsherd would have sufficed.

"If you will." She laid the blank sheet before him and glanced at the scar on the apple of his throat where the guard pricked him in the courtyard the morning he arrived. There was humor in his eyes. Was he laughing at her?

He inked his pen with black soot and wrote with quick, stiff strokes.

Her eyes touched, furtively, on his sinewy form. He'd filled out well since the first day she'd seen him. She leaned back, unable to resist a peek at his bandaged ankles. This man, the same desperate criminal she saw in the king's morning chamber.

Hard to believe.

"This style I learned in keeping my former master's estate."

She gave a start at his calm voice, then inspected his writing. If he hoped for a compliment, he would not get it. "Hieroglyphs are good enough for common workers or trade but not for someone in the king's house." She plucked up the Book of Sbayt, a book of wisdom text that Hetnu had laid out for their study. "Here is the superior form of writing you must learn, called hieratics." She turned a page, enjoying the strain at his brow. "You've seen this writing style before?"

"And dreaded it."

"It's used by the affluent for everything from poetry to official documents and speeches. You must learn this well." She turned to the first page and anchored it down with an alabaster box full of red ochre. "Begin."

He wrote badly, and she attacked his mistakes with relish, enjoying the slow grimace forming on his lips. But he was too well-behaved for a savage, and she could not resist goading him.

"So, what will you do now that you have everything?"

He was silent for a beat, keeping an eye on his sloppy symbols and a finger on the copy page of the writing book. "I will be very careful."

He took the questions easy enough. Another then. "And how long do you expect to maintain the position of vizier over the whole land before you are poisoned or killed in your sleep?"

A smile broke at his lips, but he kept writing. "You speak your mind very plainly, lady. It is a privilege of your station. Most have not enjoyed the luxury you exercise." He laid down his reed pen, and she forced herself to meet his piercing gaze. "I think it's fair to say that most will be amused with the king's new vizier." He paused to renew the ink in his pen. "And then." He paused again to study his writing, and she was sure he'd done it to irritate her.

"Then what?"

"Then, the king's subjects will prove whether they are

true servants of the king." He kept his pen moving across the sheet of papyrus as he spoke.

"And what have you to do with that?"

"When I carry out the king's instructions, others will show the king the depth of their loyalty through their obedience to me."

She snorted, and he flashed a neat row of teeth.

She squared her shoulders. "You haven't enough skill to rule and only the basest understanding of what is needed." Her voice was louder than she intended, but she was piqued by his arrogance.

"I have lived as a free man and as a slave. In Lord Nebitef's house, I rose from obscurity to manage hundreds of slaves beneath me. So you are right, my lady. I have the basest understanding."

"And this god of yours—"

"Is everywhere, and I will not compromise that truth because you wish to bury him beneath yours." His eyes narrowed in forthright challenge.

Good.

"No god is everywhere. Furthermore, you are a fraud, and I do not like you."

"As a foreign slave, branded a felon, I am well-seasoned in being disliked, but I thank you for your frankness."

She put down her reed pen, ignoring the approaching footsteps. Let the servants gossip if they must. Someone should put this savage in his place.

"And what right has the daughter of my enemy to challenge the authority of my vizier?" The king's booming voice resounded in the room. Asenat lowered herself to the floor, pressing her face into a lion pelt.

"Majesty." She drew a halting breath. The sweet scent

of spices and lotus essence hovered over her melting her bones.

"In kindness, I gave you the privilege of assessing my vizier's writing," the king barked at her back. "And you dare judge him?!"

"Majesty," Lord Yoseph intercepted. "The lady refreshes me, and I prefer her frankness to the false compliments I've received since my appointment to the vizierate."

The king's silence prickled her skin. She clenched every muscle in her body.

"I heard your answer, Yoseph. Once again, you prove yourself full of wisdom while this girl shows me the shallow depth of her gratitude. I should find a task more humbling for the daughter of the high priest of Amun, who pays my vizier as much respect as her father pays me."

"She is an excellent instructor whom I believe to be well capable."

"You see, girl." The king's voice hovered low and lethal above her prone form. "The man you think an unskilled savage has redeemed your fate. Now get back to your chamber before I judge you as harshly as you've judged him."

ASENAT RETURNED TO HER ROOMS WITH HER heart in her throat. Four servants flitted about her sleeping chamber, laying out beadnet dresses and jewelry under Hetnu's direction.

"There you are, foolish girl!" Hetnu pointed a stiff finger at her. "You've made a mess of all that I have done, and now I must save that long pretty neck of yours."

Asenat plodded past him toward her sleeping couch. "Please leave. I wish to be alone."

"Yet you shall not be." He drew his lips in tight, his face rigid.

Her stomach sank. "You've heard."

"I've heard?" He pressed his be-ringed hand to his chest. "The queens have heard. The whole court has heard. And how could they not when the sovereign of the land yells at the top of his lungs? To the bath stall with you." He directed the servants, taking Asenat by the arm as he checked the water clock. "There is no time to waste."

Three body servants tended her with firm looks and firmer brushes. They bathed her, buffed off a layer of skin, then massaged her with lotions and oils afresh, as if it had not all been done with agonizing care this morning. The women ushered her back into her room and set their hands furiously about her. A stolen glance at Hetnu brooding from a chair released a fresh barrage of scolding.

"I warned you, didn't I? I told you to watch your tongue. Now I have lost all trust in you, and your freedom hangs in the balance. You're a spoilt child, who has gotten her way in Iunu, but you do not address a king in such a manner."

"I hardly addressed him at all. And as for Iunu, you know nothing of my life there."

"I know that wherever you were, you were a proud and foolish thing, as you are here before me now." He sprang out of a chair, paced a few quick steps, then pivoted. "You have no conception of what it means for a king to hold you hostage."

His reprimand was worse than a switching. Her eyes watered in humiliation that it was the Asiatic who'd saved her. She kept her focus on the wall of women around her and on the girl braiding a girdle of colored leather strands down the side of her hip.

Hetnu strutted back and forth across the room. "The king treats you with nothing but kindness. And that with no little coaxing from me, though he has been approached with several offers for you."

"Offers for me?" Her brows creased. "But I don't wish to marry."

Hetnu shook his head, his face an utter expression of wonder that made her look away. "A woman of high birth is a king's pawn, girl. Truly, your father's sheltering has done you more harm than good if you don't know this." He pressed his temples and spoke slowly as if to reserve strength. "Have you any idea the dowry your father would lay out? The connections, the alignments that would put a man in power were he to become connected with your father through marriage to you?"

She opened her mouth to speak, but no words would come. She knew such things, yet somehow never realized they applied to her.

More servants entered the room with pelted boards full of pectorals of colorful cloisonné designs, beryl and amber stones set in silver bracelets. Gold pendants and earrings glistened under Hetnu's inspection.

A sharp intake of breath from the doorway shifted Asenat's attention. The girl entered, tossing reddish-brown curls over her shoulder with a look of disdain at her frowning mouth, as though she'd caught them all in some iniquitous act. She sent Hetnu a scornful glare.

"I suppose you thought you'd gotten rid of me. Wicked man."

Hetnu rolled his gaze upward. "Not now, Appipa. I'm busy."

She went rigid at the beautiful jewelry passing beneath

her nose but managed a civil nod to Asenat. Her gaze
flicked around the chamber, taking in every vase, every
piece of furniture and cushion as if to compare it with her
own dwelling.

"I came to see my dear friend..."

"Asenat," Asenat provided, seeing she'd forgotten
her "dear friend's" name. "It's kind of you to return the
bracelet I lent you in the broad hall."

"Yes," Appipa nodded, caressing the bracelet on her
arm, batting eager eyes at the pelted boards of jewelry
Hetnu picked over. She shifted her gaze to Asenat. "Do you
get on with the king? Is he in good health?" Her inquiry,
like sweets on a bad tooth.

"No, no, not the peridot," Hetnu ordered the slave
holding the earrings to Asenat's cheek. "Hold up the
pectoral with gold workings."

Appipa gasped at the filigree collar wrought of fine gold
netted chains, full of sparkling charms and tiny carnelian
teardrops. The new intricate style of jewelry from Crete
mesmerized all of them.

Hetnu narrowed his eyes, tapping his chin. "No." He
waved it off. "Something subtler." He selected a scarab
pendant of yellow jasper with cloisonné falcon wings of
garnet. Waving the women back, he placed it around
Asenat's neck then stepped back to view his work.

Appipa stood off to the side. She locked her jaws and
fingered through a bowl of nuts on a tray. "I hope no one
is swaying the king against me." Her squinted gaze shifted
from Asenat to Hetnu's back. "If anyone dare speak ill of
me in his presence, I will be sure to have my revenge."

"You are too sure of your prettiness," Hetnu said over
his shoulder while directing Asenat to turn. "There are a

hundred girl's like you, Appipa, all of them scratching each other's eyes out to get into the king's bed." He directed Asenat to the door. "Now, you are ready."

"Do not think you can so easily dismiss me," Appipa dogged his steps. "You are only a cupbearer here."

Hetnu stopped and faced her. His expression shifted in such a way that Asenat took his arm.

"Ready for what my lord?" She drew his attention from Appipa.

"For the last hope I have of saving you from the king's anger." He took her in a firm hold, pulling her from the room. "You are going to see the queens."

KHENEMETNEFERHEDJET WHO WAS ALSO Weret, was the god's great wife, though the term queen was used loosely for all the king's favored wives. Queen Khnemet, was also the king's half-sister like Weret, but his newest wife, Neferet, was from Pe, some backwater province in the delta region.

Asenat prostrated herself beneath the garden pavilion on a woven mat and rose for inspection.

Queen Weret leaned forward, her bobbed wig clicking with the sound of a thousand gold beads. She tapped her gold-painted nails against gold lions carved in the arm of her chair. According to Hetnu, she was a lioness herself. By sheer will she produced two sons in two consecutive years, securing her position as mother of the next king.

"Turn, girl."

That was something Asenat had done all morning. She obeyed the god's wife and caught a glimpse of the other two queens flanking Weret from adjacent lower couches.

She met the shy gaze of Neferet. Hetnu borrowed the dressing-servants from her. Asenat assessed the queen, three years younger than herself. She was the pearl of the group, with dimpled cheeks and swollen Hathor braids, a hairstyle exclusive to royal women of the king's house. She stroked her pregnant belly.

"She has no breasts," Queen Khnemet said from the opposite couch, her words filling Asenat with mortification. The second queen covered her snicker and reached back. The nurse passed a small child to her while Neferet smiled with longing in her eyes.

"Yes, too small there," Weret said. "But her bottom will more than suffice."

"Shall we recommend her to Khakheperre, then?" Neferet asked.

Asenat froze at the words. Hetnu said nothing about her being offered to the king. Going to the sovereign's bed would ruin her plans for the temple. It would ruin her life.

Weret poured herself a cup of wine, ignoring Neferet's question. The girl's face flickered with hurt. Hetnu said Weret was cold to her because she was not of royal blood. Yet the king was determined to favor his newest wife and planned to add Neferet's name to the Horus columns.

Asenat had attended the ceremony that transformed Neferet's common blood to that of royalty. Hetnu had gathered the proper officials and won the agreement of the priests to title Neferet the King's Daughter of his Body, Great one of the Hetes-Sceptre and Mistress of the Two Lands.

The weight of such glorious titles seemed too heavy for Neferet's unlearned and tender shoulders. She gave a tenuous smile from her ivory inlaid couch, attempting to ape the relaxed poise of Weret and Khnemet, who were queens born to the highest privilege.

She failed miserably.

Some commotion ensued behind Asenat. She did not dare turn to see it, but Queen Khnemet drew her fingers to her lips, chuckling as she bounced her child on her knee.

"Get out of my way!"

Asenat shut her eyes, clenching at the voice she recognized. Surely, the girl would not be so stupid. But she glanced to her left and none other than Appipa stood beside her.

"Royal Majesties, forgive my tardiness." Appipa cleared her throat, tugging at her tight sheath-dress. "I was detained by the palace jewelers who brought me a gift from a secret admirer."

Asenat looked away, mashing her lips. The secret admirer had apparently been hiding in her chamber and gave Appipa the filigree gold collar Hetnu had laid aside for a special occasion. He would be furious when he found Appipa had taken it to appear before the queens.

Uninvited.

Weret sat back. Her eyes glittered as Appipa jabbered on, unable to charm the lioness about to devour her. Only the king's approach saved her, drawing Weret's attention to the bolt of fabric the guards brought in behind him. Weret stepped down from her chair with slow reverence. Her eyes fixed on the fabric that shone like still night water. The rich, deep amethyst color was not to be found in the land.

"From where did you get this, Khakheperre?"

"It is a gift from old man Nakht of the Shrine province who is too sick to come to court."

"That decrepit old thing?" Weret stroked the cloth with

her gold-painted nails. "Who would think that wretched old toad could acquire something so beautiful?"

"Be kinder with your tongue concerning your subjects, Weret." The king shot her a look of reproach.

"I must have it, Khakheperre."

"Then you must share it, Weret. Give a small portion to Khnemet and Neferet." The king took the giggling tot from Khnemet, kissed the babe, and gave the child back to the nurse.

"I'll share with Khnemet perhaps." Weret shrugged. "But not with this little gnat you've brought from the harem to test my nerves."

Neferet gasped at the insult, and when the king moved to comfort her, Weret signaled to the guards to take the bolt of fabric to her rooms.

Appipa prepared herself for the king's attention by fingering her curls and pulling her shoulders back to perk up her breasts, but the sovereign's eyes never left Neferet.

He sat beside her, mumbling endearments as he cupped her chin, then stood, pulling her up with him. "I'll do something special for you, you'll see." He stroked Neferet's back before handing her off to her maid, his hooded gaze full of contentment.

Appipa flushed with pleasure as the king smiled at her. "You are dismissed," he said.

Asenat bowed with a sense of relief, having made the king angry enough, today.

But he touched her shoulder. "Not you."

She glanced up to find him studying her.

"You stay."

Asenat fell into step behind the sovereign and two

gardeners bearing jars of water on their shoulders. The king's garden burst with fragrant blue isi flowers, white and sun-colored dedmets, and other imported blooms, the likes of which she had never seen. He led them down a shaded path, paved with stone where they stopped at a blossoming lotus tree brought down from the peninsula. Asenat sucked in a breath at the bright pink-tipped petals, drawing a suppressed smile from the king. None of her father's gardeners had ever been able to sustain one.

"I do not consider it good for a woman to hold too much in her head." He directed the gardeners with the water pots. "It is no wonder that you are so fresh with your mouth." He took the pot from one of them to water a spot himself. How quickly he'd grown in strength since the words of the Asiatic. "Tell me about your search for the gods."

An answer stuck in Asenat's throat. She'd thought it was the slaves disturbing her notes in her private writing chest. Her mouth went dry. Apparently, nothing of hers had been kept from the good god.

"First, there is A-Amun w-who is head of the triune gods at Iunu."

"Mmm." The king pruned a few flowers beside his gardeners. This was not the answer he sought.

Her mind flashed with a vision of being carried off into the desert by one of the Libyan princes Hetnu spoke of. She bit her lip, trying harder. "There is also the Neter, who is the first being, an unseen one who created the other gods."

He stood and faced her at this answer. "And do you think this is the god of the Asiatic?" His voice took on a slightly higher pitch.

Her eyes shot to the gardeners. They would bear witness for the king if he used her answer against her.

He must have sensed her panic, for he dismissed his gardeners and stood, brushing dirt from his robes. "The priests think so. But they are forever taking credit wherever they can, even though the gods have ignored me these years." He seemed to weigh his next words as he straddled a water pot tipping it to rinse his hands. "Yoseph claims it was his god who made himself known and came to my aid." Asenat didn't know where to look while he searched her face. "And I am inclined to believe him."

"Our writings do not speak of this god, Majesty." That was as boldly as she dared to speak.

"Look again, Asenat," he said, picking up an empty watering pot and turning down the path. "I think they do."

She dined beside the sovereign, fearing he would silence her "fresh mouth" by taking her to his bed. She was his enemy's daughter, and she would spend the rest of her days whiling away in the king's harem of indolent, gossiping women.

He made it clear that their conversation in the garden was to be kept strictly, between the two of them and that she was to dig out any information she could find on this Elohim. Her mind worked nimbly on how to win the king's favor and turn his interest to her advantage.

Servants removed their trays, and she was startled by the clashing of cymbals and the sudden dimming of oil lamps.

She leaned forward in anticipation of the eerie blue mist building from the sheer curtains before a figure stepped through them.

The actor chilled her bones with his rendition of the Ghost of Amenemhat. Studying his gestures, Asenat realized it was Hetnu, of all people, who performed the skit. It was as though Amenemhat returned from the dead to give an account of his murder in the night and to caution his heir on how he must rule.

"'...But it was he who ate my bread who raised levies; he to whom I had given my hand created terror thereby; those who wore my fine linen looked on me as a shadow; and they who smeared on my myrrh poured water under me...'"

The Teachings of Amenemhat was one of Asenat's favorite texts, and Hetnu's performance was as to make one forget to breathe. She glanced sideways to find the king's lips moving to the words as did her own. The stirring text left a sense of foreboding in the room, hovering like the blue mist floating above their heads.

They sat silent for some time.

"Who holds your loyalty girl?" the king asked. "If not your father, whom you claim to repel."

"My king holds it. And he may confer with anyone at the Iunu temple on the ongoing and strained relationship between my father and me."

The king sucked his teeth. "And what would anyone dare to say other than what your father charged them to report? They fear him more than they fear me." He tapped the table, thinking. She waited in silence. "How many years since your mother died?"

"Ten, Majesty."

"Lady Rudet was a favorite with my mother. I will honor your claim of loyalty to me until you prove otherwise."

"I am grateful, my lord." She licked the tip of her lip. Perhaps she could stretch out this moment of favor. "And I would ask the good god to consider giving me leave to continue my research at the temple of Pakhet. The temple is exclusive to women, and I can study the existence of the gods with no disturbance."

The umbrageous twist of his lips told her she'd gone too far. "You are as arrogant as your father. I offer you my confidence, and you attempt to remove yourself from my observance. Do what I have bid you do. Then I will see what reward your behavior warrants."

Chapter Thirty Two

Yoseph

YOSEPH HELD STILL AT HETNU'S TUG ON HIS long sheer overskirt. He wore it over an embroidered shend'ot, a shorter formal kilt allowed only to men of high rank.

"There, you see Tjebu? Just so," Hetnu instructed in the room's strained silence. Tjebu gave a tight nod, and Hetnu rose from the floor, completely missing the subdued anger seething in the face of the king's garment maker.

They were all applauding Tjebu's expertise when Hetnu entered the room, took one look at the elegant ceremonial garment, and abruptly confiscated the bone pins to reset the hem Tjebu had just finished.

"The garments of a vizier must be flawless, Tjebu. Whether the man is capable of performing the work of his office or no." Hetnu stepped back, sucking in his cheeks to scan the reset hem, and Yoseph imagined him checking for any sign of the exonerated convict still showing. He came forward and yanked loose the overskirt's formal knot, retying it, his lips pursed in deep concentration. "Especially a barbarian fortunate enough to find himself in the light of the good god's favor."

Yoseph felt every eye in the room riveted on him. He tightened his lips. Responding to the glib insult would only make the gossip worse. Hetnu, who seemed unaware of his cutting remark, had moved on to torture the royal jewelers. He'd been given full authority to oversee the vizier's wardrobe and the entire induction ceremony. He was a reigning terror.

Yoseph had learned the demeanor of the elite as a steward of Nebitef's estate. Yet if he displayed any show of table manners or proper conversation, Hetnu insisted on superfluous improvements on how a vizier was to stand, how he was to sit and eat. Yoseph had a belly full of Hetnu's inept lectures. The royal tailors, wigmakers, and jewelers could bear it one more day if he had borne it this long. Tomorrow he would be installed as vizier.

The wall in his chamber lined with gifts had grown thrice-deep since Lady Qatsenut's visit. His tables overflowed with felicitations from every province. Now that the harvest had proved profitable, even Hetnu was forced to let out his leash. Court ladies simpered when he crossed their paths. Matrons thrust their nubile daughters forward to meet him. He was sought out for advice, handled like an oracle and all but devoured by the strong current of approval. The courtiers of the king's house had come to accept him as their latest novelty, and his popularity rose to dizzying heights.

But the high priest, Potipherah, watched him like a quiet bird of prey, while Lady Kemsiyet knew no bounds in slandering him. The smirks on some of the faces of the court officials suggested Nebsumenu spoke of their confrontation in the king's corridor. Or perhaps Dagi spread the news after viewing his humiliation.

SEAL OF THE SAND DWELLER

Hetnu had nothing but high praise for Nebsumenu's thoughtfulness in placing treasury guards at the entrance to his chamber, knowing nothing of the conflict between them. Neither did Sabni, whom Yoseph wished to keep ignorant of the incident for as long as he could.

He was exhausted by the time the servants helped him out of his ceremonial garments. Unbidden visions of a colorful overcoat flashed through his memory and the look of utter disappointment on Leah's face. It was a lifetime ago. And he was an arrogant young fool.

"Are you troubled by something, Lord Yoseph?"

Yoseph looked up and blinked at Hetnu's question. "The flowers." He plucked a slice of roast goose from the platter Duaf had laid out for him and sat down. "Are they from Asenat?"

Hetnu gave him a measured look. "No."

Yoseph could have kicked himself for the question. Any mention of the girl outside the scope of his writing lessons had proven off limits with Hetnu. He hovered over her like a goose with a single chick.

"The flowers are from one of the Asiatic slave girls in the palace who is devoted to you. The poor thing begged me to bring them."

"I ask because I've seen Asenat wear such flowers in her hair." His tongue was making a fool of him. Hetnu's scathing regard narrowed.

"Now that you bring up Lady Asenat, I have a boon to ask of you."

Hetnu who only gave out insult and command was asking a favor. Yoseph sat up with interest.

"I would ask that you keep the girl in your service for as long as possible." A wave of distress passed over the cupbearer's brow. "And I ask that you speak well of her to the king. She has a talent for drawing out the sovereign's displeasure."

Yoseph covered the smile on his lips. Since the day he saved Asenat from the king's anger, she'd punished him with stringent writing instructions, impervious to his smile that usually made women swoon. The girl was a critic, but a thinker, and not easily swayed.

"It will be no trouble to speak well of Lady Asenat. She is a fine tutor." And perhaps behaved more liked Neith, the old goddess of war for which she said she'd been named.

"The finest," Hetnu assured, smiling.

"I, too, have a request, Lord Hetnu. One that I hope you will not deny."

The room had emptied, but at the low volume of Yoseph's voice, the cupbearer pulled up a chair. A ram's head earring swung from his ear as he leaned in. "By all means speak, my lord, and we shall see it done."

"I wish for scouts to be sent out in search of my family."

Hetnu shot up from his seat bringing Yoseph eye level with a jasper-studded girdle. "Certainly not! There is already enough criticism with the king's decision to make you vizier. Shall we overrun the borders with more Asiatics? I am ashamed that your service to the king is not your sole desire."

There was a knock at the door. Chu entered and bowed with haste. "My Lord Yoseph, Sabni requests you come to the vizier's estate. It is urgent."

Yoseph left the room without another word. He needed some distance between himself an Hetnu. "Walk with me," he ordered Chu through locked jaws.

Chu kept pace beside him as they headed for the

vizier's walled mansion. Hetnu recommended Chu who was appointed chamberlain and keeper of items with right of entry on a trial basis. His reputation was marred, something Kitjau had brought to Yoseph's attention that Hetnu had not. Yet Chu was doing a far better job of collecting reports than anyone expected, reports that were previously handed to Yoseph with grudging respect. Yoseph's popularity with the courtiers did not extend to his authority as vizier. In that regard, he was still a sand dweller to the palace administrators.

He and Chu approached the lavish estate, still crawling with workmen on rafters and high walls. A path of dressed stone, bordered with alternating granite and sandstone rams, led to a pylon gate. They passed the artists finishing off the bright murals on the bleached outer walls. Ma'at holding her scales, Thoth writing his truths, and the old god Nekhen who was said to speak no lies. Pools of colored stones reflected their likenesses when they passed an audience porch where short trials would be held.

They continued through an arched alcove. Angry voices came from behind an inner garden wall. Someone shouted.

"You will pay for this. I am a prince of the blood!"

Yoseph came upon Sabni's long form leaning against a muraled wall in a shaded corner of the garden. Dagi squatted below him, scowling, his hands and kilt stained as red as the dung beetles of the choker he wore.

The expression on Sabni's face was almost humorous. "My Lord Yoseph, this artist has come to leave his mark upon your new dwelling. He pushed off the wall, directing Yoseph's attention to the wall behind him. The freshly painted bright red symbols were one of the few written expressions Yoseph understood.

Vile Asiatic.

"I came to clean it up," Dagi said, tightly.

Sabni plucked him from the ground like straw and shook him once before Yoseph motioned for him to cease.

"Of course you did, Prince Dagi. Just as certainly as you did not make target practice of me with missiles of rotten fruit and dung. Let the boy go, Sabni."

Sabni sent him a disapproving glare but gave Dagi a shove. "You are wasting your good graces, my lord. Dagi will only insult you again."

"Of course he will. But tomorrow I will be sworn in as vizier, and any leniency I have offered to the good young prince will have run out."

Dagi worked his mouth to speak but instead tromped toward the outer wall.

"You see, Sabni. Prince Dagi and I understand each other."

Yoseph blew out a gust of wind from his cheeks. Hetnu drove him to the brink of his self-control. And Dagi almost pushed him past his limits. Despite Sabni's protest, Yoseph insisted on touring the inside of the refurbished mansion alone. The place would become his residence after he was sworn into office. Stairs led to a second story, but he would keep to the first floor out of respect for Sabni's vigilant care over him since being named vizier.

He passed through the grand entrance hall, his mind running to an old dream he'd boasted about. Even his father rebuked him for such words. Perhaps slavery was punishment for his arrogance. And how had it all come to this? Vizier of all things, in the land where he'd been a slave. It made no sense.

"And how long do you expect to maintain the position of

vizier over the whole land before you are poisoned or killed in your sleep?"

His fresh-mouthed tutor Asenat had asked the question he'd been too afraid to ask himself. How long? And there were Nebsumenu's words in the king's corridor.

"It wasn't the king or your god that made you vizier. It was me."

Lord Nebsumenu both angered and terrified him. But not even slavery had crushed the arrogance of his youth. It had been both his weakness and his weapon against the tormentors in his father's camp. Perhaps it was his arrogant defense against Lady Kemsiyet's lie that cast him into prison. Or his foolishness for holding the truth for so long. What would it cost him this time in a king's house? He exhaled a hard breath and covered his face, his voice rasping. "Elohim deliver me."

Deliver him to where?

He pressed the heel of his hands to his damp eyes, longing for the tent of his father, for memories of his mother, Rachel, and for Leah's warm embrace. But what if the king had set him free at the borders? Where would he have gone? Back to the camp where men hated him? Perhaps it was better not to search them out, better not to know if his father or little brother still lived.

Shuffling footsteps made him glance up, and he ducked in time to miss the jug crashing against the column. The man let out a gargled cry and a string of foul words. His attempt to charge forward took him sideways, and he crashed into the wall.

"In here!" Yoseph shouted at the sound of footsteps racing toward him.

Sabni ran ahead of Chu and grabbed the offender. He

put the man in a chokehold and raised him to his feet. The man clawed at the thick black arm around his neck, slapped at it. Then sobbed.

Sabni took a sniff and wrinkled his nose. He let the man fall to a heap on the floor. "He's drunk."

The man decked in gold bangles and a noble's kilt gave a soulful wail. "You have taken my position from me, you dirty sand dweller," he slurred, shaking his fist. "You have caused me to lose face among my peers!"

Chu stepped forward with a derisive snort at the weeping drunk. He pivoted to Yoseph and gave a flourishing bow. "I should like to introduce your one-time opponent for the office of vizier, Lord Deduamen of the Min province."

CHAPTER THIRTY THREE

SABNI

SABNI BRUSHED THE RIM OF HIS DYED LINEN cap and studied his likeness in the polished bronze. A sharp wink of gold reflected off his arm cuff and off the heavy feldspar pectoral resting on his polished black shoulders. He looked the part of a glittering god. It was all too much.

Khakheperre had always searched for ways to promote him whether he liked it or not. And the king had finally won by promoting him to great one of tens in the vizier's crew.

But Sabni was a man of war, a soldier at heart, with little use for titles and rank. The administrative work of his new office could turn a man's body to mush, not to mention the idleness brought on by having so many clerks to do one's bidding. But the position was tied to the vizier's crew, the sole reason Sabni had accepted it. His vacillating concern for Yoseph had gone from helping a slave to almost killing him. And now his job was to protect him. But after having spent time with Yoseph, Sabni found it was something he wanted to do.

His instincts told him it would be best to get rid of

the treasury guards posted at Lord Yoseph's door, and he planned to correct the situation by recruiting some of the most trustworthy of the palace guards into the vizier's service.

Word was out that Qareg had escaped the king's prison. Guarding Yoseph would no longer be enough. He would have to learn to fight. The court ladies adored Lord Yoseph, and the thought of putting all that pretty muscle to work with lessons on handling a club and dagger brought a smile to Sabni's face. Exercising with the adze had already improved Khakheperre's health greatly.

The king was full of goodwill toward him, but Sabni would have traded the new status, the promotion, and even Heperre's favor for the answers he sought. Answers that might remove the splinter lodged in his soul. But the topic of his past remained mute on everyone's tongue. Having nowhere to aim his anger, it gnawed at him, sapping his resolve to be patient, challenging his loyalties. How long could he go on this way?

Restless, he moved to a small table to lift the lid of a cedar box. Within were the ceremonial weapons he would wear for the vizier's induction. An ivory throw-stick with gold capped ends and a jasper dagger with a blade of imported obsidian, engraved with spells. But it was the gleaming axe with a shaft of milky quartz that drew Sabni's gaze. He lifted it with care, knowing Khakheperre had set his best jewelers to the task. Sabni's eyes reflected in the polished axe head, prompting his memory of one of the names of Yoseph's god. El Roi, the god who sees.

According to Yoseph, this El Roi had once heard the plea of a rejected concubine, an Egyptian girl named Hagar who had belonged to Abraham, Yoseph's great-grandfather. El

Roi had already proven himself great in the land, and if he saw the plight of one slave girl, then surely he saw the injustice done to the city of Wai. Sabni returned the axe to the box, his senses alert to the slight breeze at his back.

"Take another step, and I'll kill you." He spun to face the entrance of his chamber. "Or perhaps I should just kill you anyway."

The man dressed in a plain kilt kept his eye on the dagger in Sabni's hand.

"Who are you?"

"It matters not who I am, only that I represent a great man who wishes to remain anonymous."

Sabni chortled. "Don't play games with me. You stink of that expensive cardamom and myrrh the priests splash on at Iunu. Potipherah would hack you to croc fodder if he'd known you'd been so sloppy. Whatever price you're offering, tell the priest I will not kill the vizier."

The stranger shrugged. "It matters little. A slave brought to such sudden power is destined to meet an early demise."

Sabni moved toward a stool. "I might agree with you if I didn't know Yoseph any better." He picked up a whetstone to drag across the blade of an old dagger. "But he's not like other men."

He'd come upon Yoseph more than once with his hands clasped tight and his eyes bleeding tears. He was a devout man of his god, sincere and seasoned by the grief of hardship. This Sabni believed with all his heart. He laid the dagger on the table. The intruder's eyes glistened with arrogance.

"My master finds that a man of your experience is the real treasure, not that useless Asiatic. Better promotion awaits you in the service of the high priest of Amun."

Sabni threw the whetstone, catching the man on the shoulder. A startled yelp ended his bluster. He fled from the doorway.

Sabni threw his dagger, next, sticking it to the opened door. A waste of a good throw, but he could hardly afford to injure a man on the day of Lord Yoseph's induction. He humored himself that Yoseph's patience had rubbed off on him. At any rate, the fool was gone, and the arrogant prattle ceased.

Soon thereafter another sound of quick short steps drew near, but these, Sabni knew.

Imehy assessed him from the doorway, raising his chin. "And that's the cleanest you've probably been since birth." He harrumphed and pulled the dagger from the door.

Sabni forced a grin.

"Not open to friendly visits I see," Imehy nodded in the direction the stranger had fled.

"No," Sabni answered. "I prefer a more irritable temperament such as yours." He stood up to get a better look at Imehy's bright yellow shend'ot. Their new rank in the vizier's service entitled them to wear the royal skirt. Imehy strutted farther into the room, giving Sabni a show with a heap of plumes in his headdress and on the long, silver pole he carried.

"I believe you're the most impressive crier I've ever seen." Sabni pulled a sturdy table in front of the bronze shield and lifted Imehy to stand on it. Usually, such an act paid insult to a dwarf, but he and Imehy had walked a long road together. "You're heavy."

"Keeps drunks from knocking me to the wind."

Sabni adjusted Imehy's kilt in the proper fashion for the

ceremony. "They'll be no more of that now that you're in the vizier's crew."

"There'll be considerably less of it." Imehy primped in the bronze and gave a lopsided smile. "Now I've only the young princelings to deal with, and nothing deters them."

Sabni drew a long electrum chain from a pouch Imehy handed him. He shook his head at the intricate links. "I don't understand why you've never gone into jewelry making."

"The royal jewelers sought me out, but I couldn't leave Lord Yoseph now. Not after all he's done for me."

Proud of his friend's sense of loyalty, Sabni drew the thin chain through the loops in Imehy's wide leather girdle as he turned.

"So what about the knife?" Imehy gestured toward the door. "The fellow must have struck a nerve."

Sabni shrugged and lowered Imehy to the floor where he jammed his toes into a pair of sandals with yellow jasper studs. "It's nothing. I handled him quickly." He guided Imehy to the shield where he admired his likeness. "You're a prince." Sabni slapped his friend on the shoulder, avoiding more talk on the stranger at his door. The man's bluster about Yoseph being destined to fall, disturbed him, as did Deduamen's sloppy assault just yesterday. Sabni had his work cut out for him in protecting the vizier, but El Roi would be watching.

CHAPTER THIRTY FOUR

ASENAT

ASENAT HELD HER PEACE. WHAT MIRACULOUS feat had Lord Yoseph performed to double the cupbearer's esteem of him?

Hetnu had spent all morning grinding her ears to powder. She was ungrateful, she was spoilt, she was undeserving of this rare opportunity to tutor the new promising vizier.

According to Hetnu, she owed Lord Yoseph a gift not only for his inauguration ceremony, but as a peace offering for her wretched behavior toward him. She reached her limit and almost stomped away from the treasures Hetnu laid out for her to choose from, that is...until her eyes fell on the fan.

It was a rare thing of masculine beauty. An elegant falcon's wing stretched almost its full span on a curved electrum wand inlaid with onyx and mother-of-pearl. She brushed it against her chin and found Hetnu searching her face, his eyes narrowed.

"What?" She arched her brows.

"Nothing." He worked his jaw but said no more. "I must check the wines and beverages for today's ceremony. Keep to your rooms, and I'll send an escort."

She dressed early for the ceremony under Hetnu's meticulous supervision and laced her fingers together, nodding her compliance. He glared, waiting for her complaint. They'd argued over the tight restrictions he imposed for her protection. But he never made clear whether that protection was from the king or from her father. Both were angry with her. Nevertheless, he left her rooms in a rush, taking her door guard with him.

Asenat hurried to retrieve the note she'd hidden. She refused to feel guilty for going behind Hetnu's back. He was bitter over being fooled in the king's scroll room and allowed her no contact with Mepi. She had no choice but to write the dear old father in secret.

She opened the note with laughter bubbling in her chest, but the grin faded from her lips. She cast the message into the morning brazier and fought down her panic as it burned. The note bore Mepi's seal but it was not from Mepi. It was from her father, Potipherah.

That they'd kept her away from him by making her the king's ward, meant nothing. She was never far enough from her father's reach. No one was.

She picked up the fan and left her suite, her veins throbbing with a violent pulse. It was the first time he was able to contact her in the king's house.

She would not let it happen again.

She disobeyed Hetnu in leaving her rooms early, but no one could argue her whereabouts. As always, she tended her daily chore of going to see the vizier.

She pressed the black falcon wing fan to her thigh so as not to damage it while moving through the crowded corridors. She was anxious for company and eager to present her gift. Some part of her had come to admire Lord

Yoseph. He was astute, yet an affable man. He knew himself charming by the women who flocked to him, yet he handled them with tact. But perhaps the greatest revelation of his character was how much his own slaves were pleased to serve him.

He was determined to learn the hieratic writing style despite the groans he sometimes tried to muffle in a casual tune. His impeccable and courteous manner charmed her out of her proud anger but not her pride. She'd set him at a rigorous pace, keeping his fingers stiff with reed pens and stained with ink-soot.

Sometimes they made light of their similar conditions. Both of them were in the king's care and policed by Hetnu's imperious supervision. But, while Lord Yoseph had gained extraordinary favor, she was disliked by the king.

She spent hours talking to Yoseph about his god and tried to convince him of the benefits of having hundreds of gods to pray to instead of just one. But he met her efforts with a stubborn determination to cling to his ambiguous Elohim.

He claimed his ancestors, a one Abram and Sarai whose names were later changed by their god to Abraham and Sarah, had come down to Egypt where Elohim showed his power to the king, just as Mepi had told her. But few scribes would bother to mention the plain-dwellers who had always flooded Egypt's borders. Yoseph was intelligent and reasonable in all things except the view of his god, but she supposed this was the backwardness of border-crossers and slaves.

The court wavered between admiration and contempt of him. He was handsome and held a quiet confidence from his years of experience, but he was still an Asiatic, and the courtiers had not forgiven his behavior at the Horus columns. But none could deny the changes his god had brought to the land.

The farmers broke out in joyful songs to Hapi, Renenutet, and even to Yoseph's Elohim at the swelling river and pungent scent of silt on the banks. Yoseph's interpretation of the king's dream proved true after years of poor harvests, and they were all astounded.

Seeing no guards out front, Asenat knocked on the door of Lord Yoseph's suite. A lady stepped out to greet her with eyes skillfully painted in three shades of malachite and kohl, though none of it hid the tell-tale lines of her age. A trapezoid pendant of blue and silver beads lay above the ample cleavage of her low-cut sheath. The fringe from her overlaying beadnet dress rolled across her shoulders as she reached back to close the door. A wave of resentment rose in Asenat's belly, startling her. She pushed it down, having no right. If Lord Yoseph had taken a lover, it was his right to do so. And he had shown great dignity in being discreet.

"What do you want?" the lady asked with crisp civility, keeping one hand on the door latch behind her as if to bar entrance.

Asenat's first instinct was to cower at the woman's imperious tone, but she forced out her words. "I am the vizier's tutor. I've brought him a gift."

The lady extended a palm, her fingers laden with rings, her wrists covered with bright silver bracelets. "I will take it."

Asenat ignored the irritation the command stirred in her. Some part of her had looked forward to Lord Yoseph's delight, knowing his fondness for falcon feathers. But she was a scholar, not a love-sick calf. She handed the fan over to the lady though her fingers itched with protest.

The lady drew the fan behind her back. She curled her lips in a pert smile that creased the painted lines around her eyes. Her gaze flicked down the length of Asenat's pleated sheath. "I'm surprised the king took the trouble to dress the daughter of his enemy in such fine apparel." Her tone was sing-song and caustic, now that she had what she wanted.

No, Lord Yoseph would not take such a woman as a lover. And Asenat would spare herself the cat-fight this sophisticated courtier obviously craved. She squared her shoulders. "Great lady, I suspect at your age, the matter of finding a mate must be of utmost importance. Your poor behavior suggests you clearly have the greater need. Therefore, you may have the vizier if you wish. I do not want him."

The woman gave a sharp intake of breath, then drew in her lips tight enough to resemble a pair of dried figs. She narrowed her eyes viciously and stepped back into the room, closing the door with a sharp click.

Asenat smiled at the door's wood-grain patterns with her dignity intact. She hadn't been the one to cower after all.

A LONG TRELLIS OF FLOWERING VINES SHADED the path leading out to the central gardens. Another of Kitjau's wonders since vines were rarely sustainable beyond the delta climate. Butterflies flitted around blossoms while groups of musicians played synonymous tunes from different parts of the grounds bordering three expansive lakes on which Re sparkled with blinding glints of light. Courtiers clustered under colonnades or trees near fish pools to converse and to pet tame antelope. The air was heady with sweet scents, and the muraled walls were lined with bright travertine sphinxes and more of Kitjau's creeping vines.

His expansive garden project had never come to fruition because the low water levels of the past years would not feed the palace canals. This year his work turned out a veritable success.

Asenat made her way through the crowd, pushing past groups of courtiers dressed in white and the vermillion made popular at court by Lord Nebsumenu's wife, Lady Satweret. Asenat regretted passing her gift to the lady at Lord Yoseph's door. That kind of woman could destroy a man's rare goodness with her ambitions.

The successful inundation soon heralded the Going Forth of Wadjet, and the king ordered the famous Iunu temple choir upriver to facilitate the vizier's inauguration. The king goaded Potipherah almost too far in disturbing the temple's tradition of the famous Iunu spring concert, but Khakheperre was determined to garner respect for his new vizier.

The choir stands had been set up. Asenat mounted the lowest step to look over the crowd. She searched for Mepi, hoping to steal a moment with him or perhaps with the high priestess of Pakhet. Hetnu had mentioned that she was chadding downriver with a small entourage for the ceremony, and Asenat would give anything to make a good impression.

Some disturbance worked its way toward her through the throng. Appipa emerged from the crush, leaving heated protests in her wake.

"There you are," she called. Her sheer sheath-dress was as tight as snakeskin in the garment that started below her breasts. The immodest topless style seemed to reap the attention Appipa craved. Only Hetnu's sparkling pectoral from Crete covered her, and she looked as tawdry as a well-dressed temple harlot. Appipa was beautiful and a wild danger to herself. If only Hetnu would attend her.

"I've been looking for you all morning." Appipa clamped down on Asenat's wrist and cupped her mouth toward the crowd. "Over here!" She waved her arm like a flagging pennant. A round-bellied man pushed through the crowd, pulling Appipa's twin A'at up beside him.

"Lady Asenat." A'at greeted her, panting from the exercise. "You remember Lord Ubenresh."

"Soon to be appointed mayor of the Shrine province under Governor Nakht." He shook off A'at's hold on his arm to straighten his heavy wig. His words were for none but Appipa, on whom his gaze was a mixture of irritation and awe. He was as taken with her beauty as he'd been the day they met in the broad hall.

The poor man.

"I told you I could find her for you," Appipa called over his head.

The crowd parted, and Prince Ameny came through. The king's brother took advantage of the new fashion at court and donned a vermillion colored shend'ot and a collar of lapis and gold beetles. He pinned Asenat with a slow, salacious look.

"See how I am forced to snare you, pretty bird? Thrice I've invited you to dine with me."

"Majesty," Asenat bowed, catching A'at's eyes flash wide with warning. How was she to answer when Hetnu tossed all three of Prince Ameny's summons in the brazier. She was instructed to avoid the king's brother at all cost.

Hetnu told her respectable families knew better than to let their daughters near the prince.

"Lady Asenat, this is our father." A'at introduced the man at Ameny's right shoulder. "Governor Deduamen, and beside him, our brother, Hotepi."

The introduction loosed Asenat from Ameny's trapping gaze. She greeted the disinterested youth Hotepi and Lord Deduamen. His hair plaits were littered with a copious amount of gold dipped cowrie shells. Hetnu had not spoken kindly of the governor who might have been vizier if it weren't for Lord Yoseph. Lord Deduamen was of an age with Lord Nebsumenu and might have been as attractive but for the profuse amount of gold at his throat, ankles, and arms. He was a draw for thieves with such a superfluous show of wealth and could be nowhere safer than in the king's house.

"You will attend me tonight at the banquet." Prince Ameny drew Asenat's attention. It was an order, not a request.

Hetnu was busy directing the placement of incense stands on the stage for the ceremony. Asenat willed him to look at her, having no authority to refuse a prince of the blood.

"I'm afraid Lady Asenat will not be available, Majesty."

Relief swept through her at the voice over her shoulder. Lord Yoseph gave a small smile and bowed to the group, the gold and amethyst beads of his formal wig swinging forward. "I have reserved a place for my writing tutor near me." He took her arm, and Deduamen stepped forward to block their exit. His apparel was nearly identical to Lord Yoseph's, down to a gold-capped cylinder seal he wore at his chest. An imbecilic protest.

"So, this is the one the king has made vizier instead of me, based on the luck of a dream." Deduamen's insulting tone invited altercation. Lord Yoseph gave no response and drew her from the strangling group. She marveled at his self-control.

"Thank you, my lord." She pressed her fist to her chest. "I am ashamed to be in such need."

"Then you may repay it at once." He smiled at her, and the lines crinkling at the corners of his eyes gave him a rugged beauty. She could not help but smile back. "I understand you are familiar with this kind of ceremony?"

She nodded once. "I've performed the role of the goddess in the ceremony before. But I cannot do it, my lord. You will have to find someone else." The court gossiped enough about Potipherah's mysterious daughter, and she had no intention of giving them an eyeful. She looked over Yoseph's shoulder to avoid his coaxing gaze. The woman who blocked her entrance to his rooms came toward them with eyes afire. She touched Lord Yoseph's back and flushed the tightness from her face.

"So, this must be the tutor you told me about." She gave him a radiant smile.

"Qatsenut." He turned to greet her, his brows lifted, his smile flat. "Asenat is the finest writing tutor in the king's house."

She batted her eyes as though they'd never met. Asenat could not resist the urge to refresh the lady's memory.

"But I met you this morning, Lady Qatsenut, and told you I was Lord Yoseph's tutor."

Qatsenut flashed her a look bearing a million curses. "Yes, I must have forgotten in all the excitement of the day."

"I do hope my lord likes the fan I left as a gift for him." Asenat indicated the fan swinging from Qatsenut's hip.

"Oh, yes." Qatsenut lifted it from a hook. "I'd completely forgotten about it." She handed the fan to Lord Yoseph, squeezing his arm as he took it.

Asenat held her composure, gratified in how he held the fan aloft to study it.

"It's beautiful."

She flushed to the core as his eyes took on the same wonder over the unique gift as had her own. "It's just a little something to congratulate you on your appointment." First raw with insult from Qatsenut, now bashful before Lord Yoseph. What a dissembler she was. His gaze held hers as he tucked the fan in his armpit. He rocked forward.

"But you will assist me in the ceremony," he said, his tone personal, as though only the two of them stood in the crowded garden.

"Yes, I will attend you," Asenat said from some cache of impudence, despite Qatsenut's blistering glare. The stage it would be then.

ASENAT STOOD BEHIND THE CURTAIN ON ONE side of the stage and observed the crowd. Appipa had gotten her wish and attracted the king's attention. Though one was not permitted to touch the sovereign, she hung on his arm as they walked through the crowd. A lion's tail attached to his gold-embroidered shend'ot dragged across the ground. His Amun crown with gold-dipped feathers sat high and lofty on his brow. Appipa's crown of fragrant curls was no less glorious and thick enough to rival any wigmaker's talent. Her lips, reddened with clay, and her snug sheath drawing the hungry gaze of every man near the king. A'at, who trailed the king and her sister, was dressed far more becomingly in a beadnet dress covering a white sheath with vermillion trim.

The king was amused by the twins, but not enough to bring them on the platform with his wives. He stood the sisters adjacent to his throne at the front of the crowd where Appipa preened and winked at him despite Queen Weret's narrowed gaze fixed on her.

As the foster child of Wadjet, Queen Weret wore a jeweled vulture diadem with cornflowers weft throughout. She was resplendent in her amethyst-colored sheath-dress, though she drew no such attention from her husband as Appipa drew from him and from Lord Ubenresh.

The candidate for mayor of the Shrine province had eagerly pressed through the crowd to stand beside Appipa. She slapped at his roving hands until the king whispered to a guard to direct him elsewhere.

Asenat lowered the curtain. She would have preferred to avoid the fanfare and commotion of the crowd. But at least the ceremony for induction into an administrative office was standard and only became more elaborate according to the position and means available. But her victory over Qatsenut made her forget the more intimate aspects of the ceremony. Nonetheless, it should all be done reasonably quick.

Hetnu whisked past her in a netted shoulder-length wig, and she grabbed his arm.

"I cannot stop and chat now." He dragged her with him to the curtain and flipped it back. He frowned at the opposite side of the platform extending beyond the stage. "Queen Weret refuses to share her shade canopy with Neferet. I had to sneak the girl a patch of linen to keep her from smudging her eye paint with tears." The ladies of Queen

Weret's ornate made no room for the king's newest wife from the harem. Neferet sat beyond the canopy's shade with a countenance as weighty as the lapis pectoral on her shoulders. Most days she was drowned in lapis earrings and charms, lapis anklets and diadems. It was a stone permitted only to royalty, and the king took every means possible to prove her his favorite.

"Poor little savage." Hetnu tsked. "This is all too much for her." He motioned, directing three slaves across the platform to place a heavy potted tree at her back to block the sunlight.

Asenat tugged on Hetnu's arm. "Look there, Hetnu. Among the harpists, second row down. The Minoan. She's the one who held me captive before the king discovered me. Her name is Yimenet."

Hetnu pulled away from Asenat's hold, dropping the curtain. "Has it occurred to you that the king might reward the girl? No need to remind the good god of what we hope he will forget. Ignore her." He gave her hand two quick pats and rushed off to direct the servants, guards, and scribes standing behind stage.

Asenat exhaled a sharp breath and donned the ceremonial mask, frowning. She had no wish to share such polite space with a woman who'd held her like a captive pet, but Hetnu was right. There were some things she hoped the king would forget.

Lord Yoseph stood at the opposite stage entrance, beyond the crowd's view. Despite the commotion around him, he stared at the floor, alone in his thoughts. Thin jeweled straps on his bowed shoulders held up his long ceremonial vestments. There was nothing left of the slave that fascinated her in the king's morning hall. Despite the rumors stirred by Lady Kemsiyet, the court ladies would swoon at the handsome sight of him.

Asenat ran her fingers over the pendant she wore and studied him. He would be in danger holding such a lofty position, and she wished she hadn't uttered such foolishness about his being poisoned.

The drums started, and she blew out a nervous breath. The chatter of the crowd ceased. Lector priests mounted the stage with fire sticks, lighting silver incense pots with a synchronized dance. They descended, and the Iunu temple choir began a hymn of Amun. Asenat recognized her cue and stepped on stage as gracefully as her nerves would allow.

She gained some confidence behind the mask she wore as the crowd cheered her portrayal of the goddess Ma'at. She made a sign of peace in the king's direction, signifying the gods' conjoined consent to the selection of the new vizier, then stepped back to the mural, affecting the pose of the goddess among the painted ennead bearing witness to the ceremony.

The blob of yellow and white passing her was Imehy, strutting to the front of the stage. He stamped a silver staff against the block, and his high plumed headdress danced in the air. A group of princelings near the front of the crowd imitated the mating calls of marsh birds, and Imehy's attempt at the vizier's illustrious titles were lost in the crowd's laughter. Yoseph sent him an encouraging nod, but a heckler drowned out his renewed efforts.

"Yoseph is a pasture name for a goat herder. Send the Asiatic home!"

There was a short silence after the shouted insult, then whispers and scattered tittering. The king leaned forward in his chair, scanning a small section of the crowd.

Deduamen stood near the front, smirking amid slaps of approval from Prince Ameny and a few of his followers. Lord Nebsumenu stood behind the sovereign and pressed his fingers to his lips. He chuckled.

Poor Imehy could not know how the hecklers enjoyed his twisted, angry face. He attempted the vizier's titles again, spitting them out through clenched teeth as the tall plumes of his headdress and staff bounced and swayed. The corner of hecklers doubled over laughing, as did a growing portion of the crowd. Imehy rushed off stage, slapping Asenat's mask with his plumed headdress.

Lord Yoseph proved himself seasoned to insult and emerged stone-faced with a confidence that silenced most of the chuckles. His mask of equanimity strengthened Asenat, and she stepped from the wall to meet him, extending her arms.

"Do you love truth, my son?" She rushed the words, unnerved at how quickly the flattering courtiers had turned on him. Lord Yoseph cupped her elbows, the classic pose of one receiving instruction from the gods.

"I do, O' Ma'at, revealer of secrets." His loud voice competed with a rising onslaught of insults from the hecklers.

Asenat's heart raced, her voice pitched higher. "And do you love justice, my son?"

"Let's see those miserable feet beneath that hem of fine linen!"

She gasped. Prince Ameny.

A nerve jerked in Yoseph's jaw. His fingers dug into her elbows, holding the ceremonial position. "I do, O' Ma'at, leader of justice." His gaze locked on hers, urging her to win this test of wills.

"And do you love me?" She steadied herself against the shrills of laughter. She hadn't heard his reply. No one had.

It was pitifully done, but done nonetheless. She accepted his embrace on behalf of the goddess before removing the gold chain from her neck with shaking hands. The king had designed a new seal more beautiful than the first, with an engraved jasper cylinder and gold-capped ends. She placed it around his neck, and he embraced her, again.

"We will finish this," he whispered, his heart pulsing like hers. He pulled back, his face unreadable. Though she wore a mask, she followed his example.

Her father's voice startled her. She stepped back at the irritation ringing in his chanted prayer. He shook a wet branch over Lord Yoseph, drenching him with holy water.

The three of them held hands in tense silence as the choir sang another hymn. The hecklers were sated, having ruined the short ceremony. Lord Yoseph remained dignified in his expression, though his pulse still raced within the grip of her hand.

When the choir began a second hymn, the sovereign sprang from his chair and handed off his scepter. He made his way to the center of the stage, his lips tucked in displeasure as he removed his own lapis signet ring. Asenat released Lord Yoseph's hand and stepped back. Khakheperre shoved the ring onto the finger of his new vizier and raised his hand. The crowd gave an obligatory, halfhearted cheer, even the hecklers joining in. Asenat closed her eyes at the king's weak and delayed response. It was not enough.

ASENAT SLOWED HER STEPS AS THE CROWD

rushed by her. Palace slaves handed out palm branches with wreaths of flowers for the procession that was to take place around the palace walls. Troupe dancers stretched and flexed, ready to prove their acrobatic prowess. Ameny and his pack of hecklers received no correction from the king, and the insult paid to Lord Yoseph seemed otherwise forgotten.

Queen Neferet was crestfallen to be sent back with her ornate of ladies. But she was with child, and the king would not suffer her to be jostled about. She caught only a glimpse of his two glorious chariots and horses, gifts from Mesopotamia along with slaves to tend their upkeep.

The parade of courtiers in white linen donned spring wreaths and waved palm fronds beside ox-carts bearing the king's family and favored guests. These lined up behind the performers and preceded the rest of the court on foot. A happy jaunt around the palace walls in celebration of Lord Yoseph's appointment, and after this mockery, a lavish banquet.

Lady Qatsenut glared down from the vizier's cart, gripping the rail in some heated confrontation with Hetnu. "I will most certainly not get down. Let the girl ride with someone else. She's had enough attention for the day."

Asenat stepped back into the shadow of a colonnade. Her cheeks grew hot. Who else could Qatsenut be speaking of but her?

"This cart is for the honored staff of the vizier." Hetnu's voice was low and sharp. "She is his writing tutor. You are not, Lady Qatsenut. Come down and take your place among the queen's ladies."

They stared at each other until Qatsenut finally gave in with an angry huff. Chu, who'd been eyeing the exchange stopped pretending to converse with another official to help Qatsenut down. She made her way to the cart of court ladies whispering and wide-eyed at her approach.

Hetnu's set down of the king's cousin would be the talk on everyone's lips, but as the king's cupbearer, his influence was greater than Qatsenut's.

Asenat pressed back against a column, mortified when Hetnu motioned her over. She felt stares from the cart of women Qatsenut had joined. "You go too far," she whispered as Hetnu helped her onto the vizier's cart.

"Control yourself, girl. The whole world is watching." He smiled, stiff and confident as he glanced at the onlookers. "You must be seen useful to the king as one assisting the vizier." He left her there with a large portion of the crowd watching her. She fought back angry tears. How they would love to see her crying now.

Lord Djehuti, who was friend to Hetnu, whispered to his son who recently joined the vizier's crew as a zab official and messenger. Rudi came to stand beside her as the king's new chariots were being brought to the head of the procession.

"Horses are gaining some popularity in the land, but I could never understand it. Can you, Lady Asenat?"

Her eyes were watery, and she had no courage to look at him. She folded in her lips and gave a little nod.

"Oxen are far sturdier and more useful. Horseflesh is sinewy and tough."

She was grateful for Rudi's effort to cheer her but afraid her voice would reveal her distress. He seemed to understand.

"Even a few of the courtiers have taken a liking to the creatures." He swept her face with a private look of sympathy, his robust and cheerful tone kept her from bawling her embarrassment. "The climate is too hot for them, I think."

Asenat found her courage and glanced at his narrow shining nose. She gave a little smile. His cheer was contagious.

"Look there!" He whistled in admiration at the king's four beautiful geldings being divided between the chariots, one of white and gold in which the king stood with the current Potiphar of his house. Lord Sabni and Yoseph mounted the second red chariot. Lord Yoseph's knuckles whitened on the rail as Sabni calmed the beast.

She was feeling better about the whole matter until she glanced at the cart holding the queen and her ladies and met Qatsenut's threatening glare. The lady would never forgive her.

The parade carts lurched forward, and the procession left the grounds. Instead of the expected trip around the palace walls, the king led the whole court down the main boulevard of the city. One hundred palace musicians, fifty of the king's best dancers, and two hundred singers preceded his grand chariot.

Peasants lined the streets, greedy for the sight of courtiers in jewels and crisp white linen. Asenat could have sworn that every slave and gaunt beggar's chest was swollen in pride at the site of Lord Yoseph.

"Khakheperre is righteous!" they shouted.

"Khakheperre is the strength of Horus!"

"Yoseph is Khakheperre's strong hand!"

The courtiers of the king's house were fickle in their affection toward the new vizier while the peasants in the streets readily claimed him. Even though he was an Asiatic, he'd been a slave like many of them. The words of his god had turned their fears for the harvest to joy.

The merry jaunt into the city dwindled to a miserable plod in the heat of the midday sun. Fat priests huffed down the boulevard, and the cheering court became irritable as rivulets of sweat streaked their painted eyes and rouged cheeks. A few gave up the vanity of their wigs and used them for fans. Every litter chair in the city was bought up. Wealthy nobles accepted cups of water from the lower class they would at any other time, have spurned.

The god's wife Weret sweated out her garment made from the precious fabric she kept to herself and ordered some of her ladies down from her parade cart to give herself extra room. Qatsenut gripped the side of the wagon, with stubborn determination.

Lord Nebsumenu had the good sense to conceal his displeasure when the king refused his counsel on the tired courtiers. Some mumbled that the god of the sand dweller had gotten hold of the king's senses, but a glimpse at his drawn features did not speak of madness but subdued anger.

The parade stopped in the middle of the city where the king's chariot pranced around the center-mark. The streets were packed with citizens and sweaty courtiers. The king ordered all to bow the knee to his new vizier. Queen Weret ignored the order, waving her fan until the king's piercing glare forced her down.

"You see here the man I have raised from my prison and chosen as vizier." He turned Lord Yoseph to face him, his voice clear and strident. "I am king. I name you vizier, and no man in the land will lift neither hand nor foot without your word." He could hardly wait for his criers to echo his words into the city. It was enough to make Asenat almost forgive his cowardice in letting Lord Yoseph suffer such a loss of dignity from a handful of ill-mannered hecklers. But the king had been inconsiderate to the aged who suffered in such heat.

He called Imehy forward and let him announce the vizier's titles again. There were no snickers nor heckling from the worn out crowd this time. The king made Lord Yoseph face the crowd.

"Furthermore, his name shall no longer be called Yoseph but Zaphenath Paneah. For in him, all the spirit of the true god dwells."

Many of the priests in the crowd were outraged by this bold declaration. Khakheperre had dirtied their linen, dragged them into the city, and now he had exalted his Asiatic vizier and his god above them.

And they would not soon forget it.

NEITHER COURTIER NOR PRIEST BOTHERED TO express their displeasure. Instead, they reserved their strength for the trek back to the king's house while baking in the day's heat. Those unable to acquire litters either trudged back on foot or paid to ride the strong backs of peasants. By the time the vizier's cart of honored guests returned, Asenat gave Hetnu her begrudging thanks.

Shade pavilions and dining tables flowed out from the banquet hall into the delightful central gardens Kitjau had built. The aroma of honey-grilled meats wafted through the air. Many of the courtiers, still dirty and soaked with sweat, went straight to the hall and fell on the food. Slaves rushed to meet their demands with grilled melon, cheese-stuffed figs, and loaves of bread packed with beans and roasted vegetables. There were succulent meats of the best cuts and confections exclusive to the king's house piled high on trays. Full bellies abated the sensibilities of the king's disgruntled courtiers. It seemed Khakheperre had timed his retribution perfectly.

Asenat went to her rooms to refresh and change for the evening banquet. She donned a curly wig and a sheath with jeweled straps on one shoulder that Hetnu had approved for her. Lord Yoseph's new name rang again and again in her mind.

Zaphenath Paneah indicated one who reveals mysteries, a finder of secrets who sustains life. Such a name would draw out critics and enemies for a foreigner who'd won such favor from a king. Mockers would challenge him on every level.

She returned to the banquet hall, her hopes of finding Mepi dashed with Hetnu's assigning her to the ornate of Queen Neferet. She took no pleasure in joining the handful of giggling girls who rose from the harem as companions to the king's newest wife. At her approach, Neferet extended her hands, pulling Asenat down to the cushions as if they were old friends. Asenat pulled away with a polite smile. Someone should teach the girl that it was unfitting for a queen to display such common manners, but it was Neferet's first formal banquet.

Asenat charged herself to be patient, but her eyes strayed to Queen Khnemet's ornate. There is where Hetnu should have placed her. She would have been better suited with Khakheperre's middle queen. Khnemet was less of a beauty, yet better composed in her dignity without the meanness of Queen Weret, whereas Neferet was too ingratiating and no more than a smiling babe-in-arms.

"Look there!" One of Neferet's girls pointed at courtiers racing for a fresh batch of grilled meat. A chorus of giggles erupted from the girls sitting behind Neferet. "We never behaved so in the harem." One girl raised her chin.

Asenat leaned back, speaking to the mumbling group of ninnies behind her. "I find it disagreeable for a queen and her ladies to laugh at those in her lord's court." She turned her head, affecting a look of disdain for such gossip. Neferet straightened beside her.

"My, but you are right, Asenat." Neferet took her hands again. "Hetnu said you would be good for me."

Asenat's brows knitted in a frown. Neferet's humble response chafed her. It was no wonder Weret harassed the girl so. She was a honey cake, and the court would eat her alive.

"Look!" One of the girls squatted and touched Neferet's shoulder. "There's a fat man dancing and filling a sack with food." More giggling followed as Asenat studied the man whose round shape and lightness of foot she recognized. The rotund Iunu priest was sure to make a fool of himself for a platter of food wherever he was.

Senib.

He was not dressed nor behaving like a priest from Iunu and danced at the front of the hall near the serving tables. The musicians picked up a tune at his light steps, and the guests in the hall chuckled as he plucked food from some of their platters, placing meat and cakes in his half-filled sack. What was he doing here?

His smile froze, and Asenat turned to see her father's sharp gesture to the guards. Senib was a blackmailer and conniver who'd broken with his temple vows, but she could not wish even him the tortuous death her father was sure to bring him to. Senib recovered his wits when the guards came at him and bowed to her father with a cocky grin. Dancing backward out to the connecting central gardens, he tore into a run, holding his sack of food. The guards were hard on his heels, and she hoped Senib was as fast on his feet as he was light on them.

The king entered the hall in a gold-shot nemes headdress and an immaculate yellow pleated robe of gold trim. Lord Yoseph followed the sovereign into the crowded hall. Lady Qatsenut strolled beside him, more stunning than ever in her sheath and red beadnet dress. Her clear effort to recoup from this morning's embarrassment was proof that Lord Deduamen was not the only one bribing the royal garment makers. Yet Qatsenut was far subtler in her attempt to match the vizier's outfit. Her large hoop earrings were of the same design as Lord Yoseph's falcon wing belt. The two of them looked the perfect couple.

Lord Yoseph still carried the falcon wing fan. His eyes found Asenat's in the crowd, and he nodded. But she looked away, pretending not to see it.

The dining arrangement for the honored vizier and king topped several tiered platforms. Beneath them sat some of the most important men of the kingdom and members of the vizier's sparse cabinet, still in great need of officers.

When Neferet tugged Asenat's arm and whispered in her ear, she rose, relieved to remove from the troupe of gigglers, yet dreading her approach to the vizier's table. She straightened her posture, taking more confidence in this second garment she wore. A traditional white sheath she begged of Hetnu instead of the vermillion made popular at court. In place of a beadnet dress, Hetnu allowed her a wide, netted girdle of gold dipped acacia beads that hung in long panels down the front and back of her sheath. He'd designed the look himself, this and her hairnet with scattered gold disks that covered her wig.

Lord Nebsumenu winked as she passed him, and she flushed at the memory of his stolen kiss. He'd asked for her, coming to her door once or twice while she tutored Lord Yoseph. But something internal warned her against the king's treasurer, and she was relieved to have missed his visits.

Shifting her gaze, Asenat was startled to find Lord Yoseph watching her. He'd seen her exchange with Nebsumenu and either he chewed a tough piece of meat or worked his jaw. Qatsenut touched his hand, drawing his attention.

Asenat approached the table, holding her breath. Hetnu gave a rare smile, eyeing the creation she wore with a look of approval in a little proud shake of his head. But the sovereign shot up from his seat. Asenat bowed as he rushed past her to Neferet's side. She'd fainted, and he reached her at the same time his physician Mentuser approached.

"My Lord Yose—Lord Paneah," Asenat amended, remembering his new name. She gave the vizier her full regard. "Queen Neferet wishes me to pass a private request to you."

"You may whisper it." He tapped the gold bird claw earring he wore, and she hesitated at his casual manner. Qatsenut was staring at her as though she were some pest. Asenat lowered herself beside him to whisper, embarrassed by his familiarity and by Neferet's silly request to have him interpret one of her dreams.

He pulled back, nodding and chewing, then made eye contact with Lord Nebsumenu at one of the lower tables. "Stay beside us. Eat." A brief smile graced his mouth. He relaxed as though the day's humiliating event had never occurred. Such resilience.

Qatsenut protested with the sucking sounds she made against her fingers as she ate and stared into the crowd, her heavy bracelets clashing at her wrists.

"I must attend the queen." Asenat excused herself, but the king helped Neferet up, and she motioned for Asenat to stay put.

"It seems the queen does not require your attendance at the moment." Lord Paneah missed the withering glance Qatsenut shot her and called for a platter of food. He took it from a servant and placed it before Asenat. "Eat," he ordered without looking up.

She worked up a thin smile and toyed with the food on the platter, taking little bites here and there. He found better conversation with Sabni and Imehy, who sat below him. Kitjau joined them, and they cackled, teasing Lord Paneah on how well he'd decked himself out for the ceremony. He laughed and took their japing with good humor. Slavery had woven a resistant mettle into his ka. He was a marvel to behold, considering the courtiers who dithered between insult and flattery.

An Asiatic slave girl came up the stairs by the table, offering a small bouquet of flowers. Lord Paneah accepted her gift with a smile, and she bowed herself off, grinning.

"Impertinent," Qatsenut said in a low voice, tilting her head.

"But as a slave, it may be all she ever has."

Qatsenut forced a little smile at Paneah's words, flicking a look at Asenat who lowered her gaze to her platter. After this, the women came in droves of giggling ladies. Matrons and young girls approached to introduce themselves to the most eligible bachelor in the kingdom. For he was certainly that. And the ladies could forgive anything with such a handsome and wealthy prize in view.

Lord Sabni received his fair share of attention, having been among the king's elite guards and now promoted to the vizier's great one of tens. He was quite amused by the whole thing and chuckled with Imehy and Kitjau, betting on which ladies would forget him and pursue the vizier with abandon.

Hetnu, who might have policed the intrusions, sat at the far end of the table with three trays piled high with food. He paid them all no mind and hunched over a platter, chomping.

The evening's entertainment started. Dancers dipped across the floor in foxtail skirts while acrobats tossed spinning fire sticks in the air to catch and swallow the flames.

Qatsenut sprung to life as the adept hostess. Flashing her brilliant smile, she deferred the conversation to Lord Paneah, yet, somehow, still managed to control it. The vizier found little to say with her beside him, and Hetnu watched from a distance, rolling his eyes as he devoured his food.

Mentuser had just returned to the banquet hall though the king and Neferet did not. He joined Nebsumenu and Lord Resnakt. Prince Ameny sat at their table, drunk and hanging over Lady Satweret who was immaculate in her vermillion pleated sheath. She squeaked more than once at Ameny's hands on her thigh, until the treasurer motioned for a guard to assist the royal prince away from his wife and out into the new gardens where he might get some air.

Scanning the crowd, Asenat searched for Mepi as a tall shadow towered over her.

"I extend my sincere congratulations to you, Lord Paneah." Her father's voice resonated above her head, and she held her breath. Lord Paneah rose to his feet.

"I am most honored, Lord Potipherah, to receive it from you."

"It is not every day that a charlatan can pull off such a miracle. When you are finally executed, I trust the memory of this event will disappear, along with your invisible Elohim, and the great Lord Paneah will be Yoseph, once again."

Asenat shut her eyes wishing she could disappear. Her father's felicitous addresses always preceded some kind of verbal slap. Even Qatsenut was left speechless while Hetnu held food in his jaws, looking between them.

Lord Resnakt staggered over, half drunk and grinning. "Both of you together," he slurred. Asenat shied a glance up at him slinging one arm over Lord Paneah's shoulders, the other over her father's. "Good. I've had a dream I wish to be interpreted."

The clash of symbols drew everyone's attention to the entertainment at the front of the hall. Even courtiers deep in their cups manage to clap to the familiar military tune as the dancers appeared.

Asenat's gaze widened on Prince Ameny. He'd found himself an Asiatic garment and covered his chin with black paint to appear like a bearded Asiatic. He led some of the younger princes in a poorly synchronized dance, paying Lord Paneah the highest insult by doing the dog walk, a humiliation meant for captured foreigners and prisoners of war. The courtiers laughed and clapped and cheered. Lord Paneah removed Resnakt's arm from his shoulder and swept out of the hall with heated steps. It seemed his resilience had limits after all.

CHAPTER THIRTY FIVE

YOSEPH

YOSEPH RUSHED BACK TO HIS OFFICE AFTER Sabni took him through a regimen of defensive fighting moves. He changed just in time for the meeting. Duaf laid out Reniqer's favorite cakes and wine. And if that weren't enough, the aroma of date-glazed duck stuffed with emmer grain and almonds wafted through the air. Reniqer's favorite dish. The show of respect might soften the broad hall leader's manner and win his capitulation. Yoseph needed him on his side if his plan was going to work.

Reniqer entered with the badge of his office slung across his puffed chest. He leaned heavily on his staff, using it as a walking stick, the gout evident in one of his swollen feet. He paused, sniffed the meal cooked in his honor, then sent Yoseph a cold glare.

Yoseph rose from his desk with a sinking feeling. He'd overdone his effort to impress the staunch official. He bowed. "Greetings, Lord Reniqer. I thank you for coming."

"I should warn you that I will not be bribed."

"Which is precisely why I've called for you." Yoseph

proffered a cushioned chair and stool for Reniqer's foot. "Please, sit."

Reniqer was, at first, caught off guard by the forthright statement, then his jowls drooped farther with his frown. He gave nary a bow nor a nod of respect. He glanced around the chamber, taking in the muraled wall of Thoth in action with Amun-Re, the shelves of fine varnished cedar holding rolled documents, and the excellent furnishings. Lowering himself to the cushioned chair, he perched on its edge, gripping his gold-capped staff and ignoring the stool set out for his gouty foot altogether.

Jafener, Paneah's new head scribe and royal sealer, sat cross-legged on a mat in the far corner of the room, stroking out symbols on a sheet of papyrus. He was one of the king's best and sent to serve after Yoseph's disagreement with Nebsumenu over the tributary gifts. Jafener confirmed the accuracy of Gebi's report, and hearing of the intended interview with Reniqer, offered to stay for support. He said the broad hall leader was a tired old toad, croaking blunt insult whenever he found occasion to do so.

"Nor will I turn my head at any corruption you choose to engage in." Reniqer struck the floor with his staff. "I am not like you cowardly sand dwellers that nip at our borders and run in retreat. But I perform the work of the king, straight and true of heart."

Yoseph arched a brow at the covert look Jafener shot him. He'd been warned. "And I am glad to hear it," he answered, bypassing Reniqer's insult. Reniqer's position was one of great importance, overseeing the distribution of the king's word to every province. But his office also governed the many corridors around the broad hall. Corridors Nebsumenu was using to steal from the king.

Since efforts at charming the stalwart Lord Reniqer had utterly failed, there was nothing left for Yoseph to do but ask. "I understand, Lord Reniqer, that you are soon to retire and that you surrendered your duties to Lord Resnakt since your gout has been so troubling. But I'd like to restore the responsibility to you, and ask that you give special attention to the night watch."

Reniqer tucked his chin in a look of disbelief. He sat up straighter. "Well it's about time," he bit out. "They think I'm too old, but I can't remember the last time the corridors were governed properly. I've complained about it, but Nebsumenu has stripped my authority and left me with nothing but the title."

Yoseph pressed a fist to his thigh. Like Qareg, Nebsumenu sought to silence any voice of authority other than his own and to bind any action against his efforts, hand and foot. And with the vizier's office vacant, the treasurer governed the passageways through Resnakt, his deputy treasurer. But Yoseph collected Resnakt's reports now, and they were false. Restoring Reniqer's true authority over the corridors would change everything.

"I am grateful for your assistance in this. You may take up your duty of monitoring the corridors immediately. And now another question. Have you any knowledge of the whereabouts of Lord Gebi, who is overseer of the lower fields and the royal tributary offering? He assisted me with my first report to the king."

Reniqer snorted. "Why don't you ask your true god since his spirit dwells in you, alone." Reniqer flashed a look at Jafener in the far corner before he went on. "Gebi was careless."

Yoseph lowered his voice to match Reniqer's. "The quay

scribes told me one story about Gebi. The guards told me another. Two of his lower supervisors said he'd gone down to the Delta region, but there was no record. I cannot allow the king's servants to be in peril for simply attending their duties."

"One can often get into trouble here for doing just that." Reniqer's words hung in the air as though he wished to say more. Instead, he glanced at Jafener and slapped his knee. "It's the same reason I was stripped of my authority." His voice was loud and hard again.

Yoseph rubbed the lines in his forehead. "My lord, if there is more you need to tell me, then I must insist that you do so since I am vizier."

"Are you, now?" Reniqer reared back, clutching his staff. "Then where is your seal of office, Lord Zaphenath Paneah, in whom the spirit of the true god dwells? Where is your ring of the king's authority? I see nothing but a polished Asiatic before me who lays out pretty cakes and prepares a sumptuous meal." He pursed his lips. "That is no more than what you did at your master's house. But it will not be enough if you truly plan to improve things here." He thumped his staff on the floor and stood.

Yoseph stood with him. "I may call upon you for future questioning."

"And I will tell you the truth if you can tolerate it."

Yoseph motioned to Jafener. "Walk Lord Reniqer out through my private exit."

Reniqer snorted. "Don't trouble yourself with an old man. You have far greater concerns to deal with."

When they left, Yoseph went to his desk and sat. He opened a box and pulled out the king's lapis signet ring. He pushed it on his finger, then put the chain bearing his seal of office around his neck. After the humiliation in the broad hall, he'd avoided wearing the jewelry stating his authority, and Reniqer was the first to notice.

Imehy came in to tend his feet, and Yoseph took his usual position on the mat in the corner of the room. His legs and feet never fully recovered from Qareg's abuse but sometimes tingled or ached.

"Your feet are looking better, my lord. No flowers mind you, but you'll suffer far fewer foot sores if we keep massaging your limbs."

Something in Imehy's voice was different. Yoseph looked over his shoulder. "You're gloomy today."

Imehy shrugged in response. The poor fellow had not fully recovered from his own humiliation at the induction ceremony.

"You should reconsider the offer the royal jewelers have made you. It's a true compliment. I'll call you to work on my feet when I need you."

Imehy shrugged again, but his gaze wandered to Yoseph's face before he looked away. When he finished, Yoseph returned to his seat while Imehy gathered his supplies. There was a knock at his door.

"May I come in?"

Yoseph waved the broad hall attendant who was also Nebsumenu's deputy treasurer into the room. No use putting this off. "Come in, Lord Resnakt." Resnakt took a seat across from him holding that bright boyish, grin Yoseph never trusted. "Send in Chu on your way out," he instructed Imehy and bent to replace the jeweled cuffs he always wore. Resnakt gawked at the deep scars at his ankles. "How may I serve you?" Yoseph asked, drawing Resnakt's regard away from his feet.

"Asking to serve me, Lord Paneah?" Resnakt flipped the new name off his tongue with a little sneer nestled in his smile. "You still sound like a steward." He glanced at the cylinder seal necklace on Yoseph's chest.

"I am steward over all that is the king's."

"Had you many visitors today, then?"

"Very few," Yoseph answered, perceiving Resnakt's true interest was not in how many had come to see him but in exactly *who* had come. Yoseph went back to tallying the sheets he'd been working on. Resnakt could hold that coaxing grin until his cheeks burned.

"Prince Ameny was ill-mannered at the banquet, though quite the character in that get-up he wore." Laughter slipped from Resnakt's lips before he caught it. He cleared his throat. "Yes. Well, I still need an interpretation to my dream and thought it best to seek you out."

Yoseph set his work down and listened to Resnakt's dream. His was the usual boast of a wealthy man. Finding gold, seeing one's face in a mirror, plunging into the river, all bore omens so flattering that one was given to dream of such things. But it was the mention of Resnakt seeing the faces of his six sons in murky waters that sent a sudden jolt of warning through Yoseph. He sat forward.

"Give your boys time away from you, my lord. A year."

"Nonsense. I keep my children beside me like a good father."

"Nevertheless, a trip would do them good." Yoseph weighed his next words, knowing Resnakt held the pride of a wealthy man. "Your life is surrounded by danger."

Resnakt's perpetual grin died on his lips. "I believe you're trying to scare me."

"No, my lord. I am not."

"And what should you know about my life?" He sat up, his easy manner gone. "Lord Nebsumenu warned me you enjoy stirring confusion in the king's house. I should not have come. As for my dream, I've already received a suitable interpretation from Potipherah." Resnakt's chair fell over sideways when he stood. "Do not dare to speak ill of my sons again."

He rushed from the room as if fleeing the warning spoken.

Yoseph stared after him, hoping he would change his mind.

YOSEPH OBTAINED A SMALL VICTORY IN refusing to sign the blind tally Nebsumenu sent him. His duty was to see the king's coffers for himself. Nebsumenu had ignored his three requests to tour the kings two houses of gold. And after a few unanswered messages, Yoseph began to think the king ignored his complaint of being ignored. The report on the sovereign's holdings was due today, the vizier's seal was needed. Yoseph made his way to the two houses of gold with Chu beside him. Still, his stomach twisted at the thought of facing Lord Nebsumenu again.

Chu had gained only a little respect in becoming chamberlain to an Asiatic vizier, especially with the rumors surrounding his family's fall from grace at court. The old scandal had brought him to demotion that rendered him nearly invisible. And this invisibility he claimed to use as he witnessed the watchmen take the corridors around the broad hall on several nights. Yoseph would have debunked Chu's excitable account, but it matched his own assessment from the storerooms and also what he and Kitjau had discussed.

"Have you received the reports from the two houses of silver yet?"

Chu nodded. "The royal granaries are slow to respond, my lord. It's an abundant harvest, just as you foretold."

"When I was steward over Lord Nebitef's estate, we'd had the king's tribute well in hand by now."

"Yes, but consider that Lord Nebitef is faithful and not among those resisting the sovereign's rights like the governors. But I will redouble my efforts to get you a report from them soon."

"I've already sent Sabni to investigate the matter." Sabni was not as knowledgeable as Chu, but he was dedicated and sharp. He was also hotheaded as a young bull, something that would not serve today's task. Even Chu's emotions ran high at times. A nuisance, since he was rarely disposed to conceal them.

Canes tapped the pavement, and mismatched footsteps shuffled up behind them. "My Lord Vizier!"

Yoseph slowed his steps, glancing sideways at Chu who gave a long forbearing gaze toward the heavens.

"Ladies Ipwet and Sahathor." Yoseph bowed to the puffing matrons. "Good day to you. I cannot stop to chat."

"Yes, yes, Lord Paneah." Sahathor clutched his arm, panting. "But we are taking bets as to which one you will choose."

"Which one?"

"Do not be coy," Ipwet said over Sahathor's shoulder. "Qatsenut is a seasoned woman of the courts. And Asenat, the learned younger one. Take them both if you like."

"No, not both, Ipwet!" Sahathor struck her friend's arm. "We will win nothing that way."

So this was the new talk on everyone's lips. Yoseph had been told to be careful with these two mothers who could slice a man to bits with their tongues. And he had no intention of sending Lady Kemsiyet any help in that corner.

"I wouldn't dare spoil the pleasure of your predictions."

"Oh come now. We will be the very mouth of Nekhen and keep it in our bosom," Sahathor implored, extending a hand weighty with rings. Lady Ipwet made a motion of pinching her thin lips together to drive home the point.

He feigned a look of grave observation. "I understand the courtiers look to you for direction in all matters of information and entertainment concerning the goings on of court life."

"True," they answered in unison.

"Then I charge you to observe and let the matter rise to a fever's pitch." He leaned in closer to whisper. "Let the world guess and beg and plead to know while you tell them nothing, not even the ladies themselves." He winked, and Ipwet covered her open mouth.

"Oh but that is worthy, Sahathor." Ipwet pulled her friend off to the side of the path to discuss how they might stir up the matter even more.

Asenat would not thank him for his suggestion to the two mothers, and he laughed to himself as he and Chu continued toward the wall of the treasury. They approached the pylon gates, and the lightness of the moment was gone.

Yoseph tensed as they kept a steady pace through the courtyard and into the main hall, ignoring the eyes that fell on them. They stopped at the podium to address the attendant. Ibiau looked up chewing, his jaws swollen with food.

"I am come to inspect the king's treasure rooms,"

Yoseph said, loud enough for those around him to hear. They'd expected him and the room stilled as Nebsumenu's footsteps echoed toward them. Everything about the treasurer's looks and manner told Yoseph to bow, but he fought his slave instinct and pulled his shoulders back. "You will open the door to the king's treasure rooms." His command was feeble.

Nebsumenu's gaze rested on the seal around Yoseph's neck. "You cannot see the rooms today, Lord Paneah. But you can allow me to add your seal mark to the report." His voice was firm.

"The king has requested I view the rooms. I will not bring him a record of your tally, but my own."

The air was charged when Yoseph started for one of the great silver doors. Nebsumenu yanked him around by the shoulder, grabbed his gold chain and dragged him back to the podium like a dog on a leash. No guard moved to help him.

Ibiau produced a small stack of documents and clay tablets at Nebsumenu's bark. A jerk on the chain pulled Yoseph level to the surface of a podium.

"You will sign that the rooms have been viewed." Nebsumenu held him firm as he and Ibiau made quick work of rolling the vizier's seal across two clay tablets and signing his mark on papyrus. Yoseph bore the humiliation with gritted teeth, his cheek pressed to cold stone as those in the hall looked on in fascination.

"My Lord, you cannot—"

Yoseph shot Chu a look, warning him to stay silent. Nebsumenu released him, and the damp clay seal struck his chest. His blood drummed in his ears as he started for one of the large silver doors again, addressing the guard. "You will allow me to view the rooms." His voice shook, but the guard worked his jaw, staring straight ahead. "I am the vizier. You will open the door!"

"Guards!" Nebsumenu snapped.

Footsteps closed in, and the guard blocking the silver door leveled his spear at the red clay stain on Yoseph's chest. His stomach leapt. Chu stood beside him as treasury guards surrounded them, aiming their spears. They parted to let Nebsumenu into the circle.

"I could end it all here." He stepped close to Yoseph, his voice a menacing whisper. "One word from me and you are dead, sand dweller."

Yoseph felt the tip of a spear pressing his side.

Chu's voice caught in a breathy grunt. "There would be questions, Lord Nebsumenu. Administrators of the vizier's crew are fast following on our heels."

The lie snapped Nebsumenu from his killing trance. He looked around. "Lower your spears." The guards' spear shafts struck the polished sandstone, and Nebsumenu stepped sideways, gesturing for his men to let them through the circle.

Yoseph and Chu proceeded toward the exit with Nebsumenu's breath hot on the back of Yoseph's burning neck. "Now get out of my treasury, you desert dog," Nebsumenu carped, following them back through the courtyard. "And remember who is the true master here."

Chapter Thirty Six

Asenat

ASENAT BROUGHT IMINI WITH HER OFTEN SINCE joining Neferet's ornate. This morning, she made her way down the corridor, holding Imini's hand and fighting a surge of laughter bubbling in her throat.

The child rose early from a sleeping mat in Asenat's inner chamber, declaring she would only appear before the queen dressed as a court lady. The servants spent all morning making a sheath-dress and diadem for Imini to wear. She strutted through the corridors, affecting the pomp of a haughty courtier. Neferet and her girls would enjoy this.

There had been a combined effort to stop Imini from sucking her thumb, but then she developed the habit of picking things up that didn't belong to her. Queen Neferet fashioned her a beautiful paddle doll to keep her occupied. She clutched the doll to her chest and pulled away from Asenat's grip to run down the corridor to Neferet's chamber.

"Imini, you will walk." Asenat covered her snicker at the child's effort to slow her polished little limbs. Hetnu had left Imini to her charge for a few days, and Asenat started her on simple strokes with the reed pen. She was quite brilliant.

Lord Yoseph or Lord Paneah, as he was now to be called, had not summoned her for writing lessons since the insult paid him in the banquet hall. The courtiers had treated him with blatant disrespect. Yet she could not forget that she'd been the first to do so, and the memory sat ill in her stomach.

Time with Imini distracted her from guilt, and she delved deeper into the study of Elohim as the king had ordered her to do, as well as share her findings with his newest queen at the king's command.

Both the sovereign and Neferet seemed to hold some secret affinity for this god whom they claimed married their hearts one night in the desert. Asenat read the accounts written by former scribes and Neferet received them as truth. Her childlike fascination with the so-called deliverance of Abram and Sarai led to unending chatter on Elohim's power and greatness. Preposterous.

She was mocked enough as it was, being an ignorant girl from a tiny province in the delta. Asenat pondered how she might break Neferet's foolish fixation on this Elohim while on her way to attend the young queen. One day, Lord Nebsumenu had caught up with her in the corridor.

"How goes your dealings with the sand dweller?" He smiled handsomely at her. "I hope you will be released from such humiliation soon."

Her lashes fluttered at the scathing comment. Defense rose up in her ka. "Lord Paneah is not what I expected at all. He is an honest and humble man." The treasurer's mouth hardened, but she held to her courage even if her voice quavered at his scowl. "I think he will do the king and the land great good if he does not lose those qualities."

She'd heard that Nebsumenu had taken the vizier to task very roughly. She did not want to believe it of the elegant treasurer. However, there was, at present, something very oily about him that she could not name.

"You say such things because you are young and know no better. But don't allow your heart to be controlled by that Asiatic, and do not give your affection to him."

She pulled away. "Please do not accuse me of carrying on in such a manner. I am a scribe, not a palace slave to be tampered with." She straightened. "You may ask any of the vizier's servants or mine if you wish to know my conduct."

"I already have."

She blinked, keeping her displeasure to herself.

"I will speak to the king, again. This position as scribe to the vizier compromises you greatly."

She held back the protest on her lips as Nebsumenu bowed and strode off. She could have told him that she no longer tutored the vizier, but Nebsumenu was neither her lover nor her keeper, and she owed him no such assurance. Yet his threat to cancel her lessons with Lord Paneah vexed her in a way she could not explain.

After her encounter with the treasurer in the corridor, she'd been careful to bring Imini with her whenever she could. Imini turned the corner to enter Neferet's suite and she'd lost sight of the child. Smiling, she shook her head and checked her fingers for signs of ink-soot that permeated the hands of all scribes when someone clamped a moist palm over her mouth. She kicked and fought the crushing grip on her waist as she was dragged behind a column.

"Quiet girl! You don't want them to find me. That would mean trouble for both of us."

Her abductor released her. She staggered to face him. "Senib. What are you doing here?!"

Senib pressed a fat finger to his lips in a plea for silence. "My lady will excuse my method of getting her attention, but I must beg that you speak to your father for me." He worried his plump hands, rolling them over each other.

"Speak to my father? He would hack you into pieces if he knew you were here."

"Can you not try?" Senib asked, the pitch of his voice climbing another octave. "Might he not forgive me with your intervention?"

"You know as well as I do that my father does not forgive. Besides, the king allows us no contact."

Senib's face pinched. His shoulders slumped. "Then pray I leave the king's house in one piece, for there is a terror far worse than your father who goes by the name of Nakht." He drew his knuckles to his mouth. "He has set his men to watch for me at the palace gates."

"You've brought this on yourself, Senib." She narrowed her gaze, discerning the truth. "It was you who started my troubles, wasn't it? I suppose you approached half of the courtiers in the king's house with information about me until you found one who believed you and offered the right price."

He winced.

"If you hadn't let your greed rule you, neither of us would be stuck here now."

"You are right, my lady." He nodded, squeezing his eyes shut. "And now, I have nothing to show for my ambition." His face was awash with repentance except for his regard sliding to the trapezoid gold and amber pendant she wore. "But perhaps you might, out of the goodness of your heart, show mercy to the downtrodden."

She huffed, crossing her arms, then unhooked her necklace and pulled the rings from her fingers to save him the trouble of begging. Hetnu would be upset to see her without jewelry, but if this was the cost of saving a man's life, then so be it.

"Thank you, my lady." He gave a hundred little bows. "Thank you for your kindness." He dipped again, and his gaze lingered at her ears. She handed over her gold hoop earrings, and he tucked them in a pouch he couldn't possibly see beneath the girth of his middle. Winking his farewell, he tipped quietly down a corridor used by servants.

Asenat continued to Neferet's rooms, unsure whether she had been kind or had given Senib an opportunity to make a bigger fool of himself.

ASENAT COULD NOT TAKE BACK HER HARSH treatment of the vizier, but she vowed to help mold Neferet into a brilliant queen who would win the court's respect. Already, Neferet had memorized the Admonitions of Impuwer and was losing her hideous dialect from the northern swamps. Asenat rounded the corner to enter Neferet's suite. The shrieking she heard from the porch confirmed her plans for writing lessons had been canceled. She entered the wide columned room full of cushions, kittens, and musicians strumming amidst heavy laughter.

Imini had shed her new garment and joined the water play on the porch. Neferet's girls were a swarm of dancing, squealing shadows, darting between the maze of colored panels. Slaves controlled high hanging pots punctured with holes, tugging ropes to change the frequency of the downpour from sprinkles to random, drenching soaks. The girls drew Asenat's laughter, racing between the panels like a pack of clacking geese. They beckoned her to join them, but she gave a quick shake of her head, having no intention of ruining her pleated sheath-dress.

In one corner of the porch, two bodies, soaking wet, emerged from behind one of the sunlit panels. "Asenat," Neferet called, laughing as a young male slave scooped her up. He was drenched and grinning as he bore the weight of Neferet's cumbersome pregnancy with surprising vigor.

Asenat looked again. It was not a slave who carried Neferet, but the king, his face open and untroubled as she'd never seen him before. He lowered Neferet to a couch. Sitting beside her, he kissed her belly and then her lips like a man in love.

"Not now, Khakheperre." She slapped at his hands, barely keeping the laughter from her voice.

A jolt of some emotion shot through Asenat's belly. She'd studied voraciously for recognition at the Iunu temple, for a kind word from her father. And yet Neferet was an unlearned girl adored by a king. The gods were clearly unjust.

The king pecked Neferet on the lips again, before he stood up and motioned to the slaves. Three rushed forward to dry her back and hair, while two more dried and dressed the king. Once again, there was the indisputable health of his body, the work of Paneah's god.

"Stare if you like, girl," Khakheperre said, having caught Asenat's gaze on him. "And be sure to tell your father how well I am faring."

"The good god knows that I have no dealings with his enemy." He would not forgive her for her forwardness in the vizier's chamber. He would not forgive her for being Potipherah's daughter.

"Don't taunt her so, Heperre," Neferet scolded from the couch. "I told you she's a good girl."

"So you say, but then why has the vizier dismissed her from his service if she is such a good girl?"

"I've been dismissed?" The question slipped out before Asenat could stop it.

"I heard he dislikes you." His words cut her to shreds.

"And this came from his own lips? Or from someone else?" She tried to keep her voice from straining. Lord Paneah never indicated as much.

The king whisked by her, without answering.

"Come, Asenat, sit beside me." Neferet patted a place next to her on the couch as he left. "Pay him no mind." Neferet took her hand and squeezed it. "He is frustrated because the vizier speaks well of you, more so than of anyone."

If the vizier spoke well of her, why had he not summoned her for writing lessons?

"You did give him my request, didn't you?" Neferet asked.

"Yes, at the banquet. Then I wrote out your dream and sent it to him." But he hadn't called for her again.

"Then I suppose Lord Paneah is too busy to attend me, but do remind him when you see him again."

Asenat worked up a little smile. How pitiful she must appear for Neferet to offer such comfort.

Imini shrieked in the distance as the girls tickled her.

"My son is laughing too." Neferet grinned, moving Asenat's hand to her belly.

She marveled at the sensation of life stirring beneath her hand and felt a surge of protection at Neferet's warm smile. This gentle girl's kindness coupled with power would make her an effective ruler.

Only two of the girls in Neferet's ornate were of noble families. One had a cleft lip and the other had a small limp, but they were happy here. Neferet even took Deduamen's daughter, A'at, under her wing. She joined them with a blackened eye, rumored to have been struck either by her sister or their father who tried to drag her to a vessel hidden near a small watergate. A'at smiled more often after Hetnu granted her a private set of rooms, though the fascination of twins still demanded a public appearance beside Appipa from time to time. A'at was Neferet's rival, born of far superior blood, yet they were becoming fast friends.

As for Appipa, she strutted around the palace in the pectoral and bracelet she refused to return. The girl used the power of her beauty cheaply. Every woman at court despised her, and the men she drove to madness.

The servants emptied the water pots and wiped the wet stone on Neferet's porch.

"Khakheperre knows how much I like the rain."

Rain was a rare wonder to behold in the land, only seen in the delta, during the winter season.

Neferet smiled, setting her favorite paddle doll in Asenat's lap. Having grown used to Neferet's shy gestures of friendship, Asenat smiled back. She was about to copy the queen's relaxed pose but grabbed Neferet's rash-covered wrists. "Majesty, your hands."

"It's nothing." Neferet sat up. "The palace physicians tell me that I am to keep away from fish and jasmine flowers until the prince is born. And of course, they are my favorite flowers, and fish the food I crave the most."

Imini's voice rang out in song at another request made by Neferet's girls who dried her off on the porch. Asenat set the paddle doll beside her on the couch and leaned back, closing her eyes against Re, sinking over the cliffs. The musicians picked out a tune, and her lips tugged upward at Imini's echoing laughter from the porch.

"Your father, Potipherah, is angry with me."

Asenat peeked at Neferet. "Then we have more in common, than ever before. My congratulations, Majesty."

"It's fine for you. You're his daughter, but I'm the low-born swamp queen."

"Don't call yourself that." Asenat sat up to face her. The courtiers of the king's house were cruel. "You don't need my father's approval or attention. Speak to another great priest."

Neferet shook her head. "Then I will make them all angry. The priests of the great temples are eager for any power my favor might bring them. Me, Asenat, who is the least of queens." She laughed and gave an airy sigh. "Perhaps I was foolish to anger Potipherah. But Heperre took me out into the desert one night to seek the temple of Elohim. There beneath a roof of stars, he made me his wife in truth. I vowed to serve only Elohim, who above all the gods, gave me Heperre to love."

CHAPTER THIRTY SEVEN

POTIPHERAH

THE COVERED LITTER BED SWAYED IN THE shadows of night, and Potipherah rubbed his aching fingers, thinking of how he might punish the little swamp queen Neferet for her disrespect. He was chief of the secrets of heaven and the king's astrologer, yet she dare deny him the right to interpret her dream. Further, that little unlearned thing named queen clung to the sand dweller's god, Elohim.

Every rustic fool within hearing praised the god of the Asiatic to whom no temples were raised. This might give credence to men approaching gods without the aid of priests. There would be no more offerings, no support for the great gods and priests, no control over the people. It was dangerous.

Potipherah's tongueless slave, Khons, slurped his favorite soup as the litter swayed. He set down his bowl and wiped his mouth, ever the attentive companion should the Potipherah choose to voice his thoughts aloud.

The darkness entombed them, and Khons seemed to grow weary. Potipherah motioned for him to rest. He obeyed, curling on his side, and soon released soft snores.

Moonlight filtered through the curtain and rolled over his prone form, reminding Potipherah of what life could become for a man who didn't keep himself sharp in his affairs and one step ahead of doom.

He'd touched on the observation earlier today with Reniqer, who led the broad hall. He and Reniqer were not friends in the truest sense of the word. But both of them had survived two kings, and they'd learned to study the nature of men, sometimes sharing their findings.

"Men come and go in the king's house," Potipherah reflected from the bench overlooking a lake in the central gardens. "But you and I, Reniqer, are more like sturdy foundations upon which newer bricks are set."

Reniqer leaned forward on his staff. "You speak of the new vizier. I think there is more to that brick than what meets the eye."

Potipherah raised his brows at Reniqer's subtle defense of the Asiatic. "Much more, apparently." He inhaled the scent of jasmine flowers, coaxing a tame antelope closer before he threw out a piece of bread for him to chase. "But I doubt the men of the realm will tolerate him."

He refrained from dispatching the Asiatic, enjoying Nebsumenu's irritation with him. The sand dweller was on to that thieving good-for-naught, and for once, Nebsumenu was forced to use his wits. Potipherah chuckled. "And how shall Lord Paneah survive in the king's house with such a terror as yourself, Reniqer?"

Reniqer cast a sidelong glance at him. "So your spies informed you of how rude I was to him. But they could not tell you my thoughts. Lord Paneah, in my humble estimation, is worth ten of the king's best men though I did not let him know it. He's wise enough to tread carefully.

But as soon as he gave me my head, I put that jackal-faced Resnakt back on the hall's morning watch." Reniqer leaned back, huffing. "Let those crooks try to trample through the king's house while I oversee the corridors at night. Nebsumenu can no longer displace my monitoring the corridors though he's minced up to me, offering his usual flattery."

Reniqer's sense of righteous anger on the king's behalf was earnest, but Khakheperre had brought this on himself. For too long he refused to choose a vizier, and where there is treasure, there is stealing, and his coffers were no exception.

"Though you are due this revenge against the watchmen, take care, Reniqer. Perhaps you should place a few guards around you until things settle down." Potipherah refilled their cups from the pitcher of beer set down between them.

"You think Lord Paneah has not assigned them to me? But I'll keep taking orders from him as long as he deals justly, and Nebsumenu has no say on the matter."

"You express great faith in the Asiatic."

"Saw you any pride in him at his induction ceremony?"

"None." Potipherah had tried to ruin the ceremony himself, warning the actress who was to play the goddess not to show up. He was not pleased to find her replaced by his daughter. "The hecklers made fine work of Lord Paneah. By the time I reached him on stage, he was trembling with well-concealed anger."

"Yet he is humble."

"Humility is appropriate for slaves, not viziers."

"It is appropriate for any true servant of a king."

Potipherah chuckled and gripped the rail inside the litter as the bearers took him down an incline. The memory of Reniqer's subtle rebuke stayed with him all day.

Reniqer misunderstood his position. He'd never been a servant of kings. Kings came and went like any other man. He was a servant of the kingdom, and his job was to know things. He knew that the king's new vizier wept and prayed often to his invisible Elohim. But already the men in his office had begun to unravel around him.

This bothersome business of watching Lord Paneah might have been settled had Sabni accepted the offer Potipherah sent to him before the vizier's inauguration. But Sabni was a young man full of subdued passions, and it was only a matter of time before he slipped from his pedestal of composure. The dwarf, Imehy, was settling in with the palace jewelers, and there was always some corruption in that corner. Lord Chu, the vizier's chamberlain, was not a man of sound reputation. A bribe would buy him off easy enough, and perhaps the king knew this when he sent his best scribe, Jafener, to serve Zaphenath Paneah, who would soon unravel himself.

The swaying litter came to a stop, and Potipherah reached over to shake Khons awake. They'd reached the grove, and he dismounted and checked the dagger under his cloak. He took the torch from his light bearer, and on a whim, brought Khons along.

They went deep into groves heavy with fruit, the perfect place for conspiracies and assignations. But he'd ordered them cleared tonight and passed only an occasional totem to Min or Renenutet.

"Now, where is that scoundrel?" Potipherah pressed Khons' shoulder and looked around, raising his torch. A twig snapped, and Khons was snatched away. He cried out, and Potipherah turned to find a dagger pressed to his servant's throat. "Release him at once."

"You said you'd come alone."

"My, but you are jittery, Qareg. Is this the thanks I get for seeing to your escape from prison? I shall know better how to deal with you in the future. Lower your blade from his throat. Lower it, I said!"

Qareg hesitated a moment longer, nicking Khons' neck before shoving him forward. Potipherah caught his servant and drew a cloth from his belt. Khons pressed it to his throat and trembled.

"You go too far. The man has no tongue and is no danger to you."

"You're either his mother or his lover to worry so about a slave." Qareg sneered.

"I value those who prove themselves valuable. You'd do well to remember that if you plan to serve me."

"I serve m'self." Qareg pressed the bloodied dagger tip to his chest.

"Not when I'm doling out the funds for your activities. You'll serve me first or glare at the world from the end of a pike." Potipherah's chest heaved. The moonlight betrayed his concern for his servant and Qareg took note of his tight face before he sheathed his weapon, grinning.

"Just testing you, priest."

"If you continue in this manner, your death is certain. Or you can tame your wild behavior and become rich."

"I'm no scrap beneath your feet. I've killed thirty—"

"I already know how many you've killed. Your record is satisfactory but nothing compared to mine."

"Then why bother with me?"

"My reasons are my own, as is the task, as is the time, all of which I will inform you when I am ready." He tossed a bag of rings, and Qareg's hand whipped up to catch it.

"That should sustain you. Keep your wild machinations sedated with wine and women until you are summoned."

Qareg jammed a few rings on his dirty fingers and tied the pouch to his waist. "It's that Yoseph I want. I want to see the shock in that sand dwellers eyes when I dig out his heart and eat it."

"I suppose one should expect as much from an escaped convict who is at the constant beck of his own temper. But there's the common fish gutting you propose, or the flourished ending that leaves people talking for years. Which do you prefer?"

The challenge brought a flicker of interest to the glazed over look on Qareg's countenance, the kind that would only appeal to a true son of Set. He shifted on his feet.

"I wonder if you're capable of such sophistication and stealth, Qareg. To kill everyone around the intended victim before you strike him, causing his torment to crest toward death." The bait took hold, and Qareg was all but salivating.

"I can do it—kill with the flourish you speak of." Qareg drew his dagger, waving it like a knife at a meal. "Qareg is the greatest killer the world has ever known."

Potipherah smiled. "With my help, you will be the greatest killer the world has yet to know."

CHAPTER THIRTY EIGHT

YOSEPH

THE BACK OF YOSEPH'S NECK STUNG LIKE FIRE as he navigated the wide columns in the king's corridor. The shoulder-length wig covered the scab where Nebsumenu yanked him by the chain and tore off skin. And despite Reniqer's new watch on the corridors around the broad hall, the treasurer had slithered through some new route leading out of the king's house with his booty.

Wearing the seal of a vizier and the king's lapis signet ring had not changed what some of the palace administrators thought of Yoseph. Even the king seemed to shut him out after making him vizier. Breaking into Khakheperre's meeting was a last resort.

Chu had begged to join him. But he had let the confrontation in the treasury hall slip from his mouth. It would have been a mark against him had Jafener not intervened and suggested a document that even the king would not resist. The king's former scribe was of a steadier nature than Chu. The king trusted Jafener, so Yoseph brought him along instead.

Their intrusion into the meeting was almost ruined

when two of the king's war dogs leapt up, snapping their jaws. Yoseph knelt and Brave One recognized him as his old care-giver, giving him a hearty greeting.

Elohim be praised.

"Welcome Lord Paneah." The king beckoned him and Jafener near. His face brightened in pleasant surprise, convincing Yoseph that none of his requests for a meeting had reached the sovereign. His gaze flicked to Nebsumenu who sat beside the king. The treasurer's countenance flashed with alarm at their intrusion.

"I'm glad that you and Nebsumenu have worked out your differences. He's handed me the report with your signature." The king looked between the two of them. "That wasn't so hard, now, was it?"

"Your treasurer is direct. The process was simply done." Yoseph glanced at Nebsumenu's guarded expression as the back of his neck throbbed. "I recommend we report the amount in your coffers more often. Perhaps once each season."

Nebsumenu's lips puckered.

"Good idea, Paneah." The king clapped. "Start at the next Going Forth of Min, then."

"Yes, Majesty. And you will be pleased to know the harvest reports are in." Jafener handed the report to the king as Yoseph continued. Nebsumenu shot him a threatening look. "The yields are lower than I'd hoped, and these amounts listed in the royal granaries cannot be accurate." Yoseph pointed to the number symbols. Those he knew well.

"I can hardly be upset about it, Paneah, when there has been little or no tribute for the past few years," the king said.

"I will look further into the matter, but I also brought a count of your oxen and a tally on the import of precious metals and stones."

The king raised his brows. "Already?" He slapped his treasurer's knee and laughed. "Look now, Nebsumenu, but the vizier seeks to put you out of a job."

Nebsumenu had kept up their private conflict, permitting no one from the vizier's crew to step into the treasury courtyard. Chu claimed to overhear that one or two of the royal treasure rooms were empty. Thus Yoseph kept with the practice of having all imports and tributary gifts stopped and counted before they reached the city, then counted again at the palace quay. He would know the exact amount of tribute brought into the king's house from here on. If Nebsumenu had stolen anything, he would have to correct his tallies, adding back anything he'd stolen.

Yoseph remained very still. Truth was his weapon. And that truth was written in the report handed to the king. The look on Nebsumenu's discomfited countenance was revenge enough for now. The only thing better than exposing a thief was waiting for the right moment to do so. The king enjoyed an accurate report of his holdings. To do more too soon would make Khakheperre fearful.

"It's wonderful." The king shook his head over the tallies of profit and handed it back to Jafener. "Read it aloud."

"I cannot stay to hear it my lord." Nebsumenu placed a cup on a tray. "I have duties in the two houses of gold that I must attend."

"It can wait. I want you to hear it, so there is no dispute between you and Lord Paneah later." Khakheperre motioned, and Jafener read the report aloud. Nebsumenu's nostrils flared above the flat lines of his mouth.

"A good report, Majesty," Nebsumenu said, cutting Jafener off. "But I fear the vizier has exaggerated with such hefty accounts."

"Jafener was one of my own scribes," the king defended. "He is meticulous in his work."

"As is our vizier." Jafener assured the king. "Lord Paneah has also taken care to have copies of each day's harvest brought personally to his office. The king has a great return in his fields with this season's crops of barley and flax, and there is still the count of wheat and emmer to come."

"Let me see that." The king took the report from Jafener, again. He read it in silence. His forehead creased before he looked up again. "All of this?"

"And more, Majesty," Yoseph said. "We are but halfway through your grape orchards, trimming the vines."

The sovereign fell back in his chair. "Nebsumenu estimated the amounts would be far less than this."

"I am glad to find myself incorrect, though the numbers on the report are extraordinary. I can have my men double check them."

"No need to do so, my lord." Jafener smiled. "The vizier's records are accurate."

"Then I am a wealthy man, again."

Yoseph nodded, confirming the king's assessment. He stood. "Jafener and I will leave you to your meeting. I look forward to working with the treasurer on the next report." He bowed and crossed the room, counting his steps before he turned back. "One more thing, Majesty. A small request."

"Yes, Lord Paneah." The king smiled. "I'm inclined to indulge you when you bring me such good news."

"I would like to restore the nursery balcony."

An ivory cup clattered to the floor and a servant rushed with a cloth to dab wine from Nebsumenu's leg. His gaze darted to the king. "The balcony is a just memorial for the king's loved ones."

"It's an eyesore in the king's house that reminds no one of the king's loved ones, but it reminds everyone of the horrible accident." The king seemed to waver. Yoseph pushed on. "Kitjau has assured me he can secure it so that no one will fall from it again."

"Make it so, then." The king nodded. "And come see me, again, Lord Paneah, whenever you wish."

Yoseph bowed and cut a sideways glance at Nebsumenu. The look on his face was one of all-out war.

YOSEPH STROKED THE FALCON WING FAN ON the side of his desk, inwardly licking the wounds to his pride. It had been near a month since he'd met with the sovereign though his last report should have earned him easier entry into the king's presence. The king's steward turned him away at the door. He tried again and again, but the king was busy. The king was resting and not to be disturbed. The king was in conference with his treasurer. Nebsumenu had built a new wall around Khakheperre, this one considerably higher than the last.

Yoseph drew in his wandering concerns though Djehuti, who sat across from him, hardly noticed. He extolled the qualities of his younger sons without so much as taking a breath. Djehuti was sharp in his work, taking on the duties in his cabinet as overseer of cattle, overseer of public works, and overseer of fields until the vacancies could be filled. Yet such diligence would not persuade Yoseph to yield.

"No Djehuti, I cannot offer positions to your younger sons. Not when they have openly insulted me at my inauguration banquet by doing the dog walk beside Prince Ameny."

"It was foolish of them, my lord. But I've heard how you are putting your hands on the necks of these wild young men of the king's house. Surely you can help raise my sons to excellence."

"Your eldest son, Rudi, is singular in his duties as one of my zab officials and his work exemplary. But Za'amun and Meru have joined the wrong crowd of young men."

"I will have them cut off their associations with troublers."

"Then make them also stop torturing their elder brother. Rudi has come to work more than once with bruises. Once with a limp and twice with sprained fingers. Why do you allow them to handle him in such a manner?"

"It is all in good fun, my lord."

"I don't see Rudi having any of that."

"They go back and forth at each other because they are spirited boys." Djehuti shifted on the stool. "Rudi takes no offense."

"But he takes the blows and too many of them."

Djehuti pushed back on the stool and stood. "I think your advice can do me no good since you have neither sons nor brothers."

Yoseph signaled an impatient dismissal. When Djehuti gave a stiff bow and left, Yoseph let out a sharp breath, remembering the quick answer he gave to one of Queen Weret's ladies at the king's garden party. He told them he had no brothers. He told everyone this. It was not a lie.

Rudi's bruises reflected what his life might have been

without his father's protection from the others. Rudi needed protection despite Djehuti's denial of the contention between his sons, and Yoseph stepped around his desk determined to do something for the boy when Hetnu rushed into the room, holding up a hand to forestall him.

"I would speak with you a moment." The cupbearer planted himself on the stool.

Yoseph sat down with a strain of divine patience. Until the vizier's mansion was complete, Hetnu had easy access, bouncing in and out of his office to offer advice and suggestions at any given moment.

"Do you know where your writing tutor is?" he asked too patiently for the question to be well meant.

"I assumed you had Asenat busy elsewhere or that she requested to join Neferet's ornate."

Hetnu tapped his chest with the pommel of his fly whisk, concealing none of his irritation. "Has the girl displeased you?"

"She has not."

"Then why do you assume when you can command?" He raised his arms in a broad gesture. "The king has put the whole palace under your finger. Call for her."

"You are quick to make reference to my power as vizier when it benefits your interest. But at my last mention of Asenat, you nearly rose up on your hind legs." Yoseph had watched the door daily, waiting for Asenat to enter. To think of her in distress while he behaved like a well-mannered slave. He ground his teeth.

"The king informed me that she is no longer in your service because she offends you."

"I said no such thing."

Lady Qatsenut's entrance interrupted their discussion.

She wore a stunning shade of green beneath her beadnet dress of faience and wooden beads. A pair of servant girls followed with two platters of steaming goose legs. It was fast becoming her custom to appear at his door, looking altogether beautiful, at the same time of day he usually had his writing lessons. What an utter fool he'd been.

Hetnu glanced over his shoulder, then back at him. "Perhaps a certain cousin of the king has put a buzz in the sovereign's ear. I trust you'll correct this." He gave a brief nod to Lady Qatsenut, passing her on his way out. She smiled when Yoseph rose to greet her.

"Where shall we lunch today?"

He took her out into the garden. She chattered with beautiful gestures, her back to the sun's warmth.

Duaf came out to taste his food, and Qatsenut pecked at her platter while a sick heat stirred in his gut. "I've been told the king has heard of my displeasure with Lady Asenat."

Qatsenut batted her eyes and took a sip of pekha while chewing just a fraction slower. She studied her platter. "You were too busy to dismiss her. I took it upon myself to help you."

"You have not helped, but you have done my tutor an injury that I must now correct."

She gave a pretty pout, running a manicured nail down the scar on his forearm. "But you do not need the girl, with so many expert scribes around you."

"The lady Asenat is herself an expert scribe." Yoseph forced himself to remain pleasant. Qatsenut was as cunning as his own mother, Rachel, had been and almost as beautiful. "Please do not take it upon yourself to ever speak for me, especially to a king."

She would not meet his gaze but speared a piece of meat on a metal prong. "So be it."

He rose without touching his food and bowed to her.

"Where are you going?"

"Please stay for as long as you like Lady Qatsenut. Enjoy the sumptuous meal you have brought. But I must leave as I am quite late for my writing lessons."

RENIQER'S RESTORED CONTROL OF THE NIGHT-watch around the broad hall cut off the route for thieves, and Kitjau's repair of the faulty nursery balcony afforded quite a view of the palace grounds. No wonder Nebsumenu had the balcony closed.

Yoseph stood on the high overlook, tapping his fingers, counting the sacks unloaded at the treasury gate below him. He had a scribe write down the numbers he gave. For more than ten days, there was no suspicious activity, and he handed off the watch to a scribe and a guard to keep an eye on the treasury courtyard. He was almost disappointed at the lack of activity, until the day he took note of a bedraggled worker hauling dirt.

At first, there seemed nothing suspicious about the man carting rocks and dirt through the alleyways of clustered buildings. He stopped to rest, but his gestures held a ghost of familiarity. When he gave a furtive glance at the balcony, Yoseph met his gaze and broke into a slow smile.

It was neither worker nor slave who carted dirt to the treasury courtyard. It was Nebsumenu. He'd donned a disguise to return his plunder to the king's house. So he aimed to match the king's report, after all.

Good.

But Yoseph would not make repentance so easy for the king's treasurer. He found the ancient watergate Nebsumenu used to sneak his loot back into the king's house and sealed it up. The treasurer's disguised meandering through the palace alleyways and servant roads suddenly ceased.

WHILE YOSEPH WAITED FOR THE KING TO answer his request for a meeting, renovations of the vizier's mansion were complete, and it was time to move in. The days had grown cooler since the Going Forth of Wadjet, and Yoseph held interviews for the open positions in his cabinet in the formal gardens of the estate. Braziers blazed against a mild winter breeze, providing just enough heat for Mepi who sat wrapped in a cloak and pelts among the interviewers. Two of the applicants were princes whom Yoseph had seen with Prince Ameny, but Mepi told him their way had been hard in life.

Neheri, a dark-skinned youth of about fifteen, displayed a suitable humility and answered the interview questions trembling. Yoseph nodded to have him accepted. But at the prince in the red and white choker coming to stand beside Neheri, Yoseph drew the line.

"First, you are late." Yoseph interrupted the scribe's question to the boy. "And what is this coming to an interview with such an ill-fitting kilt?"

Dagi shot a glance at Mepi, who began to speak up for him, but Yoseph shook his head, signaling this one was not to be considered. Dagi left the line, heading back to the main gate.

Yoseph followed, keeping stride. "Why did you even bother to show yourself here? Did you think I would forget your disrespect?"

Dagi marched just ahead of him. "I came because Mepi asked it of me," he said without turning, "Not for you. I'll not darken your door again."

"See that you don't, for I promise you will regret it."

Dagi walked past the entrance gate of the mansion and turned, signing Yoseph a gesture so crude that the guards begged to go after him.

"No. Let him be." Yoseph headed back to the garden. The boy was like a grain of sand in the eye.

That was one problem out of the way. The day was busy enough with the last of the furnishings being brought into the mansion. Fine woven rugs, chests and chairs, trays and sleeping couches with all manner of vases and works of art. Painters touched up murals, adding patterns to the floors where Yoseph would henceforth reside. Each of the fifty rooms would house some of his staff and visiting ambassadors.

With security set in place, Sabni took it upon himself to direct the moving of furnishings into the mansion. Yoseph was very fond of his great one of tens, but decided to keep the news of his confrontation with Nebsumenu from Sabni a little longer. Besides, the day held enough work for them all.

Djehuti would hear no correction on his younger sons, yet he volunteered to sit as a judge for the candidates, as did the renowned and sour-faced Reniqer to Yoseph's surprise. Hetnu could not be avoided for the honor, but neither could he sit still, seeing Sabni direct the placement of furnishings moved into the mansion.

But it was Mepi who encouraged Yoseph to use this opportunity to cleanse the king's house of corruption where he found it. The openings in his cabinet had drawn officials and scribes from almost every corner of the palace. Except for the case of Dagi's appearance, Yoseph stood back and allowed the judges to have their way with the applicants.

Reniqer, the broad hall leader, had even those best fitted for the positions shaking to the core. His intense scourging caused several waiting candidates to quietly depart after three were held for questioning. One was cuffed and escorted to the new prison behind the mansion, and another sent off to retirement to which he gladly fled. Reniqer sliced through the men in the heat of righteous anger but was never more outraged than when his no-account son, Ipuur, presented himself to be considered for one of the openings.

Ipuur stood clean shaven before the judges but stunk of the river taverns and wept shamelessly at his father's lambasting. Yoseph arched a skeptical brow when Mepi sent a secret finger sign to accept this one without condition. Ipuur was rumored to have a hidden talent well worth his weight in gold.

Seeing no further need to overlook the proceedings, Yoseph started in the direction of his private gardens. The day was a success, and he felt the light of Elohim's favor on their progress. Perhaps he could do this. Perhaps he could be vizier. He had good men around him and looked forward to the king's report at the next Going Forth of Min. This time he would be prepared for Nebsumenu's threat.

"Lord Paneah, you have made some mistake." Yoseph slowed his steps while Hetnu caught up to him, catching his breath. "Three of the candidates recommended by Lord Nebsumenu have been dismissed. I assure you that these are your best men for the job. Reniqer and Mepi also recommend them."

"The positions have been filled." Yoseph brooked no

argument, yet Hetnu took umbrage, keeping pace with his stride.

"What do you mean? How can you possibly decide who is acceptable when you exhibit no better sense than to throw yourself into a pit with dirt up to your belly?!"

"That's quite enough, Hetnu."

"You should be ashamed for the trouble you've been causing Lord Nebsumenu. I've heard about it in little snatches of conversation among the courtiers." Hetnu stuck out his chest, lifting his chin. "It is not Ma'at for you to reject the wisdom of men who know better, who have experience. Who are Egyptian."

Yoseph stopped and faced him. "I thank you for your advice in times past, but it is time that you accept that I am vizier, Hetnu, and you are not."

Hetnu reared back, flaring his nostrils. "Then behave yourself in such a manner that befits one." He stomped off in the opposite direction.

Yoseph resumed his walk, shaking off his irritation. There was no use explaining the dream he had about the three candidates. Before he knew Nebsumenu had sent them, he knew they could not be trusted. And here was Hetnu, hot on his heels, insisting he take orders, yet at the same time conduct himself like a vizier.

He'd promised himself to visit Queen Neferet who'd asked for him, but first he would stop in his private gardens to clear his head. Qatsenut had not forgiven him for failing to slip out with her to tour his new pleasure barge. She sat quiet in his private garden for some time, then left early. But he suspected the lady's true source of irritation was his renewed writing lessons with Asenat.

He owed the girl something more for his neglect of her

care. Thus, hearing of Hetnu's determination to keep her away from Mepi, he arranged his next lesson at the same time Mepi came by for a visit.

"My Ibis." She had run for Mepi's arms, almost knocking him over. The strained joy in her tight face was enough to think the girl miserable all her life. Her joy struck something within Yoseph. He left Jafener to serve them in his office and made himself busy elsewhere. When he returned, Mepi was alone, greeting him from a chair with a warm cup of cinnamon milk.

"Asenat introduced herself to me as a Lady Benu when we first met." Mepi chuckled. "A romanticized name that drew too much attention. But I already knew she was Potipherah's daughter." He placed the cup on the tray beside him. "I took the poor thing in. She is more fragile than you know." Yoseph took a seat on a low stool, patting the old father's hand. Mepi covered his. "I thank you for allowing her to see me again."

"You have both rendered me great service."

Mepi looked over him with sharp assessment. "Could you come to care for her?"

The question caught Yoseph off guard. He could not answer.

"If you cannot, then find someone to unlock her heart, so she is not destroyed by her own misery. Do it for an old man. For I love her."

Yoseph thought of Mepi's plea and hung back at the wall separating his private garden from the formal grounds. Asenat and Jafener sat on cushions at a low table, surrounded by torchlights and braziers, reviewing the dictations of palace scribes applying for positions within his cabinet.

"Mepi would never put up with some of these dictations." Asenat shook her head. "Look how the writing becomes sloppy near the end of the document."

"You've worked with Mepi in the scroll room?" Jafener seemed genuinely impressed.

"Yes, beside him, along with some of the best scribes in the palace."

Asenat's voice held it's usual arrogance. Yoseph moved down the wall to hear Imini's song piercing the evening air.

Asenat held the child in her lap and bent to accept a dried wreath of flowers Imini placed on her head. She drew her thumb to her mouth, correcting the action when Asenat flashed her a look. A smile tugged at Yoseph's lips. Her eyes spoke for her more than she knew. "Lady Benu," he whispered the name.

He remembered her scornful glare from the rooftop the night they brought him into the palace courtyard. Uneasiness lurked in her gaze at his offered apology for the misunderstanding caused by Qatsenut, but she would not have it. Instead, she got straight to their lessons working his fingers till they cramped.

He gave a low chuckle and leaned against the wall as she rocked Imini to sleep. She was so relaxed, so animated with Jafener. She was never so with him, always using her conceit like a shield. He shut his eyes, enjoying her rich, hearty laughter and the cadence of her voice. She was a handsome girl and an oddity. When her chatter abruptly ceased, Yoseph opened his eyes. Jafener was leaning in closer than was appropriate. She stiffened, holding Imini up between them. Yoseph stepped into the garden. "That will be all, Jafener."

They startled, and he came toward them.

"I should finish my writing lessons before the day advances further. You may go."

He rose, giving an awkward bow. "Very well, my lord. I have some documents to organize in your new office, and I'll look for the writ we spoke of."

Yoseph nodded, noting the man's eager offering and quick departure that proved his misconduct.

Asenat looked down at Imini, biting her lip. The songs of praying mantis, owls and frogs permeated the evening air with the gentle crackle of torches lighting the grounds.

Yoseph laid a few cushions closer to the warmth of a fire.

He lifted Imini from Asenat's arms and she passed him a shy glance, her eyes large and luminous in the warmth that passed between them. He allowed himself the pleasure of a small kiss on Imini's head, laid her on the cushions, and covered her with soft pelts. "You'd make a good mother," he said with his back to Asenat.

She didn't answer but fumbled with her reed pens when he sat down beside her. If Jafener's flirting hadn't discomfited her, then his presence had. That pleased him. She was of a stern nature, often biting her forward tongue, but she was an innocent. No one had taught her the alluring arts of a woman, and yet she was so beautiful tonight. He would have a word with Jafener, letting him know the girl was off limits.

"Shall we begin?" she asked, pinching a reed pen between her ink-stained fingers.

He smiled and followed suit. "Certainly. Am I to study words of measurement today or farm animals?" His humorous complaint won some laughter from her, and he basked in the moment of her fleeting approval. He'd dreamed of her when he first came to the king's house. But to tell her this would knot up her face, and she would scowl for the rest of the evening. She had eyes like Leah.

His heart ached.

Footsteps approached from behind as she lay a sheet of papyrus before him.

"Dismiss your tutor, Lord Paneah. I'd like a word with you." Potipherah glared at them from the opening in the garden wall, leaving Yoseph with no doubt from whom Asenat inherited her scowl.

She was like a stone carving when her father came forward to pour himself a cup of watered wine from a pitcher.

Yoseph touched her shoulder. "Go into the house through my office."

She nodded.

He rose with her to place Imini in her arms. Potipherah watched her retreat as he picked over a platter. He pinched a sliver of cheese and beef between his fingers. "How fares she?"

"Very well," Yoseph answered.

Potipherah raked him with a cool glance. "Walk with me."

Yoseph fell into step at the order, tension building between them as they made their way to a corner of the garden thick with trees and bushes. Kitjau created this clandestine spot where voices were easily muffled in the dense flowering hedges and the canopy of a sycamore tree. Yoseph invited the priest to take a seat on one of the stone benches facing each other. Potipherah refused.

"I've come to warn you."

"Of what, my lord?"

"Of me." Potipherah gave a thin smile and sat, then motioned for Yoseph to follow suit.

Yoseph indulged the priest in his game.

"You still take orders well for a former slave. I'm impressed. But I am surprised you do not exploit the pleasures of your good fortune."

"That is not what I have pledged to do."

"Better and greater men than you have done so." He paused. "Though your caution does you credit."

"A slave learns caution if he wishes to survive."

"Then, by all means, continue with diligence." Potipherah puffed out dry laughter.

"Do you plan to murder me, Holy Father?" Yoseph asked, impatient with the priest's toying with him. "I've been told my dwelling is well guarded."

"Is that so?" Potipherah's amused expression chilled Yoseph. He leaned forward, dropping his voice to a harsh whisper. "I know, for a fact, that you had a bowl of warm grain with cinnamon for breakfast and a little honeyed quail stuffed with cucumbers. So don't get high and mighty with me, Yoseph. Your position here is as precarious as the king's. I could destroy you like that." He snapped his blue fingers, and his rings flashed in the torchlight.

"Then what keeps you from destroying me now?"

Potipherah snorted. "Why get my hands dirty with your death. Given time, I'm sure you'll kill yourself with no help from me at all. If not you, then your enemies will do it for me."

"You mean Lord Nebsumenu, I take it."

"You've shown great courage in standing up to him. But he's not your greatest problem.

"Enlighten me, if you will."

"Khakheperre's a coward, even without Nebsumenu's interference."

Yoseph should have argued the point, but he hesitated. He'd told himself that his uncouth visit to the Horus columns had caused him to lose the esteem of the good god. This, with the open slander of Lady Kemsiyet and Lord Nebsumenu's influence was enough to turn the sovereign against him. He'd passed the sovereign in the corridors more than once without Nebsumenu at his side. Khakheperre always kept their discourses short, never giving direct answers, never promising to meet with him, never meeting his gaze.

"Your little fact-finding efforts on the king's coffers are commendable, Paneah. But it will take more than a sheet of numbers to convince a man full of fear to change his ways. Khakheperre is like a rat in a corner. It does not matter that you are on his side. He will turn on you because he's afraid. You'd be wise to save yourself. Yet, if you find yourself poisoned, I wish you to know that it was none of my doing. Blame Nebsumenu, or that cheeky Resnakt or Mentuser." Potipherah looked him over. "And if I pass any information to you, you are to understand that I am neither your friend nor your lackey."

"You would receive full credit for your contribution."

"I desire none."

"Then why offer me both your threats and your help?"

"Because I'm making a study of interesting brave fools who have not the good sense to preserve themselves. I plan to add you to my collection." Potipherah stood and walked to the edge of the garden where Yoseph joined him. They walked back up the path.

"You have lucked up on a season of good harvest, but

what of next year or the year after that? Sooner or later your words will fail. Sooner or later, you will be found a liar. You will need me then, Paneah. Then you will beg."

Yoseph prayed for some retort, some surge of confidence to defend himself and Elohim against the priest's words. None came.

"Another thing," Potipherah stopped, pointing a blue finger in his face. "She is not for you."

Yoseph stepped back, his lips tight. "Of whom do you speak?"

"You know well I mean my daughter. And don't bother with petty denials. I've seen you gazing at her with those long looks of yours, and I warn you to remove your eyes before I do it for you."

Yoseph flexed his jaws and continued up the path with Potipherah at his heels.

"And don't think me ignorant of how many times one embraces the goddess Ma'at at an induction ceremony."

"The king dislikes her, and I do all that I can to show her my favor."

"You are showing *me* your favor. That is far more dangerous."

They reached the garden wall separating the grounds. Yoseph faced the priest. "I have tolerated your insult long enough. Good evening to you, Holy Father." Yoseph bowed at the opening in the wall.

Potipherah stepped past him and huffed over his shoulder. "You'll get yourself a new food taster if you know what's best for you."

"A most excellent food taster has already been found for the vizier." Hetnu stepped out from the shadow of the wall. How much of their conversation had he heard?

Potipherah passed him a look over his shoulder. "The very one that should be replaced."

Chapter Thirty Nine

Sabni

SCOUTS WERE SENT BOTH NORTH AND SOUTH of the palace in search of Lord Gebi, who was overseer of the king's lower fields and tributary offerings. He'd not been seen after assisting Lord Paneah with his first report to the king. His assistants were promoted on a temporary basis. His wife was in despair. Sabni feared the worst.

Nonetheless, a final investigation was a good training exercise for the younger officers in the vizier's crew. Rudi, Djehuti's son, was the worthiest of the youths, always aiming to please, offering cheer and a good word to all the men. Ipuur was older than all of them, even Sabni, yet somehow he fit in with the younger ones. His father had cut him off and that, perhaps, the only thing driving him to manhood. Neheri, the poverty-stricken prince Paneah had taken in, would be less trouble separated from his cohort Dagi. Yet that troubler had also found work in the king's kennels.

Training these was more like sitting with babes, and Sabni felt put off, sensing some unnamed conflict with Lord Nebsumenu that Paneah skirted around. But these great men were bound to clash sooner or later. Sabni shook off his irritation at the useless errands Paneah sent him on. He was new at being vizier, and he would be a great one.

Sabni and his charges set out for the southern end of the palace grounds as the light of Re sank in the west. Lord Reniqer sometimes took an overnight room there, instead of traveling to his estate.

Rudi was downcast at his brothers' harassment. Sabni slapped him on the shoulder. "Stick with me. Your brothers are just jealous because you've moved into the vizier's mansion." Rudi tried to smile through the shiner of an eye they'd laid to him. But he was too tenderhearted for his own good, and Lord Paneah moved him to the vizier's mansion to protect him from his brothers' harassment. "I'll teach you a few tricks, and you'll fell your brothers with a proper blow. They'll starch your linen for a month." Sabni forced a smile through gritted teeth. He would correct Rudi's younger brothers himself. Djehuti made too many excuses for them.

Sabni hung back with Rudi and Neheri, letting Ipuur take the lead. He was eager to impress his father, Reniqer, and eager to make amends for being known as one of the famed drunks of the city. Reniqer sat on a bench outside his room, catching the evening breeze with a paddle fan. He lowered it at the sight of his son approaching.

"Greetings, Lord Reniqer." Ipuur flourished a perfect bow. "I am here on the vizier's behalf. Lord Paneah has concerns for you that he wishes to address."

Reniqer looked past his son, lifting his chin and smiling. "Ah, Sabni. There you are and who are these stalwart young men beside you? Such fine examples, not bent on destruction as some others who are born to privilege."

Sabni stepped past Ipuur, casting him a sympathetic look as he cleared his throat. "Yes, Lord Reniqer. Lord Paneah has entrusted this investigation to Ipuur. We are here to aid him." It wasn't the exact truth, but Ipuur's posture straightened at the mention of his importance.

"Why Sabni, I hear your words. But I see none other than you and the two respectable young men you have brought."

"But, Father," Ipuur whined. "I'm now in the service of the vizier."

"What's that noise?" Reniqer put a hand to his ear. "Do you hear utterance, Lord Sabni? I feel the hot breath of one who is as destructive as the east wind."

"But Father."

"Do inform the vizier that he has made a terrible mistake in bringing such turmoil to his ranks. I advise he follow my example and remove the troubling wind before it brings destruction as it is accustomed to do."

"The vizier wishes to know if you've had any word of Gebi," Sabni said. "He also wishes you to accept the guards he sent to protect you."

"I've heard nothing of Gebi's whereabouts and need no such attention as guards."

"If you should change your mind—"

"I will not, neither on this matter nor on other matters." Reniqer cut a glance at his son. "I bid you good day, Lord Sabni. Take the riff-raff with you when you go."

Sabni clapped Ipuur on the shoulder and turned him around. "Don't take it too hard. You'll make your father proud yet."

He sent the young men away for the evening and waited by a persea tree for the palace jewelers to quit their workrooms. There were two or three taller men in the glittering parade of dwarves that passed him, all of them discussing the value of stones. Imehy lagged behind. Sabni waited for the last minute and yanked him into the shadows.

"Where have you been, little traitor? The vizier raised you from the dung heap, and you thank him with your disloyalty. I liked you better when you smelled of sweat and ox dung. Now you do nothing but hobnob with the nobles."

"I'm a noble myself and don the royal skirt just as you. And I'll call to your memory that it was you who suggested I consider jewelry making. I have Lord Paneah's consent."

"I've seen you talking to Lord Resnakt." Sabni pointed an accusing finger. "I sense he and Lord Paneah have had words."

"That's none of my business and probably none of yours if that's what you're thinking. I know nothing of it. "

"What I'm thinking of are the times you've missed tending Lord Paneah's feet. But I suppose connections with the vizier won't impress your new companions in the jewelers' crew."

Imehy raised his chin, "I'm an important man now. I can't always find time for the vizier."

Sabni gave him a sharp smack on the head.

"Ow! What was that for?"

Sabni bowed to the dwarf. "Forgive me O, great exalted shoveler of ox dung. I sought to jog your memory of the vizier's kindness to you and release a little pressure from your swelling head."

Chapter Forty

Yoseph

YOSEPH STUMBLED AT THE PAIN IN HIS FOOT, but he righted himself. Since Imehy had not returned to tend his feet, Sabni insisted wrestling was the next best way to keep them free of cankers and his limbs vigorous. The two of them circled the wrestling mat, hunched in a fighting stance.

When Sabni forced him to the ground in two quick moves, the crowd in the wrestling yard cheered. Yoseph leapt up grinning like a jackal. Asenat glared at him and crossed her arms, her mouth puckering almost to a kiss. Sabni dropped him again.

"Pay attention, my lord. All the ladies are watching, not just one." He winked, pulling Yoseph up from the ground.

The yard was full of courtiers, officials, and slaves who came running to see the vizier make an utter fool of himself. Once again, the wild Asiatic was on display. The guards clustered on the back side of the high treasury wall cackling and gawking while they shouted down mock encouragement. Potipherah had passed Yoseph information on the goings on in the king's coffers, and he gave the treasury guards the show of his life.

Lady Qatsenut kept her face serene at the wild, undignified play, Yoseph would give her credit for that though she was as stiff as starched linen.

"Come now, my lord." Sabni grinned, drawing his attention. "Aggression is bravery. Try again."

Yoseph lunged forward, evading Sabni's grasp once or twice. Sabni pinned him and passed instructions to Rudi as the crowd laughed.

Yoseph worked his way out of a headlock and panted heavily as Prince Ameny pushed to the front of the crowd. Lady Appipa hung on his arm like an ornament. She was rumored to be his new woman. But his gaze lingered on the Asiatic slave girl, Ama, who'd brought Yoseph flowers at the banquet. Yoseph sent her a look of warning. She noticed Ameny watching her and wended her way out of his sight.

"Aren't you taking enough of a beating, Lord Paneah?" Dagi called down from a balcony packed with princes.

"I've not had a proper beating yet," Yoseph answered. "Come down, dear prince, and teach me!"

A unanimous cheer went up from the onlookers as Yoseph braced his palms on his knees, catching his breath with a good-natured grin. Dagi's smile slipped despite the backslaps and encouragement his friends gave him.

"I wouldn't want to be responsible for your death. I hear the Great Prison is no place for a prince, though they've let out the worst of the rabble already."

A wild cheer followed the insult, and more guards gathered on the wall behind the treasury building. Yoseph himself laughed. "I will not trouble the young prince, knowing it takes a man to prove such words."

"Well, if you insist on a beating, my lord vizier, then I'll give you one."

Amidst the clamor was the taking of bets as Dagi pressed through the crush, working his way to the wrestling yard. Ipuur emerged from the crowd first, to whisper in Yoseph's ear.

"All is well, my lord. Your instructions have been carried out."

"You are too presumptuous, Ipuur. The treasury guards are right above our heads. Get back to Chu."

"But your chamberlai—"

"Get back to him now," Yoseph whispered sharply. "And stay beside him until all information is passed to me." Ipuur nodded and hurried off through the crowd again. Sabni raised his brows in question, but Dagi approached. Yoseph bowed to the prince. "Of course, you will allow me to use my own poor native fighting skill against your superior knowledge."

"Do what you can." Dagi rolled his shoulders and took a fighting stance.

Yoseph flipped him, and the crowd gasped. He cupped a hand to his ear. "That last part again, lord prince?"

Dagi got up. "You are a cheat. I will sho—"

Yoseph flipped the prince again. The crowd cheered, but Dagi's hooting companions on the balcony were silent. "Enough, my lord?" Yoseph grinned.

Dagi staggered to his feet, wiping his kilt.

He charged.

Yoseph side-stepped and tripped Dagi who went face down, flailing.

Yoseph found Asenat's tight face and winked at her. She frowned at him and pushed back through the drove.

Dagi rushed him, and he flipped the prince a third time in a move both nimble and waspish. Dagi's red and white choker broke off, saving him from further humiliation.

Yoseph caught his breath. Most of the forty treasury guards crowded the high wall, and he took hope that his men were safe. Prince Neheri came forward to help Dagi retrieve the carnelian and crystal dung beetles littering the wrestling mat. Yoseph wiped the sweat from his brow and tossed the linen towel to a servant. He'd driven his point home with the young prince. The game was over.

CHAPTER FORTY ONE

——◄••►━◄••(▌)••(►━◄••►——

NEBSUMENU

NEBSUMENU STEPPED OFF THE FLOATING
docks where two servants repaired fishing nets while warning
Resnakt's curious boys back. A fine set of hidden water
steps Resnakt kept, with children running and screaming
at games of hoops and sticks. Nebsumenu took the stairs
around the dense sycamore to the garden terrace.

Mentuser's low chuckle carried through the rustling
leaves. "Got your sons to stop playing that dangerous
water game, I see."

"For the most part," Resnakt answered. "But the rascals
find creative ways to defy me. They complain they're bored,
of all things. But I've put my foot down. They'll have to
find other ways to entertain themselves."

Nebsumenu found them in the usual spot. Resnakt
kissed his month old daughter and handed her back to the
nurse who bowed and left the garden. "Don't look now, our
leader approaches. Welcome great Nebsumenu." Resnakt
smiled and raised a cup in salute.

A slave fetched a stool. Nebsumenu grabbed the man by
the shoulder and punched him in the gut. When he doubled

over, Nebsumenu pummeled him until his fist ached. His chest heaved with heavy catches of breath. He shook out his hand as the slave crawled away bleeding. Two more slaves stood far back from him. "Send them away, Resnakt."

Resnakt waved them off, exchanging a troubled look with Mentuser.

"And for Horus sake, take off that earring before I rip it off!"

Resnakt removed the Ma'at charm at Nebsumenu's bark.

Nebsumenu pulled out a handful of notes tucked at his waist, notes from Paneah's messengers, intercepted before they reached the king. "We need to keep the Asiatic away from Khakheperre." He tossed them in the brazier near Resnakt's feet. Sparks of ash shot up from the flames.

"Have no fear Nebsumenu." Resnakt sat forward in his chair. "We still hold the upper hand and the most influence. Prince Khakure is quite taken with my boys. They've become his constant companions."

Nebsumenu filled his jaws with meat, chewing to calm his nerves. "The vizier's rejected our spies from his service."

Resnakt shot to the edge of his chair. "But those men had the best reputations to be found."

"There goes our hope of keeping up with him." Mentuser snorted. "That craven Cushite, Sabni, removed your guards from his door, Nebsumenu." The king's physician reached for his scalpel. "You're too used to getting your own way. You should have taken my advice and fasted a day or two to Sakhmet. The goddess has never let me down."

Nebsumenu shot him a sidelong glance. "You're quite sanctimonious in correcting me on behalf of the goddess. Perhaps she can instruct me then on what to do about the vizier who has found out about the empty rooms in the king's coffers." The smug look fell from Mentuser's countenance.

"What?"

"I've fought to keep up with his tallies and brought some things back to the treasury, as much as I could before he blocked off the old watergate." Nebsumenu looked between them. "You'll have to help me find a way back in with the goods. And you'll both have to contribute," he said. "Just in case."

Mentuser rolled his tongue in his cheek, shaking his head. "May the goddess save us."

Resnakt ran a hand through his cropped curls. "I have six sons to raise and a new daughter. Am I to live on crumbs?"

Mentuser chuffed. "Your position as a broad hall attendant hardly supports your lifestyle."

"I've inherited my wealth."

"And squandered it long ago."

"Stop playing these pious games and just kill the sand dweller, Mentuser," Resnakt pleaded.

"He's too well guarded now."

"Kill the king then." Resnakt sat forward. "You've paid enough homage to the goddess for her to protect you for three lifetimes over."

Mentuser squirmed at the words.

"Oh, come now Mentuser, surely the goddess would overlook one or two small incidents."

Mentuser would not meet his gaze. "You're acquainted with my vows about royal blood, Resnakt. It's not possible."

"Then don't kill, just make it possible for that royal blood to die more easily. You have a skill for death, Mentuser.

Sakhmet loves you. Make an offering to her." Resnakt held Mentuser's gaze when he looked up. He said nothing.

"We'll need to catch the vizier off guard." Nebsumenu looked at Mentuser. "Paneah doesn't fall within your guidelines of being royal blood. You won't break your vow to Sakhmet."

"And what about your bargain with Potipherah?" Mentuser gave his faint morbid smile. "Safer to break a bargain with Set than with the priest."

"Paneah's got to be stopped. I've intercepted his notes to the king. I've tried to poison him. I've set out spies. We've got to keep him from giving the king a quarterly report."

"No one's afraid of you anymore with the god-kissed vizier righting things in the king's house." Mentuser scoffed. "Take Reniqer for example."

"That old leather strap's not afraid of Set himself." Resnakt leaned back in his chair, tugging his woolen cloak tighter.

"We've lost our use of the corridors around the broad hall thanks to Reniqer. We need it back." Nebsumenu was too ashamed to admit how Paneah had picked him out from the balcony while he disguised himself and tended the humiliation of carting treasure back into the king's house. "We've got to slow him down, Mentuser."

Mentuser scraped at a stick with his scalpel. "I'll see what I can do."

"Father! Father! Uncle Ameny has come," one of Resnakt's boys called up from the garden below. A peek over the terrace rail revealed Ameny handing the boys treats before he climbed the stairs to the terrace. Little bells jingled at the hem of his kilt.

Mentuser cut a long look at Resnakt who leaned back, slapping his forehead. "How does he always know when we're here?"

The prince was jovial, greeting them with a bow. "I'm securing a wife that will unite the provinces beneath my rule."

"You said something to that effect the last time we saw you," Nebsumenu mumbled.

"Seems like you can't get hold of Potipherah's girl, after all." Mentuser bent forward over his wood carving again.

"I'd have a better chance at it if Nebsumenu would stop grabbing the girl in the corridors. Save your kisses for your sweet little Satweret, Nebsumenu. Leave Asenat to me."

"I don't think she likes you, Ameny."

"And what does that matter?"

"It matters because you said you want in with us. You said you would prove yourself. But still, you don't have her."

"Yet." Ameny gave a sterile smile. "I don't have her yet. But in the meantime, I've been proving myself in other ways." He dug inside a pouch swinging from his arm and threw its contents on a tray.

Resnakt tipped out of his chair and scooted back. "What in the name of Set is that?!" He sniffed the sharp scent coming from the grey item.

"I believe it's a hand soaked in brine." Mentuser glanced at Ameny and went back to his carving.

"And not just any hand, mind you. It belongs to what's left of Gebi, the overseer of something-or-another, who helped with the Asiatic's first report. I've killed him for you."

Nebsumenu folded his arms at his chest. "I'm flattered."

"Also, I've secured someone near Paneah to serve us."

"Horus help us if you did!" Resnakt snapped, righting his chair. But Nebsumenu sat up with interest.

Ameny pulled out a small piece of potsherd with symbols scratched on it. "It's an inside source so it will cost you. This is the amount he wants. And here is a document of some tallies with the vizier's stamp, so you know I'm not lying to you."

Nebsumenu took the potsherd and read the amount. "By Set!" He shot a look at Ameny and passed the potsherd to Mentuser. "Are you trying to ruin us?"

"Inside sources don't come cheap." Ameny placed the cured hand back in the pouch and tore into a stack of ribs. He wiped his mouth with the back of his hand, chewing. "I'll make it worth your while."

"No more killing," Nebsumenu insisted, hard pressed to admit that Ameny had gotten further along with this business than any of them. "You're too sloppy and bound to throw them on to us."

Ameny chomped on a rib and shrugged. "Fine. No more killing then. I'll prove it's the little things that count."

CHAPTER FORTY TWO

ASENAT

THE GREAT HORUS COLUMNS WERE DISMANTLED within a few weeks' time with the manpower of over four hundred workers. A piece broke off, crashing into the high wall of the king's harem, yet no lives were lost. Artists and scribes swarmed the fragmented sections like bees, copying text and images from the monoliths that were once the beacons of Itjtawy. Their humbled glory was both fascinating and sad, but sandstorms had all but devoured them. It was time for change.

Ambient torchlight glowed beyond the wall of the vizier's mansion where scribes still worked through the night. Imini sat on cushions near Lord Paneah, cradling her paddle doll and singing. Her eyelids grew heavy.

Asenat was irritated with Lord Paneah's poor behavior in the wrestling yard. How could a man be so in command one minute and completely forget his dignity the next? He sat at a table, lost in the text he copied as if he hadn't made a fool of himself in the wrestling yard with Sabni. But who was she to correct a vizier?

Paneah took his writing lessons late tonight. They were

harder to get in now that he'd started the true work of his office. Asenat took his falcon fan and got up from the low table. They were having a warm spell in the weather, and the evenings had grown too pleasant to sit still.

Sparrows darted through the garden, tending their nests and drawing Asenat out to the landing to pick out the voices of workers and scribes beyond the wall. The balmy air wafted with the scent of budding flowers and ripe winter grapes, but still, she was restless. A dismal premonition swelled in her gut. A storm was coming.

Sabni felt it too. It showed in the way he tightened security and worked the vizier hard with a regimen of martial arts, wrestling, and staff fighting. But one could not guard against such inner warnings, only wait for them to manifest.

And wait Asenat did, most days in one of the rooms of the vizier's mansion assigned exclusively to her. It was a pleasant little nook where she kept scrolls and writing supplies until Paneah called for her. She was no longer required to attend Queen Neferet and her ornate of gigglers and there was no more of Neferet's ridiculous obsession with the two Asiatics, Abraham and Sarah, the former Abram and Sarai, who were saved by their great Elohim. Though Asenat missed Neferet and her girls. Yes, she missed them.

Prince Neheri, ofttimes kept her company when he wasn't running errands. A political career in the vizier's crew proved just right for the wayward and impoverished prince after all.

Duaf, the vizier's food taster, was very short with her during Lord Paneah's match in the wrestling yard. She supposed he was as cross as she was over Lord Paneah's poor behavior. After the vizier's wrestling match, Duaf was his attentive and cheery self again, always bringing her favorite snack of cinnamon custard, papyrus crisps and a mug of honeyed beer. Sometimes she sat for hours waiting to attend Paneah with her pens and inks and her Book of Sbayt. She pondered, wrote, and studied. It was bliss.

Remembering the king's order to learn more about Paneah's god, Asenat studied what other scribes wrote of Elohim, this so-called creator god. They agreed he was powerful and again confirmed what both Paneah and Mepi had already told her.

Asenat wrote her own notes on what Paneah told her about his ancestors. How his great-grandfather Abraham believed god for a son well past the years of his seed. How Isaac's wife, Rebecca, came to her husband wearing the beautiful earrings he'd sent with a servant in search of her. Paneah's own father, Jacob, tricked his brother out of his birthright and wrestled with a messenger of god to limp away, blessed.

The stories cycled through her mind, and she wondered at this Elohim said to be almighty, who chastened one king and blessed another. How wonderful it would be if this were all true. She sucked in the fragrant evening breeze, looking over the vizier's garden. The sound of workers ceased in the distance, giving way to the sounds of beetles, owls, and Lord Paneah scratching across a sheet of papyrus with his reed pen.

"Are you done yet?" She leaned forward on the stone balustrade still radiating the day's heat and turned Paneah's fan in the evening breeze. "I remember how the courtiers admired this when I brought it to you on the day of your inauguration."

"I remember too." There was a smile in his voice. "But I don't think it was the fan they were admiring."

Asenat looked over her shoulder. He stole a glance at her, then studied his symbols. She absorbed his compliment in the awkward silence.

Imini had made herself at home in his lap and was now fast asleep. He sometimes called for her, and they took their lessons together. She ran rampant in Paneah's office all evening, but he refused to silence her. He hummed and sang along as Imini danced around him, correcting him harshly if he missed any words. He shifted the sleeping child, reaching for the ink-soot and shot Asenat a grin that sent a flash of heat through her belly.

She'd always feigned indifference to him, but to find solid integrity coupled with such beauty in a man was unnerving. She struggled to keep her head around him just as much as the other women at court though she dare not show it.

He made many changes in the king's house, all of them good. He warned the palace jewelers to take no more bribes. The late-night wrestling matches and cheering from balconies had ceased, giving much relief to servants and older courtiers who longed for sleep. By his authority, palace guards could now apprehend any prince of the blood caught rabble-rousing and dicing in the courtyards at night. Even those in a drunken stupor managed miraculous control of their bawdy midnight songs when it came down to paying heavy fines.

Slaves were assigned to sections of the king's house by colored kilts and beads. Female slaves were safe from molestation and finally afforded the dignity of woven skirts if they wished to have them. None were to be touched against their will nor drawn from their duties without a beating with sticks for the offender.

But the king's brother Ameny could not be corrected. He continued in his drunken midnight songs, slapping slaves and sometimes low officials whenever the mood took him, and once with Lord Paneah watching.

Paneah inched a rolled document from Imini's hand.

"I hope she's not picking up things again," Asenat said, of the papyri sheet rimmed in red ink. "Something important?"

"She's been holding this all night." He tugged it from her grasp, without waking her. "We'll look at it later."

Asenat came inside. "I can check your work tomorrow." She reached for Imini, hating to leave the calm of the moment.

"No, stay a little longer." He called for a servant to take Imini to her bed, then held up his work to blow on it like a proud artist. "There." He placed it on the table and led her back out to the landing, clasping his hands behind his back.

Her whole being resonated as they stood together in the moonlight. She willed him to speak, but he feasted on the silence. A longing lapped through her to be as beautiful as Qatsenut. Then she would know his silence was for her. But she was not Qatsenut and forced herself to look at him.

"Tell me why Kemsiyet is still permitted to speak against your character. If her accusations are false, shouldn't she be silenced?"

He gave a lopsided smile. "One way to catch a blatant liar is to simply let them be. Kemsiyet will only gain sympathy and attention if she is suppressed."

"You are right." The whole palace knew of Kemsiyet's parties and lovers. Even her husband Nebitef kept himself away from her. "But why allow Kemsiyet to stir up such hatred against you?"

She held back her protest when Paneah took her arm, guiding her down the stairs to the garden. He limped more often now that Imehy had stopped tending his feet. He needed to prop them up.

"There will be those that hate me no matter what I do. Kemsiyet's actions will speak for her in the end, and mine will speak for me."

Asenat nodded. "That is worthy, my lord." They strolled past trees lit with sesame oil lamps as she phrased her next question with care. "Do you think all your officers are trustworthy?"

He searched her face. Perhaps she'd been too forward. She, above all, could easily be considered a spy for her father. But one of Paneah's men mentioned there could be a traitor among them.

"I thank you for your concern. If you see anything suspicious, you may come to me at any time."

She exhaled relief that he received her concern well. They continued their stroll down the lamp-lit path.

"Now, I must ask you a question."

"Yes?"

"Has Lord Nebsumenu ever kissed you?"

She stopped and opened her mouth, her explanation halting. "I did nothing to invite such attention." His gaze brushed her lips, and her pulse climbed. "I-it was so quick. The first time I came to tutor you. He greeted me in the hall and before I knew it..."

He touched her elbow. They continued their stroll. "I cannot blame Nebsumenu for wanting to kiss a pretty girl, but I'm afraid that I must now insist you join my cabinet for your protection."

"But, I'm just your writing tutor." He gave her a potent sidelong glance that she couldn't decipher.

"Recently, there were threats made to anyone assisting me. You are a woman, and they may attack you first."

A chill raced through Asenat's veins. So, her father had been busy. He made enemies often enough for someone to attack her without any attachment to the vizier's office. She was acquainted with all the men in Paneah's cabinet and hated to think of them in danger.

"Wouldn't you like to have a shrine built to your god now that he's proved himself?"

He pressed down a smile and pointed to the stars. "Look there, Asenat. If the earth were Elohim's temple, it could not hold him." There was such reverence in his voice.

"You make him sound so powerful."

"I don't hear the farmers complaining. You're always irritated by the mention of my god. I think you are drawn to him more than you know."

"I am not."

"He pursues you." His voice was warm on her ear. "But you don't like being pursued. Do you?"

Her belly fluttered at the huskiness of his mocking tone. He laughed, and she pinched her lips together. It was cruel of him to flirt with her.

"Are you counting when you stand on the wall of the quay or on the balcony overlooking the treasury courtyard?" That cut his laughter short.

"Why do you ask?"

"I've seen the way you touch your thumbs to your fingers. It's a Babylonian counting method using all the finger joints." She smiled with brilliance at the shock on his face.

"Why, you little sneak. You're probably the first to notice."

"Be well behaved then, my lord, and your secret is safe. But should you need a good setting down, I expect you to take correction without complaint." She waved her finger. He laughed.

"You're no better than Imini who took Prince Khakure to task for laughing at one of her dances. She stopped mid-song to smack him in the chest."

Asenat gasped. "She didn't!"

"Yes. And Khakure picked her up to carry her in any direction she pointed for the rest of the day. But she was angry with him and sucked her thumb the whole time."

"After all I have taught her."

"I fear Khakure has fallen madly in love." His chuckle subsided in a cleansing breath. "There are times when a good setting down makes a man feel grounded."

"Like setting a wayward Asiatic in place when he has come to undermine the king's authority?" She meant to poke fun at herself, but the smile fell from his lips.

"Yes." His voice was a bare whisper when he stopped and pulled her toward him. Her heart fluttered.

A shriek erupted from the tall hedges and trees clustered in a corner of the garden wall. They ran back up the path, seeing some movement in the dense shadows. The sound of weeping filled the quiet.

Paneah warned her back and parted the bushes. Then he was still. "Asenat," he called, his voice hard and distressed. "I need you."

She started forward at the strain on his face. He took her wrist, pulling her to the shaking fingers extending past the leaves of the thicket. The girl sobbed as Asenat pulled her out. She was scratched by the hedges, but her face was swollen, and her woven skirt torn.

She shook, squeezing Asenat's fingers, almost breaking them. It was Ama, the Asiatic slave girl who'd brought Paneah flowers in the banquet hall.

"Who's done this to you?" Paneah rasped.

"Don't speak to her that way." Asenat fought to keep from tipping over as the girl clung to her, shaking. "Can't you see what's happened?" She tried to shush Ama's sobs.

"Give her to me!" Paneah demanded, his voice full of anger. Ama shook her head and tried to back away, but he scooped her up in his arms. She flailed, screeching. He spoke in his foreign tongue and pressed his lips to her forehead. She collapsed against him, sobbing afresh as he took her inside.

Asenat followed on his heels. The storm she sensed brewing had arrived.

Chapter Forty Three

SABNI

LORD PANEAH HAD BEEN CALLED A LIAR WHEN he interpreted the king's dream and incompetent when he took on the role of vizier. On both accounts, he proved his critics wrong. Someone had flung a ravaged slave girl over his wall, and Lady Asenat's presence made no difference. Now they were calling him a molester of women. Oh, how Lady Kemsiyet rejoiced.

Imehy had avoided Sabni more than once whenever he thought their paths might cross. He seemed to be forming an alliance with Lord Resnakt. Sabni was hurt by the loss of Imehy's friendship, but every man had to make his own choice.

If El Roi was a just god, he would speak. Yet he was too slow on defending Lord Paneah, and Sabni thought to lend the god his aid, checking first with those who knew the girl Ama's daily routine.

Several messengers and lower scribes trailed behind him as he checked the slave dwellings, questioning anyone who could wash this soil from Paneah's reputation. That most slaves were afraid to speak up had the stink of Ameny written all over it.

Having scoured the palace, Sabni approached the storage buildings that replace the old ones burned in the fire. An unlikely place to look, but he would leave no gaps in his search, even if it meant questioning every occupant of the king's house.

"Ho there!" He stepped into a long rectangular room stacked with chests and fabrics. Either the workers avoided him, or they had gone down to the palace quay to bring in new supplies. Sabni glanced at his men dragging behind him. He'd worn them out over the last few days and directed them to the shade of a tree while he checked the rest of the storerooms one by one. He padded over to the last building, rubbing his tired eyes and yawning. A look inside from the doorway paralyzed him.

"My lord, is all well?'

"Sabni swallowed, unable to answer Prince Neheri who came up behind him. Flies swarmed the man blinking at him from a pool of blood on the floor. Sabni turned in the doorway and grabbed Neheri's shoulder. "Run and fetch the vizier. Bring him here as fast as you can."

CHAPTER FORTY FOUR

YOSEPH

YOSEPH LOWERED HIS VOICE TO A HEATED whisper, glaring at Chu across his desk. "You are keeper of the items with right of entry. So behave like one, and for once, keep what I have entrusted to you!"

"My Lord should not let this slide when the Going Forth of Min is upon us, and the king expects a report on his coffers. My lord should interroga—"

"You will obey me in this and say nothing."

Chu regarded him with a look of pent-up frustration. "Yes, my lord."

His stilted response provoked a stronger reprimand, but Jafener appeared in the doorway, looking between them.

"Forgive my intrusion, Lord Paneah, but Sabni has sent Neheri to fetch you. He bids you come without delay to the storerooms."

Yoseph nodded, passing Chu a look of warning as he stood. He had no room for his chamberlain's high-tempered fits. More and more Chu proved himself incapable of holding information in confidence. More and more he proved wrong for his position. "Come with me. You too, Jafener."

The men flanked him, and his friction with Chu smoldered in the air.

A small crowd formed around the last storeroom at the temple wall. The guard blocking the doorway moved to let them pass. Yoseph entered the room. Potipherah was there, his face hard and full of misery. He knelt by the man on the floor, swathed in bloody cloths.

Reniqer.

Yoseph stumbled.

A guard helped Potipherah get to his feet. "I've just arrived from the temple. You can ask any of the slaves or Sabni."

There was no need to ask. He was still dressed in his ceremonial garb of blue and white linen. A ritual fragrance of some myrrh blend hung heavy in the air, mixing with the scent of blood. His body servant, a man of exotic appearance with straight black hair, wept as he stroked Reniqer's head resting in his lap. Reniqer gave a slow blink and stared at the wall. His chest and arms were as blood-soaked as the rags set out around him to catch the flow.

"Does your servant know Reniqer?" Yoseph asked. Potipherah's face was drawn. For once he looked old and worn.

"Khons knows him by way of the same humiliation wrought upon his flesh. Have no fear Paneah. He will be gentle."

Reniqer gave a gargled cry when Khons removed the bloody rags from his mouth to replace them with clean ones. Someone had taken the time to wreak meticulous agony on this man who was revered among the king's administrators. All of his fingers had been neatly severed. His eyes fluttered, and he groaned as though awakening to the realization of his pain. "The drug his attacker gave him must be wearing off," Potipherah said.

A peal of misery erupted from over Yoseph's left shoulder. Jafener stuffed his fingers in his mouth, attempting to muffle his grief. He backed away. Reniqer had once been his writing master during his years of service in the king's house.

"Take him out," Yoseph said.

Chu nodded, weeping as he led Jafener outside. Yoseph trembled, rubbing his forehead. He should have insisted on Reniqer's compliance instead of letting him rant on how immune he was to assault.

"Blame yourself only a little, Lord Paneah." Potipherah gave a half-smile, searching his face. "I doubt you could have coaxed him to safety with a king's decree. That is just Reniqer's way."

"Call for a physician!" Yoseph barked at one of the guards.

"And who else do you think performed this torture with such precision?" Potipherah shook his head. "He's lost too much blood. He'll be dead within the hour."

"SIT," YOSEPH ORDERED ASENAT AND PRINCE Neheri. The boy had been behaving himself. Yoseph hoped the prince's recent promotion to zab official wasn't a mistake.

"My lord?" Asenat inquired, her forehead drawn in wrinkles.

Yoseph stared at her. "Have you had any secret dealings with your father?" He spoke gravely and sharp. "Any requests from him, meetings, written or hidden messages since you've been in my service?"

Her lashes fluttered. "My lord knows, tha—"

"Answer me, girl!" he snapped. His mouth turned a hard frown.

"No."

He stared at her a moment longer, looking for any physical signs of lying.

"And you, Neheri. You have been a follower of both Ameny and Dagi for some time which is no good reflection on your character."

"I have, my lord." The gangly youth straightened from his slumped position.

"You will follow them no more."

"Prince Ameny has proven to be the worst of troublers, but Dag—"

Yoseph slapped the desk. "I did not ask your opinion! An honorable man has been murdered by someone who hates, not him, but me." He swallowed against the shameful quaver in his voice.

Asenat's eyes widened. "Who, my lord?"

"Lord Reniqer was found with his tongue cut out and all his fingers severed. He did not live long."

Asenat gasped and covered her mouth.

"You will both be under watch until I can get to the bottom of this."

"For suspicion or protection," she croaked.

"Both."

"I cannot help who my father is!" Asenat burst into tears, taking Yoseph off guard. She swiped her eyes until there was no dry place left on her arm. "I have no part in such wickedness." She jerked out the words between gasps, her face an expression of soul-torment. "If I am so easily equated to the level of a convict, I'll leave your service."

"Let me unload your burden further, my lady. There are new holding cells at the back of this mansion. Perhaps you'd like to test their durability." He'd wounded her but remained still at her catches of breath. He had to be hard on her, or the king might bring her into question.

She stretched her long neck streaked with tears. "I never asked to be a part of your cabinet, my lord."

"I never asked to be a part of my cabinet either, but we will each serve it circumspectly. Do I make myself clear?" He did not wait for an answer. He could not look at her. "You are dismissed."

Neheri started to speak, then pressed his lips together. He bowed and left. Asenat glared at him as if he'd grown horns. She rose from her chair and pivoted toward the door. If a guard hadn't been stationed there, she would have slammed it.

Yoseph bit back the outcry in his throat. Reniqer died within the hour just as Potipherah said. A good man had been butchered and murdered, and an innocent slave girl brutally raped. Not because they'd deserved such torture, but because he was vizier. He buried his face in his hands and lost track of time mumbling pleas to God for help.

He looked up when Chu entered the room. The sun had moved lower in the sky.

"My lord," Chu addressed him with alerting formality. "The Lady Appipa wishes to see you." Chu motioned with a look at the door. She was just outside. His raised brows suggested the meeting might bear some fruit.

"Let her come in."

Appipa heard and entered the room, gliding toward Yoseph's desk. A shameless little fox in scant clothing. Someone should take the girl in hand, but she was the king's guest. The only thing more obvious than her beauty was her knowledge of it. Even bowing, she studied her effect on him while giving a demure little smile.

"I've come to make a complaint, my lord."

She had not come to make a complaint. She came to seduce, dressed in a sheath starting at her waist and that gold collar that barely covered her breasts.

"Very well." Yoseph kept his eyes on Appipa's face and laced his fingers together in his lap. He called to Chu leaving his chamber. "Stay and search out the barley report."

Chu nodded and studied a few scrolls. They'd found it this morning, but Chu could search it out again. He would not be left alone with such a girl. He would give her no grounds to accuse him.

"And your complaint is?"

She batted her eyes. "I've made every attempt to speak to the king. I hope you will give him my message since Lord Hetnu will not." She knelt and pressed her thighs against the low table where he sat. He rose to distance himself at the landing overlooking his garden. Across from where he stood, beyond the wall, men repaired the harem walls damaged during the dismantling of the Horus columns. The sight in front of him was far worthier than the sight behind him. This interview was over.

"You are a man most capable, I hear." Appipa came up behind him. "The king has great confidence in you. I am sure you can persuade him."

Her fingers slid over his shoulders. He frowned and turned to capture her wrists. Something whizzed between them. He yanked her down, and a volley of arrows assaulted them.

"Guards!" he shouted covering Appipa as she shrieked

against his neck. There was shouting from within the building. Arrows rained down from one of the outer garden walls, striking the stone landing where they stood.

Sabni barked an order, and five guards ran out to the landing with shields. Even then the belligerent marksmen waited for the last minute to withdraw from the trees housing them in dark safety. Sabni plucked Appipa up from the ground. She screamed well past the moment of danger, clinging to him like a monkey.

Yoseph rose and brushed himself off. "Question the girl when she calms down." He pressed his mouth to a grim line. His enemies would take down anyone in their path to get to him. Perhaps no one near him was safe.

QUEEN NEFERET WIGGLED HER FINGERS, AND Yoseph mounted the platform to her couch. He bowed and touched the back of her hand to his forehead, trying to keep his expression clear of shock. Her hair, once thick with Hathor braids wrapped in gold strands, was now thin enough to see her scalp. She flashed a brilliant smile despite her hollow cheeks, cutting his heart into a million pieces. A slave pushed a stool behind him. He sat.

"I did not know." But he did not want to know. It had been more than ten days since Reniqer's murder. He had stopped watching the treasury courtyard from the balcony. He had stopped checking the tallies at the quay. He had stopped everything.

"None of that, now." She stroked the back of his hand. "You are a busy man." She slid her small hand into his and gave a weak squeeze. "You are doing good work here. They've lied about you, and I believe none of it."

His eyes clouded. She was near death yet sought to hearten him. Ama's assault, Reniqer's murder, the king's refusal to see him. All sat like stones in his gut. Who was he to right the wrongs in a king's house? Who was he to demand justice here? He'd been a slave, and his enemies made him pay for it. They made everyone pay.

She squeezed his fingers, her dark-rimmed gaze seeking his. "You have started something Paneah, something never done here before. But you must finish it. If you do not, Khakheperre's fearful nature will turn and rend you. If you look away, then you are still a slave to your oppressors and to your fears."

He thumbed the signet ring on his hand. She saw through him like one looking through clear water. But he would not speak the dread he feared, that God had brought him here to fail and to die. That this was the punishment for the arrogance of his youth. That same arrogance that made him dare to challenge the watchmen's deeds and caused Reniqer's murder. "The king will not see me."

"Khakheperre avoids you. But it is Ma'at that you cleanse his house, for I fear it will not otherwise be done. He is a good man and has the will for change but not the courage. Leave him to me."

"I will try for you, my queen."

"No." She blinked, and he barely perceived the shake of her head. "No. You will speak truth because I believe it is what you have always done. And though it has cost you greatly, men look for someone to spur them to justice, to stand for it. We all fear its cost. You are not to blame for Reniqer's death, Paneah. He died for the truth he believed."

She closed her eyes as if to reserve strength, this girl, so meek of spirit. He did not know her past, but that she had suffered much to amass such a cache of wisdom within her. No wonder the king loved her so.

They sat silent for some time. And he thought to leave and let her rest, but she stirred and spoke again. "Now tell me. What is the interpretation of the dream I sent you?"

His chest pooled with dread. "I expect the queen has received numerous interpretations already."

"No. Though even the great Potipherah has offered. But the priests would flatter me with false hope and only dare to speak of the strength of the child I carry."

She searched his face and Yoseph worked his jaw, trying to find words.

"I shall not recover, then."

He gave a single nod. He'd blamed God for not showing him Reniqer's death, but God had shown him Neferet's.

"And the child?"

He shook his head, his heart heavy with the truth that her child would die with her.

Tears streamed past her smiling cheeks. "Then Elohim alone is kind. For only he confirms what I already knew and gives me time to make a difference while I can."

There was contentment on her countenance though he'd put off coming to her like a coward who was no better than Qareg. The hard truth had freed her, and he'd kept it from her too long. He pressed his face to the side of her couch and wept.

CHAPTER FORTY FIVE

ASENAT

ASENAT WAS DUE TO MOVE INTO THE VIZIER'S mansion, but after the terrible incident in the garden, Lord Paneah refused to let her come. Instead, he posted guards at the door of her suite and another just inside. She was preparing for bed when one of them informed her Lord Hetnu waited at her door. She came out to greet him, and he placed her between himself and Lord Sabni, then escorted her through the corridors. Both of them were somber and quiet.

She peeked at her fingernails, relieved to find no ink-soot. She hated to admit how the thought of Qatsenut's pretty yellow hennaed nails inspired her to keep her own cleaner. "So where are we going?"

Hetnu did not answer.

"Is Lord Paneah hurt?" She vowed she would not speak of him after his brutish interrogation of Reniqer's murder. The thought that her father might be responsible gave her no rest.

Hetnu shushed her as they passed a few courtiers. After a few moments, he glanced over her. "Qatsenut says I dress you far too well." He did not speak of Lord Paneah, but his casual change of subject signaled no emergency. She could easily agree with Qatsenut. Hetnu's direction had won her a level of respect even without the king's favor. She guessed that the expense for such a lavish wardrobe and collection of jewelry had not come from the king's coffers, but from his.

Hetnu gave her a smug look. "Qatsenut is jealous," he said, almost rejoicing. "You are a lucky girl to have someone look out for you the way I do. Qatsenut fears Lord Paneah will want you, despite all her conniving to get him. But I know a learned girl such as you would not stoop to such depths."

"And you are correct. I have no interest in the vizier."

Sabni gave an incredulous snort at her remark. She sent him a scathing look.

"I'm afraid you must endure the wagging tongues, my dear," Hetnu continued. "Your position has distinguished you, and it is through the vizier that you hold the king's favor. I can tell you that Appipa wishes she had such guidance. The girl is making a fool of herself, but she will have no help from the lowly cupbearer, I tell you that."

Asenat bit her lip. It was true. Appipa was destroying herself with Ameny. "She needs someone to save her, Hetnu."

"Well, it won't be me." He gave a dry chuckle. "I've never seen a better matched couple at court. She and Ameny are like two beautiful snakes ready to devour each other. But even their vanity is nothing compared to that of our vizier. Of all things, flipping a prince of the blood in the dirt."

"I think wrestling shows Lord Paneah vigorous," Sabni defended. "No other officials have gone to such lengths."

"That's because they know they shouldn't."

"And Dagi deserved it," Sabni added.

Hetnu pointed his fly whisk across Asenat's face to Sabni. "That's Prince Dagi to you."

"And that's Lord Sabni to you."

Asenat cleared her throat. Perhaps a change of subject was needed. "I stepped back from the wrestling match, and Yimenet shoved me into the vizier's platter." That seemed to distract them from bickering.

"And where was Duaf?" Hetnu asked, his gaze fixed ahead.

"Caught up in the wrestling match with the rest of the crowd. Yimenet's a sly one, Hetnu. I don't trust her."

"I'll look into it," Sabni said.

"No," Hetnu cut in, "you have enough to do with your investigation on Reniqer's murder. I'll handle this."

"Well, it's about time," Asenat said, exasperated. "I've pointed out Yimenet's actions to you more than once." Hetnu tapped her arm for silence as they drew near Queen Neferet's rooms.

"What you are about to see, you may speak to no one," Hetnu whispered.

Asenat entered the chamber filled with incense. Neferet's girls embraced each other, weeping, as priests chanted incantations. The queen lay on her couch, propped up with cushions. Her complexion wan and yellowish, her belly swollen and tight. She beckoned, and Asenat mounted the stairs. Her knees gave way, and she knelt beside the couch. She grasped Neferet's thin hand.

"Tell me the story again, about Abraham and Sarah, how Elohim kept his promise to them."

Asenat could not speak. Her tears splashed Neferet's hand.

Neferet gave a weak smile, touching her wet cheek with cool fingers. "Khakheperre would let me tell no one." She raised Asenat's hand to her chapped lips and kissed it. "Forgive me."

"I will fetch you the stories from my chamber," Asenat croaked.

"I'll walk her to get it."

The voice behind Asenat was Prince Ameny's. He touched her shoulder.

She stiffened.

"No Ameny," Neferet reached for his hand. "Come sit and read me the poems you've promised." She patted a place on her couch and shot Asenat a look.

Asenat took the hint and left without an escort. Her heart fluttered at the footsteps catching up to hers in the corridor. She exhaled relief that it was not Ameny but Neferet's servant informing her that the queen would call for her later. She entered her rooms, calling for Ama as she worked the knot out of a jasper studded girdle. With Hetnu's permission, she took the girl as her personal slave. Ama had proven more than efficient in her tasks and happy in the refuge of a lady's suite. Asenat entered her inner chamber to find Qatsenut waiting for her. The lady passed her to shut the door behind her.

"We must speak." A frown marred Qatsenut's brow. She put her hands on her hips, facing Asenat. "I want him. And if you keep me from him, it will be the worse for you."

"You mean Lord Paneah?"

"Who else?" Qatsenut moved to Asenat's sleeping couch to sit. A shadow of torment riddled her elegant repose. She was a full cup on the verge of weeping.

"Do you love him?" Asenat asked.

"I love his looks, his body, his power." Qatsenut stared into nothingness. "I must have him. He is beautiful. Unique." She looked up as if just remembering Asenat's presence. "Paneah is a man capable of the deepest devotion. I want his children and a home. You said you didn't want him, but you've kept him from me on purpose. Admit it."

"I most certainly did not. I teach him how to write. That is all."

"I've heard you are now a part of his cabinet."

"And they watch me like hawks because they think me in some conspiracy with my father."

Qatsenut spurted laughter. How relaxed she became, hearing this. Asenat crossed her arms. Without Hetnu and Paneah's protection, this woman would have surely swallowed her up. "You are your own worst enemy, Qatsenut. You know the vizier's dedication, yet you attempt to schedule outings without his consent, as if he should drop the king's business to chad downriver with you."

Qatsenut pushed back the braids of her heavy wig and shrugged. "I'm worth it."

"You miss the point to make a childish one of your own." Asenat came around to stand before her. "You treat the vizier as though he were still a slave to answer to your beck, but his master is the king, not you. Seek consent for his time rather than poking out your lips at his rejection."

Qatsenut pushed off the couch. "I hear there is a position you desire at the temple of Pakhet. The main priestess has heard of you. She is impressed." Qatsenut stroked a small likeness of the goddess Sefchet on the tray near Asenat's writing pallet. "If you will speak often of me to Paneah, then I will speak often of you to the king. Khakheperre doesn't like you, but I can sing your praises to him if you will do the same for me."

It was true that Asenat needed help speeding up her admittance to the temple. Paneah's wild behavior in the wrestling yard might have ruined her chances. But Qatsenut's words were a threat as much as an offer. If she indeed had the king's ear, she could say whatever she pleased. But Asenat wanted out of the king's house.

"Consider it done."

Qatsenut's eyes flashed in condescending amusement at her agreement. She exhaled with a smug little smile. "How silly of me to think you competing for the vizier's attention. You wouldn't know a worthy man if he came up and bit you on the thigh."

CHAPTER FORTY SIX

HETNU

HETNU SCREECHED AT THE TOP OF HIS LUNGS
when Prince Khakure, the co-regent and heir to the throne,
ascended from one of the palace lakes soaking wet. The
prince had slipped his tutors to trudge the depths of the
lake in an overturned skiff with Resnakt's six boys. Hetnu
ran to the scene and struck at Resnakt's darting rascals
with his fly whisk as he called for the guards. He ignored
Khakure's protest. A prince had no business mingling with
such low-borns.

How much more loss of dignity must the king's house
suffer?

Hetnu had the prince escorted back to his tutor, then
motioned to the men following him from a distance to slow
their pace. He used care in sweeping by the ladies Ipwet
and Sahathor. The two old biddies would be sure to slow
him down, and Sabni could be distracted for only so long.

Asenat couldn't have known the weight of her casual
mention of Duaf's attending the vizier's meal in the
wrestling yard. This was a nasty business to tend to, but it

must be done since Khakheperre had placed such trust in his Asiatic vizier.

Hetnu passed the women grinding flour by the wall in the vizier's cooking courtyard. He almost collided with the butchers hauling a skinned cow on poles and slowed to a casual pace. He threw a handful of almonds in his mouth and chattered with a few servants before making his way to the workroom across the road. He stepped inside, and his presence interrupted the heavy chortling going on.

Duaf entertained two companions and was the last to notice him enter. "Lord Hetnu. A pleasant surprise." Duaf invited him closer and shooed away the two men who bowed and left.

Hetnu planted himself on one of the vacant stools, allowing Duaf to fill his cup with his renowned beer brew. "I thought it time to visit my friend." Hetnu sipped from the cup, savoring the spiced doum palm flavor. "A fine blend." He nursed the cup before quaffing it and forestalled a shudder. This was the last of the brew he would ever taste.

"I'm glad you still enjoy it. Even Lord Paneah has asked to taste my secret blend. I am a true expert, my lord."

"Apparently at many things."

Duaf's smile slipped. He tried to refill the cup, but Hetnu covered it with his hand. "On the day the vizier and Lord Sabni were in the wrestling yard, you supervised his mid-day meal, did you not?"

"Yes." Duaf pressed his chin to his neck and locked his hands over his belly. "I take my work as the vizier's food taster as no small task. I remember his meal to be cheese, boiled cucumbers, and guinea fowl."

"And how much of the meal did the vizier eat?"

"Nothing of that meal, my lord."

"One of the king's dogs was found bloated with food spilling from his mouth." He searched Duaf's face, letting the words sink in. Duaf kept his expression clear, his hands still.

"I'm sorry to hear of it."

"And how long have you been royal food taster here, Duaf?"

"Am I being accused of something? I have never nor would ever add a poisonous substance to the vizier's meal."

"That, I believe, is correct and to your credit. Yet Lady Asenat saw you stand away from the vizier's platter during the wrestling match."

"It was an exciting event, my lord."

"Yes, one that gave the perfect opportunity for your subtle neglect in standing guard over the vizier's platter."

"I have a history of loyalty that would argue such accusation."

Hetnu's heart sank at the poor defense. Honest men gave direct denials. Liars toyed with reason. "You stepped away from his platter when you well know it is your solemn duty to protect it. And whoever added the Syrian olives left the cover askew before you could cover the vizier's meal again. I take it you were too nervous to hand the platter off after the failed attempt to poison the vizier. But you are new to such foolishness and thus tossed the plate without thinking to first remove the poisoned olives. I checked with Prince Dagi who sometimes runs the king's dogs. You might bribe the dog trainers, but the boy doesn't lie." Hetnu searched Duaf's expressionless face. "Very sloppy, old friend."

Duaf's countenance caved in, and Hetnu felt a sad relief that there would be no argument on the matter. It had been hard enough to get around Sabni and pay the three off-duty guards. This unofficial arrest was a favor for a good man gone sour, and the less others knew about it, the better.

"You'll be sent to the amethyst mines to work without food until you starve to death."

Duaf's shoulders shook, so that Hetnu thought him laughing until he saw heavy tears spot the royal food taster's kilt. He groaned like a man in pain.

"And what of my son, Cary?" Duaf's voice quavered. "He knew nothing of this."

Hetnu sighed through his nostrils. "I'll see what I can do for him, though he will certainly leave the king's service unless you tell me who paid you to taint yourself for a few trinkets."

Duaf shook his head. "I cannot tell you," he croaked, glancing up with reddened eyes. "They will come after Cary."

"So be it." Hetnu stood. That he should have to treat this man in such a manner after so many years of excellent service. But it was the best he could do. "Come now, Duaf. Redo the kohl at your eyes. I will give you time to recover yourself, and you shall walk out of the courtyard smiling. But three plain-clothed guards will follow you to your barge. You'll be fed sumptuously until you reach the mines."

"It is a great mercy you show me." Duaf choked on the words.

Hetnu left him without a bow or farewell. He hadn't believed Potipherah's warning about the vizier's food taster needing to be replaced. It was hard to accept that Duaf had fallen to such depths. Hetnu crossed the courtyard like

R. RUSHING

a man in a dream to instruct the guards standing across
from Duaf's workroom. Pasting a half smile on his face, he
patted a few children on the head as he left the yard, sick
to his stomach. Duaf would more likely take his own life
once he reached the barge. And that would make all this
mess easier to hide.

Hetnu's eyes blurred for a moment, but for once his
cheeks remained dry at this travesty. He was growing hard
in his old age.

CHAPTER FORTY SEVEN

ASENAT

"MY LADY." AMA ROCKED ASENAT, SHAKING HER awake. "The vizier is at your door. You must get dressed and go with him."

Asenat sat up on her sleeping couch, exhausted. After Neferet's request, she'd spent hours poring over her writings on Paneah's god, but the urgency in Ama's voice chased away her drowsiness.

"What does he want at this time of night?" Asenat dragged herself to the cosmetic table. She filled her mouth with minty water, swished, and spit into a bowl, then wiped her face with a damp linen cloth. Ama helped her into a crisp sheath, kohled her eyes, and set a short, braided wig on her head. The jewelry Asenat left off. Qatsenut bade her to wear little or none to sparkle on her face or throat and draw Paneah's attention. She was angry enough to comply with Qatsenut's silly request since he offered no apology for his harsh interrogation after Reniqer's murder. Other than his writing lessons, they'd said very little to each other.

"Come. We must be quick." Lord Paneah drew her from the doorway. Guards fell into step behind them. The kohl at his eyes was smudged. He wore a fresh kilt, the king's signet ring and his seal of office. But this was the first time he hadn't covered the scars on his feet with anklets or jeweled cuffs.

They passed slaves catching frogs and cleaning cobwebs in the corridors. A few of them lit torches, sending a nod of respect to Lord Paneah. They knew the truth despite the harsh rumors about him. Yet he could not discern the truth about her, that she was Potipherah's daughter but nothing like him. How could he think that she would secretly meet with Potipherah, that she would spy for him?

"We must be strong for her."

She nodded at Paneah's whisper. Her heart flipped when they entered Neferet's suite. The cloud of incense could not cover the scent of death. Neferet's girls consoled each other and kept to a corner of the half-crowded room. Three or four great priests from various temples kept to another, their faces pinched, having been denied their customary chants and spells.

Asenat's father implored the gods Amun and Shu to renew Neferet's vigor, but it was all for show, a waste. The priest of Osiris, swathed in black and green, stood back, holding his staff of spells. He would come forward to conduct the ritual of death when Neferet passed over.

Qatsenut rushed into Lord Paneah's arms with a force that knocked Asenat from his grip. He stumbled back to keep his balance. Funny the king's cousin should cry so now when she ignored Neferet like most of the court. Paneah held Qatsenut with one hand and beckoned to Jafener, who pried the lady off and took her aside. Queen Khnemet was present, bless her, but the god's wife, Weret, was probably somewhere wrapped in her precious amethyst-colored fabric, scheming against any joy she should happen upon.

Paneah took Asenat up the dais to Neferet's couch, where the sovereign groaned over his dying wife.

"Don't leave me, Neferet." Khakheperre wept, pushing back his physician, Mentuser, who tried to pull him away.

Asenat trapped a sob in her throat and knelt beside the queen's couch. Paneah knelt with her. Neferet's belly was distended and tight, her limbs were sticks. Ipuur was present, and Asenat took umbrage that he should hover so near the head of her couch. Was this not Reniqer's wayward son, kneeling closer to Neferet's face than the king himself?

"Speak." Ipuur coaxed Neferet in a soft voice. She met his gaze then looked to the king.

"I knew not Elohim, but among the gods, it was he who regarded me."

Neferet's lips moved, but it was Ipuur who spoke the words, his gaze fixed on her mouth.

"Just as Elohim regarded Paneah and raised him from your prison. Do not forget this." She touched the king's face, and he kissed her hand. "My joy is short-lived but full. Thank you for loving me so well, Heperre."

Asenat swallowed and repented her resentment. Ipuur was indeed worthy of his weight in gold.

"I go to meet the Elohim. He will send a sign to console you, my love."

The king nearly devoured her limp hand in his grief. She motioned to A'at who helped him from a stool and held him as he stumbled down the steps.

Neferet's gaze rolled to Asenat, the light in her eyes dimmed. "You have meant more to me than I could tell you. Like the sister I lost to death but shall soon meet again. Remember what I want in my tomb and chapel. Tell Kitjau." She turned her head away, her eyes half-lidded and empty. Her mouth opened with a faint exhale. Ipuur stared at her parted lips. But they were still.

The mourners began their wails, and a sob rose in Asenat's throat. Someone drew her down the stairs away from Neferet's couch. She broke from their hold and ran to the corridor. The priest of Osiris began his chant of death, and the cries of Neferet's girls rose to a chorus, drowning him out.

Asenat thought herself immune to such grief after her mother's death. But deep sobs welled within her, wrenching her gut. She covered her face, accepting a linen cloth someone pressed to her cheek. Strong arms embraced her.

"There now, poor girl," the voice cooed. "You need to come and rest."

She stumbled through two darkened passageways, full of her grief before realizing Prince Ameny gripped her wrist. He dragged her through the slave corridors. She pulled back. He struck her with the flat of his hand, knocking her wig askew. He was careful not to strike her face. That would not do for an argument of her willingness.

The few slaves they saw either disappeared or averted their gaze. The more she resisted, the more roughly Ameny yanked her. He held her and stopped to catch his breath. "Don't make me beat you girl. I'll do it." He locked his jaws and smeared his arm with blood from his dripping nose.

Someone approached from behind. "My lord, what are you about this time of the morning?" Prince Dagi addressed Ameny as though grappling with a woman in the corridors was a common occurrence.

"Nothing. Mind your business, and remember that I kept you in linen when your funds ran low."

Dagi nodded. He flicked a look at her before he bowed to Ameny and jogged off in the opposite direction.

Ameny yanked her forward again.

She knocked over vases, clawed his arm, grabbed at statues until her grasp slipped, anything to slow him.

He raised a hand to strike her. She cried out, and he covered her mouth, pulling her out to the main corridor toward two guards at a large set of cedar doors painted with hunting scenes.

His dwelling.

She fought him with her lungs burning for air. Sweat rolled off her arms, and his hold slipped. He grabbed her again. She was fast. He was stronger. One of the cedar doors opened. Yimenet stepped out and gasped, then curled her lips in a snarl.

"I thought you abed with that pup Appipa you use to make me jealous. But here I see you've found yourself a new plaything." She tugged Ameny's arm. "You don't need this cold little fish."

Ameny pulled away. "Out of my way Yimenet, or you'll pay for interfering!"

She shoved Asenat in the chest, breaking Ameny's hold.

"You seek to get your hooks into my man!"

"Get out of my way, Yimenet. We'll talk about this later." Ameny tried to weave around her. She shoved Asenat again.

"Ho, there!" The call echoed from the opposite end of the corridor. Sabni jogged toward them, panting almost as hard as Asenat. "Lady Asenat. You seemed to have gotten lost."

She would have leapt into his arms had she the strength, but she could only drag air into her lungs.

"I command you to go. I'm taking her to rest." Ameny grabbed Asenat's wrist. Sabni took the other.

"Her chamber is in the opposite direction, my lord."

"We are closer to mine." Ameny yanked her, but Sabni held firm.

"I'm sorry, my lord, but I must escort the lady to her room by order of the vizier."

Asenat heaved air, slumping with fatigue. She could not stop them from splitting her in two.

"Take her then!" Ameny cursed, shoving her into Sabni's chest.

Yimenet pulled Ameny around to face her. An argument ensued.

Sabni pushed Asenat down the corridor in the opposite direction. "Just breathe. Keep walking."

Asenat staggered, barely making out his voice above her gasps for air. The sound of a striking fist cut off Yimenet's tirade. Asenat looked back as Ameny stepped over Yimenet's sprawled form. He went into his dwelling and slammed the door.

CHAPTER FORTY EIGHT

YOSEPH

YOSEPH MET WITH JAFENER IN ONE OF THE palace gardens for a private discussion. He left, grimacing. The sole of his right foot was tender again. He clamped his jaws wondering whether Imehy had not gotten his summons or had ignored it. Perhaps the dwarf had gone over to Nebsumenu's way of thinking. Or perhaps he'd been poisoned by Kemsiyet's lies. The thought only darkened Yoseph's mood, along with what Jafener said about Chu's private dealings. He did not like what he'd heard.

Sandstorms had blown through in the last few days, and Yoseph lifted his shawl to cover his face. The winds added to the keening of royal mourners who wailed throughout the palace grounds at various intervals of the day. The lament for Queen Neferet forced the king's house to a state of sobriety beyond its usual tolerance, and many courtiers fled to country estates. Khakheperre felt the loss of his beloved wife, and he meant for the world to feel it with him.

Yoseph passed the king's newly rebuilt harem wall with a temporary barrier fixed around its perimeter. No one was

permitted to gaze upon the royal wives and concubines. He
nodded a greeting to the few courtiers who'd ventured out.
One or two returned a curt nod, but he heard the insult
one of them passed under his breath.

"You there. What did you say?" He called the men back
to him. The mocker batted his eyes.

"I-It was nothing, my lord. I mumbled to my companions."
His friends took the cue, nodding vigorously.

"You said something." Yoseph had seen these three
before. Men near his age who diced by the quay wall or
talked near the gate leading out into the city. Permanent
palace dwellers, decked in jewels and looking for ways to
cure boredom. "You called me a name." The wind kicked
up. "What was it?"

"Nothing, my lord. I swear."

Yoseph flattened his mouth. He was full of the baleful
glances and remarks he heard muttered under the breath
when he passed courtiers. They blamed him for Reniqer's
death. They blamed him for Neferet's. And now there
was rumor that the king's health was spiraling downward,
again. They would certainly blame him for that. But who
knew if any of this was true with Khakheperre shut up in
mourning. The king would see no one, least of all him. The
line Yoseph walked grew thinner, and his nerves more raw.

"You will pay me the proper respect, or I will make you
pay it. Do you understand?"

"Yes, my lord," they chimed in unison.

"Off with you." He shooed them away with a gesture
and scoffed at his indulgence of such minute gratification.
The rumors would deepen. The gossip would spread. These
were the king's subjects, living in the palace with nothing
to lose.

He passed the guards at the gatehouse of the vizier's mansion and headed for his personal dwelling. Hetnu corrected him more than once on his habits that were still too much like those of a slave. He couldn't afford the luxuries and blindness of rank. But today, he was exhausted, and because he *was* vizier, he was going to take a nap.

Thoughts of his couch grew more appealing as he drew near his sleeping chamber. Just past his entrance hall, Kitjau shot up from a bench, handing him a cup of watered wine. Yoseph motioned for him to follow. He would let Kitjau chatter while he fell off to sleep.

"I've come to say good-bye. The king has ordered I cease with plans to rebuild the Horus columns and tend to Queen Neferet's burial at She-resy."

"The priests won't like your interference," Yoseph said, then quenched his thirst with the cup Kitjau handed him and placed it on a tray. His body servant approached and removed his jewelry, eye paint, and wig, everything but his seal of office.

Kitjau took a cushioned stool. "Potipherah has already warned anyone from the main provinces not to work on Neferet's tomb. None of the major temples will assist in building her chapel. I am forced to gather all the men and materials myself." He shook his head. "Our little queen's defiance and rejection of the gods has caused quite a stir. I've had to send all the way to her hometown in Pe for artists and priests. They'll be proud to do it though I expect inferior quality from such a backwater little hamlet."

"At least the good god gave you orders." Yoseph exhaled a gust of air. "His Majesty refuses to see me."

"He spends his days grieving and fasting now. He won't even see his watchmen though Mentuser waits by his door praying to Sakhmet. It's the king's refusal to eat that makes his health poor, Paneah, not your god.

Kitjau's offering of assurance gave him little comfort. "Nebsumenu and Resnakt have taken a trip downriver." They could avoid the quarterly report altogether with the king in mourning. The weight of failure pulled at Yoseph's pride. They'd beaten him.

"The treasurer's gone, is he?"

Kitjau's tone drew Yoseph's attention. "Whatever you're thinking, forget it, Kitjau." Yoseph had been as slick with the truth as the liars were with lies, and it seemed to have gotten him nowhere. "I've degraded myself enough at the Horus columns and in the wrestling yard."

"In both instances, you accomplished what no one else had done."

"And gained nothing for the fool I made of myself. Oh, the looks I've gotten from Hetnu." Yoseph traded his starched kilt for a thin sleeping shift. How could he stop the thieving in a king's house when the king listened to no one but the thieves themselves? He dismissed the servant and drew his balcony curtain halfway closed.

"And how else would you have discovered if Potipherah's words were true about the empty room in the king's coffers? Your little tussle in the wrestling yard was the only thing that drew out the treasury guards from their posts."

"I might have gotten my men killed had they been discovered."

"You put yourself and your reputation at risk for the sake of justice. Your men follow because they believe you stand for truth."

Yoseph rubbed the lines on his forehead. Neferet had warned him that he was still a slave if he turned away from the truth. Yet standing for truth promised no favorable outcome. Reniqer's murder was proof of that.

Kitjau sprang from the stool and approached him. "What is this you wear on your chest, Paneah?"

"You know well it's my seal of office." Yoseph took the seal pendant from Kitjau's grasp. "I wear it at all times to remind myself that I am no more a slave, but vizier."

"Then stop thinking like a slave, my lord, and remind the rest of us."

YOSEPH SENT WORD FOR ASENAT AND PRINCE Neheri to keep to their rooms. He called for the rest of his men, fed them sumptuously, and took them for a walk in the vicinity of the treasury walls.

His men followed him past the temporary barrier at the harem wall. Kitjau grinned down from a scaffold as his men began untying the planks in sections. When Yoseph sent the signal, they would have to move fast.

Nebsumenu had left no instructions, and because Kitjau was always hammering at some structure in the king's house, the guards paid no heed to the workers digging out grooves around the treasury walls.

Yoseph and his men approached the treasury gates from one side. Sabni came from the opposite direction. Forty beefy guards trailed him, armed with adzes and cudgels.

The two groups filed into the courtyard following Yoseph into the treasury hall with his seal of office swinging at his chest. Ibiau, the hall's attendant, shot up from his stool, swiping some creamy sauce from his lips. "What is the meaning of this? The master is not within and you—you cannot enter. Guards!"

The silver doors on each side of the podium burst open, and more guards shot out with their spears aimed. But at sight of the forty bearing emblems of the vizier on their armbands, the treasury guards lowered their weapons. Sabni pressed to the front of the group, his black arms akimbo in a posture that begged the guards of the treasury to try him.

None moved.

Chu stepped up to Ibiau's podium and snapped open the red-rimmed document. "The king is master here you fat char—"

"Chu!" Yoseph barked. "Do not forget yourself!"

Ibiau's eyes widened on the order. His nostrils flared as he blustered in search of coherent words. "How dare you!"

"It is a Writ of Amun's Entry," Chu said. "You cannot gainsay it."

"From whence did you excavate this relic, this piece of..." Ibiau slapped the document. "Such a thing!"

"Should never have been necessary." Yoseph drew the attention of the attendant who helped Nebsumenu humiliate him during his last visit. "The king has put me over his entire house, and the two houses of gold are *in* his house. You are dismissed."

Ibiau gripped the podium, but Sabni yanked him down by the scruff of his meaty neck and dragged him to the gates. The fiercest stinger was gone. The treasury guards and scribes filed out without further protest.

Yoseph allowed himself no time to bask in the small victory. He took his men back to the treasury courtyard, informing them that they were camping out. Servants with supplies and tents and cooks with sacks of food flooded the gates past Sabni's men, who trotted back out of the courtyard. Sabni patted Yoseph on the shoulder, pulling up the rear. "Aggression is bravery."

Yoseph nodded. He could well use the encouragement. He sent the signal to Kitjau, and there was a sudden burst of shouting, commands, and pounding hammers as the workers moved the barrier surrounding the harem to the grooves they'd dug out around the treasury walls. Kitjau bellowed from the heights, bolstering his workers to a furious pace. They secured the blockade, while Sabni's men took position around the treasury walls. No one would leave the king's treasure house. No one would enter.

Yoseph exhaled an uneven breath. This takeover could lead to a battle on the palace grounds, even with Nebsumenu gone. He turned at the tap on his shoulder.

"Asenat. What are you doing here? I sent you orders to stay in your rooms, today."

"I left my dwelling at sunrise to visit the temple and never received the order, my lord. I was on my way back to my dwelling."

Her eyes were as wide now as they were when he'd first seen her on a palace rooftop. But she had the good sense to take an escorting guard who waited at the treasury gate, and there was no lie in her countenance.

"You told me I could speak to you at any time if I had concerns about your men, and I could not rest." She leaned toward him and bit her lip, her gaze shifting from side to side. "I passed Chu a few days ago in some heated whisper with Ibiau, the treasury attendant. I thought you should know."

She straightened, losing her timidity at the chaos around her. "I was not told you were seizing the king's treasury today."

He should be angry with her, but he fought down a smile at her light sarcasm. Pulling her to the side, they cleared the path for a group of slaves passing them to pile cooking wood against the inner courtyard wall. "I told no one I would do this." He turned her to face him. "I think you should stay now."

"I can take care of myself."

"Yes." He clutched her arm. "And thanks to Sabni's interference you missed the chance to prove it when Ameny insisted you grieve in his rooms." Yoseph glanced at the treasury gate. Asenat's escorting guard would have no power to refuse Prince Ameny if Asenat encountered him on the way back to her dwelling.

The workers secured the last of the planks in front of the gates. Jafener pressed by just in time, huffing with exhaustion.

"My lord!" He jogged toward Yoseph. "What is this?"

"A surprise inspection of the king's coffers. You've made it just in time."

Jafener shook his head, trying to catch his breath. "This is a great risk we take."

Yoseph patted his shoulder. "But I have the best of the king's house beside me." He looked at Asenat. "And I trust there'll be no argument from you for a change." He left her with Jafener giving her no time to answer.

"Gate is shutting now!" Sabni shouted from the other side of the barrier.

Yoseph surveyed the servants setting up camp and the bewildered looks on the faces of his men in the courtyard. If God was not with them, this could mean death.

Chapter Forty Nine

Nebsumenu

NEBSUMENU AND RESNAKT STRETCHED OUT under one of the canopies on the deck of his pleasure barge. The vessel chonted back upriver. Now that Reniqer was out of the way, Resnakt took on the role as the new leader of the broad hall. They'd set out on a hunting trip to celebrate his appointment, and made a sport of collecting desert hares and fox tails for his boys. Nebsumenu stuffed the last cheese-filled date in his mouth, and let Resnakt wear his Ma'at trinket without complaint. They had the upper hand now. Their troubles with Lord Paneah were over.

His grand attempts to finish Paneah off with a poisoned meal and a surprise attack on his dwelling had both failed. But he'd learned that the murder of a man's reputation was sufficient to set things in motion. Kemsiyet's mouth alone deserved half the credit for destroying Paneah's popularity. Ameny flipped the ravished slave girl over the wall of the vizier's estate with a flourish that proved, indeed, the little things did count.

Nebsumenu took a deep breath, refreshed by their two

week outing though it would have to be cut short. "One more day," he said aloud to a half-dozing Resnakt. "Then we'll head back upriver to cry over our little dead marsh queen." The news had traveled downriver faster than his pleasure barge could escape it. But it couldn't have been timed better, along with Reniqer's tragic demise that fascinated the court and paralyzed Paneah. Khakheperre, mawkish babe that he was, would mourn his wife's death forever. The Going Forth of Min had come and gone, the treasury report due him was forgotten. They'd have plenty of time to refill the king's coffers. The whole thing, a flawless execution.

"My lord, I'm sorry to disturb you."

Nebsumenu peeked through one eye at his barge captain. "What is it?"

"There's a small vessel trying to wave us down."

"Run him over," Resnakt slurred, reaching for a wine jug.

Nebsumenu motioned for the barge captain to help him up. He went to the side of the ship, rubbing sleep from his eyes. He called down to the small reed skiff bobbing near his barge. "Out of the way, you fool. Or I'll turn you into croc fodder!"

"It's me. Mentuser!"

Nebsumenu squinted. Resnakt staggered over to the side of the vessel.

"Gods, it is Mentuser!" He cupped his hands to his mouth. "Mentuser. You had us fooled!" He broke into laughter, slapping the rail.

Foreboding churned in Nebsumenu's gut. Mentuser was not one for jokes. He came aboard dressed in the rags of a peasant. The grave look on his face could mean no good thing.

"Order your captain upriver to the nearest town. We need to change to a smaller vessel."

"What's happened?" Resnakt asked.

"Do as I say. And both of you trade clothes with the rowers. Take off your wigs and jewelry. We'll put in at a river tavern. I'll give you the details when we get there. Not before."

NEBSUMENU SAT AT THE LOW TABLE IN THE ramshackle tavern, pulling his mug of beer to his chest. His jaw locked at the urgency in Mentuser's expression. He was rarely an expressive man. "So, what has the Asiatic done?"

"That wild dog has holed himself up in the two houses of gold and set up barricades. No one may enter or leave."

There was a space of silence before Nebsumenu could wrap his mind around Mentuser's words. "What?"

"He used some ancient writ to justify his access to the treasury." Mentuser rubbed the back of his neck, blowing wind from his cheeks.

"Ibiau will challenge him." Nebsumenu raised his chin.

"Ibiau was kicked out along with all the other attendants and guards."

"But, the king must kno—"

"He's in mourning for his dead wife, remember? He won't be seen. Not even by me." Mentuser was a shrewd thinker, but the glare in his eyes told Nebsumenu their troubles were real.

Resnakt tilted the lopsided table, reaching for his mug of beer. He looked as clever as a cow with his mouth open in dumb shock.

Nebsumenu took a pull from his mug. His chest heaved.

"If you hadn't botched your dealings with Reniqer, Mentuser. If you had just killed him straight out."

"A servant of Sakhmet does not murder." Mentuser corrected. "I simply cleared his road to death. He might have been royal blood."

Nebsumenu banged the table. "The whole world might be royal blood!"

"Mentuser doesn't work like that. He can't break his vows to the goddess," Resnakt defended.

"Shut up, Resnakt," Mentuser hissed. "If you controlled your sons better, Ameny might have never found us near your secret water steps in the first place. And you, Nebsumenu, making a pact with the prince while trying to stake personal claim on the high priest's daughter yourself. Your charm does us all more harm than good."

"Then I'll go fix it all now. And while you're both blaming me, I'll cut up that sand dweller and fill up the king's coffers." Nebsumenu motioned to rise from the table. Mentuser pulled him back down.

"Get a hold of yourself. If Paneah has what he seeks, there's nothing you can do about it. Remember what you said. Stealing requires cool nerves."

"Well, I want out." Resnakt shook on the verge of hysterics.

Mentuser glared at him, fingering his scalpel at the edge of the table. "I can offer you the quick way out if you want it. Otherwise, keep up that famous grin of yours, and keep your composure."

Nebsumenu met Mentuser's hard glare. His pulse raced. They'd made a pact, all or nothing.

"And where is Ameny in all of this?" Resnakt crossed his arms.

"He's one of the few Khakheperre will see." Mentuser looked between them "We need him. Now more than ever."

Resnakt nodded vigorously. "Yes. He's probably working in our favor."

"He'd better be." Nebsumenu raised his mug. "Though your sons would have been a better influence if Hetnu hadn't kicked them out of the palace for that stupid game we warned you about. Nearly drowned the king's heir."

Mentuser plucked a broken stick from the dirt floor. "One thing's for sure. Ameny will put in a good word for himself if not for us. Amun is foremost."

"We'll wait this out. There's been more unrest in the palace than ever before with the Asiatic in place. He's done himself in by seizing the treasury with the king in mourning." Nebsumenu drank with his companions in silence, waiting for some sense of assurance to overtake him. Mentuser looked across the room and broke into a slow smile. Nebsumenu turned to follow his gaze.

"What is it?"

"A gift from the god Set, himself," Mentuser mumbled, watching the two young men walk into the tavern and sit at the table next to theirs, separated only by a few tall potted plants.

"Isn't that one of the princes assigned to the vizier's cabinet?" Resnakt pointed at the two youths. Mentuser pushed his hand down, shushing him.

Dagi helped Neheri lower himself to the table. "You're drunk. What are you doing this far away from the king's house? Does Lord Paneah know?"

"I don't care if he does. I've missed my friends." Neheri swayed, his lips poked out in an exaggerated pout.

"We're better off without the kind of friends we've had. You'd best stay on the vizier's good side."

"He's ordered me to keep to my room, like a child. And I don't like the way he's treated you. If he knew how you were trying to support your mother and sister at court. I'll tell him I was the one who pissed his head. He'll take you in then."

"Don't worry about me. I like to run the king's dogs." Dagi leaned across the table, squeezing Neheri's arm. "Stay put. I'll run and fetch a litter to get you back before the vizier finds you gone."

The prince left his friend at the table and left the tavern. Mentuser looked around the room. "There's always a back entrance to these places." He stood up brushing his dirty kilt. "Well don't just sit there. The young prince is in the vizier's service. If we're going to question the boy, we'd best do it while the other one is gone."

Nebsumenu got up, biting back his protest at having to dirty his hands again with such work. Who would expect a scarred-up sand dweller to cause so much trouble?

CHAPTER FIFTY

———◄▮►——◄▮►——

YOSEPH

ON THE SIXTH DAY, YOSEPH WOKE AT SUNRISE to the call of the herald standing beyond the barricade. He sat up, stiff from another night on the thin mat in the courtyard and flattened his feet on the warm paved stone. His own couch, brought into the treasury building, he conceded to Asenat. They'd set her in a room alone to confirm all accounts of their findings. Yawning, Yoseph accepted the hot drink from his body servant and took a sip. His gaze locked with Jafener's across the yard when the sovereign's herald repeated the order. No words were needed. They'd all expected this.

For the last five days, he and his men audited the two houses of gold. It was a miracle they'd gotten away with as much as they had without a full-on battle.

Sabni and his men kept order around the perimeter of the barricade. There was some heated confrontation beyond the walls made by a few disgruntled treasury guards. Weapons clashed once or twice. Sabni barked a sharp warning, and the challenge ceased. After this, Yoseph and his men worked under shattered nerves. Yet it was done, once and for all.

Elohim be praised.

Yoseph's body servant pulled him from the mat, and he shouted over the wall to Sabni. The guards began hacking at the ropes connecting the barricade. "We all leave together, at once!" His shouts stirred the men and servants sleeping in the yard. It had taken all of this for the king to finally call for him. His face burned with humiliation as he followed the herald waiting for him at the gate with the staff of precedence. For an official of high rank to be summoned in such a way announced the king's displeasure to the world. The last time Yoseph was summoned with it, he'd been a slave. After today he might be slave again. Or worse.

It wasn't the king or your god that made you vizier. It was me.

He was putting Nebsumenu's resounding boast to the test. He was testing God. If Elohim had made him vizier, then it was better to please him more than the king. More than his own fears. Who was he to turn his eye from justice? Yes, lies had their own power, but truth needed a voice with which to break that power. And if he did not survive the truth he offered the king, it would still live as God lives.

Laughter welled in Yoseph's chest despite his exhaustion, and he coughed to cover it. He'd turned the king's treasury on its head to reveal corruption. He'd made enemies and set himself in the way of the king's wrath. And somehow he knew he'd do it all again.

The herald brought him to the sovereign's personal dwelling. The king's leisure room was swathed in the dark blue of mourning. His war dogs lay on the tiled floor, Brave

One only lifting his head in greeting. The sovereign faced his balcony in a blue robe shot with silver. Yoseph offered a formal greeting, and the king cast a look over his shoulder before returning his gaze to the garden.

"So you've come to make a fool of me." Khakheperre's voice was low and sharp. "While they sail my wife's body down to Abydos for her beautification, you break into my coffers with your men."

A sound from another part of the room drew Yoseph's attention. Nebsumenu mumbled a foul name and glared at him with eyes full of venom. Yoseph expected the treasurer took full advantage of the sovereign's anger and cut his sense of reason to shreds.

"No, Majesty, I have not."

Lady A'at sat very still on cushions not far from where Nebsumenu stood. Her eyes were as full of warning as Hetnu's were of censure. He collected cups and pretended to make himself busy at the wine cabinet, but his lips were pressed to a line.

Yoseph forced himself still when the sovereign rushed at him to yank off the gold chain bearing his seal of office. He threw it across the room.

"You have greatly distressed my trusted servants!" The veins in the king's neck stood out. His chest heaved beneath his robe. "You have dishonored the passing of my most beloved wife! You were less than nothing when I plucked you from the prison, and now you dare break the peace of my house with some decrepit writ!"

Yoseph ground his teeth. Those were Nebsumenu's words. And it was Nebsumenu's anger in the king's face.

"There are checks and balances needed here, Majesty." Nebsumenu's voice carried from the far side of the room.

"I agree with the treasurer. There has not been a proper check of the king's coffers. Therefore, I sought the balance." Yoseph lowered the report in his hand at Nebsumenu's approach.

"Don't play at words, sand dweller."

"I have brought the audit from my lord's treasury." Yoseph kept his gaze fixed on the king and pressed the documents to his thigh. "One that I should have been allowed to conduct but was never given such privilege."

"And how do we know you haven't messed the numbers yourself? You could have robbed His Majesty blind by now." Nebsumenu's voice grew louder. "How do we know your own men have not cheated the king, seeing his coffers filled with treasure?"

"They weren't that filled." Khakheperre's eyes fluttered at the comment. Yoseph continued. "My entire cabinet disrobed, leaving our garments in the courtyard." Nebsumenu's gaze lowered to Yoseph's hand. He drew the report behind his back. "We worked naked, with each man accountable to three witnesses. Every garment and belonging thoroughly checked, including mine. My own couch was brought into the courtyard before all my men. The feathers were pulled out, and it was burned." Yoseph hesitated. His next statement trod dangerous ground. But the king must hear it from him first. "Only the Lady Asenat remained clothed. We placed her in a room alone where she checked and double checked the amounts we found."

"You brought the daughter of my enemy into my two houses of gold?"

"Yes." Yoseph met the king's heated gaze. "She was nearly forced to Prince Ameny's chamber upon leaving Queen Neferet's room the night that she died."

"By whom?"

"By your brother, Prince Ameny. I thought it better to keep her safe since she is your ward. That no shame should come to her."

"Nonsense." The king flicked his hand. "Ameny has never forced a woman in his life. He is the son of a god. As for Asenat, I grant she'll run to her father and give him a full account of my coffers."

"She cannot as she has been sworn into my service. She has been watched and found to be obedient. Her skills were essential to our success." His defense was too anxious, and the king sensed it, giving him a long hard stare.

"It's your own hide you should be trying to save, not hers."

Yoseph held his patience. Khakheperre used his dislike of Asenat to dismiss his brother's behavior.

"I should call in all my officers and flay you in front of them, then hack up all of your men."

"For upsetting Nebsumenu, Majesty? Or for bringing you the truth on the state of your coffers?" Fatigue had unlocked the careless words. The room went deathly still until a small voice filled the silence.

"The good god will remember the promise he made to Queen Neferet before her death." The meek reminder came from A'at, sitting across the room.

"Be silent girl!" the king barked.

She startled at his anger and splashed tears onto her lap.

He huffed, but her words made him unsure of himself.

"Let us see these claims." Nebsumenu reached for Yoseph's report.

The king slapped his hand down. "You are partially to blame for this, Nebsumenu. How long have you promised me an account of my coffers?" He took the report from Yoseph. "*We* shall see nothing, Nebsumenu, as *we* are not king." Nebsumenu shifted on his feet, and the king flashed a look as though his own words had caught him off guard. His gaze darted around the room. "Get out, all of you!" he barked and faced his balcony.

YOSEPH BLEW WIND FROM HIS CHEEKS, thankful that his head remained attached to his neck.

He returned to his office, where his men waited for him, all of them feigning some type of busyness. Like him, their nerves were on edge. No one missed the empty spot on his chest where his seal of office should have been. Jafener sat at a low table, reviewing records. Asenat laid out his writing lesson for the day, insisting he prepare for the annual report on crops. She peeked up as he sat beside her, touching his chest.

"I don't know if I shall have it back." He met her gaze. Fear hammered in the back of his mind, fear that Nebsumenu would still get what he wanted. But the decision was the king's to make. "It's in the best hands, don't you think?"

She sorted reed pens, speaking in a low voice. "Truth tried by fire remains true."

Her words stunned him, more so the righteous anger in her countenance. She was ready to stand with him. She was ready to make war for truth just as much as the others.

Chu gestured at his chest. "Perhaps no one will notice, my lord."

"You did."

"Then wear your finest pectorals and bracelets that prove your station."

"The king yanked the seal from my neck. Everyone will hear of it soon enough." He was sure Nebsumenu would see to that.

A knock at the door drew their attention. A royal messenger came in the room and presented Yoseph with a sealed message from the king and a small linen pouch. When he bowed and left, Yoseph handed the scroll to Jafener, who scanned it with Chu looking over his shoulder.

Yoseph dug into the pouch and gave an audible sigh as he drew out his seal on a new gold chain. Asenat's regard reflected his relief. He placed the chain around his neck. The lives of his men were safe. For now.

"The king has read the report." Jafener raised his finger. Then his countenance fell. "But he cannot accept it because the old records are missing, and there is nothing to compare the new amount with."

"But I saw the records there. I handled them myself." Asenat turned to Yoseph. "Everything was correct."

"She's right," Jafener said. "I named each list aloud before I passed it to her."

"And he named them all correctly. I rechecked them and passed them to Chu." Asenat turned to Chu. "Did you not see it?"

Chu nodded. "I saw and confirmed all the records, along with the names of every document in the stack you handed me."

Yoseph looked between the three of them. Jafener and Asenat had both spoken to him about Chu. And there was Potipherah's warning of a spy among his men.

He dismissed everyone, and for a few days watched the door with an underlying fear as he prayed to Elohim and paced the floor. The king's guard could still come for him. And if Nebsumenu could sway the king, they would certainly come.

There was enough talk and enough doubt about Chu to think him the spy Potipherah spoke of. But Yoseph could not bring a man to judgment so easily when no more than an accusation had once condemned him to prison for so long. He needed more proof.

A gentle rap at his door brought him to his feet. "Now, here is the pleasant surprise I've been needing." He took Mepi by the arm and led him to a comfortable chair, then propped his feet up on a stool.

"I shall suggest to the king that all his viziers be first slaves." Mepi chuckled. "You do your office great credit."

"And you are worthy of my best service." Yoseph pulled up another stool to sit at Mepi's thigh.

"I'm taking my exercise today with you in mind." Mepi propped his cane on a nearby table. "You seem to lack understanding where Prince Dagi is concerned."

Yoseph reared back at the mention of Dagi, but Mepi touched his shoulder.

"You didn't let him explain himself at the interview. The boy is arrogant because he has little else. The kilt he wore to interview for one of your positions was borrowed. He gambles to make ends meet, and visits me for bread and treats for his mother and sister who live here on the king's good graces. Dagi admires you more than you know."

Yoseph huffed. "Perhaps you know one Dagi, and I know another."

"All the boy needs is guidance."

Yoseph had little tolerance for the wayward prince, yet he held his tongue out of respect for Mepi.

"I came also to hear more about Elohim. You say anyone can approach him without the aid of a priest?"

Yoseph nodded. Mepi leaned back into the cushions. "I was taught to intercede for men to a number of gods. But I have studied the scribes of old. Their writings speak of a nameless god who is not graven in marble nor beheld in form. One who has made all things but has not himself been made."

Mepi's voice grew thick. He struck a tear from his jaw. "I feared the great temples had killed him. I feared they had broken him to pieces like potsherd and divided him like spoils of war in their greed for fame." He sniffed. "I have searched in hopes of digging him out from our pile of gods and many rituals, this pure one whose representations thereof are vain. And it is here that our paths meet. For he came to me and revealed himself again." Mepi smiled through his tears. His eyes were shining.

The joy in Mepi's face made Yoseph set his troubles aside to share how Elohim had revealed himself to his forefathers, not in face but in character. He told Mepi how his great grandfather, Abraham, knew him as El Elyon, God Most High, after the victory at Dan, then recognized him as El Shaddai, God Almighty, when he changed his name, and El Olam, The Everlasting God, at Beersheba. He was Jehovah-Jireh in a time of great testing and El Roi to an Egyptian slave girl who prayed for justice for herself and for her son.

Mepi seemed to ponder this in silence. He stayed to take a little refreshment. "Now, what's this I hear about the vizier's overbold move of raiding the king's treasury building?"

Yoseph shook his head. "I've done it to my own detriment, I assure you."

"Overbold it was." Mepi raised a brow. "And long overdue."

"I've angered the king."

"You've frightened him. That's what you've done. Challenged his sincerity, questioned his principle. If Khakheperre is angry, let him be so. You've proven yourself a true servant. The good god must examine himself now. And I hear too that the king has refused your audit of his coffers?"

"Someone extracted a page from the report I gave him. Whoever did it knew what he was doing. I've put the lives of my men at risk for nothing."

"And what page is it that you are missing?"

"A page stating the amount in the last report given over three years ago.

Mepi gave a derisive huff, lacing his fingers together. "So the king hasn't had a report on his own wealth since his father's reign."

"I've had my men work backward to give the best account I can. All that was left was the current amount in the treasury to be compared with withdrawals since the old report."

Mepi raised his brows. "If that's all you need then I think I can dig out the information for you."

"What?"

"Am I not the king's scroll keeper? What kind of scrolls do you think I keep?" Mepi smiled.

"With forty scribes at your beck. I suspect you keep them all."

"Correct." Mepi tapped his finger to his temple. "There are a few select documents that come directly from the king's hand to mine. Khakheperre trusts me solely in this. Nebsumenu was treasurer for at least three years before you entered the king's house. Let that rascal explain himself since the last audit I hold in check."

"I had not realized you would have such records. But why have you not revealed this information sooner?"

"I had to study you, Paneah, to see if you were worthy. Of course, I hardly knew you would tromp like a great bull into the king's treasury building." Mepi gave a hearty chuckle before his smile faded. "But if I'd found you to be as corrupt as your adversaries, who snuggle like vipers in the king's bosom, I would have taken the information with me to the grave. That is the level of corruption here. That is how quickly bribes pass from hand to hand."

Yoseph nodded, too weary to reflect on the depth of this triumph.

"I believe even Reniqer would be proud of you," Mepi assured him with a pat on the shoulder.

"Let me send someone with you to fetch it," Yoseph offered.

Mepi shook his head. "They are in a secret place that I cannot reveal. I would call Asenat to help but we cannot involve her further in such dealings."

"Agreed, but you must speak of this to no one."

"Of course," Mepi winked. "And how is my girl?'

"She fares well," Yoseph said.

Mepi searched his face, his expression indiscernible.

"She was with us in the treasury building when we took it over."

"And that perhaps worked in your favor. Khakheperre may dislike Potipherah but he'll go lightly at punishing the priest's daughter. You've taken exceptional care of her." He leaned on the arm of the cushioned chair. "Do you think she likes you?"

The question caught Yoseph off guard. A surge of jealousy had run through him when she'd confessed that Nebsumenu had kissed her. When he stopped in the garden to take her arm, he'd done it on impulse. There was a look in those large, warm eyes that tightened his chest. He'd wanted to kiss her. Then Ama screamed from the bushes, and his reputation hung by threads. He forced a thin smile for Mepi's sake though his heart sunk in despair. "If she cares for me, I fear she would be the last to know it. Who can tell what lies beneath that stern disposition of hers and that flint-like tongue?"

"Asenat?" Mepi asked in mock surprise. "Why, the girl's all honey. If you can draw it out." He extended his hands, and Yoseph helped him rise to his feet.

CHAPTER FIFTY ONE

AMENY

AMENY SAT IN THE ROOM FARTHEST FROM HIS entrance hall where Appipa banged at the door of his suite, torturing him with her whining shrills and sobs. It was the third time this week. He might have beaten her senseless but for Yimenet's reminder. Many of the palace guards could no longer be bought.

"Sit, my love." Yimenet tugged on his arm as Appipa shrieked in the distance.

"Open the door, Ameny! Or I will tell the world how you used me! How you tried to kill me along with the vizier!"

What was she so upset about? She hadn't a scratch on her. The surprise attack of arrows in the vizier's garden was more Nebsumenu's idea than his. Ameny sniffed. His nose began to bleed. "I need to silence her."

Yimenet muffled her laughter and turned his face to hers. "Listen, my love, to her silly claims. Everyone knows a prince of the blood uses whomever he wants." Ameny's lips tugged upward as she stroked his temples. "No one will believe anything of Appipa."

Yimenet's was the voice of reason. He kissed her. She

pulled back and uttered a cry, touching her bruised lip where he'd struck her in the corridor.

"Take me away," she purred against his jaw.

He kissed her lightly once more. He owed her this pleasure of revenge against Appipa, who was much like that sparkling pectoral she always wore, demanding far more attention than she deserved.

"I can't take you away now." He captured a handful of her fragrant tresses and kissed them. "I need to think."

She littered his face with tiny kisses, avoiding the bruised side of her mouth. Her apology for interfering in the corridor seemed heartfelt enough. She was jealous, and he'd forgiven her. Though he was still undecided if she had lied about Asenat. He needed to get his hands on the girl. But if for any reason the vizier's takeover of the treasury turned sour for his thieving companions, it would be best to have Yimenet in his corner, not Appipa.

Nebsumenu hadn't answered his messages. Resnakt made excuses. And Mentuser, as always, said as little as possible. Ameny went out of his way to prove himself to these men who had used him when they needed his help. Now they ignored him. His gut instincts told him they would run, but he would not be the last one holding a sack of trouble. Amun was foremost.

Yimenet glanced up at the sudden stillness. "Appipa's gone."

He inched closer to her, delighted. The screeching had stopped. "Appipa who?" He wrapped Yimenet's long hair around his wrist as she began to play her harp. He was lucky that Yimenet didn't read, but still, one had to be careful with her. She was a few years older than he was and as much an acrobat with lies as she had once been on the back of a bull. He leaned in to kiss her neck. If he ever found out she'd lied to him about Asenat, he'd kill her.

A servant entered with a gentle knock. Ameny took the note, breaking the seal. He'd anticipated a response from Nebsumenu, but this was something far better. He tucked the note away, smiling. His contact in the vizier's crew had been diligent. This was just what he needed. "I think you are right, my love. We need a respite, you and me. A trip it will be."

Yimenet stopped playing and gasped, knocking him back on the cushions.

"Pack your things. Perhaps we'll leave as early as tonight." He stroked her shoulders and she bathed his face and chest again with kisses. If things went according to plan, he would leave the palace with both Yimenet and Asenat. And return soon.

As king.

CHAPTER FIFTY TWO

SABNI

PRINCE DAGI HAD A GIFT FOR TRAINING THE king's war dogs, and Sabni often left him with only a few tips to offer. But Dagi had not returned from an errand he was to run on behalf of the king's dog trainers. Now it seemed that he'd gone missing along with Prince Neheri. Sabni scoffed under his breath that he should worry so about the young lords.

The main thoroughfare seemed naked without the great Horus columns standing proud in their place. Kitjau had overseen their dismantling, but now he was needed at the funeral grounds in She-resy, and all that was left of the columns were two great gouges in the earth.

A servant girl passed him a note for Paneah and Sabni decided to take it to the vizier himself. He and Paneah needed to talk. He took the stairs to the nursery balcony where Paneah turned to him, his face pinched with concern.

"Any news on Dagi or Neheri?"

"None." Sabni joined him at the rail. "Perhaps the young lords took a trip farther downriver together. Just another mannish escapade they probably struck up at a moment's whim." Sabni surveyed the grounds, sounding more confident than he felt. Joining the vizier's crew was good for Neheri. But more than once, the prince had expressed his impatience on the security strictures enforced after Reniqer's murder. Sabni would give Neheri a crushing embrace and a fitting punishment when he returned, which had better be soon.

"Any word from the king?" Paneah asked.

"Not even to me." Sabni let out a breath. His rank as great one of tens had raised his authority but given him less access to the king. He could no longer stroll into Khakheperre's chamber like a casual friend but had to make appointments to do so. However, his work kept him busy. And it was only from a few of his own men that he'd heard talk about some run-in Paneah had with Nebsumenu before his takeover of the treasury. Until that day when he and his men had blocked entrance to the king's two houses of gold, he had no idea the conflict between Paneah and Nebsumenu was so intense. Paneah had no right to keep such conflict to himself, but now he wore his concern for the missing young lords like a heavy woolen cloak. Sabni bit back his complaint. His anger could wait.

The treasury takeover was a success, despite the missing page from the audit. Paneah challenged Khakheperre to open his eyes to the way his coffers were being handled. The king could honor the Writ of Amun's Entry or his own words declaring Paneah's authority over his house. Or, Khakheperre could continue to bask in false flattery and half-truths. But Sabni hoped he knew the king better than that.

"Also I figured you'd be wondering about our silent priest and sent Ipuur out to check Potipherah's lips as he spoke with Lady Satweret. They conversed about some town below Iunu where Satweret could find more vermilion dye. As if the court hasn't had enough of that." Sabni shot a look skyward, sick of the color.

"Satweret who is Nebsumenu's wife?"

Sabni nodded. "Yes."

"Keep an eye on her. Now more than ever, the dashing treasurer keeps to his office."

"Then you'll be pleased to hear that Ipuur observed him trying to persuade the king to remove Asenat from your service."

"Is that so?" Paneah said, his tone indifferent as he surveyed the grounds, but the veins in his temples flexed.

Sabni crossed his arms. "If you like the girl, go ahead and kiss her. That would tell what was what." By the look Paneah shot him, Sabni's advice, however unwelcome, had hit the mark. He cleared his throat, deciding not to leave the poor man in misery. "Khakheperre finally shut Nebsumenu up, refusing him." At this, Paneah fought hard to suppress his grin.

"Inform Ipuur that he is not to watch the conversation of the sovereign, not even on my behalf."

"Yes." Sabni nodded, "Ipuur has been zealous in his work of late. His father's murder has changed him. Unfortunately, he stepped too close to Prince Ameny on one of his drunken sprees and got his two front teeth knocked out." Sabni gripped the rail. Ameny was a thorn in the side of justice itself. The whole world covered for that unworthy wretch. "Of course, the prince refuses to report for questioning."

"Inform Ipuur that if he is willing to make an official complaint on the incident, he shall have two gold teeth to replace the ones he lost." Paneah surveyed the treasury courtyard like a watchdog, tapping the joints of his fingers. He glanced sideways, ascending some private thought. "I'm waiting for Mepi to send very important information to me."

"That reminds me." Sabni reached for the note he tucked behind his dagger. "A slave girl, pulling the linen from your couch, begged me to give you this."

Paneah frowned. "I've banned all females from my dwelling since Ama was found in my private garden." He took the note and glanced over the symbols. "Get me someone to read this at once."

CHAPTER FIFTY THREE

YOSEPH

YOSEPH WAS MOVING BEFORE THE SCRIBE finished reading the note. He refused to wait for guards or for a litter and set out for the scroll room on foot. Sabni warned that the note could be a trick, but Yoseph would not take chances.

He ordered guards to check Asenat's suite, then follow him to the scroll room. Sabni bellowed for courtiers to clear the path as they jogged the distance. Yoseph kept pace, grateful for Sabni's insistent physical training that he had at one time begrudged.

The note stated that Asenat was on her way to the scroll room and that she was in danger. But how long ago had the note been written? How long ago had she left? Their vigorous trot through the corridors could not close the distance fast enough.

A shriek reverberated through the dark and empty corridor as they neared the scroll room. Yoseph took off running with his heart in his throat. He recognized Asenat's cry before he turned into the gallery.

Ameny hunched over her, ripping her sheath. She bucked wildly, scratching him.

"Get off her!" Yoseph ran forward and threw the prince against the wall. Baskets and scrolls scattered across the floor. Yoseph pulled her to her feet and snatched down a curtain to cover her. "It's all right." He crushed her to his chest. They were both shaking.

"Mepi," she whimpered, clinging to him. She turned her frantic gaze to the upper level of the gallery. A light flickered from the old father's office.

"Behind you!" Sabni shouted.

Yoseph yanked her down, and the sweep of the cudgel missed them. He chopped Ameny in the throat. The prince doubled over, choking.

Sabni was on him, slick with sweat.

"Sabni!" Yoseph barked.

He hurled the prince into a set of shelves with a string of curses.

Ameny struggled to his feet, swaying with a face full of blood.

Sabni growled, hurling him into the shelves again. Splintered wood and scrolls flew in every direction across the gallery floor. This time the prince stayed down.

YOSEPH TALKED THROUGH PART OF THE NIGHT to Sabni and paced the rest of it. Hearing the morning oblations to Horus and Re, he called for scented water, dressed himself and kohled his eyes, having no patience for the ministrations of servants.

Last night's terror left him sick to the stomach. He left his chamber with two guards and made his way to the king's personal dwelling. He barked, warning the king's guards to let him pass, but a steward blocked the king's inner chamber. Yoseph shoved the man aside. One of the two voices coming from the room was Ameny's.

He'd ordered the prince taken to a cell last night but should have known better. However, Sabni foiled Ameny's getaway, capturing one of his vessels packed for a trip. But he was otherwise untouchable.

Yoseph's abrupt intrusion hadn't startled the king or his brother who continued his ranting.

"And here is my accuser, brother. This sand dweller, who dares to strike royal blood."

Yoseph bit back his defense and prayed God would steer his tongue. Ameny sat on a stool, chewing natron. His face and shoulders were covered with Asenat's scratches. His chest, scored by the splintered shelves Sabni threw him against. But the bruise at his throat was Yoseph's own gift to the prince who tried to club him from behind.

Yoseph remembered himself and bowed to Khakheperre, whose regard narrowed on him as he sat upright on his sleeping couch.

"Am I to understand that you impede justice in my house?

"The good god knows that I do not."

"I know nothing of the sort." Khakheperre sipped through a reed straw in a silver cup, and placed it on a tray. His body servants entered with a large bronze tub and pitchers. "You've stirred enough trouble in my house, Yoseph, for me to ponder your worth." The king would not meet his gaze, but his face was tight. He disrobed and stepped into the tub.

Yoseph recognized Ukem. The Asiatic body servant

who'd once struck him, now tucked his chin, trying to hide his face. His hands moved with efficiency over the king's form.

"My brother tells me he caught a murderess last night and that you had the audacity not only to stop him but to defend her."

Yoseph's eyes fluttered. The outrageous accusation left him tongue tied.

"If the daughter of the high priest has done murder, I'll have her head for it."

Yoseph swallowed hard and breathed. Slavery had taught him that anger was the deathblow to a man's defense before his lord. "Your faithful servant, Mepi of the scroll room has been murdered. Your brother was the one with blood on his kilt, Majesty." He forced control into his voice. "Not Asenat."

"I pulled her off Mepi's body," Ameny said.

"I pulled the prince off Asenat." Yoseph stepped closer. "He tried to rape her."

"I wrestled her to the floor, calling for help."

"She was the one calling for help. Not Ameny."

The king stepped out of the tub and dressed as the two of them volleyed accusations. He watched them from his polished bronze shield as his servants rouged his cheeks. His stiff posture confirmed an inner struggle, as did his countenance. He raised his shaking hand from his lap. "I will come to a decision about the girl later." His gaze shied from Yoseph's in the bronze. "Leave me."

Yoseph knew better. If he left now, Khakheperre would let himself be swayed by Ameny. He pulled the note tucked in the girdle at his waist and placed it on the king's dressing table.

"What is this?" The king looked at him.

"An anonymous note, warning me of the danger Asenat was in, telling me she was on her way to the scroll room. I had one of my scribes read it and went immediately."

"A lie." Ameny came over to the table and stood across from Yoseph, but his eyes were pinned to the note. "Ask anyone."

"Yes, Majesty, ask any one. And they will agree with the prince because they fear for their safety if they speak out against him." The king turned to his brother as Yoseph went on. "Lady Asenat has filed an official complaint, along with another member of my cabinet, against the prince. They are both willing to testify in your presence."

The king was speechless. His eyes narrowed on his brother, but for the first time he uttered no defense. Yoseph could only hope Ameny was moving closer to the justice due him.

CHAPTER FIFTY FOUR

ASENAT

ASENAT'S HEAD THROBBED. SHE STARED PAST Ama, stroking her bruised collar bone with the powder-brush, trying to lighten the mark. A full curly wig concealed the lump on her forehead. The scratch on her cheek burned.

Ama gazed at her in silence. Sympathy lingered in her eyes and also a hint of terror. She'd suffered her own violent assault.

Then there was Yimenet.

Asenat could no longer despise the Minoan who spent half her time chasing after Ameny and the other half covering the evidence of his attention. She shuddered, suppressing a sob.

If Paneah had not come for her...

Ama put down the lip clay to embrace her as she trembled and wept. She had done as much for Ama, but not long enough for the violence done to her. She wept for Ama now, and for Yimenet, but most of all for Mepi.

Lord Paneah and his men met her outside her suite. He took her arm, and she winced. Almost every part of her was tender from fighting Ameny off, but she would not cry out, not when she escaped the worst of the assault, and Ama had borne so much more. She took comfort in the presence of the men around her and the twenty guards in tow. They all walked toward the scroll room.

Sabni called out commands to the guards stationed within the gallery. The large room, usually full of musicians and courtiers, was near empty but for carpenters hammering nails into a new set of shelves where Sabni slung Ameny at the wall. A few scribes collected scrolls scattered across the floor, their faces drawn in the same misery as hers. Mepi was the heart of all progress here, and now he was gone.

Paneah took her up the stairs against the wall. Her vision hazed, and her head grew light. They reached the threshold of Mepi's workroom. Her knees buckled at the blood seeping between the tiles.

Mepi's blood.

Ameny told her he killed the old father, and that she would meet the same fate if she didn't retrieve the old audit of the king's coffers. He had not scared her. He enraged her. And she held her tongue despite his blows. When his grip loosened, she tore out the room and got as far as the bottom of the stairs before he caught her again. A shudder rippled through her at the memory of his attack.

"Wait here," Paneah told the group of men following them. He took her into Mepi's office and pulled the curtain. "Find it."

She stared at him and blinked. Then understanding dawned, and she moved to the statue of Thoth. Ameny knocked her head against the odd-placed sculpture. The trick was not to pull or push against it, but to find the hidden catch at its base, then turn it. The lever clicked, and the hidden drawers shot out from behind what appeared to be a simple row of cubbies.

"Thirty-fourth year of Nubkaure Amenemhat, season of Akhet," Paneah murmured over her shoulder.

She checked the color coded seals for the last years King Khakheperre reigned as co-regent with his father Nubkaure. Her eyes leaked tears. She sniffed, swiping them away. Mepi trusted Paneah. The time for secrets had passed.

"Here it is." She handed the document to him.

He exhaled a rush of air, meeting her gaze as he took it. They restored the rest of the scrolls to the secret compartment, and he instructed two guards to stay behind. No one was to enter the room.

Asenat shook when they descended the stairs. Paneah's half embrace kept her upright but she could hold her dignity no longer. Her soul-agony gave way to raw sobs. She clung to him. He called for a chair, but she begged to walk. The old mothers, Ipwet and Sahathor, had gotten an eyeful of her on the way over. She had no wish to be paraded back to her rooms in a litter with her face so stricken.

She would never again fetch Mepi a cup of cinnamon milk or embrace him on the palace water steps. She could no longer bask in his wisdom and love. Her Ibis was gone, and her bones would soon crack with grief.

The group of men shielded her from the scrutiny of onlookers. Her steps were surer with Paneah's arm around her as they traveled through passageways and down ramps back to her dwelling. But his anger revealed itself when he followed her into her sleeping chamber.

Imehy greeted them, sparkling in silver and rock crystal rings and bracelets. He bowed to the vizier but would not meet her gaze. He had tended Ama after her assault, but after that, wasn't seen outside the company of the royal jewelers.

"How is it that I have deserved the merit of your attentions when the vizier's feet have not?" Asenat puckered her mouth in demand of an answer.

Imehy blinked and looked away to pour some foul-smelling liquid into a cup to which he added a handful of herbs.

Nor had Paneah mentioned Imehy's desertion but motioned the dwarf forward while he studied the bruise at her neck. "Obstinate girl. You cannot seem to keep to your dwelling but sneak like a spy through the corridors at night." Paneah reached for the lump on her forehead, then pulled his hand back, his mouth a resolute frown. "This is not a place for childish games!"

"Mepi sent a note. He needed help retrieving the document you requested." She sought to curb Paneah's anger but the dip in his brows suggested his disbelief. She fetched the note from a cosmetic box on her dressing table, intending to read it. Paneah snatched it from her grasp. He stared at it, then tucked it behind his jeweled belt.

"I'm not yours to scold." She was flippant. Nothing was right in the world, and she ached for a fight.

Paneah took the cup from Imehy and extended it to her. "Drink it."

"I don't need anything for sleep."

You will take it just the same."

"I am not a child."

"But you have behaved like one, and I will treat you thus." He barked the words, as ready to fight as she was.

She snatched the cup and drank it. Tears slid down her temples.

Let it be death. Rejoin me to those I love.

The drug took hold fast. She swayed. Paneah's seal brushed her chest. Someone laid her down. "I hate, I ha-" She swallowed, unable to complete the thought. Her head swam as darkness clouded her consciousness.

"If it is me you hate, my heart will never mend."

She grasped to place the soft whisper at her ear, but it was a thousand echoes away.

CHAPTER FIFTY FIVE

——◀▶◆◀▶◀▮▶◀▶◆◀▶——

YOSEPH

THREE SCRIBES VERIFIED THE DOCUMENT Asenat recovered as a copy of the old record missing from the king's report. Yoseph locked it away near his desk.

As for Asenat, he wanted to shake the girl for her carelessness. Terror still lingered in her glistening eyes, just as it did in Ama's. He pulled out the note she gave him and examined it. But even without recognizing the hand, he already knew who wrote it. He pinched the bridge of his nose and drew in a ragged breath. It was good that he ordered Imehy to drug her heavily. She'd seen enough death for the day.

And there was more to come.

Yoseph glanced up as Sabni entered the room and pulled up a stool. "I'll check the roster for the guards who were supposed to be on duty in the scroll room." He poured two cups of watered wine, and Yoseph reached for the one he pushed toward him. "If I find any of them were paid off, I'll beat each of them with a leather baton myself." Sabni pulled a bowl into his lap and munched on fruit despite the look of brewing anger on his countenance.

Yoseph leaned back in the chair. "And if the guard duty was canceled, then arrest the attending scribe and beat him instead."

Sabni nodded, and they sat in silence for a while before he spoke again. "Well? Out with it."

Yoseph smiled a little. Sabni read him too well. "Your handling of Prince Ameny was excessive."

"He deserved it and then some." Sabni worked the skin off a pomegranate without looking up.

"We are the king's servants and must be cautious."

"You're still a good slave, aren't you Paneah?"

Yoseph checked his anger as Sabni spurted dry laughter and put the bowl on the tray beside him.

"What good is caution when a prince kills a venerable old man and tries to rape the king's ward?" He glared his challenge. "So don't feed me that hog fodder. We are both foreigners torn from our homes. I won't wink at Egypt's corruption because she's been good to me."

"We must maintain the utmost integrity before our peers."

"Was it integrity then, when you lied about having brothers? I know a little of your tongue having been on the borders. You spoke of them when you thrashed with fever in Imehy's care."

Yoseph searched for words. He was dead to his old life and to the men who killed it. His words were not a lie. Yet bitter memories kept their images vivid in his mind. "I share the blood of other men who were my father's seed." He swallowed the lump in his throat. "But they are not my brothers. I cannot go back to my past." He gave a weary smile at Sabni's hard face. "You are the only brother I have now."

There were no signs of triumph in Sabni at having exposed him. There was disappointment. Hurt. "Then why have you sent me off on wild chases? You hid Nebsumenu's threat from me. You never let me in on the watchmen's thieving. As your great one of tens, I had a right to know. You've used my skill and left me out of everything. Why call me brother and withhold all this from me?"

"You are right. By your actions, you have shown me more patience than I deserve. Forgive me." Yoseph met his gaze, squarely. "But I know what it is to be anxious for revenge, Sabni. I know what anger can do to a young man, how he judges poorly based on the fire raging within him. Aggression at the wrong time is not bravery but foolishness. And retreat at the right time can be wisdom."

"You mock my zeal."

"Your zeal stems from an anger I've known far too well, my brother. I sought to protect you."

Sabni slammed the tray beside him and broke it. He stood up, heaving. "I don't need your protection. I need justice. I will not forget what I owe my past or my people. I'll not remain blind because of the hope of a dream or a promise from your god!"

Yoseph remained seated. "You are not blind, but like me, you are struggling. Rein in your anger, or you will lose all the ground you have gained, and you will not see the justice promised you."

"Is that a threat?"

"There's no need to threaten when your actions do it already."

Sabni blinked. The subtle reprimand washed the outrage from his face. He sat and squeezed his eyes shut. His lips trembled.

"The dream will come to pass, Sabni, but you must wait for it. Do you understand?"

He shifted on the stool, tottering on the brink of reason. Yoseph prayed God would give him strength.

"Yes." He clenched as though an arrow were lodged in his flesh. "I understand."

"And are you with me, brother?"

Sabni looked up. "You know that I am."

"Then send guards to fetch Imehy from the jeweler's crew and call in my men, for there is grim justice to be served."

THE MEN OF YOSEPH'S CABINET FILED INTO HIS office. Imehy stood among them. Yoseph offered no explanation for his presence, neither to Imehy nor to his men. His bowels trembled at the next task he was to perform, but it was crucial for the moral commitment they all swore to uphold.

Yoseph ordered the men of his cabinet to stand or sit in a tight circle as he brought over a chair, ignoring their worried glances. As scribe of the vizier, Jafener took his usual place beside Yoseph on a cushion with his writing supplies. Both Reniqer's and Mepi's deaths struck him hard. He sniffed, sullen and still at his palette, crooking his reed pen above a clean sheet of papyrus.

"Compose for me a sanction of execution, Jafener," Yoseph said, looking over his men. "Set the date for today."

Jafener gave a solemn nod and set his pen sweeping across the page. The silence was palpable, and Yoseph well understood the fear spreading throughout the room. He once thought himself facing such an end.

"And what style of execution is to be used, my lord?" Jafener dipped his pen in the ink-soot.

"Death by impaling."

Some of the men winced. Such torture in the right hands could be quick or otherwise stretched out for days.

Jafener nodded, and the room remained still but for the scratching strokes of his pen. He set the finished document down.

Yoseph removed his seal of office from his neck and handed it to his head scribe. They all waited while Jafener copied an identical order on a clay tablet.

"Have you ever seen an impaling, Chu?"

His chamberlain startled at the address. Yoseph shot a glance at Sabni who waited. Chu opened his mouth. He was tongue-tied.

Jafener rolled Yoseph's seal across the tablet, then read each copy aloud. Yoseph nodded his approval and rose from his chair to hand the document to Chu, then sat down again to clean his seal with a piece of cloth.

"On the day we walked to the treasury building together, Nebsumenu paid me great insult and you spoke up for me. But I charged you to remain quiet about the matter. Not only did you blurt the news to Jafener, but I hear you approached Ibiau, the treasury attendant against my orders."

Chu panted as though robbed of breath. "Yes, but please understand, my lord, that Ibiau insulted you behind your bac—"

"You have disobeyed me more than once based on the tenets of your personal zeal instead of following my instructions. I've been urged to expose you." Yoseph placed the chain bearing his seal around his neck and stood to pluck the document from Chu's shaking hand.

Chu began weeping. "But I was angry on your behalf. I have kept my word in all but this, my lord. I swear it."

Yoseph offered him no comfort. Chu was his chamberlain, and his position was one of the highest confidence. He deserved to weep in fear of his life. "Imehy," Yoseph called above Chu's sobbing. "Sabni tells me you've been talking to Lord Resnakt. I counted you friend but you've not answered my summons since the Writ of Amun's Entry went missing from my documents."

Yoseph held the order to the dwarf's face. He fell to his knees, clutching the silver at his heaving chest.

"Only your willingness to assist me of late has restored a little of my faith in you." Yoseph held him in a stony glare and passed the order to his chief scribe. "Take it, Jafener." Yoseph sat again in his chair, letting silence cloak the room. "And affix your own name to it."

Jafener remained still as his reed pen hung over the order. His hand shook, and he let out a wail like a woman giving birth. Yoseph snatched the order from him. "Chu, come sign the name of your accuser!"

Chu took the order, his brows pinched in confusion.

Yoseph snapped his finger pointing to Jafener. "Kneel him before me."

Two guards picked up Jafener, who'd gone limp, and dropped him to his knees.

"You're a clever jackal." Yoseph bared his teeth. "But the scent of innocent blood is on your hands. Clear your heart of lies!"

"I did not know that Reniqer would be killed," Jafener's voice quavered.

"I counted you honorable. You whom taught me the work of my office. You who I leaned upon for the truth you swore to give. Little Imini was dancing in my office one night and found the Writ of Entry where you hid it. I had Chu confirm the page had been cut out from a set of bound documents, and he could not keep his tongue for wanting to know who had done such a thing. But he never blamed you as you blamed him. You exerted yourself, pushing me to see his guilt." Yoseph pulled out Asenat's note. "I leaned against the garden wall when Asenat told you she had once worked beside Mepi. You are the man who scribbled this lie to lure her to Mepi's office."

The guards held Jafener's shoulders to keep him from bowing toward the floor. He shut his eyes to the note Yoseph held out. Tears soaked his chest. He tried to laugh. "She joked how badly the old father forgot to keep secrets. She was right."

"You took the old records we found for the report in the king's coffers."

"I burned them." Jafener's words were barely audible through his groans and snotty tears.

"And put every man here at risk with the deed. You should have burned the note you passed to Asenat." Yoseph slapped him. "You were almost responsible for her death, but most certainly responsible for Mepi's. He trusted you."

Jafener mumbled incoherent pleas for mercy, straining as the guards held his arms. Yoseph leaned back in his chair, hearing none of them. "All that you have worked for is gone, your hard earned reputation, the future of your children and the good name of your family. Your life."

Jafener raised his head, his throat catching with sobs. "Who could have known that your good fortune would hold?" He leaned forward, both laughing and weeping like one gone mad. "That an Asiatic dog turned vizier would last?"

"You have betrayed not only me but every man in this room who gave you their trust and respect. You have betrayed the work of your office and the king. You have lied to all of us. But if none of this was enough to keep you from your wickedness, the work of my god should have warned you from such deeds." Yoseph gritted his teeth, wanting to say more. But what did it matter now? He could do nothing to cure this ill or withhold the justice due. He motioned to the guards to carry Jafener, chief scribe of the vizier, away to his death and to his eternal unrest.

CHAPTER FIFTY SIX

ASENAT

THE WORLD CAME TO A HALT FOR THE FUNERAL procession of Queen Neferet, Great One of the Hetes-Sceptre and Mistress of the Two Lands. The fleet of luxury barges chonted upriver at a snail's pace. Another fleet of servants in cooking boats and vessels trailed them, bearing furniture and garments for the traveling courtiers. They'd set out for She-resy, and the journey that might have taken them eight days took fifteen. Chu bore up as well as one could, returning to the province once lost to his family's rule because of some old court scandal.

Asenat held a place of honor on the vizier's barge as his tutor, but she'd broken Paneah's trust, and this was also a subtle incarceration. Humiliation and anguish warred within her.

They said Ameny had gone ahead of the funeral procession on some business. If the king was hiding his brother from her father, he was wise to do it. Potipherah's silence on the matter meant Ameny was in grave danger. However, Khakheperre refused to hear charges against his brother, and Asenat's willingness to testify deepened

Khakheperre's dislike of her. Her place in the vizier's crew had become both her prison and shelter against the god's anger.

She had gone into full mourning, as much as the court would allow, wearing no wig and the barest amount of jewelry. She pulled her woolen locks back into a bun at the nape of her neck and let wavy ringlets fall to her shoulders. More than once Paneah's gaze lingered on her dark brown mane. But he frowned at the mark on her forehead where Prince Ameny had struck her as though she'd put it there herself. She and Paneah had managed a companionable silence on his barge, and he'd allotted her one of the cabins below deck, though she and Ama mostly kept to one of the four shaded pavilions above. When she wasn't reading him reports or literature, he set his handsome face like a warrior, attacking the symbols in his Book of Sbayt. The constant bobbing knot in his throat, the far-off looks, and the long trembling sighs from his nostrils revealed the anger and remorse he tried to conceal.

The queen's barge sailed past them full of ladies. Rejected by Ameny, Appipa had finally joined the ornate of the god's wife and traveled upriver, unaware of how Queen Weret and her ladies laughed at her snores. She slept most hours of the day and did little else other than napping and peeing and eating. Weret kept her as one would a pet, remarking unkindly at how Appipa's once tight sheath seemed let out around her belly.

Asenat caught a glimpse of one particular lady lingering at the stern of the queen's vessel, her eyes fixed with hunger on the vizier as the barge sailed out of view. "Lady Qatsenut's in love with you, I think."

Paneah raised his head. "You're just trying to distract

me." He arched a brow and went back to his lessons. "You hate it when I do well."

Ameny's attack flashed through her mind. Paneah had pulled her from the floor. He pressed his lips to her head whispering endearments she had no intention of holding him to. He'd been anxious for her safety. "I mean it, my lord. She holds you in high regard."

Qatsenut had cornered her on the way to the vizier's barge, reminding her of their bargain. She gave instruction on how she was to be spoken of to the vizier, without sympathy or inquiry on Mepi's death. Yet, the old mothers, Ipwet and Sahathor, had offered kind condolences, however crude they were.

"Shall I marry her then?" Paneah asked, scribbling across the page.

"Marry Qatsenut? Certainly. She's beautiful."

"Beauty is not the only quality a man wants."

He baited her with the statement ready to divulge his thoughts on a woman's qualities. But she didn't dare ask him. She was no good at flirting like other women, and by the look Qatsenut sent her from the queen's vessel, she was no good at flirting for them either.

Mepi's death was still too fresh, and Jafener she had been on the verge of calling friend. She choked back a sob and spasmed with grief. Mepi deserved better, and Neferet's death ached like a deep gouge in her chest. Only now could she admit how she loved the young queen. She trembled and closed her eyes, attempting to trap her tears. "So much loss."

"It's been a heavy blow to all of us." Lord Paneah took her hand beneath the table. He squeezed it and left a linen cloth in her bent fingers.

She sniffed, dabbing her wet face, trying to regain her composure.

THEY DOCKED AT SHE-RESY AND CAMPED ON the bank of the river where a yelling match took place in the tent of Queen Weret. Khakheperre ordered his first royal wife to strip off her beloved amethyst-colored garments and don the appropriate blue of queens in mourning. The king won his argument, but his haggard face and slumped shoulders proved him sapped of strength.

Khakheperre had built a modest chapel and a small pyramid on the west bank near a fertile basin. However, the abundance of the last harvest had increased his funds greatly, and with the promise of six more prosperous harvests to come, he'd set out to expand his eternal resting place into something grander. However, Weret was livid to discover he'd allotted the smaller pyramid there to Neferet instead of to her.

The work on the king's funerary complex was brought to a halt, and the procession of courtiers meandered through a pleasant valley. The royal mourners led them forth with earnest wails that inspired tears in the coldest of hearts. But wherever there was the king's provision of food and quality beer, there his nobles would follow.

Kitjau had extended the causeway leading to the king's burial grounds to make the journey more sufferable. Slaves bore the elderly in chairs and ox-carts with a great company of sledges and servants bearing shade canopies on poles. Hundreds of bindweed wreathes, cornflower garlands and bouquets of jasmine and sweet marjoram were prepared for the opening of the mouth ceremony. Carts followed, loaded with bread, cakes, fruit, and fowl for Neferet to take with her into the afterlife.

A little fat-faced priest from Neferet's town of Pe led the cortege, his voice trembling as he quoted spells from the Book of the Dead. The great priests in attendance chuckled at his backwater accent, picking apart his poor direction of the procession. The man was a hare among jackals, stuttering under the hard and critical glares of the illustrious first prophets of the great temples, including Asenat's father who was chief of intimidators.

The king walked like a man in a dream, taking little note of the mockery. Appipa wormed her way beside him during the Opening of the Mouth ceremony. Queen Weret who walked behind them could do nothing but stare with daggers in her eyes at the back of Appipa's head. By the time the procession approached the funeral chapel Kitjau had built, Appipa hung on the king's arm.

Deduamen took the cue from his overbold daughter and tried to cut the line of intimates following the king after his officials. But the old mothers, Ipwet and Sahathor, struck him with their ebon canes, and he limped back to his place in the line beside his daughter A'at.

The king reached the ramp leading to the chapel. He stopped, and Mentuser started forward, but the king beckoned to Lord Sabni instead. Some would say Khakheperre had no need of his physician since he'd quit his fast and started eating again. But Asenat took note of the veiled concern on the watchmen's faces. They were not called to walk beside the sovereign as they had been in times past, and the three of them were composed and quiet during the entire trip. Asenat had not known the conflict between Lord Paneah and Lord Nebsumenu was so great, but after the treasury takeover, she received no more winks or inquiries from Lord Nebsumenu. Not even a look.

A hot wind stirred the long tresses of the royal mourners who stood at the base of the chapel ramp. A strange set of clouds drew near, and Asenat's father declared the darkening sky a sign of the gods' displeasure. It was wicked of him to cast such dismay with the ceremony already suffering in execution and dignity. Many began murmuring spells of protection and making signs to ward off evil.

Asenat entered the chapel with the vizier's crew and found it to be of a generous size, having not one but three chambers to capture Neferet's likeness on murals in the days of her former beauty. The king lingered at several of the muraled walls for some long moments. He could not have blamed Kitjau for failing in his task with such pressures of time and resources imposed upon him. However, Kitjau had not failed, and Asenat pushed her way through the crowded rooms of the chapel to see how the artists rendered Neferet's life in various scenes. She sighed her joy at the bright, soft colors she found to be as expressive as Neferet herself.

Scenes of life in the delta proved the young queen was not ashamed of her humble birthplace. Her life story progressed throughout the rooms, one room ending with her being taken into the king's harem, the next room starting with her marriage to the sovereign in the desert. But it was the last scene of her life Asenat had anticipated, the scene she'd rendered for Neferet on papyrus to pass to an artist.

She pushed through the crowded room to the last mural on the innermost chapel wall and gave a little gasp. She had carried out Neferet's instructions faithfully, but she was amazed that the king would allow what might be considered blasphemous with the absence of spells or gods on the chapel's innermost wall.

Asenat swallowed as tears sprouted from her eyes. Neferet stood in the last frame with an unknown girl, perhaps the sister she once spoke of. Two Asiatics stepped forward from a burst of light as if welcoming Neferet and the infant she held in her arms to eternal rest. Her fondness for the story of Abraham and Sarah made this rendering seem more a happy reunion than an end of life.

Asenat's vision blurred as tears swept down her face. How could Neferet be so foolish as to put her trust in a faceless god to succor her for all eternity? Could one god be so large? Could he bring one such joy after death?

The king came up beside Asenat. She swiped her tears as he stared at the scene, his lips parted as though trying to absorb the same wonder she felt. After a few moments, he moved away, his hope ebbing to nothing more than a tight knitted brow and a frown. He was crushed.

"It's pure sacrilege, and all for some little delta-stick of a girl."

Asenat rounded on the source of the insult, the one woman who could not keep her mouth from any deed of Lord Paneah's influence.

"Lady Kemsiyet. You dare insult our departed queen? She was a study of faithfulness and love in a wife. I believe such is a lesson you still have yet to learn."

The old mother, Sahathor, whooped at the comment. Slapping her hand to her mouth, she danced through the crowd in search of Ipwet. The look of horror on Kemsiyet's turned down mouth and slackened jaw told Asenat the words would be repeated a million times by the end of the season.

Asenat pivoted toward the sound of shouting from outside. A tangy scent filled the air. A tapping on the pavement and on the chapel roof reverberated in her ears like a thousand leaping beetles.

The king pushed past her and stepped outside. He gasped and extended his arms. The crowd below screamed and ran for their shade canopies. Khakheperre's laughter was clear and vibrant as the cold drops of water struck his skin and left dark splotches on his kilt. Few this far upriver had ever seen rain.

Asenat's chest swelled. Her eyes watered again, and she swiped them, determined not to miss such a miracle. The water-game Kitjau had rigged on Neferet's porch. Her love of delta rain. Asenat laughed as tears coursed down her cheeks.

Elohim had sent them a sign.

The king trembled, drawing a linen square from his jeweled girdle. He unfolded the cloth and raised it above his head. His guards beckoned him from inside the chapel entrance, as unstrung by the marvel as anyone.

Hetnu braved the wet platform, producing a small casket into which the king dropped the cloth. They came back inside and the rain ceased as miraculously as it had appeared. The sovereign laughed and shook the water from his robe and kilt, his eyes shining and full of joy.

"The gods show forth their anger at this blasphemy you perform here." Potipherah stepped up to the king in such a way as to startle him, but the sovereign was not disturbed. "I warned Neferet that her affection for some unknown desert god would make her unacceptable to the gods of the land."

Asenat chafed at the aspersions her father flung at

Neferet, but Khakheperre withstood the insult without losing his newfound peace. "My dear wife told me that Elohim would send back a sign if he was worthy. He has done it, just as she said he would. If you think her condemned, you are a priest, but I am a god among the gods and say that she has found at least one who accepts her."

Potipherah shifted his jaw. "His majesty is overbold in his confidence among the great gods."

"Yes," the king decided with some reflection. "And Neferet has made me so."

THE GROUND DRIED QUICKLY DESPITE THE rain, and Asenat's heart glowed as she trekked back to camp with the crowd. It seemed as though the king could be bold after all if something mattered enough to him. News of Elohim's miracle would spread, and there would be nothing the priests could do to stop it, not even her father. She walked along the edge of the paved causeway full of carts and courtiers, her gaze pulling sideways. An old man leaned against a boulder in the shade of trees some distance off the main path. He beckoned her near.

Asenat approached him, smiling. He stood bent with bowed, uneven shoulders and a lump on his back. "Are you thirsty, old father? Do you need something to drink? I can call for a chair to take you back to camp."

"Don't need your help, girl. Don't need your titles, nor the king's favor." His tone was potent with a malice that put her on guard. He pulled a leather baton from the loop at his belt with surprising agility. "But I have a message for Khakheperre."

Asenat stepped back.

He struck his palm repeatedly with the rod, and rocked toward her with a wide, bow-legged stride, his uneven steps, deceptively quick. "What's your name?"

She stepped back again and kept her eye on the rod smacking his palm.

"Asenat." He broke into a smile, the only handsome thing about him.

She did not like that he said her name. She did not like the way he said it.

"Deliver this to the king for me." He raised the cudgel, locking her limbs in place with his glare. Terror froze the scream in her throat.

"Lady Asenat!"

Sabni's bark startled her. She stumbled and turned toward his squinted gaze as he shaded his eyes from the sunlight. "What are you doing over there? Come away."

"This old father called me over." Asenat pointed to the shaded boulder, but when she turned to it again, there were only odd tracks in the dirt and the old man was gone.

AMA WENT TO FETCH BREAD AND MEAT FROM one of the cooking fires. Asenat approached her tent, shuddering. Had she met a man or an apparition? Sabni said she'd walk too far and set her on a cart until they reached the encampment. She walked to her tent and pulled back the flap. The sweet blend of almond and frankincense tickled her nose

"Majesty."

The king stopped her from lowering herself and called her over to where he sat on her stool, her scrolls spread out around his feet.

"Was it not a wonder today?" He lifted his head. His smile was radiant. "Yoseph's god spoke to my accusers in such a way that cannot be gainsaid."

Asenat smiled with him. If this Elohim had taken Neferet's life, still he did not fail her. Asenat once thought Neferet a simple village girl, but who could deny her quiet power, her humble determination? She'd changed them all.

Asenat sat on her mat at the sovereign's feet as he shared memories of Neferet, his voice thick, yet exuberant. And this, the second miracle, that for a moment, she and the king were kindred in their love for Neferet and in their belief of Elohim's power.

The king left her, and she ate in silence. Ama took their platters to wash at the riverbank, and Asenat inhaled a trembling breath. The day was full of wonder. She yawned, prepared to stretch out on her mat when her tent flap flipped up.

Qatsenut stepped in. "I see you had a visit from the king. Did you mention me? Did you tell him that I want Paneah for myself?" She tried to sound pleasant, but Asenat's patience had worn thin.

"Is that all you can think of, Qatsenut? How to get a man who pays you little mind?

"Yes." Qatsenut's voice strained to a whisper. Her face caved in with tears as she flopped on Asenat's sleeping mat. "That is all."

Drowsy-eyed, Asenat fell to her knees to comfort Qatsenut in her inconsolable weeping. It was going to be a long night.

·

CHAPTER FIFTY SEVEN

KEMSIYET

THERE WERE PARTIES TO BE ATTENDED BACK at court, and Kemsiyet prepared to board one of the barges returning to the king's house when a messenger approached her. He extended a sealed note and bowed. Her stomach flipped at the symbols she recognized. She broke the clay seal and called for a scribe to read it.

My barge awaits your arrival on the borders of Henennesut. Return with the bearer of this message, or your allowance will be cut off.

Kemsiyet snatched the note from the scribe. She searched the messenger's face for any clue that he knew the content of her husband's note, then called over her maid and gave instructions. They boarded the vessel her husband sent to retrieve her. Asenat's insult had gotten 'round fast enough to move even Nebitef to some resolve.

It was about time.

For five days, the north winds pushed the sails against rising flood waters as the vessel chonted farther south of the king's house. Kemsiyet was careful to keep a layer of self-righteous anger over the fear of facing her husband Nebitef. They hadn't held a civil conversation since his days as Potiphar of the king's house. His promotion to commander over the Ptah division of soldiers made his heart as resistant as tanned leather.

Asenat brought her to this humiliation of being summoned by him. Some of Kemsiyet's own followers had snickered at the girl's insult. And what was Asenat but some dried-up female scribe with ink-stained fingers? What could such an awkward lanky thing know about faithful wives? She would certainly never be one.

The vessel reached the borders of Henen-nesut far too soon. Kemsiyet's heart raced as the rowers took her out to her husband's formidable barge sitting in an empty part of the river. Well armed for battle, she squared her shoulders. She'd already checked with a scribe of the law and conferred with her friends on which properties she should demand. If Nebitef wanted a divorce, he could certainly have it.

She came aboard the pleasure barge to find him dressed in a kilt of blue trim. She hadn't seen him out of uniform in years. He was still strong with a solid and well-groomed form. A gold chain with a simple lion pendant hung at his chest, redolent with a scent of cassia and myrrh. Her belly clenched. It was a fragrance she used to love. He ushered her to a shade pavilion in the middle of the deck and let down the flaps.

"I'll not stay long." Kemsiyet folded her arms across her chest. "My friends are expecting me for a party."

"As always." He poured two bowls of wine.

She peered through a narrow space between the lowered

flap and the pavilion column and caught a glimpse of the oarsmen leaving the barge.

All of them.

Her heart leapt to her throat. She turned to her husband. "You wouldn't dare strike me, Nebitef."

He raked her with a look. "It's not altogether a bad idea. You could stand a strike or two." He extended a bowl. She shook her head and stepped back. She'd been careful to inform one or two of her friends where she was going. If Nebitef murdered her, the whole world would know it.

"Oh stop it, no one's going to hurt you." He quaffed both bowls of wine and stacked them on a tray then studied her until she shifted on her feet, backing up against the pavilion column. She would run if she had to.

"You were so beautiful that day in the broad hall. Despite that lying tongue of yours."

She took a step forward. "Let's settle this so I can be off. I have no wish to waste your time, and it seems that I have always done so." She turned her back to him, ashamed at the catch in her voice. Her pectoral counterweight swung across her shoulder blades. No, it was his thumb, stroking her like he used to do.

"We will make time." He gripped her shoulders with callous hands, turning her to face him.

She swallowed, willing away the longing that scorched her belly. She lowered her gaze. "You made far more time for Yoseph than for your wife." There. She'd spoken from her heart. That was the last of it.

"That was no reason to ruin the reputation of a good man." His voice croaked in soft reprimand.

No, it wasn't.

A traitorous tear cascaded down her throat. She smacked his hand away. "I wanted to hurt you."

He held her at arm's length. She braced, wanting him to hate her. She willed it.

"You are good underneath these ugly scales you've grown."

"I am not good." She snatched away from his hold.

"You have come clean of a terrible lie."

She didn't want his praise when the humiliating truth had pried itself from her heart.

A faithful wife.

How those words scored her. She had not been a faithful wife for a long time. She'd been a bitter one.

His gaze rolled over her face, and she waited for his anger to manifest. A blow, a curse here in the dark where no one could see him. She squeezed her eyes shut when he pulled her forward. His mouth covered hers, and her senses heaved and shattered. He pulled back, leaving her gasping and weak.

"Your pride has made fools of us both." His breath shuddered through his nostrils, gripping her arms. "But I forgive you. Forgive me also. I have missed the wife I love. Let us start again."

She lowered her head at the pleading in his instructive tone. Another tear spilled down her cheek. She had longed for him all this time. He drew her close and kissed her once more. And there was no other touch in the world.

Chapter Fifty Eight

Sabni

BRIGHT TORCHES LIT THE PALACE QUAY against the night sky. The courtiers shouted from their barges beyond the walls of the quay, impatient to enter. Sabni gave no heed to the logistical disaster he'd caused and ordered every vessel returning to the king's house, thoroughly checked. Until Ameny was found, a murderer was loose in the land. The angry courtiers would just have to wait.

Kitjau was nestled away on a barge far down the northern wall, inside the quay, away from the mayhem. The king made good on his promise to reward his architect for his work on Neferet's funeral chapel and gifted Kitjau with a luxury vessel weighted down with treasure and ready for travel. No one would be sadder to see him go more than Prince Khakure who, under Kitjau's tutelage, acquired a passion for building forts.

Kitjau would detour to the border city of Tjaru to drop off the bolt of Queen Weret's precious fabric at one of her estates, then head for the Great Green by way of Djedu. From there he would sail for Byblos, his homeland.

It was Weret's way to put something out of reach whenever the king insisted she share it. Even now the god's wife perched herself high on a landing to overlook Kitjau's barge. She'd probably stand there like a watchdog until the vessel left in the morning.

Besides checking the names of those returning to the king's house, there was the task of recording all those who left. Sabni passed one of the busy dock scribes and took Rudi in a half embrace. "We are sorry to see you go." He patted Rudi's shoulder, attempting to hide his irritation. Djehuti was a fool to send Rudi home with his brothers when the boy distinguished himself so well in the vizier's service.

"My father needs me to return." Rudi swallowed his complaint and directed the porters to load his belongings, but disappointment showed in his feeble smile. Djehuti was led about by the bit of his spiteful wife. If her good-for-nothing sons could not prosper at court, then even Rudi was made to suffer for it. His younger brothers, Za'amun and Meru, had learned a new level of flippancy, having spent time among the royal princes, and they swaggered past Rudi onto the departing vessel.

Sabni motioned a good riddance to the rascals, then took Rudi's shoulders. "Remember the moves I taught you. Thump Za'amun's head on the ground once or twice, and Meru will henna the soles of your feet." He patted the boy on the back, fighting the urge to make him stay.

Rudi gave a tight nod and strode up the plank with drooping shoulders. He was a good-hearted young man, the best the land had to offer, yet no good at standing up for himself. Sabni sent his brothers a scathing look until some disturbance drew his attention farther down the stone landing.

"This makes no sense!" The woman squawked at the scribe taking her name. "You cannot hold me here. I am a servant to Prince Ameny, the king's brother."

Sabni pushed his way through the crowd to a small bright skinned woman, shaking her head in animated complaint. The porters reloaded her bags on the vessel, more convinced by her than the flabbergasted docking scribe.

Sabni came up behind her, looking down on the top of her head. "You say you are Ameny's servant?"

She pivoted into the wall of his chest, and he delighted in her rich, sea-colored eyes. Her appearance was shabby, but for the polished counterweight of her menat necklace. He squinted. "Didn't I see the prince strike you in the corridor?" She'd cut her hair. There was a mark on her lip.

"I don't know what you're talking about." She turned away from him without so much as a blink.

Impudent little liar.

"Come now, admit it. You play the harp in the king's house and wear the turquoise of musicians." He leaned forward for a whiff of her fragrance and took her hand. The pads of her fingers were calloused. "It is you."

She snatched her hand away, and he was sure that only his height kept him from a slap.

"But, perhaps, if you claimed to be a palace musician in the king's service..." He let his words trail off, but she was too perturbed to take the hint.

"What do you know about it, oafish brute? Let me go, and I will trouble you no more." Was that a threat in her eyes? She was delightful.

"All right then." Sabni straightened. The scar at her mouth said she was better off without Ameny anyway.

"I'm afraid you must be held for questioning since the whereabouts of Prince Ameny are unknown."

A high-pitched scream pierced the clamor in the quay and cut off her strident protest. The god's wife Weret had forgotten her dignity and leapt up and down on the landing like a monkey on hot stones.

"My cloth!" she screeched "Someone save my bolt of fabric!"

Sabni had never seen the sour-faced queen so frantic. But the laughter died in his throat at the smoke rising from Kitjau's barge.

The first flames shot up, and he trotted toward the vessel. His heart thumped at the single man moving on deck like a demon of Set. He stabbed rowers too weak to fight him off. Sabni's gaze locked on his, and the man sent him a squat-faced grin before he took a running leap into the water. That demon of Set titled greatest of fifty.

Qareg.

Sabni roared, bursting through the pack of men racing toward the vessel. The flames consumed the deck. It might already be too late.

Chapter Fifty Nine

—◦◦◦━━◄▶◦◦◄█▶◦◦◄▶━━◦◦◦—

Nebsumenu

"THERE'S A FIRE IN THE QUAY." MENTUSER rushed into the treasure room, placing four sacks on the tables. "I sent the guards to help."

"Good. Gives us time to work without distraction." Nebsumenu nodded and kept his hands moving. It was best they tend to this business alone without witnesses. He, Mentuser, and Resnakt restored the room with jasper, debens of gold, sealed pots of myrrh, and pectorals of brightly colored stone among other treasures.

"Stop dallying!" Nebsumenu carped at Resnakt who picked through his sack of jewelry, laying out each piece with slow reverence.

"Some of it's mine." He pouted, clutching a silver pectoral to his chest. "You woke me from a good nap, and for what, but to clear out my own coffers."

Nebsumenu snorted at Resnakt's complaint. They'd all been forced to add some of their personal belongings along with what they returned to the king's coffers. The king hadn't offered to share Paneah's report, but it was best to refill the treasure room with more, not less. This had proven a greater challenge than they expected. Resnakt's whining didn't help.

Jafener's services were costly but Paneah had executed him without delay. This was a relief since dead men left few traces. "It'll be all right, Resnakt. After the king tours his coffers, you can steal it all back, again." Nebsumenu peeked over his shoulder and shook his head. Resnakt was captivated with some sparkling trinket and hadn't heard a word he said.

It was a mistake to let him organize the jewelry, but they were otherwise making good time. Mentuser was better focused and working with all speed as he sent up prayers for their protection. Two more trips to the concealed cart in the ox stalls and they'd be done.

"You were right, Mentuser. This was the best time to restore the room." Nebsumenu gave a little snicker. This was exhilarating, like a game. They would all laugh about it later.

Mentuser had assured Khakheperre they could best serve him at the palace while he took time to mourn his wife. By the time the king chadded downriver again from the burial grounds, the treasure room would be full to bursting.

Security had tightened around the palace with Sabni in charge. His early return made them edgy, but he was stuck in the quay directing courtiers. Nearly all the palace guards had been called, and Nebsumenu sent most of the treasury guards to help. The fire was a gift from the gods themselves. Sakhmet was with them.

"Two more trips," Nebsumenu mumbled as he concentrated on organizing a group of polished charms on the table. A pretty display was bound to distract from the quantity of items in the room. Let the sand dweller explain that to the king once they'd filled the room out. "Two more trips."

Resnakt drew in a sharp gasp. "I've found it. Exquisite."

"Whatever it is, put it back," Nebsumenu called over his shoulder as he worked the knots out of a chain of three silver strands.

"Have you eyes in the back of your head, Mother?"

"Don't be smart, Resnakt. Just get back to work." Mentuser's dry chuckle suggested Resnakt was distracted yet again, but there was no time to scold him. They would restore the room by the skin of their teeth for Khakheperre to tour on his return, and then lay low before dabbling in the treasure rooms again.

"My sons are quite enchanted with Prince Khakure's fort models." Resnakt was finally working again. "They're bored and troublesome at home. I think I'll let them tour the Walls of the Ruler with the prince, after all."

"No, Resnakt, not now," Nebsumenu said.

"Why not?"

"Because Paneah interpreted your dream. Can't you see it's some sort of trick?" Nebsumenu looked back and gestured for Resnakt to keep unloading his sacks. "Khakheperre's been touchy lately. A trip might be construed as guilt. Everything should appear natural. We have nothing to hide."

"I practically cleaned out my coffers. Now I can't even send my sons away?" Resnakt scoffed. "I'll need something to cheer me up."

"Someone's coming." Mentuser put his back to a wall, gripping his old scalpel. Nebsumenu turned to alert Resnakt who looked past him, his eyes round.

"Majesty." Resnakt gave a hasty bow.

Nebsumenu's heart dropped to his stomach. He faced the king, keeping his movements relaxed, natural. "Majesty." He bowed. "Back early." The king hadn't taken Mentuser's advice, after all.

"I'm too restless. Out for a stroll," Khakheperre's said. "You told me I could come see the rooms anytime."

Nebsumenu smiled. "Of course, Majesty, but alone?"

"No, indeed." The king whistled and his war dogs trotted into the room. Nebsumenu shot a look at Mentuser. The dogs were trained to kill.

"I've brought Brave One and All Seer with me." He stroked one of the dogs' heads. "Brave One's as fierce as any guard."

The dog snapped and growled. The king grabbed his collar. "Mentuser, I didn't see you there."

"Majesty." He stepped forward from a shadow and bowed, lowering his hand slowly from where he kept his scalpel at his waist.

"You find us here personally tending the treasure room Lord Paneah suggested was empty." Nebsumenu sent Mentuser a quick desperate look.

Cut him down you fool. What are you waiting for?

But Mentuser kept an eye on the king's dog who watched his hand and bared his teeth.

"I trust very few after Lord Paneah's insult to me." Nebsumenu held the king's attention. "You find us here alone because I fear he might have bribed even some of my own men. But a man who has raped a slave in your house cannot keep hidden for long. Yet I trust that the good god will see this in time."

The king clasped his hands behind his back and scanned

the room. He never asked about the sacks they emptied. He never looked at them.

Nebsumenu felt Mentuser's glare like an imprint on his face. He waited for a signal. Nebsumenu moved his hand, and one of the dogs leapt. The king snatched his collar just in time.

"Down, Brave One!"

Nebsumenu stumbled back, clutching his chest.

"Let us humor Lord Paneah for now." The king took both dogs by the collar. "And humor me also, Nebsumenu, for you have ever been a pillar of my throne."

The king gave a halting gesture, riddled with apology. Nebsumenu relaxed. How so like Khakheperre, a milksop perched atop a throne. "If you would like a more detailed tour in the morning, Majesty, of course we are at your disposal."

"I think not." The king yawned. "I am satisfied."

Nebsumenu bowed, willing Khakheperre from the room.

He started for the door, but something slid from a table and the king whisked by him.

In the wrong direction.

"You've dropped something, Resnakt."

Nebsumenu exchanged glances with Mentuser. They had to do it now.

"Keep it safe," Khakheperre said behind them. He started for the door and Nebsumenu braced to strike the king when he passed by again. But Mentuser gave a sharp shake of his head. The dogs were too close.

They bowed as the king left the room. When the sound of his footsteps faded, Nebsumenu walked over to Resnakt and pried a heavy pectoral from his grasp. He whimpered as Nebsumenu held it up.

Five peridot Ma'at charms danced from the bottom of the collar. There was space for one missing. Nebsumenu's gaze swept from Resnakt's dangling earring to the look of horror on his face.

"You woke me from my nap," Resnakt squeaked. "I forgot to take it off."

Nebsumenu struck him hard across the face. "Fool, you may have killed us all!"

CHAPTER SIXTY

YOSEPH

BY THE TIME THE OLD RECORDS OF THE ROYAL coffers were added to the king's report, Yoseph had gathered audits of all the king's holdings. Provincial reports from the harvest, the king's lands and tributes, his livestock, his groves and the state of his mansions with head counts of his slaves, all of it, stroked out in curved hieratic writing.

Yoseph reviewed the report several times with Djehuti and Chu, understanding some of the symbols Asenat had taught him. The audit of the king's coffers had proved again that one or two treasure rooms in the two houses of gold had been used as a watering trough for thieves.

Yoseph chewed a little bread for breakfast. According to Hetnu, Duaf, his food taster, had left on some family business and was not expected to return anytime soon. Kitjau was spared from death despite the night of the fire in the quay. He'd left his barge at the last minute for a farewell dinner with friends. Fifteen of his rowers sleeping on deck were stabbed, and six of them were dead. The men had been drugged for this well-planned attack.

Sabni plunged into the water chasing after the murderer,

but no one had heard from him since. He was still angry and had every right to be so when Yoseph had lied to him. But for years, he'd lied to himself as one does when he runs from a painful truth. He had brothers, and all but one of them had stolen his life.

Yoseph's body servants had perfumed and dressed him in a fine starched kilt of blue edging and trimmed him in jewels. His jasper seal of office glistened beneath the heavy gold collar he wore, and the king's signet ring adorned his left hand. Four guards escorted him through the corridors. Khakhepherre had finally summoned him for the report on his coffers, and Yoseph planned to milk their meeting for all its worth.

He passed through a corridor around the broad hall, sickened by the sight of Resnakt dressed in the dignified robes of its leader. He held the gold-capped staff that once belonged to Reniqer. Yoseph managed a civil nod, though Resnakt deserved no such honor.

"My lord Paneah," Resnakt called to him. "Have you by chance seen Lord Nebsumenu?"

Yoseph fought back the urge to tell Resnakt just what he thought of seeing Lord Nebsumenu at any given moment. "According to my roster, Lord Nebsumenu has not signed out of his duties so he must not be far away."

"Aah." Resnakt gave a weak nod. He wet his lips as if wanting to say more, but Yoseph did not linger. He made his way to the king's corridor. With Nebsumenu gone, there was no one to intercept his sealed messages, no one to bar his access to the sovereign.

The king's voice rang in reprimand and Yoseph left his guards in the corridor as he headed for the sovereign's leisure room. He stopped in the doorway.

"You dare resist me?" The king challenged the girl who fought him for control of her sheath strap. Her eyes were wide with panic, her shoulders locked.

Khakheperre leaned in, his tone low and menacing. "Let go of the strap now. Or else."

Yoseph stepped forward. "Perhaps Lady A'at misunderstands, Majesty." The girl was terrified. "Let me take her to your harem where she can be properly trained. I will send for another to please you." He extended a hand to the girl, never liking the king less than in this moment.

The room was silent but for her hysterical gasps.

"This one's not fit for a harem. They'd eat her alive." Khakheperre loosened his grip on her strap. "Kiss me then," he ordered, but A'at stubbornly tucked her chin. Khakheperre snorted, snatching a peck from her lips before he spun her away. "Back to your room, little country mouse. And do not come out until you are called for."

A'at fled the chamber, and Khakheperre adjusted his robes as he walked out on his porch. "Come out, Paneah. It's too hot in there."

Yoseph followed, pressing down his glower.

Hau, the king's fanning slave, snored from the far side of the balcony. His long frame stretched out on a thick mat under a shade canvas. Khakheperre did not stir him but stopped at a tray between two chairs to pour wine.

Yoseph came up behind him, eager to discuss the report he set on the tray. He sat in one of the chairs, but Khakheperre moved to where a hammock swung from two poles nestled in the shade of a persea. He plucked a small yellow fruit, the Heart of Horus they were nicknamed, placing it on a table near him.

Yoseph turned the cup in his hands, trying to form his

next words with care. "My lord does not molest women. Such an act is beneath the good god."

The king reached for the persea fruit and tossed it from hand to hand. "Yes, it is. And despite Kemsiyet's gossip and the event in your garden, neither do you molest women. Any more than my watchmen are thieves. Let this war between you now come to an end. I toured my coffers. You were mistaken about the empty rooms."

Yoseph checked his anger at the king's plea-offering on behalf of his watchmen. "Were treasury guards present when you toured the rooms, Majesty? Did you visit in the day or in the night?"

"Tell me what you think of her." Khakheperre motioned to his leisure room and reached for his cup, ending their discussion on his visit to his coffers.

"I've had little time to study A'at." Yoseph struggled to keep his voice light. There were more pressing matters to speak of, Khakheperre's murdered subjects, Jafener's execution. "She's Appipa's twin and was part of Neferet's ornate, wasn't she?"

"And was in her confidence." Khakheperre plucked a leaf from the tree branch. "By Horus, I miss Neferet." He sat up to stare past the great pylons of his private dwelling. "I used to see the Horus columns from here. But I won't put them back up now that Neferet's gone. I've commissioned two statues of her to replace the columns. My courtiers didn't like my little wife, but I'll make them take note of her for as long as I live." He gave a heavy sigh and lay back on his hammock again, covering his face with his arm. He rocked silently for a moment. "What do you think of Asenat?"

Yoseph's pulse raced beneath the gold cuffs at his wrists.

"Is His Majesty planning to take her as wife? She is a fine scribe." She would be miserable in the king's harem.

"And she is also the only reason you ever pushed yourself into my presence uninvited. Perhaps Qatsenut would be a better influence on your manners."

"Qatsenut is a beautiful woman."

"Qatsenut is as lush and ripe as fruit itself. And among all the lush fruit in my house, you prefer a green fig." The king sat up and reached for his cup.

"Ripe fruit spoils quickly. Unripe fruit has yet to mature. I trust you will remember Asenat has served you well." Yoseph rose and pulled his chair closer to the king's hammock.

"So you say, but I understand she wants to ruin the rest of her life as a priestess of Pakhet."

The king shot him a look that told Yoseph he could ask for her if he wanted. It would slake Khakheperre's thirst for revenge against both Potipherah and Asenat. Yoseph had no wish to be a seen as a means of the king's revenge in her eyes. He could keep her safe. But they would both know it was he who kept her from Pakhet. And she would use it against him. Still, the request danced on the tip of his tongue. "It is the life she wants."

"Yes. And I am reminded of that as often as I see Qatsenut. My cousin is not easily outdone. She will make you a good wife, unlike Asenat who has gotten Ameny into a fine mess."

"Your brother has done murder and gotten himself into a mess."

The king threw his cup against a wall. "What would you have me do, Paneah? Would you put your own brother to death!"

"Let this not be the day one of your wise men spoke of. The day when one sits quiet, turning his back while one man kills another."

"How dare you." The king shot up from the hammock pointing his finger. "I drew you from the pit and made myself a fool for the words of your god."

"And he has performed his word."

"He's extracted a cruel price. She who was most precious to me is no more. Those held in my confidence have turned against me." There was panic in the king's voice.

"God has not turned your men against you but revealed your enemies, Khakheperre. Neferet went to her death in peace, and your whole court beheld a miracle in the desert. Elohim has fulfilled his word.

"But there are some things that he has not done for you. He has not prevented your governors from cheating you, nor staunched the flow of their defiance, nor repaired the broken dikes, nor restored boundary stones to their right settings. These things he has left for *you* to correct." Yoseph plucked the report from the tray. "Here is an audit of all you hold. See for yourself who cheats and who defies you."

Khakheperre stepped back and shook his head. "I don't need a report when the harvest has brought me more than I've had in years."

"And what is one good harvest when your governors steal from you? They build granaries for themselves and fill yours with chaff."

Khakheperre tromped back inside to his leisure room.

Yoseph followed. "You cannot keep lying to yourself, Khakheperre. Your governors call you king and throw you crumbs."

"I am Horus who leads the two lands."

"Then lead the two lands, and do not let your subjects treat you like a governor with no province."

The king reached his couch. Yoseph sat beside him and placed the report in his lap. Khakheperre knocked it to the floor.

"What is it that you think you can do? I have kept you alive, and you've made my enemies mock me."

"If you turn your gaze from wickedness in your house and in your land, injustice wins. Your governors will continue mocking you if you do nothing. Let me go out. I will set them straight on your account."

"No. You will be safer if you govern from here."

"But for how long, Khakheperre? Your enemies encroach, and you cower. I bring you the truth of murder in your own house, and you will not hear it."

The king covered his ears. "I cannot do it, Paneah. I must not!"

The violent shake of his head, the wild look in his eyes, his clenched fists pressed to his ears.

Yoseph drew back.

"You knew your men stole from you. You knew they dipped into your coffers."

"It has always been done." The king answered in a strained whisper. "There is nothing I can do about it. I thought you might confirm my suspicions, but you have gone too far, Paneah. Let them be. Say no more."

Yoseph could hardly speak. Khakheperre shook. His hands covered his face. Yoseph pulled them down. "You are afraid, Khakheperre, but no coward. You accepted the word of a slave as interpretation of your Horus dream. You challenged the heart of your whole court to make me your vizier. When your subjects mocked my inauguration ceremony, you took them to task for it. You stood up for Neferet because you loved her. You changed laws to make her a queen. So do not say that you cannot do it. Say that you will not." Yoseph released his grip on the king's wrists. "But if you will not do this for yourself, then do it for your son Khakure, for he must come after you, and for Reniqer and Mepi, who died trying to bring you the truth as much as I have."

CHAPTER SIXTY ONE

————•)•((•——•)•((•■•))•)•((•——•)•((•————

NEBSUMENU

NEBSUMENU CHECKED OVER HIS SHOULDER
again as the boatman maneuvered the skiff through the
heavy river traffic. The rising inundation waters sped them
on their journey. He smiled, glad he'd lucked out on a good
rower. Why then was he so jittery?

He'd gotten a good three days head start and paid the
boatman to move at top speed without asking questions.
He only imagined that someone followed them.

Perhaps it was his own guilt. He'd broken his pact
with Mentuser and Resnakt and left without telling them.
Resnakt would be the last to catch on while Mentuser
would probably head south toward the birthplace of his
patron goddess, Sakhmet, for protection. Good. As long as
the trail led away from him.

He'd lost the cool nerves required for stealing as well
as his influence with Khakheppre. That became clear
when the king gave Paneah back his seal despite argument
against it. And Khakheperre had not called for him again
after coming upon them in his treasure rooms.

It was time to cut and run.

He'd sent his wife Satweret downriver, ahead of him, with enough treasure to reestablish them elsewhere. He opened the note she left before her departure, relaxed enough to finally read it.

His gaze brushed over the message, and he crushed it, then pulled his hand down over his face. Stupid little twit. And, she held all their reserve. "We'll have to stop on the north side of Iunu at one of the dye markets there."

The rower nodded and kept up a steady pace of driving through tight spaces between vessels and dodging barges.

Nebsumenu looked back over his shoulder and shook off the feeling of being followed. When he caught up with his little wife, he'd beat her for this.

Chapter Sixty Two

Asenat

TWO POLISHED BLACK GRANITE STATUES OF Queen Neferet stood on blocks of pink quartz in the center of the main thoroughfare. Surrounded by shading trees, stone benches, and sparkling fish pools, the setting covered the gaping holes left by the Horus columns. Asenat passed the statues, stifling her grief. She wished she'd been a better friend.

She turned into the enclosed walls of the vizier's mansion and came into his office where a few servants helped her lay out her writing supplies. She'd brought all she thought she would need to ensure Paneah's preparation for his first harvest report. He leaned against the doorway at his landing, facing away from her as he spoke with someone.

"But no one has seen him, my lord." Chu moved into view. "Ibiau has taken charge of the treasury in his absence. His wife Satweret has gone downriver on a shopping excursion, but she took a fast skiff, and we've lost track of her."

"Noblewomen on shopping excursions do not take skiffs. They take barges. Have no doubt that she outran you on purpose." Paneah exhaled, rubbing the lines in his forehead. "Find her."

Chu bowed himself out and passed her a nod as he left the room. Paneah followed him inside, dismissing everyone. She set out the ink palettes and reed pens, concealing her relief that her father was not mentioned as suspect in any of this. But nothing would change the fact that she was Potipherah's daughter.

She looked up. Lord Paneah stood beside her and would not sit at the pen and sheet she laid out for him. "My lord?" Her cheeks warmed at his searching gaze.

He extended a hand to her. "Come, I have something to show you."

She had never held his hand, but her hesitation was silly. She took it, letting him pull her up from the cushions. Her stomach fluttered at the strength of his grasp. He led her to two chairs. She sat, resisting the urge to scoot back when their knees almost touched. She clasped her hands in her lap. Two cedar boxes and a cloth-covered item were on the small table beside them. Paneah opened the first box and presented her with a scroll. Mepi's seal was broken and resealed by the king's signet ring.

"Read it," Paneah said.

She broke the seal and read the document aloud, almost hearing Mepi's voice in her ear.

Year seventeen of Khakheperre Senuseret, season of Shemu, month of Ujat.

I bequeath my lands in Khem to Henhenit my house woman. She is henceforth free and shall receive a third of my goods and coffers. Wenen, my young man, I set free also. He shall have an eighth of my coffers and my townhouse in Tjeny. Asenat, who is the daughter of my heart, shall have my estates in Hut-repyt, Hebenu, and Ipu and the balance of all that I have. Let no man gainsay it.

Mepi,

Overseer of the King's Scroll Room and Collector of Ancient Works

Asenat lowered the document. Her breath caught in her throat. "I have not been a good daughter to him." She swiped the tears running down her cheeks.

Paneah leaned forward, squeezing her limp wrist. "You must accept Mepi's gift." He indicated a small chest, next to the table. "He has also left you his personal musings."

Asenat sniffed and nodded. She would refuse nothing of Mepi's, however unworthy she felt.

Paneah reached for the covered item on the table and placed it in her lap.

"What is this?"

"Neferet has made all her girls wealthy, but this, she left for you." His gaze directed her to the covered object. She removed the cloth and covered her mouth. It was the paddle doll Neferet always placed in her lap. Paneah spoke, but she could not hear him above her sobs as she held the doll at her breasts. He placed a piece of potsherd in her hand, and she scrubbed her eyes to read Neferet's poorly scratched out message.

'Do not be afraid to love, my sister.'

Asenat closed the message in her hand, and Paneah pressed a linen cloth to her wet face, then wiped her nose. He took the items from her and moved his chair closer to tug her into an embrace. She wept on his neck, then pulled back and tried to wipe the kohl-darkened tears that streaked down his chest. She was an open wound, bleeding tears and gasping.

He took her hands and held them until her agony settled. "I am sorry to have reminded you of such loss. But there is good news." He placed another scroll in her lap. She sniffed and broke the clay seal bearing the king's mark.

"It says the king will allow your admittance to the temple of Pakhet," he said before she could unroll it. "I will have to find a new writing instructor." His unblinking gaze held hers. "But I am not happy for it."

THE WEST WINDS HELD BACK THE HEAT OF THE season long enough for the king to hold the reading of harvest reports in the new central gardens. It was hard to be in this beautiful place, knowing it was the last of Kitjau's excellent work.

The king's architect joined prince Khakure to tour the Walls of the Ruler while the king had another barge built and loaded with treasure for Kitjau before he set out for the Great Green. Egypt held half of his blood and half of his heart. Byblos held the rest. The king's house would not be the same without Kitjau, nor without Reniqer, nor the scroll room without dear Mepi.

The world had lost its color in Asenat's eyes, and it was sheer misery on all accounts.

Lord Paneah had not relied on the tallies sent in by the fifty-three governors, mayors, and provincial representatives, but had sent out his own men to count the harvest profits firsthand. This he did to curtail the poor attention given to the king's granaries in the provinces.

His diligence outraged the governors who were not

accustomed to being checked on by the vizier's delegates. They balked at their orders and came to the king's house to hear the reports themselves. The reading of the harvest reports was considered a formal affair. Governors and nobles donned shend'ots and the ladies their beadnet dresses over sheer linen.

The provincial rulers were at liberty to interrupt the vizier's report as he announced his findings to the king. And by the stern and disgruntled looks on their faces, Asenat suspected they would give Lord Paneah high water over the slightest discrepancy. The king ordered Paneah not to speak of the governors, which made the report even harder to read without lying.

Contempt for the king welled in Asenat's gut. He allowed murder in his house, the brutal rape of a slave girl, and unexplained losses in his coffers. And he did nothing about it.

As chief scribe of the vizier until she left for the temple of Pakhet, Asenat stood to the right of Paneah, facing the crowd. As chamberlain and keeper of items with right of entry, Chu stood to the vizier's left. Asenat glanced at the stalwart profiles of Lord Paneah and Chu. How wrong she'd been about each of these men. She was proud to stand beside them now.

Lord Paneah bore his weight on his left leg. His right foot showed signs of another sore forming. Asenat and Chu urged him to take a stool, but he would not. It was his pride. He'd been accused of misdeeds in the king's house. His indignity at the Horus columns. The murder of the king's officials. The courtiers would call any sign of sickness upon him a curse from the gods. So he stood straight and true before his critics. But the strain on his face suggested the pain exhausted him.

Ipuur stood behind the three of them, drawing winks from some of the women in the crowd. He'd become quite the lady's man with the new teeth Paneah commissioned to replace the ones Prince Ameny had knocked out. A set of polished acacia wood teeth for everyday wear and the gold ones he wore for special occasions like today. The king had yet to summon him or Asenat to hear testimony against his brother.

Sabni had not reappeared since the fire in the quay. His absence grieved Paneah, whose platter was full with the province lords set on their haunches, scowling at him. And the faithless courtiers of the king's house, who had at first marveled at the new handsome vizier, but who now came out to mock him.

Asenat would guide Paneah through the reading of the reports, a daunting task since he'd learned only a few symbols of the hieratic writing style. She resorted to writing out basic hieroglyphs and primitive word pictures to help him keep up. They'd practiced again and again until Paneah had memorized most of the information, but now there was the slightest tremble in his fingers as he sorted the pages.

The barge from the temple of Pakhet was chadding downriver to collect Asenat within a day's time, and Paneah was disappointed she could not stay for the Taking of the River ceremony. Itjtawy was the most beautiful part of the land to showcase the gods sailing on their barks. The people celebrated and worshiped, littering the river with red lotuses and water wreathes.

Asenat would miss the tradition. But it was for the best that she was leaving, and she would not flatter herself that the gloom in Paneah's eyes was for her. His needling displeasure was due to the strenuous duty he performed for the king and because of his sore foot. Nothing more.

The lovely Qatsenut would cheer him. She stood at the front of the crowd, elegant in her sheath with a girdle of yellow and gold painted acacia beads caressing her round hips. Asenat sent her a kind nod, but Qatsenut cut a look sideways, and shifted her shoulders. Her regard was for none but Paneah. He'd finally found the time to dine with her on his barge, and there was light jesting and expectation at court concerning the two of them.

The mothers, Ipwet and Sahathor, had dogged Asenat and pulled her to a corner. They shook their gold-laden fingers and brought her to account for not snatching the vizier up for herself. She was flattered that they'd actually bet on her, but how could she ever have compared to the beautiful and polished Qatsenut who would make Paneah a proper wife. Her nails would be hennaed and her hands decked in elaborate rings, not stained with ink-soot. She would give him a beautiful home, children. She would make the courtiers love him again.

The absent Governor Nakht sent his usual apologies to the king along with a few small gifts, none of which compensated for the loss of Queen Weret's precious bolt of fabric.

The god's wife sat across from the king on the other side of the platform, her composed expression one of thinly veiled misery over the loss of her amethyst-colored cloth, yet far more than she'd shown at Neferet's funeral. Or perhaps her misery was due to Deduamen's daughters, both of whom the king seated behind his throne. A'at's face was full of its usual meekness, and Appipa's full of arrogance. Pregnancy forced her to a greater measure of modesty in her appearance though she was more ravishing than ever. She seemed to enjoy flaunting her fertile condition though it was doubtful that the child in her belly was the king's.

The sovereign was quick-tempered today, so much so that even Hetnu offered wine while standing some distance back from the throne. The king motioned, and Lord Paneah began with Governor Nakht's province.

Hetnu's suggestion of this proved to be a good start since Nakht was absent. There would be no debate over numbers, and for the next few moments the reading of the reports went miraculously well. Lord Paneah progressed without incident until Lord Deduamen pushed his way to the front of the crowd.

He emerged, dragging his son Hotepi with him. Asenat braced as he stopped, stiff with drink, beside Qatsenut. He glittered in gold rings and charms, once again copying the vizier's long gossamer robes. The slight inflection in Lord Paneah's voice told Asenat that he'd noticed Deduamen's presence. Lord Paneah continued without pause though murmurs rose from below the platform where Deduamen stood.

"How do we know the sand dweller's even telling the truth?" Deduamen slurred. "He hasn't learned to read."

Asenat mashed her lips together, marking with her finger the place where Lord Paneah read. She was on the verge of answering Deduamen when Paneah shot her a look, warning her to stay silent.

But Chu would not be silenced. "The vizier is in very good company, my Lord Deduamen, as there are a great number of governors who do not read, you being one of them." His cut brought a roar of laughter from the crowd. Even the king snickered into his wine cup. But Asenat's blood boiled. Lord Paneah had done everything he could to bring order to the king's house, and the people only sought to punish him for it.

Deduamen knitted his brows together and scowled. He took an off-balanced step forward and faced the crowd. "Did not this Asiatic perform some meaningless investigation during the time of mourning for one of the king's wives? Why do we waste time here when the king's own watchmen do not show up? Even the prayerful Mentuser is absent."

Khakheperre stood up on the stool of his throne and searched the platform. "Where are my watchmen?" The crowd stirred, and he gestured with a piqued impatience as Ibiau, the attendant of the treasury hall, minced forward and presented a note. The king smacked it from his hand.

"I gave no one permission to leave." His sharp tone silenced the crowd, and Deduamen cowered behind a woman wearing an ostrich-plumed headdress.

Asenat scanned the crowd for a hint of vermillion, that would indicate Lady Satweret's presence, but Nebsumenu's popular wife was not in attendance.

"Go and fetch my watchmen." The king gave the order, not to the attendants who approached him, but to his guards.

THIS WAS THE THIRD DAY THE PROVINCIAL governors and courtiers were ordered to return to the central gardens to do nothing but stand. No one was allowed to leave the palace grounds, and the barge from the Pakhet temple had come and gone without Asenat. But who would dare ask permission to leave? Who would dare move with the king's anger so fierce and snapping?

There was a recess during the hottest part of the day, but there was no music, nor banquets, nor entertainment of any kind. Deduamen made no more outbursts but remained hidden in the crowd, away from the king's dark gaze. The intensity of the day's heat would have left them sweating out their linen if not for Hetnu's careful suggestion. He convinced the sovereign to erect shade pavilions above the crowd to catch the cooling west winds.

Hau, the king's fanning slave, labored over Khakheperre who sat on the throne clenching and unclenching his scepter and fists. He would not seek advice from his council, nor accept a cup of wine from Hetnu, nor look once at Lord Paneah who stood at the podium.

Potipherah came to join the priests, resplendent in his usual gold collar and long embroidered skirt. Asenat squinted her gaze at her father, the way he stood among the king's counselors and smiled. And his smile was something he never offered in kindness.

Her legs cramped, and she pressed her hand to her stomach to dampen a rising growl of hunger. It was almost time for a mid-day break from the heat. She glanced up, and coming through the crowd were guards bringing in Lord Resnakt.

He was bound and weeping.

Mentuser filed in behind him, neatly dressed in a traveling kilt instead of the formal shend'ot. His lips moved in the customary prayer of his office. He bowed with the proper subservience, and his gold and carnelian medallion sparkled on his chest. His hands were unbound, and he pulled back his shoulders in a state of self-possession, enough to make one think his arrest preposterous.

Khakheperre raised his voice above the clamorous

speculation growing in the crowd. "What's this? My watchmen are returned to me, but unwilling?" His voice rang with mocking joviality. "Mentuser, my trusted physician. I fear to ask why you've left my side."

Mentuser could not seem to form an answer above Resnakt's wails that surged and dipped like sorrowful songs while he panted like one mortally wounded.

One of the guards holding Resnakt up addressed the king. "Majesty, we found my Lord Resnakt hiding on a floating dock near a concealed set of water steps. He was boarding a fast-skiff." A look of revulsion crossed the guard's face. "We captured him as a fishing net emerged from under the floating dock. Entangled in the net were Resnakt's sons."

"Were they hurt?"

"All six boys." The guard swallowed. "Drowned."

A sharp intake of breath ran throughout the crowd. Asenat covered her gaping mouth as Paneah grasped the podium. The king forestalled a shudder and gestured a sign of protection for his offspring. He fell back in his chair, glaring at the leader of the broad hall.

"So Resnakt, you let your children drown beneath your feet to hide from the justice due you." The king fell silent and seemed to stare through the sobbing broad hall leader. He motioned over his shoulder. "Come forward, Imehy." The dwarf stepped out from a curtain and approached the throne.

"I long suspected you were passing water on me, Resnakt, with your flattery and wig dressing while you wore treasure from my coffers. I planted the vizier's dwarf among my jewelers to see what he could discover. But Elohim brought me to my own treasure rooms to find you holding the very collar that matched the trinket dangling from your ear, the trinket you stole. Still I would not accept this truth, even when it was plainly presented to me." The king shot a glance at Paneah and looked away. "And where is my treasurer, Nebsumenu?"

"We still search for him, Majesty," a guard answered.

The king stood. "Then you are all dismissed until tomorrow." Among the groans in the crowd, someone hailed the king from the back of the gathering.

Sabni had returned and pushed two hooded figures dressed in cloaks through the press. The smaller one weeping, the larger one gagged. He brought them to the base of the king's platform and pulled back their hoods, forcing them to their knees. The king motioned for them to stand and the crowd gasped.

Khakheperre was very still, and in his familiar cowardice looked to be on the verge of dismissing everyone. Somehow his regard came to rest on Asenat, and she found her lips moving in the text they heard when they supped together.

"...those who wore my fine linen looked on me as a shadow, and they who smeared my myrrh poured water under me..."

The king dragged his gaze away from her mouth. How could he not be shaken? Nebsumenu had been his anchor and his base. Nebsumenu had been his chief confidant.

He did not dismiss the crowd. He did not move from his throne, but reached back for the arms of his chair to lower himself like a sick man.

"Nebsumenu. My friend." The sovereign gave a trembling smile. "You have returned."

The treasurer had disguised himself like a peasant fresh out of the field. The thin lines of his sculptured beard were buried in stubble, as were his chest and limbs. This was also true for Sabni and proof that he'd pursued Nebsumenu for some time. His wife Satweret sniveled beside him with her shoulders hunched as though trying to shrink herself.

It was almost comical how Sabni cut the gag from Nebsumenu's mouth, and he sprang vigorously to his own defense.

"Majesty." He bowed, his voice calm and elegant, despite the patched peasant kilt he wore.

"You will explain why you are dressed thus," the king said. "Why you have left my house without my knowledge or permission." The king snapped his fingers, and his crook and flail were brought to him on a gold tray. His trembling hand hovered over the scepters. He chose the flail and pressed it to his chest.

Nebsumenu rubbed his wrists where Sabni cut the ropes. His face bore the look of insult with his pinched mouth, but his gaze shifted around the crowd.

"It is outrageous that a faithful servant of the king is no longer safe in his lord's house."

"I will decide who is faithful and what is safe." The king pointed his flail scepter.

"I was threatened by the vizier and forced to steal away." Nebsumenu addressed the crowd. "Has this sand dweller not chased away the king's own brother?"

Asenat jerked forward to voice her protest, but Paneah yanked her to his side with a sharp whisper. "We have done our part. The king must now do his."

Nebsumenu gestured to the other watchmen. "I

instructed Resnakt and Mentuser to say nothing while I went for help."

"The vizier has not chased Ameny away. My brother is under suspicion of murder." The king's words stirred the crowd. He raised a hand for silence. "But tell me, Nebsumenu, why should my treasurer go for help when the palace is full of guards?"

"I feared the guards in the king's house had been bought by the vizier. Look how Sabni has manhandled me." He extended his arms showing the wounds on his wrists where Sabni had bound him.

The king expelled a dry chuckle.

"I was on my way with all speed to your mansion in Tjaru to gather soldiers true of heart in your servi—"

"Lord Sabni." The king raised a hand, cutting off Nebsumenu's complaint.

"That much is true of his speed, Majesty. The little craft he hired to chad him downriver, maneuvered like a crock in the water. I found him seven days out at a town below Iunu where he stopped to collect his wife. Lady Satweret was picking out vermillion dye. Otherwise, your treasurer might have made it all the way to the borders."

A cold chill blew through Asenat when her father covered his mouth to chuckle deep in his chest.

He'd played some part in this, after all.

The king sat forward in his chair. "And did you find the proper shade of vermillion, Lady Satweret?" He indicated her stained white sheath.

Satweret trembled and cast a wide-eyed look at her husband. She whimpered as her pretty visage creased. She knew that this was the end of her shopping excursions, the end of her popularity at court, the end of all ends.

"I was desperate to save your servants, Mentuser and Resnakt," Nebsumenu insisted. "Good men such as Reniqer and Mepi have already died in your house. Even the young prince Neheri must have discovered something about the vizier while in his service for no one has seen him."

"Lies do not hold. You have stolen from the king!" Paneah snapped.

"And of course, you have seen this." There was a faint sneer in Nebsumenu's voice. He was once again the elegant treasurer, persuasive, commanding. "You, a sand dweller who wrestles in the yard with princes and behaves like a laborer in a pit. Who could trust a man with such a lack of discretion?"

A few from the crowd mumbled affirmation of this, and Asenat's heart fluttered with dread.

Lord Paneah stepped to the edge of the platform. "Kitjau informed met that you even pilfered the king's coffers in broad daylight, so I came to see for myself. On the day that I waved to you from the worker's pit around the Horus columns, Lord Mentuser and Lord Resnakt were beside you. Neither the guards nor the gate scribes checked your exit as you told me they would. I had the treasury records checked. There was no mention or written order for the two sacks you carried out of the gates that day. The courtiers came out to mock me in the worker's pit, but they also saw you stealing."

A rumble of speculation rose, and Nebsumenu lost a finger of boldness. "Kitjau is not here to confirm your words." He turned to the crowd with a mocking grin. "Perhaps someone else then? Who saw me as this sand dweller claims, stealing from the sovereign?"

No one in the crowd answered. They would not stand with

Lord Paneah. They would choose the elegant Nebsumenu
who was their kinsman, a liar, and a thief. Asenat covered
her face, gasping for air.

*Elohim, give me reason to believe you as Neferet did.
Prove yourself or they will rip Paneah to shreds.*

"I was there!"

She stumbled and clutched the podium. Prince Dagi
pushed his way forward. He bared his teeth as tears washed
down his angry face.

"Liar!" he cried, pointing at Nebsumenu. "I saw them
do it." His voice cracked. "I was perched on the statue of
Horus. I saw Nebsumenu and Resnakt and Mentuser take
the sacks just as the vizier said!"

"Do you see the influence of this man on your house,
Majesty?" Nebsumenu pointed to the vizier. "One prince
goes missing. Another is taught to lie. This sand dweller is
a troubler."

"I am the mouth of Nekhen and lie not!" Dagi shrieked,
balling his fists, the cords in his neck strained. "You are the
liar. You have killed Neheri!"

Mentuser's eyes widened. He stepped forward. "The boy
knows not of what he speaks."

"Nebsumenu and Resnakt held him down while Mentuser
sliced him by the riverbank when he could not answer their
demands. I tried to go for help but my limbs were stone."
Dagi's face broke up, and he staggered. He broke loose
from Sabni's hold, rounding on Mentuser.

"You are no longer a pure priest of Sakhmet." He pointed
his finger in judgment. "You have broken your vow and
killed a royal prince. Sakhmet will no longer hear you! She
will no longer protect you!"

Mentuser stumbled back, raising a hand as if to block

the words. "No, do not utter such things aloud. Do not let the gods hear you. I did not kill the prince. He bled out, and the gods took him. Not me!" He fell to his knees, shaking, and touched his forehead to the ground. "You should not have made me cut him so deeply, Nebsumenu. Tell them Resnakt. I am yet a pure priest of Sakhmet." He groaned into the dirt, weeping. "I am pure."

CHAPTER SIXTY THREE

YOSEPH

COURTIERS FOUGHT FOR SPACE AS THEY LINED the walls of the third courtyard of the vizier's mansion. The executioners covered the limestone pavement with wood chips and a thick layer of sand. Some of them sharpened blades while others stoked the oven fire, heating the cauterizing irons to a bright glow.

There were some things worse than death.

Administrators and provincial governors were ordered to attend. The rest of the onlookers who were unable to squeeze into the courtyard perched themselves high on the walls patrolled by guards, but the king indulged his jaded subjects this once.

Khakheperre was a dark, unmoving sphinx on his throne. Only by the veins that twitched on the back of his hand did they know him mortal. Some claimed that beneath his Horus crown was the visage of Thoth, come down to hearten him and judge the wrongdoers, transforming even the war dog at his feet to the image of Ammut, the demon heart-eater.

The group was brought into the yard. Roped like cattle,

they wept and moaned. The high officials, once known as Nebsumenu, Resnakt, and Mentuser, were now "the accursed," and the judgment of their crimes would be shared by all the members of their households.

Yoseph dared to plead in the king's ear for Mentuser's blind and crippled father and for Nebsumenu's nieces, three tender girls below marrying age. The sovereign refused. But one of Resnakt's concubines begged unrelenting for the infant she clutched, and though the king's face was hard like basalt, he flicked a gesture and a guard took the child. The babe's mother wept, grateful for the good god's mercy. The infant would be nurtured on the breast of a slave until she was old enough to be sold.

Yoseph trembled, signing the clay tablet with his given name, Zaphenath Paneah. The king's scribe rolled his seal, affixing his mark to the king's decree.

The bonds of the accursed, once called Nebsumenu, were cut from the group. He was still gagged when they dragged him to the block. The king pushed forward in his chair and cupped a hand to his mouth as though he might show mercy, and order him killed outright.

"When you remove his gag, I want his lying tongue," the king said as a servant sloshing a jar full of brine rushed forward to stand near the executioners. "And give me one of those thieving hands." His light-hearted tone invited hecklers to join in, but no one in the crowd laughed or moved. Only a chorus of wails from the group tied together filled the air. They awaited dismemberment of their ears, eyes, noses, lips or limbs before being sent out into the desert where one hoped for death before marauding tribes and starving jackals took hold.

The executioner gripping the axe, a beefy pocked-faced

man, slung a handful of sand on the wide slab and grinned. The accursed, once named Nebsumenu, slobbered incoherent pleas when they removed his gag and pressed him to the block. A hush fell. The sovereign signaled, and the axe came down.

Now, the screams began in earnest.

CHAPTER SIXTY FOUR

---◄·)·◄·►◄·)·◄⬛►·◄·)·►·◄·)·◄·►---

HETNU

*SEARCH OUT A FAR-FETCHED MATTER.
Especially when the stakes are high.*

Djehuti's advice clung to Hetnu in the same way he
clung to the rail of the vessel taking him down the canal.
He clenched every muscle in his body, begging his stomach
to either quit its rebellion or complete it. He'd retched on
his fly whisk and flung it in the water. If he never heard the
term "watchmen" again, it would be too soon.

He'd praised these men to the heavens, at times
correcting even the king for doubting them. Yet it took less
than two harvest seasons for a slave from the prisons to
discover and reveal their corruption. The hounding truth
tormented Hetnu.

*Even Khakheperre caught the scent of their betrayal. But
not you, fool.*

Nen was away on some errand, and another of Hetnu's
nondescript servants met him at the water steps of his
estate. The man greeted him, bowing and jabbering some
apology Hetnu did not care to hear. He waved the servant

off and wandered through his grounds, letting his feet find their way to his sleeping chamber.

The scent of flowers in the evening air was not enough to make him forget the blood, the flies, the vomit. The screams. The courtiers watched in bloodthirsty fascination, throwing rocks and sticks while the accursed waited their turn at the block. Hetnu swayed but could not make himself faint. And he could not make himself look away.

His limbs were heavy by the time he reached the columns of his porch. He let the moonlight draw him out to his private garden where a low-burning lamp flickered in the shadows of a tree. He approached the man resting in one of his chairs holding something in his arms. Someone. A child, her head reclined, her mouth open.

"My baby!" Hetnu rushed forward, his heart nearly bursting from his chest.

Potipherah pressed a finger to his lips, commanding silence. "You'll wake her, fool." The priest turned Imini deeper into the crook of his arms. She groaned, pressing her wet thumb against his chest. The little traitor.

Potipherah met his gaze. "Afraid I snapped her neck? That's just like you." He huffed, stroking Imini's back as he searched her face. "She sang and danced for me, you know. A sheer delight. I became a real father. Not playing at it like you." He turned his head, casting Hetnu a noxious glance.

Hetnu snapped his fingers at the woman standing behind a tree. Imini's nurse rushed to take the child, her face glistening with tears as she avoided his scowl. She took Imini from Potipherah's arms and bowed herself out. The sound of her fast shuffle up the path faded, and Hetnu promised himself he'd flay someone for this later.

"Now, tell me. How does it feel to have your daughter taken from you?" Potipherah laced his long blue fingers together. "For that is exactly what you have done to me."

"I did not take Asenat from you. The girl ran."

"Nor did I take Rudet from you, though you would not believe it."

"No, Rudet you stole from me. As for Asenat, I have nurtured the girl, something you've failed to learn in your fathering."

"She is my daughter, Hetnu. Not yours."

"I think our chat here is done." Hetnu shot out of his seat.

"By all means, call your guards. But have them carry you away for being such a buffoon with the king's watchmen."

The words pierced Hetnu. His knees weakened. He sat.

"And don't start that crying, again! Gods, how you make me sick! Between all the king's supposedly trustworthy administrators, the sand dweller serves him best. He's far more useful than you."

Hetnu swallowed a lump of misery rising in his throat. "You harassed the king. In the corridor of his state chamber. I saw you. I saw the blue marks on Khakheperre's chest."

A grin crept across Potipherah's face. "I roughed him up a bit, yes. But did you see how that little scamp worked his way out of the hole I was about to crush him in? I made him feel something besides what's beneath his kilt and in his stomach." Potipherah gave a satisfied far-off look. "And his worthless watchmen are no more."

"Evil son of Set! You are responsible for this embarrassment to the king's house. You set your will on destroying them!"

Potipherah shrugged. "There was hardly anything left

for me to do after our Lord Sand Dweller applied his hand to the mix. He's very thorough. My humble contribution was barely needed." He gave a low chuckle. "Did you see the way Mentuser tried to get out of it? That burst of fear that made him fly at the guard, hoping to be impaled on the spear? It didn't work, but I think it kind of Khakheperre to have all those skilled fingers strung from a leather necklace for him."

"That's quite enough, Potipherah."

"And the ever charming Nebsumenu, attempting negotiations until they cut out his tongue. It took five guards to hold him down. And the pretty, slow-witted Satweret never caught on that I snared her with sacks of dye from my own estate."

Hetnu remembered their mutilated faces and lurched forward, bracing for his stomach's upheaval. The accursed were given a day's ration of bread and water, then relegated to the eastern desert and whatever brutal gods ruled there. Their cries he would never forget. "It was horrible."

"It was the spectacle of a lifetime, and for Khakheperre a crowning achievement."

Hetnu's eyes rounded on the priest in understanding. "You are hoping this shame outshines the king's victory. You hope it outshines the work of Yoseph's god." Hetnu shook with indignation. "To go to such lengths! You've forgotten that you are but a man, Merisu. Do not dabble with power belonging to God!"

"Call me by that name again, and I'll rip out your tongue." Potipherah stood and shook out his robes. The quick smile he gave never reached his eyes. "I was divining the heavens long before your desert dog arrived. Remember that. Change is coming fast to the king's house, Hetnu.

Change that will give you no pleasure. But it comes just the same."

CHAPTER SIXTY FIVE

AMENY

THE GIRL ON AMENY'S LAP STUNK WORSE THAN the brothel, but he wrapped his arms around her and drank from her tankard of palm beer. After entertaining thoughts of fleeing the country, he found he had not the courage nor will to leave his homeland. It was only here in Egypt that Amun was foremost, and it would not be so elsewhere.

He slurred a bawdy tune, capturing the girl's grimy fingers as she reached for the chain at his neck.

"Gold." Her eyes flashed with greed. He pulled her hand away, kissing her dirty fingers.

"Time for that later."

A hump-backed man rocked toward him in the haze filled room, like a demon of the afterlife come to carry him off.

"Greetings, my lord. I am Governor Nakht."

Ameny reared back when the old man yanked the girl up with surprising strength. He slurred a protest at the loss of her warm bottom against his thighs.

"There." The man struck the grime from his hands. "That should save you a month's worth of lice at least."

"I was enjoying her company, and you are far too ugly to take her place."

The old man chuckled. "Oh, but you can do far better, my lord for a prince of the realm."

Ameny scowled. Drinking was easier with the girl's assistance. He concentrated, raising the mug halfway to his mouth when he had a sudden burst of memory. "Nakht of the Shrine province?"

"The same, my lord. A prince of your caliber should not be in such dangerous territory."

"No longer a prince," Ameny tilted, flapping his arm. "No longer a man. I am a dog. Forgotten."

"Come upriver to the south for a while. I'll take care of you until these false accusations of murder have been put to rest."

"Nothing false about them." Ameny closed his eyes. The tankard found his lips. Bliss.

"I beg you, my lord. Let me keep you safe until your brother forgets the matter."

Ameny emptied the tankard, some down his throat and some down his chest. He gave a long burp. "Done." He slammed the tankard down.

"Good." Nakht gave a ringing clap of his hands. He grabbed the girl by the hair and pushed her on to Ameny's lap again, then leaned forward to refill the tankard. "I shall fetch my covered litter and whisk my lord away to luxurious comfort."

Nakht gave Ameny an affirming pat on the arm. Ameny snickered at the old man's hobble toward the doorway. A fat man blocked his view and yanked the girl up again.

"You fool! Don't you know who that was?"

Ameny threw his head back and squinted at the familiar

round face covered with a light scruff of beard. "Senib!" He slapped his thigh. "You've come to see me!"

He was yanked to his feet before he knew it and pushed out the brothel's back entrance. He flailed like a man in a strong river current when a few men hoisted him into a litter chair and covered him with a large, flat sack.

"Down the alley," Senib ordered the litter bearers with haste. "Away from the light."

Ameny peeked through his eyelids. His hand flopped against Senib's bald head as he walked beside the chair. "You've come and found me, old friend. And all this time I thought I was going with Nakht."

"There are few things worse, my lord, than being taken into the care of Governor Nakht. At least death by my hands will be merciful." Senib reached in the bottom of the litter and grabbed a cudgel. "I'm going to bash your brains out, stuff you in a sack, and toss you in the river for trying to turn me over to Potipherah. You forsook me after all I promised to do for you. I had to flee for my life from both Potipherah and from Governor Nakht. But it was worth it to get my revenge on you, my lord. It was worth it."

Ameny's head rocked with the swaying rhythm of the chair. He smiled at Senib's threat. Perhaps death was better. The glorious notable death of a bludgeoned prince. The thought of nobles mourning him put Ameny in a good mood, and a tavern song sprang from his lips.

"Shut up that awful noise," Senib ordered.

Ameny sang louder. They reached the edge of a field.

"Lower the chair," Senib snapped at the bearers. "Shut up, Ameny, or I'll kill you now with my bare hands!"

Ameny gurgled as Senib's pudgy fingers dug into his neck. He gripped the arms of the litter until Senib's face blurred before him. If this was death, he wouldn't fight it. Senib's moist hold released him, and Ameny doubled over, wheezing a few breaths between laughter.

"You're no murderer, Senib, despite all your boasting. You said you'd have a proposition for me were I ever parted from Potipherah." He leaned back, and Senib fingered his gold necklace.

"There's more where that came from." He managed a convincing wink, and Senib dropped the necklace and stepped back, shrugging some defeated gesture.

The temptation of gold was too much, and he steered the litter bearers in a different direction.

Ameny frowned. No courtiers to mourn him after all. The men carried him into the night. He nuzzled under the sack, yawning as Senib mumbled, walking behind the litter.

"I'll get my money's worth out of you first, before I kill you, prince. And I know just how to do it."

CHAPTER SIXTY SIX

POTIPHERAH

POTIPHERAH SAT IN THE UPPER NORTH GARDEN, staring all afternoon at the wall that blocked his view to the king's balcony. The sun was setting by the time one of his acolytes approached to tell him the whereabouts of the vizier. He dismissed the man and left his litter behind for a stroll to the quay.

He happened upon his daughter Asenat passing through an archway and pulled her to a corner bathed in shadows before she could protest. "I sent you a message and I don't like being ignored." He grabbed her wrist, and motioned to the high wall of the quay. "Nor do I like the company you keep."

Her pulse raced under his thumb, and she tugged at his grip and glanced at the vizier, positioned high on the wall. "I'm the king's ward, not yours. I will no longer give an evil man an account of my life. You are a killer."

He smacked her bottom then pointed a blue finger at her pert scowl. "Don't get high-handed with me, girl. And take comfort that your vizier lives another day because you are on your way to Pakhet."

Asenat yanked away from him and stepped back. "I'll soon be out of your reach. Something I could have wished for my mother." She skittered off before he could land another blow to her backside. But he had no intention of letting his obstinate daughter ruin his good mood tonight.

Taking the stairs two at a time, he was breathless and smiling by the time he reached the vizier on the high wall in conversation with a few of his officers. He interrupted. "Dismiss your men."

Paneah hesitated but waved the men farther down the wall. He clasped his hands behind his back, and Potipherah followed his gaze to the small vessel pulling out three piers from where they stood.

"There is something I like about you, Yoseph." Potipherah pretended to absently scan the expanse of the quay. "Though my colleagues have begged me to set up your death. And if my daughter weren't leaving for that miserable little temple of Pakhet, I might be persuaded to oblige them. But she leaves within a few days, and therefore I am forced to like you."

"I'm sorry the first prophet of Iunu is *forced* to like me."

"Don't worry. I keep it in check." He followed Paneah's gaze to the craft leaving the quay. It was built for the utmost speed. "Your trackers should have no difficulty chadding downriver to find your clan of plain-dwellers. Hetnu picked the best time of year to send them out with the flood waters pushing through." Paneah's brows flickered as he attempted to keep the shock from his face.

"Was that supposed to be a secret my lord vizier?" Potipherah asked, and pointed to three small boats farther back in the line of vessels leaving the quay. "But look there. Those are my trackers, killers who'll follow your men and use any means possible to retrieve the information you've given them. You'll do as I say then, Yoseph, or I'll have them obliterate your desert clan down to the last infant."

Potipherah studied him as he liked to do in such moments when he knew he horrified men. Something akin to fear rippled across the vizier's face before he gave an expression of forced calm. It was disappointing, but then, he had been a slave and, therefore, used to controlling the water that should be running down his legs at this moment. The sharp apple of his throat bobbed a few times before he recovered enough to speak. That was something.

"Why?" Paneah asked.

"The governors of the south want me to destroy you, and I was going to wait for the next harvest to fail, but you've exceeded my expectation, already." Potipherah flicked him with a glance, then inhaled the night air. "And because a barbarian such as you who has been made vizier must be made to know his place."

And with that, Potipherah walked away, keeping to the habit of leaving a man stunned whenever he threatened him. But curiosity got the best of him, and he pivoted back to the vizier. "But tell me, who is this Reuben? This Dan and Naphtali you call out in your dreams? Are they brothers? Sons?" He arched his brows in question.

"How dare you."

"I've dared much worse, I assure you. Your word on the harvest was mere luck. You'd do well to remember how quickly I can crush you like a dung beetle."

"And the miracle of rains in the desert?"

"Happenstance." Potipherah shrugged. "Therefore, do not let yourself be run away with delusion. If you defy me,

Yoseph, then neither luck nor Elohim will keep me from ripping you to shreds. And I will do it. Slowly."

THE IUNU TEMPLE BARGE CHADDED DOWNRIVER as full of blue and white pennants as it was priests. But Potipherah chose to relish his victories alone and trailed the temple barge back to Iunu in his private vessel.

Khons poured him a drink under one of the shade pavilions on deck, spilling wine. He garbled some apology, but Potipherah pushed his body servant back, dabbing the stain on his kilt.

"You're tired, that's all, Khons. Go and rest yourself a while. I've worked you too hard." He gave Khons a good natured smile and waved him off. His fingers ached, but he could copy the gentle manipulation he'd seen Khons apply for temporary relief. The pain had decreased greatly, now that he'd taken care of the business at court.

The Pakhet barge would be picking Asenat up tomorrow. He'd already set up spies to surround her and warned the chief priestess of the temple to advance his daughter without delay. She would be in good hands at Pakhet until he decided what to do with her. The girl was being groomed for greatness.

She'd spent too much time in the company of that Asiatic, and Potipherah thought to see her off, not that she would welcome it. But under the circumstances, it was best he depart for Iunu as soon as possible.

By all rights, an arrow should have found it's way to the vizier's chest or a cup of poison to his belly. Paneah's unnatural resilience was fascinating. He'd defied even Nebsumenu's charms and tricks. The treasurer had been on to something about him. Could it be true that his god had indeed blessed him? A thought rolled over in Potipherah's mind. He could use a man like this.

Then there was Prince Ameny. Potipherah toyed with the possibilities of how he might go about torturing the king's brother for attempting to assault his daughter. He'd instructed his spies to keep the prince alive if they found him. It would be his privilege to see to Ameny, personally.

It was a shame Khakheperre hadn't spent more time building a tomb like a proper king. Too late for that now. Dispatching Kitjau would have been a nice flourish, and though Qareg's assassination attempt failed, he took out enough rowers on the vessel to drive a point.

Potipherah had ordered Kitjau's death on principle. Khakheperre needed to be taken down a notch or two for having insulted the great gods and priests of the land on behalf of his little dead wife. He had no business paying such tribute to the god of a barbarian.

A rage had burned within him when Khakheperre dared to take his daughter as a ward. But Potipherah made no complaint, biding his time for revenge. That time had come, and he was about to teach the sovereign a lesson that he would never forget.

Or perhaps, never remember.

Reclining on cushions, Potipherah let the rowers' rhythm and song lull him to a state of placidity. Things would be much altered when next he returned to the king's house. He raised a cup of wine in challenge before he took a sip.

"Take that, Elohim, god of the desert dog."

Khons rested in the next shaded stall, and Potipherah addressed the barrier between them. "I'm going to have my jewelers fashion you a magnificent girdle when we get back to Iunu, Khons. You'll be the envy of every manservant in the kingdom." In answer, a bowl clattered, and a heavy thump shook the deck.

"Khons?"

Potipherah lifted the barrier between the stalls. His heart plummeted. Wine soaked the woven rug near Khons' face. He knelt and raised the head of his servant, but Khons' eyes stared through him, vacant and unblinking. He stroked Khons' thick black hair in disbelief. "Khons," he whispered, shaking him. But there was no answer.

CHAPTER SIXTY SEVEN

SABNI

AFTER THE KING'S JUDGMENT, THE ACCURSED and their families had been wiped from all records. There was little chance of retaliation against the good god since the members of their households were punished with them. All was secure and well.

Yet Sabni gave up trying to sleep and donned the short dark leather kilt of a soldier to blend into the night. The accursed, after all, had other family members, not of their households, who'd escaped the king's wrath. The ivory hilt of Sabni's dagger and the dim moonlight would be the only things to register him to the keenest sight. This made it easier for him to scan the shadows near the wall of the king's dwelling, exactly where his feet took him.

Some of the torches had gone out around the wall and the war dogs barked from their pens. Khakheperre apparently preferred to brood alone after the failure of his watchmen. And sometimes he preferred to cheer himself by calling in the guards at his gate to laugh with the men and give them a meal, then send them back to their posts.

Nor was it unusual to hear the sound of clacking

instruments if Khakheperre wanted to lighten his mood. Yet the hairs on the back of Sabni's neck stood up and he kicked up a trot toward the sovereign's dwelling. He jogged a little faster up the path to the formal entrance. At the same time, someone rushed toward him in a sloppy run.

A stagger.

Hau, the king's mute fanning slave, blasted a sound like a muffled horn from his throat. He fell to his knees on the landing, his face covered in blood. Sabni tore up the ramp past him. He bellowed, "All guards to the king!" as he flew to Khakheperre's innermost chamber, the sound of striking weapons sharp in his ears. As long as weapons clashed, the good god might live.

He leapt over several wounded guards and almost lost his footing in a pool of blood. He opened the doors to the king's leisure room and froze.

The closed balcony curtains and snuffed out torches bathed the room in darkness. There was grunting, shuffling and the flash of metal. Sabni's eyes strained to see Khakheperre fight with a blackened shape more skilled than he. His attacker drew him to the center of the room. The king struggled for breath and swung his adze in wild fatigue, favoring his right side where a blade had caught him. He was being lured into position for the kill.

"His legs, Heperre!" Sabni plucked an axe from a dead man's back.

Khakheperre landed a chop to the man's thigh. He cried out and dropped his weapon. Khakheperre kicked it away. Sabni hurled the axe but the mud-covered assassin ducked, then ran for the balcony and leapt off.

"Physician, here!" Sabni snatched up a sheet for the king's wounds and lit a torch, revealing the bodies of six unknown men and four night-watch guards, one of them headless. Sabni picked up the jagged flint dagger that Khakheperre had kicked away from the assassin. He knew its owner.

Qareg.

He was about to hurl the blade when Khakheperre cried out.

"No! Give it to me!"

Sabni passed the dagger to Khakheperre as he fought for breath and swallowed, turning the dagger over in his hand.

"Did you see, Sabni?" He panted. "I struck him."

Sabni dabbed blood from the king's face checking for deep cuts. "You were a brave aggressor, striking at your enemies, my lord." He moved quickly over the king's chest and limbs, fighting the urge to go after the assassin. But Heperre needed him now.

The king stared past him. *"'If I had made haste with weapons in my hand, I would have made the cowards retreat in confusion.'"* He gave a sharp intake of breath as Sabni ran careful hands down his legs. Sabni knew the text.

"The Teachings of Amenemhat, your forefather."

Khakheperre gave a jerking nod. "It is what I have failed to do in life, strike back at my oppressors." He winced as Sabni cleaned the gash at his side. This and a few cuts along the king's arms and chest were the worst of the damage other than his left eye, swelling shut.

More guards poured into the room. "Where is the physician? I'll get him myself." Sabni pulled away, but Khakheperre grabbed his wrist.

"Stay."

"Your wounds, my lord."

"Will heal, though they sting like demons' teeth. I must speak to you."

There was a forthrightness in the king's voice that said he was ready to speak of secrets long kept. "It can wait, Khakheperre."

"No, it cannot. My fears have bound me like a slave. But I've been given a second chance, and I will be coward no more."

CHAPTER SIXTY EIGHT

ASENAT

AMA SHAVED OFF ASENAT'S HAIR, PROTESTING with tears. Asenat commanded her to silence. It was time to approach the ritual of dressing with austerity and leave off the layers of jewelry, intricate wigs, and powders Hetnu had introduced her to. She wanted Paneah to see her this way before she left for Pakhet. This was the memory of her that he should keep.

In her long temple robes, she went to his office to greet him one last time. There was accusation in his gaze sweeping over her shining head. The knot bobbed in his throat. He searched her face, and his jaws locked. She'd shocked him, and he returned the favor by declaring himself busy and keeping her farewell short. Who was he to disapprove of her appearance? This was Egypt, not some desert clan or wilderness ritual. What did he think she would look like as a temple acolyte of Pakhet?

She walked back to her dwelling and caught the sound of footsteps and canes too late.

"We heard you were leaving for the temple." Sahathor

took her by the wrist and shook it. "You were with him daily, girl. How could you fail so?"

"We surely thought it would be you. Not that trumped up minor goddess, Qatsenut." Ipwet scowled.

Sahathor leaned into Asenat. "Perhaps you should have used your breasts a little. You see what it's done for Appipa."

Ipwet gave a nod of agreement. "You're not very pretty, but we think you would have brought Lord Paneah round."

"Console yourself, my dear Ipwet." Sahathor shook her head. "The girl's womb will rot among the forgotten carcasses of Pakhet."

The old mother's coarse words struck Asenat like a blow, and she fought down the panic that swelled in her chest. She would be a part of something great at Pakhet. This was the right thing to do.

SHE TOSSED AND THRASHED IN THE SHALLOW depths of sleep that night, then rose at the first faint light breaking through the curtains of her porch. Paneah's farewell sat sour in her stomach, but today she was leaving the king's house. One step on the temple barge would free her. She'd no longer be the king's ward, nor a scribe of the vizier, but the exclusive property of the temple. Dread bucked her stomach. Paneah's glower flashed in her mind, but she would not attend it. This was the right thing to do.

Her father chadded down to Iunu. She would chont up to Pakhet and put herself a safe distance from him. The vizier would govern in the name of the king and marry Qatsenut. All was Ma'at.

By mid-morning, all her things were packed. She strode

one last time through the main thoroughfare to lay a bouquet of flowers at the twin statues of Neferet. A soft wind blew through the sheltering trees like a kiss from the little queen. Asenat's eyes clouded.

May you find comfort at the breast of your Elohim.

She kissed the foot of one of the twin statues and moved on. The courtiers of the king's house had not deserved Neferet. As for the scroll room, Asenat had no heart to visit it again. The pain of losing Mepi ran too deep.

She moved bravely toward the bright orange pennants of Pakhet waving from the temple barge in the quay. Hetnu called out to her, trotting forward. She stopped to wait for him. It had been her plan to leave with no further farewells, but Hetnu had done so much for her. She owed him a last embrace.

He took her arm and doubled over, catching his breath. "You must come with me."

"What?"

"The sovereign requires your presence."

"I have the king's permission to leave."

"You are still his ward until you reach the barge of Pakhet," he rushed out between breaths. "Thank Horus I caught you in time."

Asenat glanced at the pennants and took a notion to pay the king back for his ill treatment. Ama waited for her by the vessel with their sacks. She could run for it, and once on board, there was nothing Khakheperre could do about it. Once more her freedom hung in the balance with the king's undecided dislike of her. She stomped her foot. "All right, I'll come. But you did not catch me. I stopped."

Officials and courtiers filled the banquet hall, all of them summoned with the staff of precedence. She held her chin high at the snickers her acolyte temple robes and bald head inspired. Her appearance was a far cry from the fashionable lady that Hetnu had established at court.

She sat a few tables from Lord Paneah who faced her direct line of sight. He gave her a single nod and looked away. It cut her to her heart.

The courtiers now honored him with reverent bows and addresses. And Qatsenut placed herself at the hub of his new revered status.

She cast Asenat a belittling smile as her clay-reddened lips moved in animated conversation with those sharing her table. She took up the falcon wing fan and waved it like a dancer, stroking it across her chest.

Asenat pulled her gaze away, wishing she'd sat with her back to the vizier, but the room filled up, and there was nowhere else to move.

Lord Ubenresh sat at a table nearby, his expression one of woebegone despair in his turned down lips and sinking brows. Appipa waddled past him on her father's arm as if the banquet were given in her honor. She wore Hetnu's sparkling pectoral over a sheer wedding garment to show off her swelling belly. The bracelet she took from Asenat in the broad hall still sparkled on her wrist, and her hairstyle strongly suggested the Hathor braids exclusive to royal women.

A'at followed behind her sister and father in a sheath and overdress of amber beads. A red welt rose on her cheek. Poor girl with no Neferet to protect her now.

King Khakheperre entered the hall from the raised platform, and the courtiers shot to their feet. They gasped and shrieked as the sovereign limped, favoring his right side, bandaged in linen. His arms, chest, and legs were cut up with scratches and nicks.

The king smacked at the hands of three physicians. Sabni helped him to his throne. He peeled back his lips in clear discomfort as he lowered himself into his chair. The room was abuzz with protest and demands for justice. Khakheperre waved a hand for silence.

"You see here before you the attempt of assassins who entered my chamber." The courtiers shouted their protests again, and the king saved his strength. He sipped from a cup Hetnu offered, waiting for the clamor to cease.

"I will not blame the assassin for his skill. I will blame myself."

The crowd's anger crested again, but the king begged their silence.

"While I have built myself a strong fortress, it was not enough. My enemy has studied the habits of my home and found his way into my inner chamber. He knew my own house better than I, and if he'd correctly estimated my skill with the blade, I would not be speaking to you now, but would be preparing for my journey into the West." He leaned forward letting a slave adjust the cushions in his chair as he took up his Ames scepter before his stern gaze traveled around the room. "From now on, I shall be a worthier king."

Ibiau, attendant of the two houses of gold, was called to the front of the hall and arrested. A raid on his home revealed treasury records stored there. He was to be held until the royal scribes had gone over them. Several more treasury officials were demoted and four dismissed from their post.

Among the waves of anxiety spreading around the room were moments of elation. Ten lower officials whose work had been found to be circumspect were promoted. Chu was promoted to governor of the province once lost to his family. Tears coursed down his face. It was an honor to witness his joy.

Khakheperre opened a floodgate of judgment and spent a greater part of the day working his way through the hall. The more he laid down justice, the stronger his voice and the more upright he sat on his throne, altered before the very eyes of his court.

The corrupt royal jewelers found in his service were sent to prison while he offered Imehy a chief position, but the dwarf declined it to rejoin the vizier's crew. His decision to do so left Sabni grinning from ear to ear.

"Lord Paneah, come forward," the king ordered.

The vizier picked his way to the front of the hall where the king made him face the crowd. Qatsenut's chest inflated ten times over, and Asenat could not blame her. The king once boasted that in this man lived the spirit of the true god. His words proved themselves truer and truer by the day.

The king stood at the edge of the platform, his gold sandals at the height of Paneah's shoulder. "Here you see before you a man who came into my house a slave but proved himself worthy of my esteem. In this, I judged him correctly though I give myself little credit for following his advice. He has shown integrity and courage, even when I resisted the truth he brought me, which was in itself, a great wealth."

"I have received his report of broken dikes, removed boundary stones and neglected rotting crops. I will send him out to check the loyalty and love you claim to have for me. Therefore, make yourselves ready, for he shall visit every province in the land, leaving no boundary stone unjustly placed. He shall right wrongs in my name with the seal of authority that I have given him. And you will heed his instructions or suffer the consequence."

It was all well said, but Asenat could not understand what any of it had to do with her. The Pakhet barge sat in the quay. Then the king's gaze fell on her, and she clutched her chest.

"Lady Asenat, come forward."

She hesitated, then rose to her feet. Her heart fluttered in her chest with each step she took to the front of the hall. She fought down panic by reminding herself that the king was still handing out praise. He had finally come to approve of her and he would praise her for serving the vizier before sending her to Pakhet.

"Today, Lord Paneah I give my ward to you as wife. Having her beside you may keep you alive because of who her father is. But on that same note, do not trust her because of who her father is."

Mortification heated Asenat's face and chest. Paneah squeezed her hand, and she fixed her gaze on the floor. The king's anger would always mark her as the daughter of his enemy no matter what she did.

"Lady A'at, come forward."

Paneah pulled Asenat to the side as A'at came to stand at the base of the platform, her head lowered to hide the mark on her cheek.

"Look at me, girl," the king ordered. "Who struck you?"

A'at closed her eyes, trapping some of her tears.

"I will settle this business on the supposed royal bloodline of my rival." The king found Deduamen in the crowd. "At first, I thought myself humiliated to marry one of the daughters of my so-called blood enemy. But today, I take A'at as my wife, seeing she needs me even more than I need her. She is the best of her father's house, and he was a fool not to see it." The king wiggled his fingers, encouraging A'at to mount the platform. She did so, swiping tears. He placed a green embroidered cloak on her shoulders, coaxing her to raise her head.

"All is well, little counselor." He took her hand in his grasp. "See how well our bruises pair us together? We are meant to be." He winked at her with his good eye, and a sob escaped her lips.

"And what about me?!" Appipa shouted from her seat. "I'm ten times the worth of my plain sister, and I'm the one dressed for a wedding."

"Ah, yes. Appipa, how could I forget you." The king's voice took on a hint of amusement. "Come forward."

Appipa hefted herself up with her father's assistance and waddled to the front of the room, heedless of the low rumble of laughter.

"You are special." The king inclined his head. "At least you think you are. But your beauty is like fine linen on a pig's back. For you are a girl of little sense who gave every man at court a happy eyeful and left them little to ponder in your scant apparel."

Appipa's eyes rounded at the king's words. Her rich brown skin turned red.

"It was cruel of you to throw yourself at me when I suffered the loss of my wife, Neferet. You are full of my brother's get, and yet you expect my attention. I hold you up as a lesson to all girls of supposed good breeding. I will not have you. But there is one who has begged for you though I argued with him the sense of it. Heed my advice and take his offer, for the only other one is the vessel of Pakhet that waits in the quay."

Appipa sniffed and drew a trembling hand to her mouth.

The king decided for her. "Ubenresh. Come get your woman. Today I give you Appipa as your wife."

Ubenresh was up before the king finished speaking. He rushed at Appipa like a raging bull to worship her with kisses. She fought him off, screeching at the top of her lungs, and the hall erupted in laughter.

ASENAT HAD TAKEN SEVERAL DAYS TO PREPARE for this moment, yet she startled at the knock on the door of her inner chamber. She thought Paneah might not come. Then she hoped he wouldn't.

"Come in."

She dismissed Ama from the room as Paneah entered and shut the door. He scanned the chamber. Some of her things were unpacked, but she had good reason for that.

She proffered the armed chair across from hers. He sat, his gaze narrowed on her acolyte robes and bald head. If he would just hear her out. Her plan would suit them both. It was Ma'at.

"You called for me." It was not a question. His words were short.

"I have a request."

He did not interrupt. He did not ask what her request might be. He did not nod for her to continue. He crossed his arms and glared, his cheeks sucked in, his lips puckered.

She reached for the scroll bearing the king's seal on the tray beside her. She offered it to him then gave a little nervous laugh when his arms remained crossed. "I've forgotten you do not read." She looked away from his glare and broke the seal.

"Good news." She forced vigor into her words. "The king has relented."

"On what?"

She ignored his sharp tone. "On my need to travel with you throughout the land."

"And why would the king do that when he gave you to me as wife?"

"Because the sovereign understands there is no need for me to burden your journey. This letter says he will let you take a second wife while I am kept under guard at Pakhet."

He snorted.

"If anything happens to you, my life is forfeit." Asenat rolled up the scroll. "Much better, don't you think?" She forced a smile. "Everything will be as it should." She extended the document. His glare nearly scorched it.

"Who put you up to this?"

"No one put me up to it."

"Has the king offered a second wife to me?"

She lowered her gaze, willing him to accept the king's allowance. It made sense.

"Qatsenut." He whispered the name through clenched teeth, then leaned forward on his knees expelling a rapid flow of foreign words.

"She would make a fine second wife." Her heart raced.

He uncrossed his arms. "What an ally you've found in Qatsenut. How convenient that your life is forfeit if anything happens to me. But what if something happens to you?"

"Then Qatsenut will take the place of first wife."

Silence thickened the air and she grasped the disclosure of her own words.

He flexed his jaw, pinning her with an impatient glare. "Yes."

Her mouth fell open. She closed it. "You mean Qatsenut?...She wouldn't hurt me. She's onl—"

"Qatsenut is an experienced courtier who would run the country herself if the king would allow." He gripped the bridge of his nose and closed his eyes.

Asenat fidgeted. She must convince him. She would make a terrible wife. She was better off at the temple. He was better off with Qatsenut.

"Once you said you were not mine to scold, Asenat. Now you are." He shot up from the chair. "My barge leaves to tour the land in a few days. Call back Ama and pack the rest of your things. You are my wife Asenat, and you're coming with me."

END OF BOOK 1

Coming Soon
the second installment
in the
Servant Ruler Series
Harvest of the Sand Dweller
Where Zaphenath Paneah,
Lady Asenat,
and the vizier's crew
tour the land in the king's name

Thanks for reading
Seal of the Sand Dweller

Please Review!
If you enjoyed Seal of the Sand Dweller, then please leave a review at your favorite book review site. Your review is the next best thing to word of mouth in supporting any author whose work you enjoy.

Find a review link here:

www.rrushing.com/sealofthesanddweller

About the Author

R. Rushing writes Biblical and Christian Fantasy fiction and reads the Bible with open-mouthed fascination. There's enough political and kingdom intrigue, battles and conflict for a lifetime of lessons.

Rushing lives in Virginia with her husband, Ben, and loves to write in the vein of compelling stories such as Ben-Hur and The Robe.

Seal of the Sand Dweller is the first installment in the Servant-Ruler Series.

Explore exotic realms.
Enjoy compelling fiction.
Expect an incredible God.

Join R.Rushing's newsletter for a free gift and news on the next installment in the Servant Ruler Series
Sign up at
http://eepurl.com/dfpsAL

Also
Join me on Social Media
FACEBOOK
www.facebook.com/AuthorR.Rushing
INSTAGRAM
www.instagram.com/r.rushing_author
WEBSITE
www.rrushing.com

ACKNOWLEDGEMENTS

Plans fail for lack of counsel,
but with many advisers they succeed.
- Proverbs 15: 22

Writing takes courage. I'm grateful for my family who encouraged me on many days.

Thanks to Christy McGill who read my whole manuscript through even before I got an editor. Brave soul, that one. A special thanks to Allison Garcia, Anne Western, Kim Hudson, Traycee Lydia Garner, Regina Magnum, Tamara Shoemaker, Morgan Reyelts, and to all my beta-readers and friends who cheered and shoved me to the finish line.

Thank you Shenandoah Valley Writers' for getting me through the early stages of my story, and to the American Christian Fiction Writers chapter in my hometown was huge blessing in that we all share a common goal of magnifying Jesus Christ in our work.

Above all, I thank God for putting this book in my heart and helping meet put in the hands of readers.

CAST OF CHARACTERS

Hear the names pronounced at www.rrushing.com

The King's Family

Khakheperre or Heperre
the king

Khnemet
queen

Khenemetneferhedjet or Weret
the god's great wife and queen

Neferet
queen

Prince Ameny
the king's brother
his servant, **Urshe**

Prince Dagi
the king's relative

Prince Khakure
the king's son and co-regent

Prince Neheri
the king's relative

Qatsenut
the king's cousin

Servants

Hau
the king's fanning slave

Hetnu
the king's cupbearer
his adopted daughter, **Imini**
his house steward, **Nen**

Kitjau
palace architect and gardener

Mentuser
the king's physician

Tjebu
the king's garment maker

Ukem
the king's body servant

Palace Administrators

Gebi
overseer of the lower fields and tributary offerings

Ibiau
treasury attendant

Mepi
overseer of the king's scroll room and collector of ancient works
his servants, **Henhenit** and **Wenen**

Potipherah
the king's chief counselor and high priest of Iunu
his deceased wife, **Rudet**
his daughter, **Asenat**
his servant, **Khons**
his acolyte, **Khety**
renegade Iunu priest, **Senib**

Reniqer
leader of the broad hall
his son, **Ipuur**

Resnakt
attendant of the broad hall and deputy treasurer
his son, **Bebi**

Nebsumenu
the king's treasurer
his wife, **Satweret**

Palace Courtiers

Ipwet and **Sahathor**
gossiping matrons

Kemsiyet
Yoseph's former master's wife

Yimenet
palace musician

Palace Slaves

Ama
Asiatic slave-girl

Imehy
slave-healer and stall worker

Yoseph
slave from the garrison

Vizier and Staff

Zaphenath Paneah
[formerly Yoseph, garrison slave]
Vizier

Chu
vizier's chief officer

Duaf
vizier's food taster

Jafener
scribe of the vizier

Provincial Governors and Administrators

Djehuti
governor of the Upper Laurels province
his sons, **Meru, Rudi, Za'amun**

Deduamen
governor of the Min province
his son, **Hotepi**
his daughters, **Appipa** and **A'at**

Nakht
governor of the Shrine province
his son, **Nodjme**

Sonebau
provincial governor

Ubenresh
candidate for mayor of the Shrine province

Wegaf
provincial governor

Other Players

Nebitef
commander of the Ptah division of soldiers
and Yoseph's former master

Qareg
garrison assistant

CPSIA information can be obtained
at www.ICGtesting.com
Printed in the USA
BVHW030216101121
621267BV00006B/160